THE EDEN LEGACY

Will Adams has tried his hand at a multitude of careers over the years. Most recently, he worked for a London-based firm of communications consultants before giving it up to pursue his life-long dream of writing fiction. His first novel, *The Alexander Cipher*, has been published in sixteen languages, and has been followed by two more books in the Daniel Knox series, *The Exodus Quest* and *The Lost Labyrinth*. He writes full-time and lives in Suffolk.

WILL ADAMS

The Eden Legacy

HARPER

Harper
An imprint of HarperCollins*Publishers*
77–85 Fulham Palace Road,
Hammersmith, London W6 8JB

www.harpercollins.co.uk

This production 2013

Copyright © Will Adams 2010

Will Adams asserts the moral right to
be identified as the author of this work

A catalogue record for this book
is available from the British Library

ISBN: 978 0 00 793038 8

Set in Sabon by Palimpsest Book Production Limited,
Falkirk, Stirlingshire
Printed and bound in Great Britain by
Clays Ltd, St Ives plc

MIX
Paper from
responsible sources
FSC™ www.fsc.org
FSC™ C007454

To Max, Oscar and Rose

ACKNOWLEDGEMENTS

I've long been fascinated by Madagascar, for its unique evolutionary history, its extraordinary geology, its beauty and its remoteness, so it seemed the ideal setting for this story about shipwrecks and maritime exploration. The island lies directly between the Cape of Good Hope and India, after all, so its reefs have long presented a lethal threat to shipping – as evidenced by the wreck-site of the *Winterton*, featured in this book.

All the characters in this book are of course fictional, as is the Eden Reserve itself (to accommodate which, I've had to extend the coastline a little between Salary and Bedakoy). It is, however, very loosely based on a number of wildlife and marine projects I visited in Madagascar. In particular, I'd like to thank Al Harris and everyone else I met at Blue Ventures for their help. They do terrific work at Andavadoaka, and it's a wonderful place to visit. I'm also grateful to Francesco in Salary both for his hospitality and for sailing me out to the site of the *Winterton*.

My heartfelt thanks, as ever, to my agent Luigi Bonomi and my editor Julia Wisdom, whose encouragement and unfailingly wise advice is immensely appreciated. I'd also like to thank Anne O'Brien for checking the manuscript so diligently and thus saving me from the embarrassment of my own mistakes. Any that remain are, of course, mine and mine alone.

PROLOGUE

The Mozambique Channel, 1424

Mei Hua was with the admiral in his private quarters when the great ship struck the reef. It started with a low scraping noise that made them glance a little anxiously at each other; but a storm was blowing outside, and you were forever hearing new noises on board, even after three years. The scraping died away and they smiled at each other, amused by their own nerves, and carried on with their separate tasks: she making tea; he writing instructions for his beloved globe so that the enamellers could finish it before they reached home. But suddenly there was a thunderous crash and the bow rode upwards and they came to such a shuddering halt that it sent them both tumbling in a tangle across the floor.

A moment of silence, as though the ship itself, and all on board, couldn't take in what had just happened. But then the noises started, timbers groaning like a dying giant, men yelling and a terrible splintering noise right above their heads as one of their masts toppled and crashed upon the deck.

Mei Hua looked around, in shock as much as fear. The porcelain tea service and the oil lamps had all broken, but their spilled oil had formed islands of blue flame upon the floor that were already catching on the scattered silk bedclothes and hangings. She got to her feet and began stamping them out before they could take hold. The door flew open and three bodyguards rushed in, one with a great gash in his scalp, a whole side of his face gleaming with fresh blood. They joined her stamping out the fires, like a troupe of comic dancers. Then the men helped the admiral to his feet and swept him away to take command of this disaster, leaving Mei Hua on her own.

The rules of the ship were clear and uncompromising. As the admiral's favourite, she wasn't allowed unescorted out of the harem or the admiral's private quarters. If a crewman should so much as see her, both she and he would be put immediately to death. But there were no eunuchs here, no guards either, and she had to get to her infant son, make sure he was safe. She went to the door, peeked out. The passageway was dark and abandoned.

A terrible shudder ran the length of the ship. It felt like the end had come, but then it just died away again; and it made her realise that the old rules meant nothing any more.

She covered her face with a scarf, made her way to the steps. Two officers came charging breathlessly up, desperate not to be trapped below when the ship sank. She let them pass then hurried on down. The ship lurched slightly to the side; she had to put her hands against the wall to keep her feet. A man limped towards her, whimpering and cradling his arm. Another man was crying out for help from inside his quarters, his door broken and blocked. She tried to open it for him but it was no good, and her son wouldn't wait any longer. She hardened her heart and left him.

Down more stairs, the air thick with incense from the sticks they burned to mitigate the stench of a boat too long at sea. Water splashed around her ankles. A soldier was lying face-down in it, his arms above his head, prostrating himself to the gods he'd just gone to meet. She took a thin-bladed knife from his belt, stepped over him and on. The water grew deeper, splashing around her knees and then her thighs. Lamp-light flickered ahead; she could hear the shrieking of her fellow concubines. She reached the harem's antechamber to see that fat monster Chung Hu and two other eunuchs on guard outside the barred door, following their orders to the letter, keeping the women and children confined even as they drowned.

Chung Hu saw her and bellowed in anger. He'd always hated women, as though he blamed *them* for cutting off his balls, taking his vengeance with countless small cruelties. She turned and fled, fighting through the water. Chung Hu came after her, yelling to his comrades to follow. The water grew less deep, making progress easier, but for Chung Hu too. He grabbed her shoulder; she turned and stabbed him with her knife, its thin blade sliding sweetly through the jelly of his eye into the malignant grey mass behind. He fell with a grunt face-down into the water. His two subordinates stared at her almost in awe, as though they'd thought Chung Hu invulnerable; but then a great wave of water washed by them and reminded them of their peril. They fled past her to the steps, taking the oil lamps with them.

The water was waist deep by the time Mei Hua made it back to the antechamber, the concubines still shrieking in terror and despair. She felt out the two wooden bars and lifted them free. Sheer weight of water pushed the door open, allowing all her friends and their children to spill out, wailing in relief. In the darkness, she had to shout for her son. Li Wei had him. Mei Hua took him gratefully, clasped him against her chest, ran with the others for the steps. Water was flooding down from above; they had to fight to reach topside. The open deck was crowded, not just with crew and soldiers and other passengers, but with livestock too: piglets, dogs, oxen and chickens that had got free from their pens and now were running loose.

The concubines scattered in all directions, each intent on saving herself. Mei Hua went in search of the admiral. Bao Zhi was his son, after all, even if he refused to recognise him. A splintered spar swung down from high above and speared the belly of an old man in astronomer's robes, hoisted him up again into his beloved stars. Old men were fighting like furies for the lifeboats; she begged one or other of them to take her child, but they were only interested in saving themselves. She offered the admiral's jewellery as payment, but what use were gems in a shipwreck? An officer grabbed her ruby necklace anyway, pushed her down and swung his club at her. She turned and took the blow upon her backside, then scuttled away, hugging her wailing son against her breast, stroking his hair and whispering reassurance.

A sheet of lightning lit up the sky. She could see rain and spume that she hadn't even noticed until now. She was almost at the prow, she realised. She'd never been this far forward before. A second sheet of lightning showed the great dragon figurehead rearing up above her, its wings spread either side as though in flight, Mei Hua riding upon its back as it soared above the world. *The things they'd seen, these last few years! The places they'd visited!* Yet what did that count for now? She suffered a sudden and exquisite longing to see her mother just one more time, to show off Bao Zhi to her sisters. And so close, too. Just yesterday, the admiral had shown her on his globe how far they'd already journeyed, how few weeks remained to home and their heroes' welcome.

Another great shudder ran through the ship. Another mast toppled. Everywhere on deck, people were screaming. Mei Hua sobbed with fear and hugged Bao Zhi against her. Six nights before, she'd dreamed of a woman in red walking towards her across the water, beckoning to her, holding out her arms. Tianfei, the Celestial Consort, come to welcome her home.

But not like this.

Not like this.

ONE

I

A coral reef, the west coast of Madagascar

Sixty-three metres underwater, even brilliant sunlight becomes feeble, and the glorious pageantry of the reef and its fish is reduced to bureaucratic greys and blacks. Effort put into bright liveries down here was effort wasted, and nature abhorred such waste almost as fiercely as she abhorred vacuums. The only real brightness, therefore, came from the white sand that covered so much of the sea-bed; but even that was diminished by the litter of dead sea-grass and coral, by the scattering of darker stones, shells and gnarled black rock, and fogged by the clouds of sediment that Daniel Knox and his fellow divers had kicked up during the two hours they'd already spent at the bottom.

A tap upon his arm. He turned to see Miles, his boss and dive-buddy, stopping his filming for a moment, pointing up and to his left. It took Knox a moment to see what had caught his eye: a big fish, perhaps twenty metres away, though it was hard to gauge distances underwater. A shark of some kind, to judge from its distinctive silhouette and the easy menace of its movement, though too far away for him to be sure which. Bulls, tigers, makos, white-tips, black-tips and even the occasional great white were common enough along Madagascar's west coast, particularly on the exterior of these reefs, where food was plentiful and the water was hyper-oxygenated from constantly being crashed against the coral. But they were none of them as dangerous as their reputations, so long as you kept your nerve and did nothing stupid. That was why they alerted each other whenever they saw one, so that they wouldn't be panicked into a rushed ascent or some other mistake should it suddenly come close.

He nodded to let Miles know he'd seen it, checked his equipment. He touched his dive-knife first: it was reassuring just to have, even if it wasn't there to defend against a shark attack so much as for cutting through the mesh of discarded nets that so often plagued reefs like these. He checked his gauges next. His oxygen partial pressure looked a fraction high, and his spare gave the same reading, so he adjusted his feed accordingly. Hyperoxia was an easy trap to fall into when diving on a closed-circuit re-breather, as he'd discovered off the Azores the year before. But the modest extra risk was more than compensated for by the fact that the re-breather could scrub carbon dioxide from his exhaled air, then add more oxygen, allowing him to stay underwater almost indefinitely.

A cold current swept him sideways. He let himself be taken by it, then reoriented himself and resumed his exploration, making sure that Miles was filming away, both to provide footage for their documentary and to enable their shipboard project crew to follow along. Not that they'd had that much to film so far, despite it being such a perfect-looking wreck mound, nearly eighty metres long, covered in deep sand studded by rocks, dead coral and a scatter-pattern of artefacts. It lay at the foot of a steep rock shelf that rose sharply from the sea-bed like a gigantic underwater podium on which corals had grown over the centuries to within a foot or two of the surface at low tide, a real hazard for the ships of old, navigating by their crude charts and rough reckoning, on prayer and sacrifices to the gods.

The shark had circled around and now passed close enough by that he could see the ugly pale yellow of its underbelly, the dark spots and stripes on its blue-grey back. A tiger, ten to twelve feet long. He shared a glance

with Miles. They were notoriously unpredictable creatures: they'd take a bite out of you just from curiosity.
But there was little to be done about it. Sharks liked to
attack from underneath; ending the dive and beginning
their ascent now would be far more dangerous than
staying put. He turned back to the sea-bed. They'd already
recovered the two Chinese cannons that they'd known
about before they'd arrived. They'd also found a number
of early Ming coins and several shards of fifteenth-century
porcelain, plus broken coarse-ware, nails and ironwork
that were harder to attribute, but which all presumably
came from the same wreck. But *what* wreck? Everything
they could date pointed to early fifteenth-century Chinese,
which made it overwhelmingly likely that this ship had
once been a part of one of Zheng He's famed treasure
fleets, which had sailed near this channel around that
time. But those vast armadas had been made up of all
kinds of vessels, and most of them had been ordinary
junks and supply ships. Magnificent finds, of course, and
historically significant. But not what they were after.

Another current swept him towards the tiger. He
grabbed instinctively for the sea-bed, fingers raking the sand
before hooking something solid. He held it till the current
had relented, looked down. It was reddish-brown and
scabbed, and it protruded in too smooth a curve from
the sea-bed to be natural. He brushed away sand to
reveal the top of a rusted iron ring, perhaps a foot in

diameter. He checked to make sure that Miles was filming, then beckoned Klaus to bring over one of their water-dredges. The fat grey pipe quickly sucked away the sand and sediment until he'd completely exposed an iron doughnut at one end of a fat long metal rod, like the eye at the top of an impossibly large needle.

The second dive-team arrived with a second dredge, set to work in parallel. The iron shaft grew longer and longer. It could surely only be an anchor. Knox felt his excitement build. Just as it was possible to make an educated guess at a person's height from the length of their stride, so it was possible to estimate a ship's size from certain of its component parts. The Chinese treasure ships had reputedly been equipped with anchors eight feet long, fitted with iron flukes to hook on to rocks or dig into sand, and so hold the ship in position. Knox had to remind himself to keep breathing steadily as they exposed a good six feet of shaft. Eight feet. Ten feet and still going. Twelve. And finally they found the first fluke. Knox glanced around at Miles, still filming like the profes-sional he was, but pumping his free fist in triumph; and the exultation of all the others was magnified by the strange distortion of their goggles. For it was surely un-deniable now. They'd found what they'd come looking for.

They'd found a Chinese treasure ship.

II

The Nergadze estate, Georgian Black Sea Coast
It was the first time in two years that Boris Dekanosidze had laid eyes on Ilya Nergadze, and what he saw shocked him. The great man was a frail shell of himself, shrunken, pale and bald, lying huddled beneath thick blankets on his medical bed despite the cloying warmth of the room. He had a translucent oxygen mask over his mouth and nose, sensors and tubes on his arms and throat, banks of monitors and other medical equipment on either side, while a disturbingly androgynous male nurse in a starched white uniform sat on a high chair overlooking him, like an umpire at a tennis match.

So the rumours were true, then: Old Man Ilya was dying.

Ilya's bed was mechanised, allowing him to raise himself almost to a sitting position as Boris walked towards him. With a weak and trembling hand, he clawed down his breathing mask so that it hung around his throat like a grotesque medallion. 'Good to see you, Boris,' he croaked, raising his head so that Boris could kiss him respectfully on both cheeks.

'Good to see you too, sir,' he said. 'It's been too long.'

'Yes,' murmured Ilya. But even that much conversation seemed to exhaust him. He let his head drop into his pillow, pulled his breathing mask back up.

Sandro Nergadze, Ilya's son and heir apparent, had followed Boris to the bed. Now he cleared his throat to gain the nurse's attention. 'A few moments, please,' he said.

'Five minutes,' said the nurse primly. 'Your father must have his rest.'

'Five minutes,' agreed Sandro, with a tight smile. He was courteous for a Nergadze, but that didn't mean he liked taking orders from the help. He rested his brief-case on the bedside table, then accompanied the nurse to the door, closing it emphatically behind him before returning to his father's bed and standing across it from Boris, so that his father could follow their conversation with his eyes, even if he was too tired to take part in it himself.

'Well?' asked Boris. 'What can I do for you?'

Sandro pursed his lips before replying. 'You know as well as anyone, Boris, that our family has its fair share of enemies.'

Boris nodded. He'd been Sandro's head of security until everything had gone to shit, after all. 'Of course, sir.'

'Things have grown even worse since our Greek . . . *setback*.'

Our Greek setback, thought Boris. *Is that what they're calling it these days?* Some two years before, during Ilya Nergadze's ill-fated run at the presidency of the Republic of Georgia, the campaign team had got a tip that their nation's greatest lost treasure, the golden fleece, had been rediscovered in Greece. But their efforts to bring it back here and so boost Ilya's flagging popularity had back-fired spectacularly, culminating in the death of Ilya's grandson Mikhail and the destruction of the family's business empire and political aspirations. 'I can imagine.'

'It's not merely that we have more enemies now,' continued Sandro. 'It's also that they've grown bolder, less respectful. People no longer *fear* us as they did. We've introduced extra security, as you no doubt noticed. We've also been compelled to start a programme of active threat monitoring.'

'Active threat monitoring, sir?'

Sandro gestured towards the French windows, the fine view over treetops down to the Black Sea. 'It's the damned Internet,' he said. 'It's the easiest thing in the world, these days, for our enemies to learn about us. They download satellite photographs of our estates. They check for our names at public events. They search the archives of local newspapers. They gossip about what cars we drive, what planes and yachts we own. All from the comfort and safety of their living rooms.' He turned back to face Boris. 'But it works both ways, particularly if you hire the right people.'

Boris nodded. The Nergadzes had never begrudged spending money on their own safety. 'As you have, no doubt.'

'We've set up various websites and chat rooms,' said

Sandro. 'We've seeded them with the kind of confidential information that our enemies would dearly love to know. Some of it's even true. We make these sites hard to find, so that only our more dedicated . . . *followers* can find them. Then we monitor them, particularly for return visitors. Mostly these prove to be journalists or business rivals. Nuisances, not menaces.'

'But not always?' suggested Boris.

Sandro opened his briefcase, drew out a single folded sheet of paper. 'One of the most persistent comes from a British marine salvage company called MGS,' he said. 'Quite small. Just fifteen full-time employees, though they add subcontractors for certain projects. They're scheduled to run a month-long survey of the eastern Black Sea this autumn.'

'Ah,' said Boris, glancing towards the French windows.

'This is a printout of their *Who We Are* page,' said Sandro, passing Boris the sheet. 'Recognise anyone?'

Boris unfolded the page, eight thumbnails of young and middle-aged men, presumably senior staff. But the portraits were too small for him to tell much about them; and the names and job titles meant nothing either. 'Sorry,' he said.

'Bottom row,' prompted Sandro. 'Second from right.'

Boris looked again. A man called Matthew Richardson. His photo wasn't just small, it was blurred, too, as though taken on the move. And now that it had his attention, there *was* something faintly familiar about him, though he couldn't at first work out what. But then he realised who Sandro and Ilya thought it was, if only because they'd never have summoned him here otherwise. He flinched from an unpleasant memory like flesh from a flame, shook his head. 'Daniel Knox is dead,' he said emphatically. 'He had kidney failure from the burns he took when he and Mikhail . . .' He trailed off, not wanting to finish the thought.

'That's what they told us,' agreed Sandro.

'Why would they have lied?' asked Boris. But he realised the answer even as he spoke. They'd have lied to protect Knox from the five million euro bounty that Ilya Nergadze had put on his head in retribution for killing his grandson during the golden fleece fiasco. Boris breathed in deep before he looked again at the photo. There *was* a superficial resemblance; he couldn't deny it. And the man in the photo had shaven his scalp and grown a thin beard, much as you'd expect from someone trying to change their look. But he also had higher cheekbones than he remembered Knox having, the bridge of his nose was broader, and he looked darker, older, angrier and altogether more formidable. He shook his head as he looked back up at Sandro. 'It's not him,' he said.

'Are you certain?' asked Sandro. 'Bear in mind you might not be the only one who's had plastic surgery.'

'Then how can you possibly expect me to identify him

18

from this?' protested Boris. 'I'd need to be able to get up close to him, see how he walks, hear his voice and how . . .' He broke off as he realised belatedly where this was going. 'No way,' he said flatly. 'The Europeans have my biometrics. They have my DNA. They'd grab me the moment I landed. I'd never get out this time.'

'Relax,' said Sandro. 'We're not suggesting you go back to Europe. As you say, it was hard enough for us to get you out last time.' He allowed a little time to pass, presumably to let Boris reflect on the fact that he'd still be in his Greek hellhole prison if the Nergadzes hadn't had him sprung. 'But this man isn't in England at the moment. Or even in Europe. That's why we brought you here so urgently. We only learned of it ourselves this morning.'

'Where, then?'

'On a salvage project,' said Sandro, opening his briefcase again, taking out a bulky white envelope that he offered across. 'Off the west coast of Madagascar.'

The envelope's flap was tucked inside itself. The edge of the stiff paper cut Boris's thumb as he released it, coaxing out a thin line of blood that left a series of smudged red partials on the contents as he spread them on the bedside table: ten thousand euros in several bundles of banknotes; a sheaf of press-cuttings about some Chinese shipwreck; a first-class ticket in his new name, flying via Istanbul and Johannesburg to the Madagascan capital Antananarivo; a separate ticket on to some provincial airport he'd never heard of called Morombe. 'And what do you expect me to do when I get to this place?'

'We want you to track down this man Richardson,' replied Sandro. 'We want you to determine whether or not he is really Daniel Knox.'

'And if he is?' asked Boris.

Sandro glanced down at the floor, his discomfort evident. But a noise to Boris's left startled him. He'd almost forgotten that Ilya was there. The old man clawed his mask down once more so that he could speak; his mouth and eyes were cruel and fierce, though his voice was so weak that Boris had to lean in closer to him to make out the words.

'I want you to kill him,' he said.

TWO

I

The tiger shark reappeared while Knox and the rest of his dive-team were at three metres, finishing their decompression. It circled several times, looking unnervingly interested, but then the inflatable arrived to pick them up, and the noise and churn of its outboard seemed to deter it, for it turned and swam away.

The *Maritsa* was chugging slowly towards them as they surfaced. It usually stayed well clear of the wreck-site, partly from respect for the nearby reefs, made doubly dangerous by the freak waves that sometimes came out of nowhere along this coast, but mostly to make it hard for anyone watching to mark the site of the wreck with a notional X. But the stern crane was the easiest way to recover artefacts the size of the anchor, which meant positioning directly above it.

As an archaeologist, Knox was accustomed to taking plenty of time examining artefacts in their context before recovering them; but that wasn't possible here. They only had the *Maritsa* for six weeks, and once they were done they couldn't lock this site up as they could on land, put a fence around it and hire security guards until the following year. It would be open season for any unscrupulous treasure hunter with some scuba gear or even an industrial dredge, so they needed to recover what they could, while they could.

They climbed the starboard gangway, stripped off on the stern deck, hosed themselves down with fresh water. A door banged open on the strengthening wind, and Ricky Cheung emerged from the conference room, puffing at one of his evil roll-ups. Ricky was the head of this salvage operation, an overweight Chinese American in his mid-fifties with perpetually tired eyes, as though he'd just woken. He waited a moment for a fair-haired woman in outsized sunglasses and a baseball cap to follow him outside, with Maddow the Shadow, his personal cameraman, bringing up the rear. Ricky spotted Knox and waved cheerfully, then led his small party over. 'The hero of the hour,' he beamed. 'Great job down there.'

'Thanks,' said Knox.

Ricky nodded, turned to the fair-haired woman. 'This is the one I was telling you about, Lucia,' he said. 'Matthew Richardson. Though everyone calls him Danny for some reason.' He turned to Knox with a frown. 'Why is that, actually?'

'My father was Matthew too,' said Knox, with practised ease. 'Calling me Daniel saved confusion.' In truth, he'd been such a mess for the first few months after Athens, especially from Mikhail Nergadze's brutal murder of his fiancée Gaille, that he'd often not responded when people called him by his new name. At work one time, Miles – one of the few people who knew the truth about his past – had grown so exasperated by this that he'd yelled out his real name instead, provoking the obvious questions from his new colleagues, forcing him to come up with an explanation on the hoof. His handlers at MI5 had been admirably understanding about it, retrospectively tweaking his new identity to make Daniel his middle name; and he'd been Daniel ever since, except in interviews and other formal contexts.

'Must have been one hell of a thrill,' said Ricky. 'Finding that anchor, I mean.'

'Yes,' agreed Knox.

'Most archaeologists go their whole career without ever making a find like that.'

'Quite.'

Ricky's expression clouded briefly, as though he

suspected Knox was making fun of him; but he quickly brightened again. 'Lucia is here to write an article about me,' he said.

'About the salvage, actually.' She removed her sunglasses, showing off striking blue eyes. She was in her mid-forties, at a guess, with an attractive, open face and the kind of pale freckled skin that needed protection from the Madagascan sun.

'Pleased to meet you,' said Knox.

'I'll leave you two together, if I may,' said Ricky. 'All those questions you had about history and archaeology, Danny Boy's your man.' He nodded cordially to them both, then walked briskly over to the stern crane, where the hoisting of the anchor was just getting underway, and barked out redundant orders for Maddow the Shadow to capture for posterity.

'What a wretch!' scowled Lucia. 'That's your triumph he's stealing.'

'He's been working towards this for thirty years,' said Knox. 'I've been here less than a week.'

'I've never met a man who talked about himself so much,' she said. 'I thought he must be a flamenco singer. You know: aye, aye, aye, aye, aye.'

Knox smiled politely. He knew better than to give a journalist easy copy about dissension in the ranks. 'You have some questions for me?' he suggested.

'Yes.' She gave him a warm smile, calibrated to win

his sympathy. 'I'm a travel writer really, you see. It's how I pay for my holidays. I come to a place like this for a month with lots of ideas for possible features, but I'm never quite sure which will pan out and which won't.'

'I understand.'

'I was supposed to be heading down to the Eden Nature Reserve today.'

'The Kirkpatricks' place?'

'You know them?'

Knox gave a noncommittal shrug. 'They're pretty well-known along this coast.'

'They were supposed to have left a message letting me know when would be a good time to visit. But there was nothing at my hotel, and so I wanted to bag another story, just in case. My concierge suggested I come out here, and even arranged it for me, which was terrific of him; but of course I never had the chance to do any background reading, and your boss is a hard man to interrupt once he gets going. All that stuff about China and the treasure fleets – honestly, I had no idea what he was talking about half the time.'

Knox nodded. Ricky was notorious for giving lectures rather than interviews. 'So you'd like a little background?'

'That would be wonderful. Yes.'

'Okay,' said Knox. 'Then let's head on back to thirteenth-century China.'

II

Sandro Nergadze was walking Boris out to the courtyard when he touched his elbow and drew him to one side, out of earshot of staff and bodyguards. 'A question,' he said.

'Yes?'

'How do you feel about Davit Kipshidze?'

Blood rushed to Boris's cheeks; anger clenched his heart. Davit was a former rugby lock he'd used a few times for strong-arm work, because the man was a giant and just having him standing beside you prevented a whole heap of trouble. But the moment their Greek enterprise had turned to shit, he'd broken like a little girl and blabbed his mouth off. He said bitterly: 'You should have left him in Athens to rot.'

'And have him reveal our secrets in open court?' asked Sandro rhetorically. 'Besides, he's one of us. His father did some excellent work for us; his sister is married to my cousin. And a lot of our people like him. They say what happened in Athens wasn't his fault, that he should never have been on that kind of a job in the first place.'

Boris bridled. He'd picked Boris for that mission himself, as Sandro knew full well. 'He'd always done okay before.'

'Of course,' said Sandro smoothly. 'It's just that I'm hearing more and more that we should give him another chance.'

For the second time that day, Boris realised he'd been slow to see where Sandro was steering the conversation. 'No,' he said. 'I'm not taking him with me. What if he gets spotted at the airport? He'll take me down for sure.'

'Relax. We'd send him on a later flight. You'd only meet up again in Madagascar.'

'I don't trust him. I *won't* trust him. He wouldn't do it anyway. He's too much of a do-gooder.'

'He might, if he didn't know your real purpose.' Sandro nodded through the front door to the courtyard, where a white van with tinted windows was parked on the cobblestones. 'All he knows so far is that we've a possible job for him. What if we were to tell him only that Knox may still be alive, and that we want you both to go see if it really is him; and if so, to persuade him to a truce?'

'He's not *that* stupid.'

'You're wrong,' said Sandro. 'Men like Davit always assume the best about their fellow men. That's why people like him. Besides, he *wants* to believe it. This is his opportunity to redeem himself for Athens.'

'It'll take more than this,' snorted Boris.

'And he'll be useful to you. He's the only other person we have who knows what Knox looks like, after all. He's strong as a bull and he's good with equipment too. Remember that computer business he tried to start?'

'So?'

'My father is taking a personal interest in this matter,

as you've seen. We'll therefore be supplying you with a satellite videophone.'

'Are you fucking kidding me?' scowled Boris. 'You want me to top Knox live on TV? What if those bastards in Tbilisi are watching?

'You think we're idiots?' asked Sandro. 'All our equipment is fitted with our own encryption software. We use it all the time for our more . . . *controversial* businesses.'

Boris nodded. The Nergadzes had made their original fortune smuggling arms for heroin. If Sandro was confident that a communications link was secure, it was secure. 'Okay,' he said grudgingly.

'Good. It'll make it much easier for us to communicate and provide the necessary . . . *logistical support*.'

'Logistical support,' snorted Boris. Sandro did love his euphemisms. What he meant was that they'd have to get him a gun once he arrived in Madagascar, because there was no way to take one on board a plane, not these days. 'And what will Davit think about that?'

'I don't imagine we'll be having that conversation in his presence,' said Sandro. 'Do you?'

'Okay,' said Boris. 'But I'm not doing this for free. Not on camera, for Christ's sake. You offered five million euros for Knox's head. I assume that's still good.'

'We retracted that offer once we learned Knox was dead.'

'But he's not dead.'

'We'll pay you one hundred thousand euros for the identification, whether it's him or not,' said Sandro. 'If it is him, my father has authorised another four hundred thousand for . . . for carrying out his wishes.'

Boris nodded. Five hundred grand was proper money, and there'd surely be opportunities for more. The Nergadzes' reputation and business empire had been badly hit by the fallout from the Greek debacle, but Ilya was still richer than God, and he clearly craved this revenge before he croaked. And revenge was like champagne: the more it cost, the better it tasted. 'What about Davit?' he asked. 'You don't expect me to split my money with him, do you?'

'No,' said Sandro. 'I'll make a separate agreement with Davit. Your money will be yours. His will be his. Agreed?'

'Fine,' said Boris. 'Agreed.'

'Good,' said Sandro, nodding at the van. 'Then let's go talk to him.'

III

Lucia took a microcassette recorder from her bag. 'You don't mind, do you?' she asked.

'Of course not,' said Knox.

She nodded at the crane, the metal beginning to groan

and shriek a little as it took the weight of the anchor and began lifting it from the sea-bed. 'And maybe we could go somewhere quieter?'

He led her up a gangway and past the ship's decompression chamber, leaned against the starboard rail. The wind had picked up; the sea was getting frisky. The ship's dynamic positioning system had been turned on, however, and its GPS sensors, gyroscopes and thrusters were keeping them impressively steady, a vital capability for using a crane on a sea-bed sixty metres deep. A large wave swept past them to break against the reef. On its far side, he could see the white cotton sails of several fishing pirogues in the lagoon, all of them heading for shore. 'Better?' he asked.

'Perfect,' said Lucia. 'You were about to sweep me off to thirteenth-century China.'

'The time of the Mongol Khans,' said Knox. 'Genghis was a conqueror. He rampaged through Russia and China and put the fear of God into Europeans.' Literally, as it had happened: Christians had feared he and his armies were the end-times prophecy of Gog and Magog made flesh. 'But his successors were different, particularly his grandson Kublai.'

'In Xanadu did Kublai Khan a sacred pleasure dome decree,' suggested Lucia.

'That's the guy,' agreed Knox. 'He saw himself as a *ruler* more than a general, and China was the jewel in his

30

crown. He established a new capital at Beijing, tried to win over his new Chinese subjects by appointing them to key positions. But it never really took. The Han and the Mongols each considered the other inferior. And these were tough times anyway. China was hit by the black death almost as badly as Europe, and there was massive flooding, hyperinflation, poverty and famine. The Han began to rebel, as did other ethnic groups. The first uprisings were quashed but each new one weakened the Mongols' grip a little more until the empire finally collapsed in 1368. One of the rebel leaders, a Han called Zhu Yuanzhang, seized the Dragon Throne and proclaimed himself first emperor of the Great Ming.'

'That being the start of the Ming Dynasty, presumably?'

'Yes. Zhu Yuanzhang held power for thirty years or so, but his succession proved a problem. His eldest son, the Crown Prince, died before him, forcing him to pick between his own most capable surviving son – a man called Zhu Di – or to skip a generation and appoint his grandson Zhu Yunwen instead. He went for his grandson.'

'Don't tell me: Zhu Di got mad.'

'It depends on who you believe,' Knox told her. 'We know that Zhu Yunwen was worried sick about rivals. After his ascension, he barred Zhu Di from even paying respects to his dead father – a major humiliation – then stripped his supporters of rank, effectively forcing him to give up or fight back. He chose to fight back. Skirmishes with the imperial army turned into a low-level civil war. In 1402, Zhu Di marched on Nanjing, China's new capital, and his nephew fled. Then he declared himself the Yongle Emperor. Emperor of eternal happiness.'

Lucia smiled. 'No worries about raising expectations, then.'

'He didn't do too badly, all in all. He excised his nephew from the history books and purged his supporters; but that was pretty standard. He fought off the Mongols and the Vietnamese, introduced land reclamation and other successful agricultural policies, rebuilt the Grand Canal and moved his capital back to Beijing. He also commissioned a series of magnificent armadas.'

'Ah. Our famous treasure fleets.'

'This was unprecedented. The Han Chinese were Confucians; only China mattered. If the barbarian world had business with China, it had to make the journey itself. But Zhu Di didn't think that way. He wanted to show off, and maybe let it be known around the region that he wasn't a man to mess with. His nephew was rumoured still to be alive, after all, so the last thing he'd have wanted was any lingering questions about his legitimacy. Whatever his reasons, he ordered a man called Zheng He to build a vast fleet then sail around the China Seas to establish diplomatic and trading links, suppress any unrest in China's overseas territories, that kind of thing.'

'Zheng He. This would be the eunuch, right?'

'Yes. He was actually a Chinese Muslim whose family had fought with the Mongols, and he was taken captive and then castrated when still just a boy. It happened a lot back then. But he made a name for himself, become one of Zhu Di's favourites.' Lucia raised an eyebrow, making Knox laugh. 'Not in *that* sense,' he assured her. 'Zhu Di liked the ladies. Koreans, for choice. But that was precisely why he trusted eunuchs: they wouldn't cause mischief in his harem, and they had no dynastic ambitions of their own.'

'Okay. So Mr Eternal Happiness commissions his favourite eunuch to go sailing. And there were multiple voyages, right?'

'Seven in all, though the final one was much later, more an afterthought than anything. Mostly they visited the places you'd expect: Sumatra and Java and the other main Indonesian islands. Vietnam, Thailand, Sri Lanka, Malaya, India. Places which were pretty well known to the Chinese. Their fourth voyage made it to Arabia and East Africa, but it's the sixth that's the most intriguing. Zheng He didn't actually go very far himself, but various of his vice-admirals each led a contingent of their own, and we're not entirely sure where they went, not least because there was a great fire in Beijing shortly after they set out, which the emperor interpreted as a divine admonishment against his treasure fleets, so all records of the voyage were destroyed.'

'And this anchor of yours would have come from this sixth voyage, right?'

'Most likely,' agreed Knox. 'Though Chinese ships were hopeless at sailing against the wind: they pretty much had to go wherever the weather took them. That was fine, most of the time, because the trade winds are very reliable between Africa and China. But if some Chinese ship from one of the other fleets *had* been blown off course at the wrong time, it might have had little choice except to end up here. And these armadas were *huge*. There were supposed to be three hundred and seventeen ships in the first voyage alone, carrying over twenty-eight thousand people. Even allowing for some exaggeration, that's pretty damned impressive. The demand for wood was so intense that they deforested whole regions of China. Most of the ships were supply boats, troop transports, that kind of thing. Others were for cargo, for these were trading missions too, swapping Chinese silks and porcelain for highly prized goods like pearls, ivory and exotic woods. But each fleet also included a number of what were known as treasure ships. These were floating palaces, really; or perhaps more accurately *embassies*, designed specifically to impress and intimidate foreign powers. They were reputed to be over four hundred feet long and a hundred and eighty feet wide. That's like floating a football stadium out to sea. This was ninety-odd years before Columbus, yet these beasts were more than twice as *wide* as the *Santa Maria* was *long*. They had nine masts, the tallest of which was said to have stood over three hundred feet high.'

'Three hundred feet?' Lucia pulled a face. 'Is that even possible?'

'A lot of historians and shipbuilders think not. They say the treasure ships were more likely to have been six-masters, only about two hundred foot long.' He gave a little grin, nodded over the side of the ship down towards the sea-bed. 'But that's what makes all this so exciting: we won't know one way or the other until we—' Cheers and hoots erupted at the stern. He looked around to see that the anchor had just breached the surface of the water, like some great whale coming up for air, streams of seawater cascading from it and the steel cable and the hoist straps at either end as it was slowly raised higher and higher.

'Wow!' murmured Lucia, producing a camera from her bag.

'You want to go closer?' asked Knox. She nodded eagerly, so he led her back down. The crane arm began to turn, bringing the black and rust-red anchor around over the deck, its cables and straps creaking loudly from the stress, everyone standing well clear. When the anchor was above the open hatches of the hold, the crane operator stopped it and gave it a few moments to come to rest. Crewmen gathered on every side, holding their hands out to stop the anchor from swinging, buffer it from banging against the sides as it was lowered into the hold, where the project's conservators were already waiting.

'It truly is something,' said Lucia, snapping away. 'I hadn't imagined it would be—' She jumped visibly at a loud bang from behind her, as though something electrical had blown. They all looked around. The ship listed a little to port, and the anchor began to swing again, like a gigantic pendulum nudged by a celestial finger. Knox glanced over at Miles and saw the anxiety on his face that he knew would be mirrored on his own.

One of their dynamic positioning thrusters had blown. And that meant trouble.

THREE

I

Kirkpatrick Films' Head Office, Covent Garden, London
Rebecca Kirkpatrick was doing her best to concentrate on what Titch Osmond, her Chief Financial Officer, was telling her, but it was hard, what with Nicola's scribbled note in her lap. She glanced surreptitiously down at it yet again.

Pierre Demullin (???) called. From Madagascar (!?!). Will call back later.

All those exclamation and question marks; they'd got beneath her skin. She was constantly getting calls from all over the world, and it was hardly a secret that her mother had been Malagasy, if only because of her own mix of Polynesian, African and European looks. So what about this particular message had made all those exclamation marks necessary? She breathed in deep, trying to maintain her calm. It wasn't *that* surprising that Pierre should call. He was her childhood neighbour and her father's closest friend, as well as her sister Emilia's lover and the father of her infant son Michel. Yet Rebecca hadn't spoken to him in eleven years, and the truth was she couldn't imagine what would have prompted him to call her, not out of the blue like this.

'Your mind's not on it,' said Titch. 'Shall we do this later?'

Rebecca smiled with artificial brightness. It wasn't as if there was anything she could do before Pierre rang back, after all. 'It's fine,' she assured him. 'You were telling me about our cash-flow.'

'Yes,' said Titch, flipping on through his ring-binder. 'We need another sixty-seven to see us through to July.'

'Sixty-seven?' She wrinkled her nose. 'Is that all?'

He gave a wry laugh. 'Sixty-seven's not nothing, you know.'

'Can't we borrow?' She glanced down at Nicola's note again. It wasn't quite true that she couldn't imagine why Pierre might call. That was the thing that was unnerving her. He'd certainly be the person to contact her in an emergency if neither Adam nor Emilia could get to a phone.

'You think I haven't tried?' frowned Titch, as though

she'd cast a slur upon his character. 'No one will lend us any more.'

'Why not? We're profitable, aren't we?'

'On paper, yes.' He looked up and momentarily caught her eye before hurriedly looking away again, his cheeks flaming. A couple of months before, out at a working dinner, he'd seized her hand in both of his and declared undying love. She'd put it down at the time to alcohol and the recent break-up of his marriage, but little moments like this made her wonder if it wasn't more serious than that. She devoutly hoped not. She was deeply fond of Titch, and valued him highly, yet she felt nothing remotely romantic for him. He bowed his head and turned another leaf in his ring-binder. 'But we have no assets to speak of,' he continued, 'and we keep hitting these cash-flow problems, and those two together are like a big flashing red light to the banks.'

'So what do you recommend?' The question was, what kind of emergency would keep *both* Adam and Emilia from the phone?

'Well,' said Titch. 'We have three main avenues. I'm talking as the company here, you understand. The first thing we can do is, we can go after the people who owe us money.'

'You mean me, I suppose?'

He twisted his pen around in his hands. 'Mostly, yes.'

'How much is it now?'

'Two hundred and eighty. A little over. And our loan arrangement did specify repayment within—'

'And the second option?' If anything had happened to Emilia, her father would have been the one to call. If anything had happened to her father, it would be Emilia. She closed her eyes for a moment, not willing to pursue her logic further.

'We've been expanding really quickly lately. Taking on staff. But most of our projects are costing us a lot more than they're bringing in.'

'You want me to fire people?'

'You asked me to outline our options. That's one of them.'

'What else?'

'This is a fine business you're building, Rebecca,' said Titch. 'We've already had unsolicited approaches from several companies. They'd pay top dollar.'

'No,' she bridled. 'This is *my* company.'

'Please, Rebecca. At least think about it. You're a great presenter. I mean, a *great* presenter. But you're not a businesswoman. You're not here often enough, for one thing. You're always off filming. And your heart's not in it, not really, not if you're honest with yourself.'

'I won't take orders.'

'No one would give you orders,' laughed Titch ruefully. 'They wouldn't dare, frankly. If you left, there'd hardly be a company any more.'

He was stroking her ego, she knew, yet it worked all the same. 'There must be some alternative,' she said. 'Can't we ride it out until America comes in?'

'There's no guarantee America *will* come in,' Titch told her. 'And, anyway, we won't know for weeks at least; and we won't see any real revenue for months after that. In the meantime we have our salaries and rent to pay, our suppliers to—'

A double rap on the door. Nicola poked in her head, smiled brightly. 'You said to let you know when that Frenchman called back,' she said.

Rebecca's mouth went dry and her heart started thumping hard. 'Pierre?'

'He's on hold right now.'

'Okay. Put him through.'

'Will do.'

'You couldn't give me a moment, please,' Rebecca asked Titch. 'I really have to take this.'

'Of course.' He rose to his feet. 'We'll finish this later.'

She nodded and took a deep breath, wiped her palms upon her trousers. On her desk, her phone began to ring.

II

The *Maritsa* lurched into another wave valley, sending the anchor swinging back across the open hatch like a wrecking ball. Knox crouched down and waved to the two conservators in the hold to get clear. Another wave passed beneath them. The *Maritsa* rolled harder; the anchor gained momentum. Klaus put out both hands in an effort to stop it, but it simply pushed him backwards until he tripped over a davit and fell on to his backside. It should have been funny, but no one was laughing. Something this heavy could do untold damage. It swung towards Lucia; she dithered about which way to evade it for so long that Knox had to push her clear, sending her sprawling across the deck.

The crane operator glanced overboard, clearly thinking of dumping the anchor back at sea; but there was a team of divers still underwater, and it would put them at fearful risk. Knox waited for the anchor to reach the end of its next swing, grabbed hold of its end and hauled himself up, then began using his weight to work against the roll of the boat, like a child slowing a playground swing. Miles saw what he was doing and clambered up too, and together they calmed the anchor enough for the crane operator to lower it safely through the open hatch. The moment it passed beneath deck level, they leapt free, allowing the other crew to close the hatch, cutting down the anchor's room to swing, its ability to cause damage. They heard it thump hard into the hold floor then roll briefly until it found its angle of repose. They opened the hatch back up. The conservators were already on either side of the anchor, releasing it from its straps. Ricky had somehow got down there already, shouting out his usual orders for Maddow's camera. Knox looked around. No one appeared badly hurt, though Lucia was still on her backside, looking a little pale. 'Sorry about that,' said Knox, helping her up.

'Christ!' she muttered. 'The *size* of that thing! I'd have been *jam*.' She brushed herself down, gave him a dry smile. 'You're not planning to bring everything up this way, I hope?'

'It'll be fine,' he assured her. 'One of our thrusters broke at a bad time, that's all. We've got spares. And we're unlikely to find anything else that size.'

'If you say so.'

Movement out on the water caught his eye: Garry at the helm of their Bayliner, bringing Dieter Holm for his presentation. He leaned over the gunwale to watch the motorboat slapping inelegantly through the rising sea, shipping far more water than was prudent. 'Were you planning on getting back to Morombe tonight?' he asked.

'Uh-oh,' said Lucia. 'I don't like the sound of that.'

'This weather's not great,' he said. 'If it doesn't improve soon . . .'

'Would there be somewhere for me to sleep?'

'Of course. And it probably won't come to that.'

'Then I'll keep my fingers crossed. In the meantime, is it okay if I ask another question?'

'Sure. Fire away.'

She gave him a slightly crooked smile, as if to apologise in advance. 'It's just that your boss was telling me about some family folklore of his.'

'Ah,' said Knox.

'Apparently one of his great, great ancestors originally arrived in California on some huge boat from China. He assured me this was at least five hundred years ago, more like six, a good century before any Europeans got there.'

'It's perfectly plausible,' said Knox. 'The Spanish discovered the Philippines in 1520, and it kicked off a pretty substantial trade between Manila and Mexico. Some Chinese certainly came over to the Americas then. Maybe Ricky's ancestor was among them.'

'That's not what he's claiming.'

'I know it's not,' said Knox. Ricky was convinced that his ancestors had arrived in America on one of Zheng He's treasure ships, long before Columbus and the Spanish: that the Chinese, therefore, were the first true discoverers and settlers of America.

'So? Do you think he's a crank?'

'People called Schliemann a crank,' replied Knox. 'He discovered Troy. And plenty thought Columbus a crank. He discovered the New World.'

'And you'd put your boss in their class, would you?'

'Sometimes people make important discoveries because

they stick to unorthodox beliefs even when the world's laughing at them. Most people would have given up long ago, but Ricky's kept at it, and I admire him immensely for that.' It was true enough. Thirty years ago, Ricky had set about proving that his family tradition was for real, scouring America's western seaboard for evidence of fifteenth-century Chinese ships. When he'd come up dry, he'd searched the east coast instead, before working his way south through Latin and South America, combing beaches, talking to local museums and amateur historians, following up each and every promising lead. When he'd run out of American coastline, he'd turned his attention to Atlantic and Pacific islands instead, then Africa. In all, he'd announced the discovery of a treasure ship no fewer than seven times. The first six had led only to his public humiliation, yet still he'd carried on. And finally he'd come to Madagascar, where he'd seen a rusted cannon in the grounds of a tourist hotel here in Morombe. No one had thought much of it until then, because cannons were common on this coast, from the vast number of ships sunk over the centuries doing the run from Europe to the Indies. But Ricky had recognised instantly that this cannon was different. This cannon had been fifteenth-century Chinese.

'So do you agree with him?' asked Lucia. 'That a treasure ship could have made it all the way to America, I mean?'

'I'm a scientist,' he told her. 'I go where the evidence takes me.'

FOUR

I

Rebecca's heart was in her mouth as she picked up the receiver. 'This is Rebecca,' she said.

'Rebecca? *Cherie? C'est Pierre ici.* Pierre Desmoulins.'

'Pierre. What is it? What's happened?'

'Please.' His voice sounded strained, thin, far away. 'You're not to panic. We know nothing for sure yet.'

'Tell me.'

'Cherie, they find your father's boat out at sea. *Personne à bord.*'

'When?'

'Last night. But no one see your father or your sister since yesterday morning.'

'Emilia?' Rebecca's heart plunged. 'Not Emilia too.'

'I'm sorry,' said Pierre. 'But you mustn't give up hope.'

'What about Michel?' Michel was Emilia's infant son.

'He's safe,' said Pierre. 'Emilia leave him with Therese before she go out.'

'Are you searching for them now?'

'Not me myself; not yet. I'm in Antananarivo for a conference. I only just learned of this myself. I wanted to tell you as soon as possible. But sure, everyone is looking, of course they are.'

'I'm flying out,' said Rebecca. Now that the worst had been confirmed, she felt detached yet strangely calm. 'I'll be on the first flight.'

'Good. I think that is wise. And I'll make sure to—' But then the line went dead.

'Pierre?' she called out. 'Pierre?' But now there was only dial-tone. Connections with Madagascar were always precarious. She put the phone down, stared at it dazedly, half-expecting Pierre to ring back. Her door banged open before he could, however, and Titch walked in, looking anxious, as though he'd overheard enough to alarm him. 'What's happened?' he asked. She repeated numbly what Pierre had told her. 'I'm so sorry,' said Titch, appalled. 'What can we do?'

'I need to get to Madagascar,' said Rebecca. 'As soon as possible. Now. This afternoon.'

Titch nodded. 'I'll take care of it.'

A sudden vision of her father the last time Rebecca had seen him, a little bowed by loss, his hair white and his eyes permanently moistening; and then of her sister Emilia, three years her junior, just a headstrong teenage girl back then, effervescent with ideas that came too quickly for her mouth to keep pace, but now a woman with an infant son. A black cavern opened inside Rebecca; she suffered a moment of terrible vertigo. Her door opened again and Nicola bustled in, her eyes down, concentrating on not spilling her plate of ginger snaps and frothy mug of hot chocolate. She set them down on the walnut desk, touched her shoulder sympathetically. Rebecca took the mug in both hands, savouring the sharp comfort of its heat, staring blankly down at the film of dark skin that thickened and wrinkled upon its cooling surface. Out in the main office, she could hear her staff working their phones, checking visa requirements, moving meetings, cancelling appearances, swept up by the drama of someone else's tragedy. Ken shouted out that the first flight left Heathrow later that afternoon, flying to Antananarivo via Paris, only business class available. Three thousand five hundred and twenty-eight quid. Should he take it? If so, how should he pay? There was a beat of silence in the office. Rebecca's breath caught in her throat. She took one hand off her hot chocolate and clenched it beneath the table, only too well aware that her own credit cards would never take such a hit.

'Company account,' said Titch.

'But I thought we weren't allowed to—'

'Company account,' repeated Titch, more firmly. 'We'll sort it out later.'

Nicola began reading out a list of prevalent diseases, Lindsay checking them against Rebecca's vaccination record. Bilharzia, meningitis, rabies, intestinal worms, dengue haemorrhagic fever. Rebecca felt dismay as the list went on. Cholera, filariasis, TB, yellow fever, typhus, hepatitis. She'd lived in Madagascar eighteen years, remembered none of this. A high-risk malignant malarial region with chloroquine and fansidar resistance. Lariam gave her nightmares, doxycycline turned her skin orange; she'd need Malarone instead. They'd a month's worth in the storeroom. Titch brought in a box, along with a thick sheaf of euros that he slipped clandestinely into her bag. Then he sank to his haunches and spoke slowly and clearly. Everything was in hand. A taxi was on its way to take her home to pack and then on to the airport. Her ticket to Antananarivo was bought and paid for, as was her ongoing flight from Antananarivo to Tulear, the airport nearest her home. They were still working on a driver to meet her at Tulear Airport with a hire car; he'd text her the details the moment he had them. In the meantime, she was to forget about their earlier conversation; he'd handle everything until she got back. She took and squeezed his hand in gratitude. Their eyes met; he seemed on the verge of saying something else, but then thought better of it. The buzzer sounded. Her taxi was already downstairs. She packed up her laptop, her international power adapter and spare fuse, was hurrying to the door when she glanced back, saw her staff gathered in a rough semicircle, their faces solemn and troubled, like mourners at a graveside, as though they'd already accepted the worst.

She stopped and took a pace back towards them. 'They're not dead,' she said defiantly. 'You hear me? They're not dead.'

Titch came over and took her in his arms, squeezed her so tight that she could feel their hearts banging. 'They're not dead,' he murmured. 'You'll find them. If anyone can, you can.'

II

Knox arrived in the conference room for Holm's presentation to find only Miles already there, his feet up on the conference table, scrunching up sheets of paper from his pad, trying to score three-pointers in the waste-paper basket, and not doing very well to judge from the mess he'd made of the floor. 'Just us?' he asked.

'That's how Ricky wants it,' said Miles. 'We'll brief the others later.'

Knox nodded. The conservators had their hands full with the anchor; the crew with fixing the thrusters and checking hull damage from the anchor. And their MGS colleagues, while expert divers, were mostly veterans of the armed forces or the oil industry, with limited interest in the science or archaeology of the site. Besides, half of them were still on the afternoon dive, and would need to be briefed this evening anyway.

He took a chair, but found it difficult to keep still, so was soon up again, pacing the room. Their first job here had been to take scans and sediment samples. Dieter Holm and his team had been working round the clock to analyse this new data and build a three-dimensional profile of the wreck-mound from it, so that they'd have a better idea of how to go in. Tonight, therefore, was the start of the salvage proper, and Knox felt a peculiar kind of excitement he hadn't felt in a good two years.

This room was where most of the press and TV interviews were given, so Ricky had hung the walls with props: portraits of Zheng He, artists' impressions of his fleet, photographs of artefacts on the sea-bed and reproductions of medieval world maps. Knox stopped before one of these now. It was known, rather optimistically, as the Zheng He map, and it showed both hemispheres of the world, with Asia, Africa and Europe in one, America in the other. Though it dated from the eighteenth century, Ricky and many others were convinced it was a copy of an earlier

map, made by Zheng He himself in around 1420; and
that it therefore provided compelling evidence that the
Chinese had found and mapped America. Knox might
have been more open to this dating had it not been for
the use of Mercator projections a hundred years before
Mercator had even devised them, and the presence of the
word 'America' thirty years before Amerigo Vespucci had
been born.

'Ron's threatening us with another bloody curry
tonight,' said Miles, scrunching up a fresh sheet of paper.

'Hell,' said Knox. 'I only just got my stomach back
from last time.' He moved along to a photograph of the
wreck-mound. It was extraordinary the progress marine
archaeology had made these past few decades, but it
hadn't all been good. The arrival of deep-sea technologies
had enabled enterprising treasure hunters to track down
and then plunder the richest wrecks, indifferent to their
historic value. A backlash had started and international
agreement had been reached, forcing modern salvagers
to pay far more care and attention to the wrecks themselves, not just their cargoes. As a consequence, the basic
processes of wreck-site formation were now pretty well
understood. This wreck, for example: it was a fair bet
that it had sustained a hull breach on the nearby reef. It
would have had to have been severe, because the Chinese
had used sophisticated watertight bulkheads to limit
damage. Hull breaches typically sank ships in one of

two ways. Either the weight of water would put such extra stress on the hull that the stern would simply snap off from the bow; or, more commonly, the water would wash from side to side, making the ship roll ever more violently on the waves, until finally it would reach its tipping point and so capsize. Artefacts would spill from its deck as it sank, leaving a scatter-pattern on the seabed, just like the one they'd found here; while the ship itself would be pinned to the bottom by its ballast, ironwork and cargo. Prevailing currents would push sediment up against it, like snowdrifts against a wall. They'd also ratchet up the stress on the hull's caulked timbers until they snapped, exposing their unprotected innards. Barnacles, wood-boring molluscs, soft-rot fungi and cavitation bacteria would go to work. In seas this warm and fecund, the hull would quickly rot, as would any textiles, food, human and animal tissue and other organic material, leaving behind the merest traces of themselves. And, as the walls separating the internal holds and compartments rotted away, all the metal and stone artefacts would tumble together into one vast undifferentiated heap, like the grave goods of some warrior king buried beneath a great tumulus of sand, precisely like the one pictured right here, sixty metres beneath the sea.

The door opened abruptly and Dieter Holm strode in. He didn't say a word, simply set down his cardboard box on the table, then turned on his laptop. He was short and slight, with gelled-back silver hair, gold-rimmed half-moon spectacles and a sharply pointed white beard that suggested he rather fancied himself a bit of a devil. He had an outstanding reputation as a marine scientist, and Knox had been eager to meet him; but he'd barely arrived aboard the *Maritsa* before throwing a dreadful tantrum about his quarters and the constricted lab space. Knox didn't altogether blame him, for Ricky had promised a state-of-the-art salvage ship, and the *Maritsa* was hardly that; but his reaction had still been pathetically over the top, leading his team straight back to Morombe, where they'd taken over a villa and set up shop.

The door opened again, and Ricky came in, followed by Maddow the Shadow. Knox couldn't help but wonder if he'd been lurking outside, for he had a remarkable knack of being the last to arrive at any meeting. 'Great,' he said, taking a chair. 'You're all here. Then let's get straight down to it.'

'As you wish,' said Holm. He took three comb-bound folders from his box, slid them across the polished tabletop. 'These contain my analysis of the latest data,' he said. 'But essentially I can summarise the key finding in just three words.'

'And?' asked Ricky.

Holm's smile grew thin yet somehow triumphant. 'There's nothing here,' he said.

FIVE

I

Ricky had folded his hands loosely in his lap. When he heard Holm's pronouncement, he clenched them into fists. 'Nothing here?' he demanded. 'What do you mean, nothing here?'

'I mean exactly that,' answered Holm. 'There's no ship-wreck here. There never was. And, by extension, there is no buried cargo.'

'How can you say that?' protested Ricky furiously. 'What about all the artefacts we've found? The cannons? The anchors?'

'Who knows?' shrugged Holm. 'Perhaps they spilled overboard during a storm. Perhaps one of your Chinese ships was threatened by pirates, and its crew jettisoned them for speed.'

'Nonsense,' said Ricky.

'Or perhaps someone bought them on the Chinese black market, then scattered them around the sea-bed.'

'How dare you?' erupted Ricky, jumping to his feet. 'How *fucking* dare you?'

'I'm not suggesting it was you.'

'Of course you are!'

'What about the sonar anomalies in the wreck mound?' asked Knox.

'Rock formations,' said Holm.

'They can't *all* be,' protested Ricky.

'They *can* all be,' retorted Holm. 'And they all are. I admit some of the original readings were highly suggestive; but the latest data are incontrovertible.' He touched one of the folders. 'Check for yourself, if you don't believe me. And even if the sonar scans and magnetic imaging weren't conclusive, which they are, our sediment analysis would be. If a treasure ship was buried here, the sand on top of it would be rich with traces of wood from its hull, of jute and tung oil from its caulking; we'd have found flecks of rust from nails, from anchors and other ironwork; we'd have found the residue of gunpowder. We haven't. Barely a whisper, not in any of the samples you took. No traces, ergo no wreck. What you announced as a shipwreck mound is essentially just one long ridge of rock covered by sand.'

The silence in the stateroom was so complete that Knox could hear the hum of the fan in Holm's laptop, the soft reproach of a wave as it slapped their hull. But then Ricky pointed at Holm. 'You're out,' he told him.

'That won't change the truth about—'

'I said you're out. Get off my boat. Get off.'

'As you wish.' Holm primly closed his laptop, slung it over his shoulder, walked to the door.

'You signed confidentiality agreements, remember?' shouted Ricky, following him. 'Not one word of this better get out.'

'How do you plan to stop it?'

'I'll sue your fucking arse off,' said Ricky. 'You'll never work in this industry again.' He slammed the door behind him, turned around. 'And turn that fucking camera off,' he bawled at Maddow the Shadow.

'Yes, sir,' said Maddow, dropping it from his shoulder.

'And get out.' He opened the door again, waited for Maddow to leave, then slammed it only slightly less forcefully. 'Jesus!' he said, coming back to the table. But his demeanour changed even as they watched, from anger and disbelief through anxiety to a real and palpable panic. He sat down heavily, put his head in his hands, began breathing fast and shallow.

'What is it?' asked Knox.

He looked up, still breathing hard. 'How do you mean?'

'I mean, you're not just disappointed by this news. You're *scared*.'

'I don't know what you're talking about,' said Ricky.

'Yes, you do,' said Miles.

A look of self-pity twisted Ricky's face. 'You guys don't know how hard it was raising money,' he said.

Knox frowned. 'I thought you got it from Beijing.'

'I did. But then there was that damned coup.'

Knox glanced at Miles. This salvage had originally been scheduled for the previous year, but an unexpected coup had seen off Madagascar's former president, and the new guy had appointed his own people to the various ministries, forcing them to postpone. But this was the first they'd heard that it had affected their Chinese government funding. 'Go on,' he said.

'It was the financial crisis,' said Ricky. 'My people in Beijing suddenly had more urgent uses for their money. But they recommended me to a guild instead.' He gave a bright false smile. 'A commercial and industrial guild. Very big in Nanjing, which is where the treasure fleet was built; and also in Guangdong, where a lot of the ironwork was done. That's why they were so keen to be a part of this.'

'A commercial and industrial guild?' frowned Miles, who'd spent several years salvaging wrecks in the South China Seas. 'Which one exactly?'

'I forget their name. The guild of peace and righteousness. Something like that.'

'The New Righteousness and Peace Guild?' suggested Miles.

'Yes,' said Ricky uneasily. 'I think that may have been it.'

'You're telling me that we're in business with the Sun Yee On?'

Ricky didn't reply, other than for his smile to grow a little grislier. But that was enough for Knox. 'The who?' he asked Miles.

'They're triads,' said Miles, in a matter-of-fact tone that accentuated rather than concealed his underlying cold fury. 'I came across them quite a bit in Macao. They've been trying to clean up their image and reputation recently. Lots of joint ventures with the police and local party officials, that kind of thing. Buying political goodwill with patriotic projects like this. But they're still triads.'

'They were recommended by the culture ministry,' protested Ricky. 'How bad can they be?'

'They're fucking *triads*!' yelled Miles. 'How could you be so stupid?' He shook his head in dismay. 'Jesus! I can't believe this. We're screwed.'

'*He's* screwed,' said Knox, nodding at Ricky.

'No. *We're* screwed.' Miles glared furiously at Ricky. 'He only ever hired us because he'd already used up all his own credibility, so he needed ours. Frank and me flew out here ourselves, remember? We talked to the fisherman who found the first cannon. We dived the site ourselves and took the sonar readings. Without our endorsement, he'd never have raised the money, not even from scum like the Sun Yee On. So they're not just going to blame him when they find out the truth. They're going to blame us too. And, trust me on this, you don't want to be on the wrong side of these people.'

'Hell,' muttered Knox.

Ricky gave a ghastly smile then got to his feet and went to the sideboard for a bottle of whisky and some glasses. 'We rather seem to be in the same boat,' he said, as he splashed out shots for them all with a slightly trembling hand. 'So what do you say we put our heads together and see if we can't come up with some kind of solution?'

II

Rebecca was in her bedroom packing for Madagascar when she suffered a stomach cramp so severe that she had to crouch down and bite her finger not to yell out. She'd been trying to avoid the memory ever since her conversation with Pierre, but it was no use, she couldn't suppress it any longer.

Some eighteen months ago, her sister Emilia had called to let her know that she was thinking of attending a forestry fieldwork course in southern England. Though she'd said it casually enough, they'd both known it was a big deal. Rebecca had left home many years before after a rift with her father of such bitterness that she'd never been back since, hadn't so much as set eyes on her father or sister. Emilia had been working diligently towards a reconciliation, and this had been her boldest effort yet. But the timing had been awful. Rebecca's programmes had made her an overnight sensation, in great demand on the chat-show circuit. Her Madagascan upbringing was so exotic that she was constantly being asked about it. The truth had been too difficult for her to face, so she'd sidestepped these questions by fabricating a false idyll of her childhood. But should Emilia come to town, she was terrified the whole story would worm its way out, and she hadn't been ready for that. 'I'm not sure where I'll be,' she'd blurted out. 'I may be away filming.'

'Of course,' Emilia had said woodenly. 'Maybe some other time.'

But there'd never been another time. And now there never would be. She breathed in deep, then quashed that treacherous thought. She was going to get Emilia and her father back alive. That was all there was to it. She zipped up her bags, carried them downstairs, handed them to her taxi-driver to pack away in his boot. 'We off, then?' he asked.

'Five minutes,' she told him. 'I need to lock up.'

'You're the boss.'

She went back inside, was about to record a new message for her answer-phone when she realised she didn't know how long she'd be away. She had ten days at the most in Madagascar, for her first series was about to debut on American cable and she'd booked a gruelling promotional tour to give it its best shot. She left the message as it was, then she went through her house room by room, turning off appliances at the wall, looking for anything she might have forgotten. It seemed to take forever; all these rooms she never used. She'd bought the house from a City couple with four young children, another on the way. Her viewings had been chaotic, toys everywhere, broken furniture and crayon daubs upon the wall, yet the pervasive joy and life and companionship had intoxicated her. She'd somehow convinced herself that she'd be buying all that along with the house; but all she'd actually bought was more emptiness.

She turned on her conservatory lights, looked out over her small garden. Her first night here, she'd heard a baby crying. Her heart had stopped on her; she'd imagined for a moment that the previous owners must have left one of their brood behind. But when she'd hurried outside, it had only been a black cat. Its mewing had sounded so like an infant in distress that it had made her wonder whether it was deliberately taking advantage of maternal heartstrings. Nature was ingenious at finding such weaknesses to exploit. She'd made a documentary on the subject, featuring similar cases such as cuckoos, those brood parasites that laid their eggs in the nests of other birds to pass on the cost of child-rearing, taking advantage of a glitch in the mental software of some songbirds that made parents give most of their food to the biggest and most aggressive of their nestlings, so as not to waste resources on sickly offspring. They did this irrespective of what their nestlings actually looked like, so they'd end up feeding cuckoo chicks larger than themselves, while their true offspring starved.

Rebecca had always revelled in such uncomfortable truths. She loved to cause consternation, to jolt people into contemplation of their darker nature, hurry them past their mirrors. Exploring such behaviour wasn't just her career, it was how she now understood the world. Whenever she saw people doing the most mundane things, queuing at the supermarket, holding a door open for somebody, walking their dog . . . she'd wonder why they were doing it, what the payoff was. And the deeper she'd dug into evolutionary psychology, the more uncompromising her view of the world had become. We were carbon-based breeding machines, that was all. Our consciousness was merely the hum and glow of organic computers at work. Reasoning and emotion were chemically induced. Virtue and vice were survival strategies; free will an illusion. Her work had had a subtle impact on her own life, as though a psychological uncertainty principle was at work, allowing her either to experience or to understand a particular emotion, but not both simultaneously. Whenever she felt any unusual emotion, she'd examine herself like a specimen. *Is this envy?* she'd wonder. *Is this greed? Is this what other people feel? Am I a freak?* And whenever any new man tried to get close to her, she'd scrutinise them with almost scientific zeal, examining their conversation and behaviour in minute detail, sometimes even deliberately provoking them with outrageous comments and actions simply to see their response, until invariably she'd drive them away. She did this even though she'd bought herself a house large enough for a family, and yet lived in it alone.

A bang upon her front door. 'You okay in there, love?' called out her driver. 'Only if you want to catch your plane . . .'

'Coming.' She switched off her conservatory lights and turned to go.

SIX

I

'We've leased the *Maritsa* for six weeks, right?' asked Knox. 'All the equipment too?'

Ricky knocked back his whisky, pulled a sour face. 'So?'

'So we won't be saving your Chinese friends much of anything by calling the project off now.'

Miles shook his head. 'You don't know these people. If they find out that we knew this was a bust and didn't tell them—'

'But we don't know it's a bust,' countered Knox. 'Not for sure. We have a sea-bed studded with Chinese arte-facts, remember, not to mention a very compelling sonar reading.'

'Which has been refuted by a more recent one,' pointed out Miles. 'And by the magnetic imaging.'

'Yes. And by the sediment samples too. But what if someone had tampered with those readings and those samples?'

'What?' asked Ricky. '*Who*?'

'Don't get ahead of me,' said Knox. 'I'm just asking: *isn't it possible*? I mean, how hard would it have been for someone to have switched our samples with sediment from elsewhere?'

'Why would they do that?'

'To trick us into giving up the site, of course, so that they can come back later and plunder it at their leisure. I mean, if we're right about there being a treasure ship here, its cargo could be worth tens or even hundreds of millions of dollars. Wouldn't that be worth switching some samples for?'

'*Holm*!' spat Ricky. 'I never trusted that bastard.'

'Calm down,' said Knox. 'I'm only suggesting it's a possibility. And if so, shouldn't we make certain, one way or the other, before we call off the expedition? Wouldn't our most prudent and responsible course be to take new tests and samples, but this time make sure they can't be interfered with, maybe even fly some duplicate samples back to Europe for checking. Who knows, maybe we'll get different results. But, even if not, it'll buy us another week in which to start managing the expectations of your friends back in China. And we've also got Miles and me and fourteen other professional divers on board, we've got a motor-boat and two inflatables and all the survey equipment we could wish for. Maybe the wreck isn't where we thought, maybe it's five hundred metres west, or a kilometre south. Let's use our extra time to find it.'

'You're right,' said Miles. 'We'll survey the whole damned sea-floor.'

Knox stood and went to the window. The sea was still too rough for the motorboat, and it was getting dark. No way would it be heading back to Morombe tonight. He turned to Ricky. 'I'll bet Holm's still on board,' he said. 'He could really screw us if he wants to. Might be worth trying to smooth things out with him.'

'Leave him to me,' said Ricky. 'What about you two?'

'We need to brief the guys, thrash out a new schedule.' He looked at them both for approval. 'Agreed?'

'Yes,' said Miles.

'Yes,' said Ricky.

'Good,' nodded Knox. 'Then let's go do it.'

II

Boris felt a mild euphoria as the plane took off on the first leg of his journey to Madagascar, pressing him gently back into his seat. Part of it was simple relief: he'd had to show his passport three times already, and not a sniff of trouble. The Nergadzes knew better than to skimp on such things, of course, but he was an old enough hand never to trust equipment until he'd used it in the field. And it felt good simply to be working again. He was by nature a man of action, and these past few months had chafed badly. But he was buzzing for another reason too.

Fifteen months he'd spent in his various Greek hell-holes before the Nergadzes had finally sprung him. *Fifteen months*. Boris had always fancied himself tough enough to handle serious time. It hadn't proved that way. Prison had ripped him apart. Part of it had been simply a consequence of being abroad, unfamiliar with the language and the ropes. Another part of it had come from not backing down from a fight with the wrong person on his third day, and being punished for it thereafter in unspeakable ways. But it had been more than that. The Athens fiasco had ruined his whole life. Even after getting out, it had been nothing but shit. As head of security for Sandro Nergadze, he'd been powerful and feared. Now he was nothing. People who'd once cowered from him pushed past him as if he wasn't there. This world was all about respect. He needed to earn that back. And the best way of doing that was by making someone else pay full price for it, and so let the world know he wasn't to be messed with. And who better a victim than Daniel Knox, the man who'd caused him all this grief?

SEVEN

I

It was late by the time Knox made it to bed. He was worn out from his day, yet sleep eluded him. He'd been an archaeologist long enough to take his lows with his highs, so while he was disappointed by Holm's bombshell announcement, he'd get over it just fine. But the longer the evening had gone on, the more he'd realised what a financial and reputational disaster it threatened to be for Miles and his brother Frank, his co-founder of MGS, currently holding the fort back in Hove. The two men had been good to Knox, giving him this job after Gaille died, sticking by him through his first year, though he'd done precious little to warrant such loyalty. He felt bad for their troubles, anxious to help.

Madagascar was barely a blur against the pre-dawn sky when he rose. He brewed coffee and took a cup to the control room, started revising the dive plan along the lines he and Miles had discussed with their divers the night before. He logged on as he worked. Internet access was via a local mobile phone network, and consequently expensive, sporadic and slow, but it was fine for email. His in-box was all routine, except for one message from Braddock at the Landseer Trust.

Dear Mr Richardson,

Just heard some troubling news and wanted to let you know asap. The Kirkpatricks' sailboat has been found drifting, and Adam and Emilia are missing. Don't get too alarmed – they often vanish into the forest for days at a time – but I thought it best to alert you at once as you may want to defer decisions on flights etc. I will, of course, update you when I hear anything more.

All best,

Braddock Lightman

He remembered Lucia's remark the afternoon before, how she'd been trying to get hold of the Kirkpatricks, but had failed. *No wonder.* He tried to put the news aside as he worked on his schedules. He already had plenty to occupy him. But it nagged at him all the same. People vanished into the forest, sure, but not from boats, not unless something terrible had happened. A sudden vivid memory of Emilia Kirkpatrick on the afternoon some fourteen months before when she'd burst so suddenly into his life, jolting him from the malaise he'd been in since Mikhail Nergadze had murdered Gaille while he'd looked helplessly on. He owed her an incalculable debt for that. He couldn't just ignore it.

Something else troubled him too. Their Eden project was only a few weeks away. Was it possible that the Kirkpatricks' disappearance was connected to it in some way? It was another five minutes before he gave in. He printed off the email and took it to Miles's cabin, banged on his door to wake him, then went inside and flipped on his light. 'Read this,' he said.

'Oh, Christ,' muttered Miles. 'Those poor people.' His heart wasn't in his words, however, partly because he'd never got to know Emilia anything like as well as Knox had, partly because he had enough worries of his own. But then he realised why Knox had woken him, and he sat up abruptly. 'No, mate,' he said. 'I need you here.'

'Not as badly as she needs me there.'

'There'll already be a huge search going on. People who know the area. How much difference will you make?'

'Maybe quite a lot, if it has something to do with the *Winterton*.'

'How could it?' frowned Miles. 'No one else knows about that.'

'Someone must. They got us our licences, remember? So people in the government must know. Anyway, it's only thirty-odd metres deep. Some fisherman or diver could easily have found it by accident. And if they have, and that's why Adam and Emilia have vanished, what chance will the police have?'

'The Kirkpatricks wouldn't want you telling the police,' said Miles. 'Not unless there was no choice. Don't you remember how adamant Emilia was about secrecy?'

'But that's precisely why I need to go down there myself,' said Knox. 'If it's got nothing to do with the *Winterton*, fine, I'll come straight back. But if it does . . .' He realised this wasn't enough. 'Look,' he said. 'She's a friend. I owe her more than you realise. I'll get the new schedules finished before I leave, and you don't really need me otherwise, not *really*, not for a sea-bed search like this. You've got plenty of better divers than me.'

Miles shook his head, but in concession rather than disagreement. He looked wryly up at Knox. 'We were going to fire you, you know,' he said.

'Yes,' agreed Knox.

'It wasn't just that you weren't pulling your weight – though you weren't. You were so damn morose all the time; you were bringing everyone else down.'

'I know.'

'Morale matters in small businesses like ours.'

'Yes, it does,' acknowledged Knox. 'Frankly, I could never figure out why you kept me on so long.'

Miles gave a dry laugh. 'I guess we felt bad for you after . . . what happened. We figured you just needed time. And then *she* turned up.' He squinted at Knox. 'You never did tell us what happened that weekend.'

'No,' agreed Knox.

'Fine,' he sighed. 'Go check into it. Bring her and her father back, if you possibly can. But, whatever you may think, I need you here too. I've come to rely on you more than you realise. So I want your word you'll shift your arse back here as soon as humanly possible.'

'You've got it,' vowed Knox. 'And thanks.'

II

Rebecca landed midmorning at Antananarivo's Ivato Airport, and emerged into the crowded, dingy arrivals hall to find Pierre himself waiting for her. He was easy to spot, standing nearly a head taller than most of the Malagasy thronging around him, and looking like some latter-day pirate, with his bulging goitre of black beard, his vast dark eyes and his gold hoop earring. He saw her at the same time, bulled his way through the crowd to her, took her shoulders and kissed her on both cheeks, then reached around her and hugged her, his beard tickling her cheek. She was still holding her luggage, so she had to wriggle her shoulders to make him let go. 'Any news?' she asked.

He shook his head as he stepped back, brushed a finger beneath his eye. 'I can't believe it,' he said. 'My little Becca.'

'Please, Pierre. I need to know what's going on.'

'Nothing to tell,' he shrugged. 'I speak to the police in Tulear earlier; there's no sign of them.' And he took her bags from her, led the way towards the terminal doors.

'Where are we going?' she asked.

'My car's outside.'

'Your car?'

'If we leave now, we can be in Tulear tonight.'

'I'm flying,' she told him. 'That way I'll be in Tulear this afternoon. Why don't you come with me?'

'I can't. I have my car.'

'For Christ's sake!' she said.

'You want me to leave it?'

'I want you to do whatever it takes to find my father and sister,' she told him. 'Emilia's your lover, Pierre. She's the mother of your child. My father's been your closest friend for over thirty years. And you're worried about your damned car?' She shook her head at him. 'What the hell are you still doing here? Why aren't you back home already, leading the search?'

Pierre went a little red. 'I wanted to be here for you,' he said. 'I cannot bear for you to arrive home with no one to greet you, not after all these years, not to news like this. And I think maybe you'll need someone to drive you.'

'I told you. I'm flying.'

'Yes. But I didn't know that.'

She shook her head at him, still indignant, yet finding it hard to justify. They were close enough to the automatic glass doors that they kept opening and then closing again, offering brief glimpses of bright sunshine. She turned and walked out through them. The newly laid tarmac in the car park was glistening from a recent shower, and the moisture had coaxed out a cocktail of pungent smells: from the brown-grey zebu pats, like amputated elephants' feet, scattered as fertiliser on the grass verges; from the sweat-stiffened clothes of the porters, labourers and touts; from the choking silver-black exhaust fumes spewed by the ramshackle taxis, buses and trucks. Yet, deep beneath those, she could detect hints of gentler scents, of frangipani, vanilla and hibiscus. She breathed in deep. Smell was the most evocative of the senses, they said. Eleven years! *Eleven years!* Yet still it seemed instantly like home, oppressive with memory. For a moment she felt eighteen again, insecure and terrified, about to leave behind everything she'd ever known. She shivered as though a ghost had walked through her.

Madagascar: the Great Red Island, the Eighth Continent, land of her birth.

III

The Bayliner was already crowded by the time Knox heaved his dive-bag and overnight bag down the gangway and aboard. Garry was at the wheel, with Dieter Holm behind him, looking thunderous, alongside Ron, their ship's steward, off into Morombe for fresh supplies, and Lucia on the cushioned rear seat. He added his bags to the general pile, went to sit beside her. 'What's this, then?' she smiled. 'Deserting the sinking ship?'

He debated a moment, decided he might as well tell her. She was headed to Eden too, after all, and was bound to find out eventually. 'You know how you couldn't get hold of the Kirkpatricks?' he said. 'Turns out they've gone missing. I'm going down to help with the search.'

'I thought you didn't know them.'

'I didn't say that. I only said that they were pretty well known along this coast.'

She threw him an amused look. 'So should I now doubt *everything* you told me yesterday?' But there was no sting in her voice. She was a journalist; she knew how the world worked. 'So how do you know them?'

'I only really know Emilia. She spent a few days in England a little while back. I met her then.'

'Ah. Like that, is it?'

Garry opened the throttle up at that moment, and the roaring engine spared him from having to answer. But Lucia's question set him thinking. It had been a difficult time for Knox, struggling wretchedly to find a way to live without Gaille. Before losing her, he hadn't fully understood how completely their lives had become conjoined, how *dependent* on her he'd become. The days had been manageable, thanks to his job at MGS, but his nights had been soul-destroying, unbearable. Miles and Frank had done their best to cajole him from his funk. They'd invited him to the pub, to their homes for dinner. But the forced jollity of those evenings had been awful; he'd come to dread them not simply for themselves, but also because he'd brought everyone else down, and he'd hated that. So he'd started saying no, returning instead to his one-bedroom rental, where he'd lain on his couch eating pizza and drinking himself to sleep in front of the TV. His self-discipline had dribbled away. He'd started turning up at work hung-over, unkempt and smelling of last night's booze; and though he'd known his dismissal was surely imminent, he hadn't cared one jot.

That was when Emilia Kirkpatrick had come into his life.

It had been late one Friday afternoon, during a particularly cold snap. She'd had an appointment with Frank that morning, but a flight delay had screwed that up, and Frank had headed off to Harwich to look over a boat. They'd all been locking up for the weekend when she'd arrived, and as everyone else had had plans for the evening, it had been left by default for Knox to deal with her. He'd told her to come back on Monday, when Frank would be able to see her; but she'd flown in from Madagascar for this, and she simply refused to leave, so he finally agreed to hear her out over a drink at a local wine bar. One glass had led to a second; a third had led to dinner. And, suddenly, perhaps as a result of being out for the evening with an attractive and sympathetic woman, his grief for Gaille had overwhelmed him, he'd started pouring out his heart, even weeping a little at the table, causing such consternation amongst his neighbours that he'd felt compelled to leave. Emilia had helped him to a taxi, had escorted him back to his flat, then had taken him to bed, where she'd kept him for much of the weekend, listening to him with extraordinary tenderness and patience now that the logjam had finally broken in his heart, allowing all his hurt to tumble out.

And on the Monday morning, when he'd driven her into MGS to make plans for the *Winterton* salvage, he'd realised to his surprise that he'd actually been looking forward to the day. For the first time since losing Gaille, he'd felt some glimmer of gladness to be alive. And so, yes, as he'd told

Miles, he did owe Emilia. Without her intervention, he'd almost certainly have been out of a job by now, drinking himself to death in a one-bedroom tip somewhere on the outskirts of Hove.

EIGHT

I

Boris had to wait over an hour at Antananarivo Airport for Davit. The arrivals board was broken, and he began to fret they'd miss their connection to Morombe. But the big man finally showed. 'Hey, boss,' he said, looking rumpled and weary from his flight, yet nonetheless cheerful.

Boris nodded sourly to let Davit know he hadn't forgotten Greece. 'We need to get moving,' he said.

The plane to Morombe was an antique Twin Otter. It reeked of fumes and was so cramped that Boris had to duck his head to walk down the aisle to his seat, while Davit had to bend almost double, then sit sideways. It struggled to make it off the ground, its engines straining for altitude before faltering altogether, allowing the aircraft to plunge back towards earth, causing several passengers to scream out and making even Boris grip his armrests, before they picked up again.

He looked out and down. Madagascar's capital was hemmed in by lush green paddyfields that shrank quickly behind him. They crossed mountains, forests and lakes. Though they were quite low, Boris couldn't see a single road. Turbulence tumbled and jolted them. Through the threadbare curtain separating the cabin from the cockpit, he saw the pilot thump one of his dials with the heel of his hand. The fumes grew worse. Across the aisle, an old woman opened a sick bag and vomited into it with impressive decorum, like she was clearing her throat. Afterwards, she rolled up the top of the bag and held it clenched in her lap like a packed lunch, but the smell leaked out even so, making Boris feel nauseous himself. It was an immense relief, therefore, when they bounced across Morombe's bumpy runway and then the door opened and the steps arrived and they climbed down on to the sun-baked concrete, and he could stretch his back and arms. 'That was fun,' he muttered.

'Tell me about it,' said Davit.

They collected their bags, went to find a taxi. There were just two of them, battered and yellow, but neither driver spoke English. They all looked at each other in dismay. 'Hotel speak English?' asked Davit.

The taller of the drivers grinned and gave them the thumbs up. They climbed into his cab, bumped along a potholed road into town. Young Malagasy men stared sullenly through the windows, assessing them for wealth. They pulled up outside a compound protected by high wooden palisades. 'Hotel speak English,' said the driver.

They paid him off, went inside. Two windsurfer boards and an outboard engine were lying on reception's red-tiled floor, but there was no one in sight. Boris called out impatiently. An elderly man appeared, rubbing sleep from his eyes. 'You speak English?' asked Boris.

The man shook his head. 'Claudia!' he yelled. 'Claudia!' An attractive young Malagasy woman with milk-coffee skin and braided shoulder-length hair arrived through dappled shadows. The man gestured at them. 'English,' he said.

She nodded and smiled warmly. 'You want a room?'

'Two rooms,' said Boris.

'I show you our very best.' They followed her along a sandy path. Furled sunshades leaned against stacked loungers. Mopeds and beach-buggies were coated with bird-lime and dust. A small wooden boat was turned turtle on the sand. There was no sign of any other guests here at all. Business looked dire. They reached a pair of cabins raised a foot or so above the ground, their porches offering fine views of the beach and sea. Claudia removed the padlock and led them in. It was gloomy inside, even

way. The coastal track didn't go all the way to Eden; besides, a bridge just south of town had been brought down by the recent cyclone and it hadn't yet been repaired. The only way to reach Eden was by fishing pirogue.

He explained this to Lucia, who took it in her stride; she'd been planning on taking a pirogue anyway, so that she could write an article about the experience. They agreed to share a pirogue as far as Eden; after that, she'd take it on by herself south to Tulear, from where she was flying out in two days time. They each had things to do in town, Knox to change money, Lucia to check out of her hotel, but they decided to head along the beach and hire a pirogue now, so that they could leave their bags behind. As they trudged along, their feet plunging deep into the powdery sand, Knox wished he hadn't packed quite so much. But Adam and Emilia had disappeared at sea, so he needed his dive-gear; and he couldn't exactly turn up without a change of clothes.

The piroguiers sitting by their boats sniffed business; they jumped up and hurried to meet them. The dearth of tourists caused by Madagascar's coup was evidently biting hard. Knox outlined their plans, asked the price, sparking a Dutch auction in which the young men underbid each other to win the work. Two of them reached the same price, but only one spoke decent French, making their decision easy. The young man's name was Thierry. He led them over to his pirogue, where his brother and partner, Alphonse, was mending nets. Knox gave the pirogue a once-over. Its thin, canoe-like hull had been chiselled from a single trunk, then fitted with slat seats and a weighty torpedo of an outrigger to make it more stable. It looked fine to him, as did the mast and sail lying on the sand alongside.

'Any chance of making Eden tonight?' he asked.

Thierry gave the universal sailor's shrug. 'It depends on the wind,' he said. 'But it's not a problem. My brother lives at Ambatomilo. Or we can make a tent and sleep upon the beach.'

'Sounds perfect,' smiled Lucia. 'I love a night on the beach.'

'Can you look after our bags?' asked Knox. 'We need to go into town.'

'Of course,' said Thierry. 'We wait for you here.'

'Great,' said Knox. 'See you later, then.'

III

A black dog took a liking to Boris as he walked down Morombe high street, sniffing at his heels and looking hungrily up at him. He scowled at it and aimed a boot at its ribs, but still it kept following. It was an appropriate enough companion: he'd rarely ever visited a more depressing place. The road was so badly broken that the few cars treated it like an obstacle course, weaving cautiously around islands of tarmac. There was litter everywhere, squashed packs of Boston cigarettes, lemonade bottles and the like. A young diabetic beggar with a swollen and ulcerated foot strummed a home-made mandolin, while a dispirited woman sold napkins and sweet potatoes from a tray, and children raced cars they'd made from sardine cans around her feet.

He passed a camping store with cooking utensils and hunting knives in one window, foreign-language guide-books and maps in the other. Hard to know how it made enough money to stay open, for he'd still seen no tourists. He bought a guidebook and a map of the coast from Morondava down to Tulear that he flapped open and studied as he walked. According to the press-cuttings Sandro had given him, the *Maritsa* was anchored on the far side of the reef, several miles offshore. Even getting close enough to this man Matthew Richardson to see if he was Knox or not would be hard, though the man in charge of the salvage certainly seemed to enjoy his publicity, so maybe Boris could claim to be a journalist or something, request an interview. But better by far if he could somehow coax Richardson ashore, away from the sanctuary of his friends.

He was musing on ways to achieve this when he looked up to see the man himself strolling along the pavement towards him.

NINE

I

A young man in baggy basketball shorts and a tattered Black Sabbath T-shirt was waiting for Rebecca at Tulear Airport, holding up the torn-off side of a cardboard box with her name crudely scrawled in black marker-pen upon it. He looked disconcertingly young, despite his affectations of maturity: the thin moustache, the soft-pack of cigarettes and lighter tucked into his upturned sleeve, the cheap mirror sunglasses pushed up over his long brown hair like an Alice band. Maybe he realised the impression he gave, because he'd barely introduced himself as Zanahary before launching into a manic explanation of what he was doing there: his elder brother had twisted his ankle jumping from the roof of their house and had sent him in his place. He was a very experienced driver, he assured her; very safe. Too weary to make an issue of it, Rebecca retrieved her luggage then led the way out into the sunshine.

The hire car, a gleaming dark-blue and silver Mitsubishi pickup with four spotlights on its roof, at least looked in good shape. It would need to be. She had some business in Tulear to take care of first, but after that it was still a good three hours drive north to the Eden Reserve, over a broken-up sand, mud and rock track. She checked the tyres for tread, then made sure there were spares in the back, along with canisters of fuel, oil and water. Then she opened the passenger door, to be greeted by a blast of hot air. The air-conditioning fans had been ripped out and the dashboard was covered with promotional stickers half-peeled off, leaving ugly strips of white pith everywhere. It stank of cigarette smoke, its ashtrays too bulging to close, and the seats were covered with tacky protective plastic, so that the backs of her legs glued to them at once. Zanahary climbed jauntily in the driver's side, tapped a cigarette from his soft-pack and raised it to his lips with 1950s chic, elbow high and folded, as though it were an expensive piece of jewellery he wanted to bring casually to her attention.

Rebecca shook her head. 'No,' she told him.

'But—'

'Not in the car.'

It was just fifteen minutes drive into Tulear. They stopped at a general store for a sack of rice and some other provisions for which she had plans, then drove on to the offices of her father's long-time lawyer Delpha. He'd been a regular visitor to Eden during her childhood, bringing bags of sweets and wooden dolls he'd carved himself. She'd been intensely fond of him, yet eleven years had passed, and she was apprehensive of her welcome. The receptionist beamed vacantly when she gave her name. Monsieur Delpha was busy at this moment. If madame would please take a seat . . . But he must have heard her voice, for his office door opened and there he was, older and frailer than she remembered, his hair glowing white, his dark-brown skin sprinkled with fat black freckles. 'Rebecca?' he asked, squinting uncertainly across the gloomy reception area. '*C'est vraiment vous?*'

'Yes,' she said. 'It's me.'

His face cracked; tears sprang into his eyes. She hugged him for a little while, giving him time to compose himself. He stepped back and dried his eyes. 'I thought you'd never come home.' But then his face fell. 'I only wish the circumstances—'

'Yes,' said Rebecca.

'If there's anything I can do . . .'

'There is, actually.' She glanced at his receptionist, reluctant to discuss family matters in front of someone she didn't know. He nodded and led her into his office. The walls were warm with leather-bound books, the half-drawn curtains on the high windows giving it a rather somnolent feel. She sat down, ordered her thoughts. 'I need help,' she told him. 'The trouble is, I don't know *what* help. I've been away too long. I don't know anything any more. I mean, is there even a proper search going on? If not, how can I get one started? Who should I talk to? Who can I trust? Who should I bribe? Who should I yell at? Maybe I'll need a boat for the search. Where's my father's? Can I just take it? What about Eden? What about Michel? And those are just the questions I know to ask.' She shrugged to express how far out of her depth she felt. 'So I need help.'

Delpha had jotted down notes as she was talking. He glanced over them now, then nodded and leaned back in his chair. 'You must speak to Andriama about the search and investigation. He is our chief of police here in Tulear.'

'And can I trust him?'

Delpha considered a moment. 'I have always found him honest myself. But there are rumours. There are always rumours, you understand. About everybody. About me, too, no doubt. Andriama talks loudly about rooting out corruption in Tulear, yet corruption persists, and every year he adds another room to his house. Maybe these rumours are nothing but envy, or his enemies wishing him harm. He certainly has those. He is not afraid of powerful people.' Delpha glanced down, then up again. 'As for your father's boat, you know it was found drifting by some South African yachtsmen?'

'Pierre told me.'

'They've claimed salvage rights. Under international maritime law, that entitles them to half the value of the boat. There'll be other bills to pay too, before the Port Captain will authorise the boat's release. Customs, immigration, police, that kind of thing. But don't be alarmed. Your father was insured against all such eventualities. I know; I organised it myself. But the paperwork is at Eden. Bring it to me, and I can have the boat released to you at once.'

'Thanks.'

He consulted his notes again, then adopted a more sombre look, to let her know he had a difficult subject to broach. 'You must excuse me for what I am about to say. I mean no ill. I hope and pray your father and sister are alive—'

'They *are* alive,' said Rebecca.

'. . . but you must also plan for all eventualities. Your father would expect it.'

'Yes.'

'You realise that, as your father's and your sister's lawyer, I am forbidden from discussing their affairs with you, at least until they're—'

93

'I understand,' Rebecca assured him. Delpha's scrupulousness about such matters was one reason her father had trusted him so completely.

'But I can discuss *hypothetical* situations. Imagine a wealthy man, if you will. A man who elects to divide his money equally between those of his children who survive him. One of his sons, Rupert, let's say, is childless. But the other, Etienne, has a young daughter who will be his beneficiary when *he* dies. You are with me?'

'Yes.' Rupert was clearly Rebecca herself; Etienne Emilia.

'Good. Now imagine two different courses of events. In the first, the father dies. His wealth is divided between Rupert and Etienne. Then Etienne dies a few days later. The law is clear: Etienne's share in his father's wealth passes to his daughter. But now imagine a second course of events, in which Etienne dies before or at the same time as his father. In this instance, all the money will pass straight to the father's sole surviving son. Etienne's daughter will inherit nothing.'

Rebecca frowned. It almost seemed that Delpha was advising her how to cheat Michel out of his rightful inheritance; but she knew him too well to believe that. 'What are you getting at?' she asked.

'I am just outlining a legal situation,' he said. 'You see, under Malagasy law, if a person's assets pass on to a child when that child is too young to administer those assets himself, then they will in effect pass in trust to that child's legal guardian. Typically, their surviving parent.'

'Ah,' murmured Rebecca. 'Pierre.'

'Of course,' continued Delpha, 'if that parent has the child's best interests at heart, then there is no problem.'

'And Pierre doesn't have Michel's best interests at heart?'

'That's not what I said at all,' said Delpha. 'I was merely outlining a hypothetical situation.'

Rebecca nodded to let him know she'd got the message. 'Thank you,' she said.

II

Boris raised his map to conceal his face until the man had passed him by. He walked on a few paces before glancing around, saw him hurry up the broken front steps of a local bank. It was Knox; Boris was sure of it. The jaunty athleticism of his walk, the set of his jaw, his hairline. More than that, it was a gift from the gods. It might be days or even weeks before he got another chance this good.

But how to take advantage of it without getting caught?

There was no time to fetch Davit – not that he'd be any help at this kind of work anyway. He checked his pocket to make sure he'd brought his camera-phone

with him, for he'd need to take some footage to keep
Ilya happy, then he hurried back to the camping store,
concocting a plan on the hoof. He bought a six-inch
hunting knife with a serrated blade, a day-pack, a baseball cap and the groundsheet for a tent. He packed his
book and map into the day-pack, slung it on his back.
He removed the groundsheet from its packaging, flapped
it out and draped it over his left shoulder, the quicker
to deploy. He checked his reflection in a shop window,
tugged the peak of his baseball cap down over his eyes
as he walked across the street to lean against a wall
from which he could monitor the bank's front doors.

Then he set himself to wait for Knox to come back
out.

TEN

I

There had been times, these past few months, when Davit Kipshidze had seriously considered killing himself. Perversely, he'd been okay in jail in Greece. Back then, he'd had hope. After all, the Nergadzes had vowed to spring him and bring him home. Since they'd made good on their promise, however, he'd slowly come to realise that his old life was forever lost to him, and he *hated* the one that had taken its place. He was a gregarious man by nature, he needed friends and family around. But the police were watching his friends and family in case he showed up, so he couldn't risk seeing them any more, for their sake as much as his. He therefore sat alone for days on end in his cramped first-floor apartment, watching TV and listening nervously to cars and the chatter of pedestrians passing by outside.

Lounging on the porch of his beach hut, he stared out over shimmering white sand down to the gentle breakers of the sea. How good sunshine felt after a long winter. How good it felt not to fear the knock upon his door.

Claudia appeared around the edge of his cabin, carrying clean sheets and a broom. She smiled at him as she went inside to strip and change his bed. He stood and went to watch. The view of the sea was nice, but it couldn't compete with a young and pretty woman. 'So how come you speak such good English?' he asked.

She looked around. 'I live with nice American family,' she beamed. She held up her right hand, splayed her fingers. 'Five years.'

'In America?' he frowned.

'In Tulear,' she told him. 'A big town south of here. They have this big, big house there for all the children who have no mothers and fathers.'

'An orphanage?'

'Yes. An orphanage.'

'I'm so sorry,' he told her.

'Why sorry?' she frowned. 'It nice there. They church people, they very kind, they always have food.' She nodded at happy memories. 'I like it there very much.'

'So why leave?'

She pulled a mock-sad face. 'I grow old. Many children need a home, not enough beds.' She looked a little guilelessly up at him. 'Now everything is work, work, work.'

'Is that right?' he laughed.

She laughed too, stuck her tongue out. She had slightly crooked upper front teeth, he noticed, that overlapped just fractionally, like the ankles of a coy bride on her wedding night. His chest went a little warm. He'd missed it sorely, these past two years, the company of a pretty woman.

She finished making his bed then picked up her broom and began to sweep out the cabin. She flicked a little sand at his feet, then again, harder, giving him another of her enchanting smiles, so that he couldn't possibly take offence. He played along, holding up his hands in mock surrender as he retreated before her assault. She followed him out on to the porch, flicking more sand as she came. He broke into a jig, like in the movies when the baddie with the six-shooter makes the hapless victim dance. It made her laugh so hard that she had to cover her mouth with her hand. She leant forward to sweep beneath the porch bench. Her singlet drooped as she did so, revealing the tattered bra within, tantalising glimpses of flesh and shadow. She looked up and caught him staring, grinned happily.

'Claudia,' called out the old man from the hotel compound. 'Claudia!'

'I go now,' she said. 'I see you later, yes?'

'I hope so.' He leaned on the porch rail to watch her leave, and was glad to see her put a little extra swish in her stride, just for him.

II

Knox jogged down the bank's front steps, exasperated by the absurd paperwork required just to change some euros. But it was done at last. Now for some supplies. He walked across town to a small but lively market, a riot of colourful clothing and sparkling costume jewellery, with produce spread out on rickety wooden tables: yellow-brown bananas, orange-green mandarins, plum tomatoes not quite ripe, clumps of garlic and onions, stubby carrots, creamy white manioc, coconuts both hairy and husked, clutched fists of lettuce, pumpkins, papaya, glistening steel bowls of rice and beans.

The brilliant sun in the unpolluted sky gave the slightly eerie impression of being underwater. Greasy tables of zebu steaks buzzed with fat sapphire-and-emerald flies. Salted sardines glittered like spilled chests of silver coins. A crone sat astride two wicker baskets of orange-red crabs, thrusting her bamboo cane into the writhing intestinal mass, irritating pincers until they snapped and clenched the cane so tightly she could lift them out and shake them off into a bucket. He bought fish, rice and other supplies to eat that night in case they didn't reach Eden by sunset, added some biscuits and bottled water.

Time to get back to the pirogue. He took a moment to get his bearings. He could see a line of palm trees above some shacks to his right, their fronds swept back like hippies walking into the wind. That had to mark the shore. He set off towards them before catching a glimpse of the beach down the far end of a narrow alley between two lines of huts. He turned and ambled along it, utterly oblivious of the man following a dozen paces behind.

ELEVEN

I

Tulear's Commissariat Centrale de Police was a yellow two-storey building near the centre of town, its front pockmarked like a war zone. Rebecca asked for Chief of Police Andriama at the desk, and a young man in jeans and a brilliant white short-sleeved shirt took her upstairs to his office and grandly threw open the door. A breeze from the open windows riffled loose papers on the desk, forcing Andriama to slap them down before they scattered. He noticed Rebecca at the same moment, however, and seemed to forget about his papers, springing to his feet and coming over to welcome her, taking her hand in both of his, stroking it like a pet hamster. 'At your service, madame,' he beamed, exposing blackened stubs of teeth rotted almost down to the gums. 'How may I help?'

'I'm Rebecca Kirkpatrick,' she told him. 'I'm here about my father and sister.'

'Ah. Yes. Of course.' He instantly let go of her hand, assumed a more sober expression. 'Such terrible news. Sit. Please sit.' Like so many Malagasy, he was a cocktail of races: short and wiry like a Polynesian, dark-skinned as an East African, yet with the satin black hair of a Chinese. 'Such a good man, your father,' he sighed. 'Such a good friend to Madagascar. And your sister, too. So young. So pretty. Such a terrible loss.'

'Loss?' Rebecca's heart clenched.

'Forgive me,' he said. 'But surely you appreciate the situation—'

'Are you giving up already?'

'Certainly not. We're doing all we can.'

'And that is?'

'My officers have been to your father's house and the local villages. They have spoken to many, many people, including two fishermen who saw your father's boat outside the reefs.' He pulled a face. 'At least, that's what they say, but you know the people up there, they'll say anything to please. After that, nothing until evening when the South Africans found your father's boat drifting and abandoned. I have copies of their statements, if you want to see?'

'Please.'

He rummaged through his drawers, produced some poor-quality photocopies of several hand-written pages that she flicked through while he talked. 'There were some traces of blood on the guard rail and on the deck,' he said. 'The university is testing it at this moment. Most likely your father's or your sister's, but unless we can check it somehow to make sure . . .' He drifted meaningfully to a halt.

She squinted at him. 'You want me to get you their blood-type information?'

'Your father and sister run a clinic up at Eden, don't they? I'm sure they'll have records.'

'I'll have a look. In the meantime, perhaps you could continue telling me about your search. The helicopters. The boats.'

He smiled politely. 'You must understand something, Miss Kirkpatrick. Madagascar is a poor country. Tulear is its poorest region. Even at the best of times, our resources are strained. This is far from the best of times. Besides, whatever has happened to your father and sister, it is almost certainly not a police matter.'

There was a knock on the door at that moment, and a middle-aged man with lustrous black hair poked in his head. His face lit up when he saw Rebecca. He was Mustafa Habib, he told her, advancing uninvited into the room, an excellent friend of her father's. Rebecca wouldn't remember him herself, but he'd known her as a child. She did remember him, as it happened; an import–export trader who'd procured obscure equipment for her father. When she told him so, his eyes gleamed with pleasure. He took a card from his wallet. 'If there's anything I can do. Anything at all.' He coughed diffidently. 'I know this is indelicate, but I must say it all the same. Unfortunate personal experience taught me how painful it can be to arrange . . . *sensitive* matters in foreign countries. If you should need any help at all, it would be a privilege. Your family has done so much for our country.'

'Thank you.'

'You have transport? A driver?'

'Yes.'

'A place to stay? My own home is of course humble, but you would honour us with your—'

'I'll be staying at Pierre's.' There was little she could achieve in Eden tonight, and she was anxious to meet her nephew, make sure he was safe. 'Then home tomorrow.'

'Of course.'

She turned back to Andriama. 'You were telling me how my father's disappearance wasn't of interest to you.'

Andriama sighed. 'All I said was that it's probably not a police matter. Our coast here is treacherous, all these tides and currents and reefs. When you were younger, you must have seen for yourself the occasional freak wave. They can come out of even the calmest seas and catch the most experienced fishermen by surprise. Why not your father and your sister?'

'So you're not even considering kidnap or robbery?'

'Of course we consider such things. But your father was not wealthy enough to kidnap, and sensible kidnappers would surely have taken hostage either your father or your sister, so that the other could be free to put the ransom together. Anyway, wouldn't we have had a demand by now? As for robbery, your father and sister were well known and loved along the coast. Everybody knew they'd share what they had for the asking. It would have been *fady* to rob them. You know *fady*? Forbidden.'

'I know *fady*.'

'Besides, what kind of thieves would let a valuable boat simply drift away? No. Robbery makes no sense. It was an accident. A tragic accident.'

'You've given up,' she said.

'I'm being realistic.'

'They're not dead.'

Andriama assumed an expression of sadness. 'I pray that you are right,' he told her. 'Truly, I do. But I fear the evidence is—'

Rebecca patted her heart. 'They're not dead,' she told him. 'And I'm going to find them.'

II

Boris popped the buckle of his new knife's sheath as he followed Knox down the alley, gripped it firmly by its hilt. The feel of it brought back vividly his first time, nearly twenty years ago now, as a young farm-worker seeking general vengeance for the rape and murder of his mother, one of the many atrocities of Georgia's brutal civil war, but the only one that had mattered to him. They'd been waiting in ambush beneath a thin line of trees for an approaching patrol. He remembered still lining his man up in his sights, the way he'd fallen in the snow, the inhuman sounds he'd made as he'd struggled against his fate, reaching out a beseeching arm for the comrades who'd already turned and fled. Bullets had been too precious to waste, so Boris had drawn his knife as he advanced upon his man. It had been so obvious that he was dying, however, that he'd just stood there watching with his companions until it was over; and, afterwards, he'd been struck most by his own detachment, his lack of feeling anything at all.

Some fence-posts had collapsed ahead, brought down by the weight of a makeshift fly-tip that had spilled out into the alley, stinking and buzzing with flies. Boris couldn't have asked for anything better. Getting this kind of operation right depended on knowing exactly what you intended to do. He therefore rehearsed it in his mind like a high-jumper before starting his run-up: left hand over Knox's mouth to keep him quiet, right hand sawing through his throat. Then heave him up and over the fly-tip, take some pictures with his camera-phone before covering him with his groundsheet, kicking rubbish over him. With luck, even if his disappearance provoked a search, it would be a day or more before he was found. Plenty of time to fetch Davit and make their escape.

He quickened his pace, turned the knife around in his hand, the better to carve through Knox's throat. He was just two paces behind him when a pair of girls playing tag ran shrieking into the end of the alley ahead. They saw Knox and Boris, shrieked gleefully some more, turned and fled. Knox must have seen the flicker in their eyes; he glanced around and saw Boris so close behind that it made him start. 'Christ!' he said. 'I didn't realise you were there.'

Just for a moment, Boris considered going for it anyway, but then he remembered that this man had bested Mikhail Nergadze in single combat – Mikhail Nergadze, the only person who'd ever truly put the fear of God into Boris. He hesitated just a blink, but it was enough, his opportunity was gone. He hid his knife against his wrist, offered an apologetic smile, then walked on by, out on to the beach, cursing his bad luck, wondering when next he'd have so good a chance to take his revenge and make himself rich.

III

Knox arrived back at the pirogue still brooding on the man in the black shirt. There'd been something familiar and unsettling about him. But then Lucia arrived, and the activity of departure pushed it from his mind. They all dragged the boat down to the sea's edge, stowed their luggage and helped Lucia to her place. Then Knox, Alphonse and Thierry pushed the pirogue out through the gentle breakers and vaulted aboard.

Thierry took the stern, from where he could steer. Alphonse sat sideways in the bow, where he raised the mast and set the sail, before furling it back up. Knox and Lucia each sat on one of the thin central slats. There was so little wind that Thierry and Alphonse grabbed a paddle each, went to work. Knox found a third paddle for himself. It was chiselled from heavy wood, but he soon picked up the rhythm, their blades banging like heartbeats against the pirogue's hull.

He glanced back at the shore. The man in the black shirt was walking along the beach, almost as though keeping pace with them. After Mikhail's death, Knox had lived in constant fear that some lowlife would learn his identity and that he had a five million euro bounty on his head. But the years had passed without incident, and he'd come to think himself safe. He remembered suddenly the *nearness* of the man in the alley, the flicker of frustration upon his face, and his old fear returned with such force that he half-missed his next stroke, splashing seawater into Thierry's midriff. He turned to apologise and sort himself out, and by the time he looked again towards the shore, the man in the black shirt had vanished.

TWELVE

I

The road north from Tulear was even worse than Rebecca remembered. It was just about acceptable for the first twenty kilometres or so, but then it disintegrated into a track of sand, rock and rutted mud that eventually petered out into nothing a little north of Eden. Even making allowances for its wretched state, however, Zanahary drove like a flustered nun, inching across the occasional hazards like they were unexploded ordnance. It grew too much for Rebecca to bear. 'Let me drive,' she said.

Zanahary shook his head. 'Insurance,' he said.

'Then let's at least take a break,' she said. 'I need to stretch my legs.'

He pulled over gladly, reaching for his cigarettes even as he threw open his door. She waited till he was out then slid across into his seat, locked the door from the inside, turned on the ignition and pulled away. There were tears in his eyes when she slowed enough for him to catch up and clamber in the passenger side. He stamped on invisible brakes as she sped away along the track, twisting in his seat and muffling shrieks. Perversely, his fear only made Rebecca all the more rash. She came too fast upon an archipelago of rocks, hit one hard with her front right, bounced clear into the air. She cursed out loud; that was an axle gone for sure. It was a nightmare breaking down on these roads; you could wait forever for another vehicle. But somehow they landed between two hummocks and then bounded on to safe, soft sand. It was a dreadful, reckless piece of driving; it braced her and made her careful. But on Zanahary it had the opposite effect. 'You drive like my brother,' he said, as though fear was now pointless. 'He mad too.'

There were cassette tapes on the dashboard. She pushed one into the player. The percussive Malagasy music took her back years. She turned the volume up, nodded to its beat. The wheel felt good in her hand, the driving position gratifyingly high. Navigating these tracks was all about anticipation, about trusting your hands and feet. The forest fell away to their left to reveal the sea, tall wading birds prowling the shallows, sea-grasses painting dark patterns in it, like God's handwriting. The cassette finished. Silence embraced them. Huge butterflies drifted like perfume across her windscreen. A crested coua fled down the track ahead, swerving aside at the last possible moment. The track bumped and wound through settlement after settlement. Fitsitika. Fiserenamasay. Tsifota. Tsiandamba. The tiny hamlets of her childhood had grown up into villages of thatch huts and tin roofs held down by fifty-kilo sacks of rice refilled with leaking sand.

'What that song?'

Rebecca glanced sideways at Zanahary. 'How do you mean?'

'That song you sing. What song?'

'I wasn't singing,' Rebecca told him, for she couldn't remember the last time she'd sung in anyone else's presence. Yet now that he'd mentioned it, she could hear one of her mother's old lullabies echoing in her mind, and it left her feeling a little uncertain of herself, so she took another cassette from the dashboard, and put it in to play.

II

Knox was beginning to feel blisters on his palms when the first gust of wind shivered the water and then it arrived in force. They all smiled relief at each other as they put down their paddles. The two piroguiers adjusted the rigging and unfurled their sail, and soon they were skimming so fast across the water that Alphonse had to step out on to the outrigger to give them extra stability. His sense of balance was extraordinary, standing on a narrow block of wood as water splashed off his feet like a water-skier, while Thierry clamped a paddle beneath his arm and used it as a rudder, working the rigging with his feet.

Knox opened a bottle of water and a pack of biscuits, offered them around. Lucia arranged her baggage along the bottom of the pirogue to form a makeshift deckchair on which she'd now stretched out and began to snooze, despite the two sides of the hull creaking loudly against each other. Knox devised a similar arrangement for himself, then sat low in the pirogue and watched landmarks grow large and then recede. Ahead were some fishermen, their nets trailing out behind them, sailing in a tightening spiral, like the whorls of a seashell, before beating the water with their paddles to startle fish into their trap. Gulls hung in the air above, and far away to his right, he could just make out the black crescents of a pod of dolphins at play.

Knox took his box-file of Eden project notes from his case, settled it in his lap, began going through them. As long as people had sailed out of sight of land and home, they'd striven for ways to calculate their position. For short distances, a combination of landmarks and directions sufficed: sail one day east to such-and-such an island, then south for a day to your destination. But this was inefficient and of little use to anyone swept off course by storms or unhelpful winds. What was needed was a way to determine position at sea without reference to land.

It was the great Alexandrian Eratosthenes who'd originally devised the concept of latitude and longitude. Latitude drew parallel bands upon the earth, like the equator and the tropics. Longitude, by contrast, divided the globe into segments, like an orange. Latitude was easy enough to calculate, even in open seas, by measuring the sun's position at its zenith, then checking the result against a table of the sun's declination for that day. But longitude proved a beast. In theory, it was easy enough: all you needed was to know the time relative to some fixed point, and you could work everything out from there. But keeping sufficiently accurate and reliable time on board ship was an immense challenge. It wasn't just the rolling motion of the ship that had to be overcome, it was changes in air pressure and the corrosiveness of sea-air too. Most of all, a shipboard clock would somehow have to counter the changes in temperature that shrank or expanded the internal workings of clocks, rendering them inaccurate.

Europe began growing rich on new empires. But as trade boomed, so did shipping losses. A solution was needed urgently. The British instituted a Board of Longitude; the French a Royal Academy. Astronomers looked to the skies for inspiration, trying to use the moons of Jupiter as a universal clock. But in the end it was the obsessive inventor John Harrison who made the breakthrough, designing a bimetallic strip to cope with temperature variations, then crafting timepieces of such precision that one lost a mere five seconds on its maiden test run to Jamaica.

By a cruel irony, however, not every vessel benefited from his breakthrough. The *Winterton*, a British East Indiaman, had been sailing north up this very channel one night in 1792. Her captain had been justly confident of his position, thanks to his gleaming new Harrison chronometer. Unfortunately for him and his crew, however, the clock-makers had been years ahead of the cartographers, so that his outdated charts placed Madagascar well to the east of its true location. Despite relatively benign conditions, therefore, the *Winterton* had sailed smack on to the reefs a mile or two south of the Eden Reserve, where she'd lodged upon the coral for three days, despite the crew's best efforts to refloat her, and had then broken up.

The nose of the pirogue plunged unexpectedly into a wave, splashing Lucia awake, spattering Knox's pages with translucent tears. Alphonse held up his hand in apology, made some adjustments to the rigging, and they began again to skim over the top. Lucia settled back down and Knox resumed his reading.

The *Winterton* wreck-site itself was well-enough known, but the fate of its cargo was less certain. This was a question of more than academic interest, because the *Winterton* had been carrying three hundred thousand pieces-of-eight, pay for the British armies in India. Several chests of silver had been brought ashore; more had been recovered over the years by divers. But half or more of the silver was still unaccounted for. It was this that the Kirkpatricks had found, and that had brought Emilia to England, and which Knox and his MGS colleagues were going to salvage once they were finished with Ricky and the treasure ship.

He closed the box-file. The sun was low in the sky, and their friendly westerly had turned into an unhelpful southerly that was chopping up the water and forcing them into such sharp tacks that they were barely making any forward progress. He glanced around at Thierry. 'Eden,' said Thierry, pointing to a distant headland. 'But not tonight.'

Knox looked regretfully south. The headland looked frustratingly close. 'Is it walkable?' he asked.

Thierry leaned out to discuss it briefly with Alphonse, shook his head. 'Not at night,' he said. 'Too dark. But we make camp here, we start before sunrise, you'll have breakfast at Eden for sure.'

'Fine,' said Knox. 'Let's do it.'

III

It was time for Boris to make his first report to Sandro. He watched closely as Davit set up so that he'd be able to do it for himself next time. 'This is the IP terminal,' Davit told him, plugging a device the size and shape of a slim black hardback to his laptop. 'It links to a network of geostationary satellites. The nearest is over Africa; to our north-west.' He took a compass from the case, set it flat on the table, aimed the terminal until the display told him he'd found the satellite, and then had locked on. He brought up a program on the laptop, waited a few moments, double-clicked the mouse. 'Okay,' he said.

'That's it?' asked Boris.

'That's it,' confirmed Davit. 'You have broadband.'

'And how do I call Georgia?'

Davit entered the number for him. A switchboard operator answered; they ran through the security protocols. A new box popped up onscreen, Sandro looking irritably to his left before turning to the camera. 'You got there okay then?' he said.

Boris turned to Davit. 'I'll call you if I need anything.' He waited until he was gone. 'It's him,' he told Sandro. 'It's Knox.'

There was a second or so of delay, then Sandro squinted at the camera. 'You're sure? Already?'

'I was just taking a look at the town. Guess who came walking straight towards me?'

Again that delay. It was only satellite time-lag, Boris knew, yet it was disconcerting nonetheless. 'How can you be sure it's him?' Sandro asked. 'Did he recognise you?'

'No. It was just the way he carried himself.'

'The way he carried himself,' echoed Sandro. He gave Boris a long, hard look. 'Listen, I hope you don't think we'll pay you for topping some random stranger. We'll want proof that this is Knox before you do anything.'

'It's him. I'm telling you.'

'Good. Then proof should be easy, shouldn't it?'

Boris sighed, but he knew better than to argue. 'Any progress on that gun?' he asked.

'Petr's found some dealer to drive you down a selection. We think he's okay, but you know how these things are. You might be wise to scout out somewhere neutral for the handover; unless you're comfortable with him coming to your hotel.'

Boris nodded. 'I'll look around in the morning.'

'Good. Then let's talk again tomorrow.' The screen went black. Boris disconnected then dismantled the laptop and terminal, sat there brooding. He'd been Sandro's head of security for years, had never had his integrity doubted like that before. It rather stung him. But then he wondered if he wasn't perhaps missing something. Ilya Nergadze had always been quick to anger and hungry for revenge, but Sandro was too pragmatic for such vendettas. As head of security, Boris had often seen Sandro handle his father in such situations. He'd never say no directly. Instead he'd agree enthusiastically that something needed to be done, then work in subtle ways to make sure that nothing happened until Ilya had forgotten about it. *Was that what was going on here?* Ilya was dying, after all. Taking Knox to the grave with him was all he cared about, consequences be damned. But Sandro wouldn't be thinking that way, for Knox's murder was certain to kick off a shit-storm. He'd never openly obstruct his father, not least because Ilya was quite ruthless enough to cut him out of his will. *But behind the scenes . . .*

Boris considered alerting Ilya; but only briefly. Sandro would soon be head of the family, and then Boris would be dependent upon his continuing goodwill. He shook his head in frustration. If Sandro wanted proof, Boris would just have to provide it. The only question was how.

THIRTEEN

I

Darkness began to fall around Rebecca. She turned on her headlights. The stars were out by the time they reached the small town of Salary, fires being lit for the evening meals, rice softening in blackened cauldrons as families gathered to trade stories of their day. She stopped in the dusty heart of the village, stepped out. Malagasy music pounded from a café on top of a dune, muffled by the low rumble of a generator. A crowd gathered slowly around her, trying to make it look as if they weren't staring. She recognised one or two from years before, but most were strangers. A man in a glittery blue shirt jogged down a dune, precipitating tiny avalanches of sand. Jean-Luc.

He'd always been striking: tall, handsome, confident, better educated and more ambitious than his fellows. He'd put on weight, but it suited him, made him look substantial and prosperous. He took her hands, kissed her on either cheek. 'Rebecca,' he said. 'It's been too long.'

'Any news?'

'No.' He shook his head. 'No news.'

'You've been looking?'

'Of course.' His eyes flickered, however. He tried a smile. 'You must understand, we have families to feed.'

'You have families to feed,' said Rebecca. She put her hands on her hips, looked around from face to face. 'My father was good to you. He never let you go hungry. *Never*. My sister was your friend. She nursed you and your children whenever you were sick. But now that they need you, you have families to feed. My father and sister *were* your family. You think they'd have stayed home if you'd gone missing?' Heads bowed in shame all around her, a congregation before their brimstone preacher. She dropped the Mitsubishi's tailboard, dragged out the sack of rice she'd bought in Tulear, let it thump to the earth. Two zebu were tethered to an ancient tree, grazing the meagre grass, flicking their tails and shuddering their muscles to scatter flies. 'Whose are those?' she asked Jean-Luc.

'My father's. But—'

'How much?'

'They're not for—'

'How much?'

He sighed. 'Three million.'

She took out her purse, gave him all her cash. 'I'll get you the rest next time I go to town.' He took it reluctantly, started to say something, then thought better of it. 'I need a knife,' she announced. 'Who has a knife?'

There was scurrying. A young lad with a ragged cleft-palate scar came through the ranks a few moments later holding out a long-bladed knife. She took it from him, tested its point and then its blade with her thumb. Not as sharp as she'd like, nor as clean, but it would have to do. She seized the zebu's jaw in the vice of her elbow, wrenched its head back and up. It took a couple of faltering steps to adjust its balance, leaned trustingly against her. They were strong creatures, but bred to be docile. She plunged the knife through the tough hide of its throat into the softness of the liquid canals inside, felt the puncture of the larynx, holding it there for just a moment before sawing in a jagged, sideways motion, the radiated heat striking her a moment later, and then a geyser of blood spraying everywhere, people shrieking and jumping back, her legs and hands and stomach sticky, and the zebu grunting and trying to buck away too late, crashing to its knees and then on to its side, life-blood pumping in a slackening flow on to the dry brown earth, one eye looking reproachfully up at her. 'There,' she told them. 'That should feed your families. Let me know when you need more.'

Jean-Luc glared at her, aware he'd lost face. She wiped the knife on her shirt, handed it back to the boy, then climbed on to the Mitsubishi's flatbed. 'Three million ariary to whoever finds my father,' she announced, the blood granting her a certain grotesque authority. 'Five million if he's alive. The same for my sister. You hear?' She looked around their faces. Ten million ariary was a life-changing sum for a Malagasy. And the bush telegraph was a wondrous thing. By tomorrow, word would have spread all along the coast. As for the reward money, she'd just have to cross that bridge when she came to it.

II

Alphonse and Thierry unknotted the rigging, lowered the sail and the mast, then the four of them together heaved the pirogue up past the high-tide mark of the beach. Thierry found a section of flat sand and fashioned a makeshift tent from the sail and two paddles, just about big enough for them all. Alphonse collected wood and built a fire on which they boiled rice and grilled fish, before sitting in a line looking out over the sea and eating it with their fingers.

'You never told me what the verdict was,' said Lucia.

'How do you mean?'

'Your science presentation. Did the Chinese discover America?'

He gave her a sideways glance; she must have been aware of all the rancour and commotion on the *Maritsa* last night. Maybe this was her way of angling for the story. 'I'm never quite sure what people mean by that,' he answered carefully. 'It's always struck me as a little arrogant to say the New World was *discovered* by Columbus or the Chinese or whoever. What about the tribes-people who crossed the Bering Strait sixteen thousand years ago? Don't they count? Or the Norsemen of the Vinland sagas? Or the men of Bristol, who fished off the American coast long before Columbus. Discovery's just a euphemism. What people really mean is *conquest*. And, no, the Chinese didn't conquer America.'

'Nice sidestep,' she smiled.

Knox laughed and nodded across the fire at Alphonse and Thierry, helping themselves to more mounds of rice. 'Did you know that these guys sometimes sail their pirogues all the way across this channel to Mozambique? Two hundred miles of treacherous open sea in a fifteen-foot canoe, armed only with food, fresh water and a pack of cigarettes. People do extraordinary things in boats, and they don't always leave evidence behind. Frankly, I'd be amazed if no Chinese had ever made it to America before Columbus.'

'Really?'

'Look at a map sometime. Sail north from China, you can have land to your left all the way around Kamchatka to the Bering Sea, then down Alaska to British Columbia and the western United States. Or, if you don't fancy the cold, you could always island-hop via the Kurils and the Aleutians. Did no fisherman or merchant *ever* make it there, not even by accident?'

'*Reaching* somewhere isn't the point,' observed Lucia. 'It only counts if you report it back.'

'And maybe they did,' said Knox. 'The Chinese certainly believed in a place called Fusang, ten thousand kilometres to their east, pretty much exactly where California is. The third-century emperor Shi Huang despatched a group of settlers there; by all accounts they settled happily enough. A Buddhist monk called Hui Shen followed with a party of missionaries.' Bizarrely, Hui Shen had had an almost-exact Irish counterpart, a sixth-century abbot called Brendan, who'd led a crew of monks west in search of a promised land filled with fruit and meadows and all good things, encountering talking birds and mysterious floating crystal towers on his way. Brendan had existed for sure, and his transatlantic odyssey was certainly plausible. When the Vikings had reached Iceland, they'd found it already settled by Irish Christians. And while Norse longboats had been nothing like as sophisticated as Chinese treasure ships, Leif Eriksson had still managed to sight the North American coast from one, while others had established a settlement in L'Anse aux Meadows in Newfoundland, the only indisputable evidence of Europeans reaching the New World before Columbus.

Lucia nodded. 'So Zheng He and his admirals would have expected to find land where America was?'

'They certainly wouldn't have been surprised by it. Though that doesn't mean they got there, of course. Or anywhere close.' They'd finished their food by now, so they took their plates down to the shallows, rinsed them clean. 'But you have to remember that Chinese ships were absolute pigs to steer. They could hardly sail into the wind at all, and so were utterly dependent upon the monsoon and the other trade winds.' He gestured out into the Mozambique Channel. 'If they'd come this far south, and missed their window, their choice would have been to wait out another whole year or risk sailing wherever the wind blew them.'

'And if it had blown them to Fusang . . .?'

'Exactly,' smiled Knox.

FOURTEEN

I

Rebecca drove the Mitsubishi down to the beach to wash off the blood and put on clean clothes before continuing on to Pierre's house. It was dark and deserted when she pulled up, and there was no sign of his car. No great shock, frankly, for it was a full day's drive back from Antananarivo; but she was surprised not to see any of his wives or children.

Pierre had built himself the kind of throwback colonial life that was only still on offer in places like Madagascar. His father had been in the French army, stationed out here before Independence. Convinced it would be the next tourist paradise, he'd bought this whole stretch of coast and forest, including the Eden Reserve. But nothing had come of it, and he and his wife had been killed in a car accident. Pierre, their sole heir, had flown out intending to sell up; but he'd never left. He'd realised that, by living prudently, he'd never have to work again. And the women here were so beautiful.

Mating strategies fascinated Rebecca. Every living creature was the product of an almost infinite regression of successful reproductions: yet each itself had only a limited chance of leaving offspring. To an evolutionary biologist, therefore, sex was war; children victory. It was a battle Pierre had set out to win. He'd started by building guest cabins, even though no tourists had ever come here back then, and had recruited a string of young Malagasy women, ostensibly as staff, but in reality to share his bed and bear his children. Even that hadn't been enough for him, however. After he'd sold her father a good chunk of his land on which to set up the Eden Reserve, more and more zoologists and other intrepid travellers had started making the trek up here.

A Dutch marine biologist called Cees had arrived for a week with his fiancée Ardine, an otherworldly young woman with crinkled red hair, freckled soft white skin and long, bony witch's fingers that had glittered with silver rings and semiprecious stones. When Adam had taken Cees diving one day, Pierre had pressed Ardine to let him show her a sacred grotto in the spiny forest. Rebecca had been perhaps ten years old at the time. Without being quite sure why, she'd found herself deliciously titillated by this, and so had followed. The forest trails were difficult if you weren't used to them. Pierre had kept catching Ardine when she stumbled, plucking thorns from her clothes. The climb down to the grotto itself was narrow and awkward. Pierre went first, then reached back up for Ardine, letting her hips slide through his hands so that her top had rumpled up and his thumbs brushed the undersides of her breasts.

Rebecca had stretched out on the rocks above the pool to watch Pierre strip naked then dive into the water. Ardine had been wearing bikini bottoms beneath her trousers. She'd paddled in the shallows. There was a natural stone bench in the water. Pierre had teased her until she'd sat beside him. He'd taken her hand and talked passionately; she'd blushed and looked away. He'd put a hand behind her head to hold her as he'd kissed her. She'd flapped and struggled, but not for very long. There was something about Pierre that women seemed unable to deny.

Afterwards, Rebecca had often watched Pierre go to work on their female guests. He was powerful, handsome and capable of immense charm. And he had absolutely no shame. Rebecca had learned from him how often people simply defer to strength of purpose. It didn't much matter what that purpose was, only how fiercely it was held. Some male mosquitoes loiter above salt-water hatcheries, pouncing on females as they struggled from their shells, impregnating them before they could defend themselves. Male *Heliconius* butterflies punched holes in chrysalises to force themselves upon the females inside. Pierre had something of that ruthlessness. Vulnerability thrilled him. To cuckold gave him joy.

Her father had known all this, but when you were the only two Europeans within a day's travel, friendship was the only sane option. Besides, Pierre had proved useful. Running a reserve here meant endless bureaucratic meetings in Antananarivo, the constant greasing of palms. Her father had hated that side of Madagascar, but Pierre relished it. He enjoyed, too, delivering papers written by her father at Antananarivo's never-ending cycle of wildlife conferences, like the one he'd just been at this past week, so that he could then use his tales of life on the frontline to seduce any impressionable young delegates.

'Becca! Becca!' Rebecca turned to see a Malagasy woman in pale clothes approach over a grass-topped dune, an infant in one arm, another in a sling around her neck. 'Becca!' she screeched again, waving exuberantly.

Rebecca squinted through the darkness. 'Therese?'

Of course Therese! Had Rebecca forgotten her old friend so quickly? Had she aged that much? For all her scolding, Therese radiated such joy to see her that Rebecca couldn't help but be warmed. As far back as she could remember, Therese had been part of her life, for she'd developed such a passion for medicine and nursing as a young girl that she'd spent her free time helping Rebecca's mother out in Eden's clinic. In fact, she was now running it herself the two mornings a week it was open, as well as in emergencies.

'Michel?' asked Rebecca, indicating the child in Therese's arm.

Therese shook her head shyly. 'She mine. Xandra Yvette. Xandra for Pierre's grandmother. Yvette for your mother. She so kind to me.'

'She's beautiful.'

'Yes,' beamed Therese proudly. She opened the flap of her shawl. 'This is Michel,' she said. 'Your nep'ew.'

Rebecca took him in one arm. He was smaller than she'd expected, yet heavier. He had tight purple slivers of lips, dark upturned nostrils and clenched eyes. He looked so like Emilia that Rebecca's chest fluttered. She touched his cheek. His eyelids sprang open, revealing the shiny conkers within. He grasped her finger and pulled it towards his mouth.

'He like you bery much,' beamed Therese.

Rebecca couldn't tear her eyes from him. From nowhere, she had a sudden, wild vision of taking him back with her to England, rebuilding her life around him. But she stamped down on the treacherous thought. She was here to rescue Emilia, not bury her.

'You hab news?' asked Therese.

'Nothing,' said Rebecca.

Therese pulled an anguished face. 'Your bu'ful sister, so kind, so *young*. Your won'ful father.'

Rebecca's heart tightened. 'We'll find them. We'll get them back.'

'Yes.' Therese brushed her cheeks with the heel of her hand, then smiled radiantly again, sunshine after a squall. 'Sure! We get them both back, now you are here. But tomorrow, yes. Tonight you eat. Not go Eden. No food at Eden. All dark and empty and nasty. Yes. First eat, then sleep, ebryt'ing better in morning. Okay! Yes!' She crooked a finger at Zanahary, standing by the Mitsubishi. 'And you too, li'l boy. Come eat. Come. Come.'

They walked down the dunes to a blazing fire, three of Pierre's women and nine of his children eating and laughing together. Therese heaped a plate high with boiled white rice and fish stew for her. It was hot, spicy, delicious and filling. Tiredness quickly overwhelmed her; she fought a yawn.

'Bed for you,' said Therese, noticing. 'I show you now.' She carried the two infants with her. Michel began to squirm and bawl, setting Xandra off. Therese peeled back her shirt, gave them a nipple each. 'I miss Emilia so much,' she said sadly. 'We hab our babies together. We share ebryt'ing. *Ebryt'ing*.'

The way she said it, it was like she was trying to communicate something. 'Everything?' asked Rebecca.

'Ebryt'ing,' confirmed Therese. 'It much easier when you hab good friend.' Rebecca watched fascinated as the infants suckled; she couldn't tear her eyes away. 'You be good mother,' said Therese suddenly. 'Why you not hab children yet?'

'My life isn't right,' said Rebecca, who'd forgotten how direct Malagasy women could be. 'Maybe one day.'

'One day!' snorted Therese. 'Yes'day one day. Today one day. You get busy, girl, or one day soon be gone.'

II

Boris took a table in the hotel's large but completely empty restaurant, ordered a beer then spread out his map of the coast, wondering where Knox was headed in his pirogue.

'What news from home?' asked Davit, coming to join him.

'I saw Knox earlier.'

'You *what*? Where?'

Boris nodded seawards, to avoid explanations. 'He sailed off with some fishermen,' he said. 'They headed south.'

'And you're sure it was him?'

'Yes.'

'Why didn't you talk to him?'

Boris laughed. Truly, Davit was an idiot. 'He blames us for the death of his girlfriend. How do you think he'll react when he sees us?'

'Oh.'

'Yes. Oh.' He lit a cigarette, blew smoke at Davit's face, though just enough to the side that he wouldn't be sure it was an insult. 'We need to get him on his own before we can explain what we're doing.'

'Makes sense,' agreed Davit.

'Glad you think so. Trouble is, we don't know where he's gone.'

'I could ask Claudia. I'll bet she knows the guys he went off with. Or maybe she could ask around for us.'

'Discreetly, though,' said Boris. 'We don't want Knox hearing about it.'

'She'll need something to go on,' said Davit. 'What did the fishermen look like?'

Boris thought back. 'Their sail had a great big Western Union logo on it,' he said.

'Great,' said Davit, getting to his feet. 'I'll go ask her now.'

III

Thierry and Alphonse shared a cigarette while Lucia asked them pointed questions about getting to Tulear in time for her flight. It depended on the wind, they told her; but it certainly wouldn't help her cause if she stopped off at Eden on the way. She turned apologetically to Knox, told him that she'd need to press on. The three of them called it a night shortly afterwards, but Knox wasn't yet tired. He sat on the sand and stared out over the sea, listening to its rhythms. Once, he caught a glimpse of something pale, though he couldn't be sure whether it was mist, a sail or just imagination. But it made him think again of the man in the black shirt, the possibility that the Nergadzes had finally discovered his new identity.

While lying in hospital, recovering from burns and the grief of losing Gaille, one of the ways he'd kept himself going had been with daydreams of revenge upon the Nergadzes. Knowing that time had a habit of diminishing grief and thus the need for vendetta, he'd made a vow not to let that happen. Since taking his job at MGS Salvage, he'd worked to honour that vow, learning everything he could about Ilya and Sandro and their summers on the Black Sea, devising the plan for a survey along that stretch of coast, clearing it with Frank and Miles and raising the funds himself, tapping up MGS's contact list and others with an interest in the Black Sea's secrets – which had been easier than he'd expected, for the place exerted a powerful pull on the imaginations of underwater archaeologists. Once you reached around two hundred metres beneath the surface, the water was so bereft of oxygen that almost nothing could survive in it, not even worms or bacteria, meaning that – almost uniquely in the world – there was every chance of finding ancient wrecks in perfect condition.

The closer the expedition had drawn, however, the more he'd recognised the essential contradiction of his private mission. He'd loved Gaille for her gentleness and compassion; she would have wanted him to mourn her and then move on, not waste his life on vengeance. But when anger was all you had left of someone you loved, it was hard to let it go.

A gibbous moon had risen low behind him, its light bright enough to stretch shadows on the pale sand. He frowned at it, as though it was trying to tell him something. He gave a little laugh when he realised what. With the moon up, he surely had enough light to walk by. He opened the flap of the tent, woke Thierry to tell him his intent. He paid him and his brother off and said goodbye to Lucia, then he hoisted his dive-bag to his shoulders, picked up his overnight case, and set off south along the beach.

FIFTEEN

I

Rebecca was too tired to do anything but undress and collapse into bed. She dozed off, only to be woken by a shutter banging on the breeze and the sound of singing. Most likely Therese and the others just playing the radio, but it got to her all the same. Whenever someone beloved died along this coast, the Malagasy would dance and drink until dawn, sometimes for nights on end. She couldn't help but think that these songs were for Adam and Emilia.

As a child, not understanding death, Rebecca had been enchanted by the distant music of these wakes, not least because they left the fishermen too exhausted to go out the following day, and so her father, an ardent carnivore, would use it as an excuse to butcher some meat. He'd always insisted you had to be prepared to kill what you ate, however, so Rebecca had long feared that her turn would come. That hadn't made it easy when the time finally arrived. The chickens were her friends; she'd personified them and given them names. He'd folded his arms implacably, however, so she'd chased them half-heartedly around the clearing. One chicken hadn't fled as fast as the others. She'd held it upside down until it had gone to sleep, then laid its neck upon the chopping block, picked up the axe. That was when it started to wake.

People talk about free will. If it exists at all, it's in such moments, when you choose your path. Rebecca had suffered nightmares for weeks afterwards; the moment of impact; the chicken running, its head held on by a flap of skin, blood spurting in gouts. Yet she'd been glad she'd gone through with it. The courage to inflict pain was invaluable in this world. Emilia had lacked that toughness. She'd turned vegetarian rather than kill, except for fish, of course. Fish were easy. You just threw them on to the beach where they thrashed around helplessly until—

— *Eleven years. How could you have stayed away eleven years?*

— *I'm here now.*

— *It's too late. You know it's too late.*
— *Don't say that, Emilia!*

Rebecca put a hand to her mouth to stop herself crying out. Her ache wouldn't wait any longer; she needed to go home. She dressed and wrote a note for Therese, set off. Eden was just twenty minutes away along the track, but it was spooky and treacherous by night, so she went along the beach instead. The dunes glowed like snow. The sand here was sacred. The locals used it for divination and scattered it around their houses for protection against witchcraft. She kicked off her sandals, let her feet sink into the dry cold talc. Pale shore crabs sensed her approach and rose to flee, their moon-shadows instantly giving them away. Then they hunkered down and disappeared again, their colouring a perfect match for the sand. How could you keep out memories in a place like this? How could you remain detached? Her father had once sailed her and Emilia south to a beach with darker sand and correspondingly darker crabs. He'd released a bowl of these albinos, so luminous suddenly, so visible to predators, their deaths now assured. Rebecca had known intellectually about the survival of the fittest before then, but for the first time she'd understood it in her gut, had appreciated the full savagery and elegance of natural selection.

She drew closer to Eden. Now even the trees were familiar, the frown-lines of seaweed on the beach.

Memories thronged, crushing as crowds. Adam hoisting her on to his shoulders, bellowing and charging into the surf. The tingle of sand on her palm as she'd patted the walls of castles, then the tide sapping the walls. Waging jellyfish wars with the local Malagasy boys. Scouring shallows and rock-pools for molluscs and shell-fish. The way Adam had turned grey and old after Yvette's death, as though an organ had failed. And, yes, that brutal first time she'd caught him staring at her with his face all twisted and sour, and she'd realised with heart-stopping clarity that her beloved father, the giant of her childhood, the Great Man Himself, *hated* her.

II

Davit found Claudia washing shirts in a large tub, squeezing them out before hanging them on a line stretched between two cabins, while a wizened Malagasy woman on the porch watched her closely, as if hoping to find fault.

'Work, work, work,' said Davit.

'Work, work, work,' agreed Claudia, wiping suds from her nose with the heel of her hand.

He nodded at the old woman, not wanting to cause trouble. 'May I borrow Claudia, please?' he asked. 'Only I've a problem in my cabin.' Claudia translated for him;

the woman nodded sourly. They walked off together down a darkened path towards the beach.

'What problem?' she asked.

'No problem,' he assured her. 'I just wanted to get you alone.' She smiled with such guileless pleasure that he couldn't help but smile too. 'But I do have a question. A favour.'

'Oh,' she said. 'Yes?'

He told her about the pirogue with the Western Union sail, how he and Boris wanted to know where it had gone. She assured him she'd ask around later, for she still had a shift to do in one of the local bars. He looked at her in astonishment. 'You've still got another shift to do?'

'Yes.'

'Work, work, work,' he said sadly, because he was beginning to realise it was true.

'Work, work, work,' she agreed. Their gazes met for a moment; he touched her hand. She gestured back along the path to the high mound of clothes that still awaited her, then she nodded goodnight and went to wash them.

III

Eden. What else would you call the garden paradise of Adam and Yvette? Rebecca had always found her father's sense of humour suspect. The reserve comprised some fifty hectares of spiny forest, including eight kilometres of coastline, but its heart was this natural clearing in the forest, accessible by a short drive from the coastal track. It was dark and empty and smaller than she remembered, but otherwise unchanged.

To her right was the lodge, a large and sturdy one-storey building of whitewashed stone that housed her father's office, the clinic, the dining area and a few other rooms. Her father's old Jeep was parked in front of the veranda, along with the track-bike he'd used to reach places even the Jeep couldn't go. Ahead of her, chairs and tables surrounded the outside cooking area, while a clothesline doubled as a badminton net. And, to her left, the generator annexe and cabins raised on stilts to keep them dry during the occasional fierce rains. Adam had built pretty much all of it himself, with modest help from the local villagers (the world's least reliable workforce: they'd drop tools in a heartbeat whenever the fish started running). Her father had loved such work, fitting stones together like jigsaw pieces, learning the different properties of the local woods, the hard *cassave* for houses and masts, the light *farafatry* for boats. His eyes would glitter as he'd demonstrate how to twist *faraihosy* bark into rope or tap *babo* for fresh water.

She went over to the lodge, but it had a new steel front door, perhaps in response to the recent coup. There were new steel shutters too, closed and bolted, denying her access. She'd just have to wait until morning, borrow keys from Therese. The cabins were unlocked, however. Her father's was closed only on a latch. There was a white candle by his bed. She lit it, held it up. The place was filled with poignant reminders of him: silver hairs caught in a comb; a black-and-white family photograph of them all together; drawstring blue pyjamas beneath his pillow.

She went back out. The night had grown perceptibly cooler and the stars had all vanished. Bad weather was on its way. She was tempted to head back to Pierre's, but she needed to see Emilia's cabin first. Michel's cradle was by her bed, brightly coloured mobiles of reef-fish dangling low above it. Her heart gave a twist as she recalled the morning, a year or so ago, when Emilia had phoned to let her know that she was pregnant. She'd tried to offer congratulations, but her words had come out strangely hollow. Afterwards, too dazed to work, she'd left the office and had walked for hours. In a book-shop, she'd picked out a paperback on motherhood, had made a wall of her back to hide it from the CCTV cameras, as though it were the most lurid pornography. It had been a rush just to cradle it in her palm: the sharp-edged springiness of its leaves, the creak of its spine, that intoxicating scent of newness. Every day for a week, she'd visited a different maternity store, running her hands over the displays, the silk and satin trickling like fine sand through her fingers. It had been madness. She'd been too well known. Shoppers had murmured with staff; rumours had begun to circulate. An ambitious morning TV presenter with glittering eyes had asked her flat out whether she had exciting news to share. Rebecca had had to tell her about Emilia. It was the first time she'd volunteered information about her family on television, and because her father had once been a TV presenter himself, her childhood had suddenly been in play.

'What was he like, your father?' the woman had asked.

Rebecca had simply frozen. How to answer such a question? Was she supposed to talk about the gentle, wise man he'd been before the leukaemia had taken her mother? Or the sporadic drunk he'd then become, the red-faced ranting machine who'd yelled at her and threatened her with his fists? Was that the man she was being asked about?

His abuse had lasted years. He'd felt wretched after each episode, had vowed never to lapse again. But he always had. And, anyway, it hadn't been the yelling or the threats that had most upset her, it had been the knowledge of the hatred that underlay it, not least because she hadn't the first idea what she'd done to deserve it, and he'd never said. And while part of her had been glad that Emilia had been spared his wrath during these outbursts, another part of her had bitterly resented the manifest unfairness of this, and so she'd begun in turn to pick on her younger sister, something for which she'd come to hate herself.

In the end, they'd colluded on the solution. Adam had pulled strings with his old Oxford colleagues to get Rebecca a place to read zoology. Distance had allowed her heart to heal, but the scarring still remained. For years afterwards, Rebecca had refused any direct contact whatsoever with her father. But Emilia had eventually brokered a wary truce, a first tentative exchange of letters, emails, even the rare phone call. But whenever either Emilia or Adam suggested anything more, Rebecca would freeze up, the process would be set back months.

In the bottom of a chest of drawers, Rebecca found a home pregnancy kit and a packet of domperidone, a lactation stimulator. Rebecca smiled. Emilia had been planning for motherhood all her life. Where other girls had wanted breasts to titillate the boys, Emilia had only ever wanted them to gorge her babies. Where others had fantasised about their life partners, Emilia's dream man had always been one who'd get her pregnant and then leave.

— *Pierre! How could you choose Pierre?*
— *A woman needs to be held.*
— *But Pierre!*
— *A child needs a father.*

— *But Pierre!*

— *As if your choices are so much better.*

Outside, she heard an engine. She went to the door, saw headlights through the rain that had started falling. Pierre back from Antananarivo, no doubt. But then the lights went out and a pickup truck lurched with unnerving stealth up the drive. She stepped back out of sight, blew out her candle. The pickup swung around; its engine stilled. Both doors opened and two men jumped down, faces concealed by baseball caps and scarves. They hurried through the rain to the lodge. To Rebecca's shock, they unlocked the front door and vanished inside, making her wonder whether they'd taken keys from her father and Emilia, and had come here to plunder the place while they knew it would be deserted. She watched the pale fireflies of torchlight flutter around the edges of the shutters as they moved through the various rooms. It would be madness to go challenge them by herself, but there was no reason not to check out their pickup, make a note of their licence plate. Her T-shirt was a treacherous bright white, however, so she tiptoed quietly over to Emilia's chest of drawers and began searching for something dark.

SIXTEEN

I

The charm of his moonlit walk had long since worn off for Knox. His feet were either plugging in the soft sand or stumbling as he negotiated rocky hummocks and tangles of mangrove. When he took off his shoes to wade across an inlet, something snakelike slithered from beneath his sole. He lifted his foot so abruptly that his dive-bag swung on his shoulders and he fell sideways into the water, yelling out a heartfelt curse.

The night grew cloudy, cold and dark. He took off his pack, pulled out his diving lamp. He reached another rocky outcrop, treacherous with spume. Lightning flickered ahead. A miniature whirlwind brought a hoop of dust and dead leaves towards him, whipping and twisting and bowing. It began to rain, light patters at first, but quickly growing strong. He looked for shelter, but there wasn't any. He fought his way past more mangroves and then kept going, a hundred paces at a time, the rain growing heavier around him, the lightning drawing closer. He was on the verge of giving up when he finally saw a small white building ahead. Its door was locked and its awning offered precious little protection. He shone his lamp through the small window, revealing diving gear hanging up on the far wall and a compressor for filling scuba tanks. He surely had to be close to Eden now.

Hurrying on with renewed energy, he soon reached a sign directing him up a track to a clearing of wooden cabins and a large, low building. He hurried between parked vehicles to the shelter of the veranda, was surprised to see that the front door was ajar and that torchlight was flickering inside, as though there'd been a power-cut. He shouted out as he put down his bags, and two men appeared a moment later, wearing baseball caps and scarves around their mouths, obviously up to no good. They yelled out and charged at him, knocked him backwards off the veranda. Knox slapped instinctively at an ankle as it passed, and one of the men went sprawling. He leapt upon him but the second man came back and aimed a kick at Knox's face, forcing him to defend himself, allowing his companion to squirm free. They ran for the pickup, locked themselves certain to rebound. 'It's a salvage ship,' he told her. 'They're doing a project up near Morombe.'

'That's right,' said Rebecca 'I read an article on it. Looking for some Chinese shipwreck, right?'

'That's the one.'

'What were you doing up there?'

He hesitated again, reluctant to be drawn into all these lies. But he didn't see what choice he had, other than to betray his vow to Emilia. 'I'm a freelance journalist,' he told her, borrowing a trick from Lucia. 'I was up there to write an article on the salvage.'

'And is that why you're here too? To do an article on Eden?'

'I'm always looking for strong stories,' said Knox. 'But mostly I'm here because I've got a few days off, and I'd heard great things about this place.'

She pulled a face. 'I'm afraid we're really not set up for visitors at the moment.' Then she looked out at the continuing downpour, and relented. 'But you can stay tonight, of course; and there are some nice guest cabins just along the beach from here.'

'Thanks. That's really kind.' A pool of water was gathering around his feet, making him realise just how filthy and wet he was. 'I don't suppose there's a shower I can use, is there?' he asked.

She looked bleakly outside. 'I think I'd need to turn on the generator.'

'Then don't worry about it,' he told her. 'The Good Lord provides.' He took his wash-bag and towel from his bag, went out on to the veranda, closed the door behind him, then stripped naked and strode out into the deluge to wash.

II

Rebecca lit an oil lamp, turned it up bright and looked around. A red guestbook and a wire tray of leaflets stood upon the high counter. Spare keys hung from a rack behind the desk. A menagerie of snakes, chameleons, butterflies, tortoises, birds and lemurs stared back at her from framed photographs on the walls. The intruders had left damp footprints on the floor. She followed them to the door of her father's study, looked inside. It was much as she remembered, save for the laptop upon his desk. The camp-bed was still in the far corner, for those occasions when Eden had been overrun by volunteers; and his shotgun was still in the glass cabinet behind the desk. She quickly checked his shelves of books and CDs, but there were no obvious gaps from which something might have been taken.

She went back through reception. The front door had blown ajar, revealing that the downpour outside had grown incredibly fierce, so that the ground was half covered in shallow lakes, and great serpents of dark water were slithering away on the slight camber of the site. Daniel had his back to her, rainwater running down his back before splitting like a delta at his buttocks. His shoulder was ploughed by the distinctive ridges of burn scars, with more upon his back, but there was little else wrong with him that she could see.

He squeezed a stubby caterpillar of toothpaste on to his brush, held it out into the rain, threw back his head to let water drum into his mouth. Lightning lit him up like Christmas, glinting off the silver chain around his neck, illuminating the tattoo of a star on his right biceps, reflecting in twin yellow points from the tapeta-rich eyes of night creatures around the clearing. Thunder cracked; raindrops hammered like furious dwarves at the earth, throwing up tiny coronets with each impact. Daniel didn't even flinch. She suffered, then, something like premonition; a certainty that there was more to this man than met the eye, that somehow he'd have a part to play in her life.

The door blew closed again. She shook her head at herself, went through to the main room, a large, open-plan mix of cafeteria, games room, lecture-hall, library and dormitory. She'd sleep in here herself tonight, put Daniel in her father's office. The kitchens next, then the restrooms, storeroom and clinic. Nothing seemed out of place, though she'd been away too long to be sure. Daniel was in the lounge when she went back through, wearing an olive T-shirt and baggy blue shorts, holding an oil lamp of his own that made his skin glow. 'This may sound crazy,' he said. 'But don't I know you from somewhere?'

She gave him an appraising look. Men often tried to pretend they didn't recognise her; it seemed to make them feel better about themselves for some reason. But if this one was lying, he was good. 'You may have seen me on TV,' she told him.

His eyes narrowed, then he snapped his fingers. 'That's it,' he said. 'You're Rebecca someone. Rebecca Kirkpatrick. You do wildlife programmes.'

'Yes,' she agreed.

'Cool.' He sat down on one of a pair of armchairs hunched around a low table. 'So what are you doing out here? Are you on a shoot, or something?'

'Not exactly, no,' she said, sitting opposite. 'This is where I was brought up. My father and my sister . . .' She stopped short, surprised by a pang of emotion.

'Are you okay?'

'I'm fine,' she assured him. Outside, the rain was easing. It would be daybreak in a few hours; she should get some sleep. Yet, more than anything, she felt the need to talk. 'It's my father and my sister,' she told him. 'They've gone missing.'

heart out to him last night, sharing confidences about her childhood here that she'd never before told anyone – and him a journalist! She'd known even at the time that it was rash, yet once she'd started she hadn't been able to stop herself. Besides, there was something about him that she'd trusted then and trusted still. And, for all that she'd told him he'd have to leave today, she found herself rather hoping that he'd stay.

It was cool out. She took a familiar track into the spiny forest, walking with her arms folded across her belly until exertion warmed her. The narrow path was badly waterlogged in places. Her shoes kept plugging and popping, her feet became drenched and cold. But she didn't turn back. She'd put this off for over a decade already. It wouldn't wait any longer.

Moisture made everything sparkle. Birds sang; grasshoppers fizzed from her advance. Termite mounds were rusted with rain. A huge web glittered like stretched silver thread above her head. Last night's deluge had been an aberration. This region was parched most of the year. The peculiar gyre of the Indian Ocean and Madagascar's mountainous spine kept her east coast saturated but her west coast dry. Plants had to gather enough water during the rare rains to last them through the droughts. The flowers and trees therefore armoured themselves with needles to protect this precious liquid. Spiders and chameleons too. Madagascar's tenrec and the hedgehog were a textbook example of convergent evolution, little balls of spines. Like the hedgehog, the tenrec was a hibernator, fattening itself during rains, using torpor to survive the dry season. It was a common strategy on this coast. The mouse lemur, the world's smallest primate, could plunge its body temperature to just seven degrees above freezing. As a child, Rebecca had had a knack for finding these tiny, wide-eyed prosimians in their snug tree-holes. When you cradled them in your palm, their whole bodies would pulse extravagantly with terror. They were wise to be afraid, for she'd found their bones in the droppings of raptors, snakes, owls and fossa, but they'd never had anything to fear from her. She'd always loved lemurs, not least because so many of the species were fiercely matriarchal. They knew how gender relationships should be. Female ring-tailed lemurs had first pick of food and space, they cuffed their men around with impunity.

Only after leaving Eden did Rebecca realise what a privileged childhood she'd had. Her contemporaries at Oxford University had drawn their knowledge of nature from books rather than from the world. Slightly to her consternation, they'd envied Rebecca her upbringing. Madagascar was the *haj* for biologists. Eighty-eight million years ago, the island had finally separated from the supercontinent of Gondwana, where it had lain sandwiched between Africa, India and Australia. Since then, its fauna and flora had evolved independently. And

Madagascar's diverse ecosystems of volcanic highlands, reefs, rain forest, spiny forest and savannah meant not only an extraordinary proportion of endemics, but astonishing variety.

She climbed a gentle hill. The thalidomide-limbed trunk of a baobab towered like an ancient Egyptian pylon at the entrance to an old, familiar glade. Rebecca's mother had loved it up here, for the solitude and for the view it offered out over the lagoon. She'd come here all the time until she'd fallen too sick, and then she'd made Adam promise to bury her here. He'd kept his word. Her low stone tomb stood at the heart of the glade. Its white walls were roughly plastered; run your palm across it, it would scrape your skin. A flight of six steps led down to a sealed doorway. A faded colour photograph of Yvette as a young woman was embedded in the wall to the left of the doorway, protected by dulled glass. She'd been Merina, with dark, Polynesian looks and a dazzling smile which she'd somehow kept until the end, like the grin of the Cheshire cat. Beyond the door, stone slabs lay either side of a narrow aisle. On the left-hand slab lay her mortal remains, wrapped in rich red cloth. The right-hand slab was empty, waiting for Adam. He'd known even then he'd never remarry. He'd teased Yvette that at last he'd get to choose which side he slept; but he'd given her the left in death as in life, as she'd known he would. He'd deferred to her in everything that mattered. It had been his pleasure.

A brick oven against the left wall of the tomb was filled with puddled grey ash and the charred remnants of photographs and a cassette tape. Yvette had made Adam vow to keep her informed about her family, at least once each year, on the anniversary of her death. He'd record one of these cassettes to tell her what everyone had been up to, adding photographs of Eden, the boat, the reefs and the villagers, then he'd make a great pyre, dousing it with fuel and immolating it. Old friends visiting from England had teased Adam for this, because he'd once been scornful of religion. But he'd become a Catholic just to please her; and he'd taken it seriously too.

After Madagascar's hospitals had given up on Yvette, she'd refused to let Adam fly her out to a European hospital. She was a Malagasy; this was her home. For the most part, she'd faced her death with courage. Adam, too. Rebecca had found their candour and good humour unbearable, worse even than their rare shouting matches. They'd read Elisabeth Kübler-Ross's *On Death and Dying* to each other, laughing whenever they recognised aspects of their own behaviour, as though it were a book of jokes. Rebecca had been desperate for Yvette to fight her disease, if not to beat it then at least to hold the line. Her confused welter of adolescent emotion had manifested itself in sulks and tempers. She'd been angry at Adam for letting Yvette die, at their useless doctors, at the cancer cells overrunning

Yvette's body, at the birds that squawked so loudly to deny her rest, at the sun for its dry ferocity, the wind for its noise, the calm for denying her a cooling breeze. All of creation had seemed a conspiracy.

In her final months, Yvette had suffered occasional deep bouts of depression. In part agitated by Rebecca's own foul moods, she'd berated herself as a terrible mother for having spent too much time with the local Malagasy children, not enough with her own. Rebecca's efforts to reassure her had rung so hollow that they'd only made Yvette gloomier. Their time together had become desperately uncomfortable. Rebecca had started avoiding her altogether.

One day, Adam had sent her off for supplies. On her return, he'd been waiting for her at the lodge's front door, a hushing finger to his lips. She'd feared terrible news. She'd feared the end. But Adam had led her into reception, out of earshot of Yvette's cabin, and closed the door. He'd motioned her to a chair, then told her the brutal truth about leukaemia: that when it progressed this far, it almost always proved fatal. People facing death – and those who loved them – tended to pass through certain emotional states as they came to terms with this; that these were well known and natural, and included denial, isolation, anger, bargaining and depression. Rebecca could see for herself that Yvette had reached this latter stage. Depression often afflicted people who feared they'd wasted their lives. 'Let's face it,' Adam had told Rebecca bluntly. 'When you isolate yourself from the world, as we've done here, you make that choice for your own benefit, not for your children's. I know Yvette hasn't been as good a mother to you as she might have been, but while she's feeling this dispirited, I need for you to pretend—'

This had been too much. 'How dare you!' she'd screamed, flailing at him. 'How dare you! She's the best mother ever! She's done *everything* for us! *Everything*! You don't deserve her! You never deserved her! She's too good for you! *You're helping her to die!*' This last accusation had been like a splinter in her soul. Once it had come out, she hadn't been able to speak any more, overwhelmed by sobs, trembling with emotion. Adam had taken her by the wrist and dragged her into his office. Yvette had been propped up by pillows in a camp-bed, her wheelchair parked alongside. There'd been a moment's silence. Yvette had pulled an anguished face and stretched wide her arms. Rebecca's heart had twisted. She'd run helplessly across the room and flung herself into her mother's embrace.

Yvette's health had improved after that. She'd become comfortable. Rebecca had even allowed herself hope. But it had been a mirage. In Kenya, recently, she'd watched an elderly antelope brought down by lions. Once its fight was lost, it had lifted its head and watched its own evisceration with the same acceptant, haunting silence as Yvette had displayed in those final weeks. Death shouldn't be like this, Rebecca had thought. Death was the worst thing in the world and needed to be fought, even when hope was gone. But Yvette had already passed beyond reclaim. She'd become indifferent to the world. Too late, Rebecca realised that Adam had tricked her into their reconciliation so that Yvette could achieve peace with herself, and so die.

Flower-beds dug around the tomb had been planted with orchids. Yvette's favourites, from her highland home. They needed copious and regular water to survive in this arid climate. Rebecca remembered ruefully her ostentatious grief during Yvette's funeral, her tears and wailing, her rejection of comfort, company, food and drink. People will see my grief and know how deeply I've been hurt, she'd thought. They'll compare me with my father and find him wanting. But here, in this lovingly tended tomb, was irrefutable proof that Adam had felt true, deep and lasting love; a memorial to her mother, a place she hadn't visited in a decade.

Only one person had been found wanting, and it was her.

II

Knox woke with a start to discover that the sun was up and the day was growing warm. As he rose to wash and dress, he realised he still had his medical pendant on. Miles insisted on the damned thing whenever he was on an overseas job, but it was inscribed with the MGS logo and would blow his story about being a freelance journalist, so he took it off and packed it away, then brewed coffee on the gas cooker and wondered what to do.

A small stack of promotional leaflets for the nearby guest cabins lay on the reception counter. He took one outside to read while he drank his coffee: French and English text wrapped around touristic photographs: sunbathers glistening with oil on the white sand; angel fish in crystal-clear water; a bearded man Knox took to be the proprietor bouncing across the waves in an inflatable Zodiac; a sailboat silhouetted against a nectarine sunset. He looked up at the sound of footsteps, saw Rebecca arriving from the spiny forest, raised his cup in greeting. 'Coffee?' he asked.

'Love some,' she nodded.

He refilled his own mug while he was at it, took them both back out, sat down beside her on the veranda bench. She held her cup beneath her nose, breathed in deep, then looked sideways at him. 'Doesn't count as a proper holiday if you have to shave, huh?'

'Something like that,' he smiled. The sky was bright, mist rising from residual puddles. Grey-headed lovebirds frolicked and chased in the surrounding trees. A radiated tortoise crept slowly along the line of shade, making the most of the morning cool to feed. 'Tame buggers, aren't they?' he said.

'This is their sanctuary. No one hunts them here.'

'People hunt them?'

'Sure. For food. And for the pet trade.'

'So what'll happen to them now?' he asked. Only once the question was out did he realise its unfortunate implication. He winced and held up a hand. 'I'm sorry. I didn't mean it like that.'

'It's okay,' she assured him. 'I need to think about it.' She looked around, as though seeing it through different eyes. 'I'll certainly keep it going,' she told him. 'My father and Emilia would want that. But I'm not coming back. My life's in England now.'

Knox nodded. 'It should be easy enough to find someone to run a place like this.'

'Harder than you might think. Managing a nature reserve is bloody hard work. People dream about places like this, but it's not all sunshine and reefs.'

'I'll bet.' Her words reminded him of the promotional leaflet, however. He passed it to her.

'Oh.' Her face fell. 'So you're moving on, then?'

'Not unless you still want me to.' He pointed to the picture of the sailboat. 'I was just wondering, is this the boat you were telling me about last night? Your father's, I mean. The one you want to collect from Tulear.'

She glanced down at it. 'Yes. Yes it is.'

'A flat-bottomed sloop,' he told her. 'Not quick, but a piece of piss to handle. And I'd need someone who knows the reefs, of course. Or the passes between them, at least.'

She looked up at him in surprise. 'You can sail?'

'Sure,' he told her. 'I'd imagined it was bigger. But something like that, no problem.'

Rebecca nodded slowly. 'I know the reefs,' she said. 'It's been a while, but I don't suppose they've moved.'

III

Davit was sitting on his porch watching half-heartedly for a pirogue with a Western Union logo on its sail when Claudia came around the corner of his cabin. 'Hey!' he grinned. '*There* you are.'

'Yes,' she smiled. 'Here I am.'

'Any luck?'

'Sure.' She climbed up on to his porch, sat upon the balustrade and swung her legs. 'I ask my friends. They say this pirogue belongs to Thierry and Alphonse. They say they take two foreigners with them, a man to Eden, a woman on to Tulear.'

'Eden?' asked Davit.

'You have a map?'

Boris had hired himself a motorbike after breakfast, had headed off on some mysterious errand; but he'd left his guidebook on his porch. Davit fetched it now, opened it up to a regional map as he returned. Claudia came to stand beside him when he sat back down, leaning against his thigh. Braids spilled like a bead curtain over her face as she looked down. She pointed away to their south. 'This is my orphanage I was telling you about,' she said.

'And Eden?' he asked.

'Yes.' Her finger moved with deliberate slowness, stretching out the moment. 'This is Eden here.' Her leg felt gloriously warm against his own. He glanced up at her. She scooped her braids back behind her head with her left hand. 'You like a massage, maybe?' she said.

'You give massages?' he asked doubtfully.

'Yes. I give massages.'

He glanced around. There was still no sign of Boris, and with Knox in this Eden place, there seemed little point watching out for him. Besides, what harm could a massage do? 'Sure,' he said. 'That would be great.'

'I get my oil.'

He went inside, stripped down to his shorts, lay face-down upon the bed. Claudia came back in, took hold of the door. 'Open or closed?' she asked.

'Open,' he said.

She knelt beside him and set to work on his neck and shoulders. Her fingers were weak compared to the sports massages of his rugby-playing days, but it was pleasant all the same. She tapped his shoulder; he turned on to his back. The mosquito net glowed around them in the half-light, lending a certain medieval grandeur to the moment. She massaged his chest and arms and thighs, then sat herself at the far end of the bed, took his foot and set it against her chest, the better to work his ankle. He could feel the warmth and softness of her breast against his sole. His foot tugged down her top a little way, revealing a glimpse of nipple. She gave him a look of mock reproach and adjusted herself, then ran her thumbs hard down his metatarsals, as though trying to empty a tube of its toothpaste. 'Is nice, yes?' she murmured.

'Very nice,' he agreed.

She slid her hands up past his knee to his thigh. She did it again, and then a third time, going a little further on each occasion. He felt that strange numbness of mind setting in, the kind that made men forget about things like shame and consequences until it was too late. 'How old are you?' he asked; and his voice sounded like it was coming from far away.

'Twenty-three,' she told him. 'You want to see my card?'

'No,' he said.

She nodded and set down his leg, then went to close and bolt the door. Then she walked back towards him, stripping as she came.

EIGHTEEN

I

Rebecca was ransacking her father's desk for insurance documents when Zanahary arrived in the Mitsubishi, her belongings in the back. They brought everything indoors, packed overnight bags for themselves, locked up and set off south for Tulear. She took the wheel herself, Daniel alongside her and Zanahary on the flatbed behind, where he could smoke all he wanted. 'That stuff I told you last night,' she said, once they were on their way. 'It was in confidence, yes? You won't write some dreadful feature on me?'

'Of course not,' Daniel assured her.

'My father's very highly respected. I'd never forgive myself if that got out.'

'I already gave you my word,' he said. He selected a cassette tape, turned the volume down low. 'I'll tell you something, though: if anyone had treated me like that, I wouldn't be so worried for their reputation.'

'It was only after Mama died. She was everything to him.'

'No reason to take it out on you.'

'No.'

'And it was just you, right? He never went after your sister?'

'Not Emilia, no. He absolutely doted on her. He did fall out very badly with Pierre, I remember; but they made that up in the end.'

'And what about after you left for England?'

'That was the end of it. He only ever got angry when he was drunk, you see; and he never touched another drop after I left.'

'You believe that?'

'Emilia vouched for it. She wouldn't have lied; not about that.'

'Is that why you never came back? Scared you'd set him drinking again?'

'I made him unhappy,' she said. 'It's a horrid thing, making someone you love unhappy.'

169

'Why would you make him unhappy?'

'I don't know. Not for sure.' They crossed a slender thread of stream. Two Malagasy women, their fine African faces covered in yellow masks to keep their complexions pale, gathered dried washing from its far bank. 'The only thing I could think of was that I looked quite like my mother when she was my age. Some of the things he shouted, it was like he was shouting at her.'

'Angry at her for dying,' suggested Daniel. 'Taking it out on you?'

'Grief isn't always logical, you know,' she said. 'Besides, I was a poisonous little brat. I knew how to push his buttons.'

'You were fourteen years old.'

Tears sprang into her eyes; she turned away to wipe them. 'We argued a lot,' she said. 'He made me go to church. I *hated* church. I didn't believe in God, but even if I had, I wouldn't have wanted to worship him after he'd taken Mama. And it offended me that Papa did. He'd raised us to think like scientists. Religion always seemed so . . . *cowardly*.'

'So you taunted him about his faith until he got drunk and came after you?'

A greybeard was walking towards them down the road, carrying a green turtle on his shoulder. Rebecca shook her head at him as she passed. It was illegal here to kill turtles of any species, to hunt their eggs or sell their shells or meat, but no one paid any attention. Turtle killing was still a great event in some of these communities. They'd sacrifice them on mangrove altars, offer libations to their ancestors for future success, not realising that each one they killed made their future success less likely. 'He didn't really believe,' she said. 'Not *really*. It was a way of keeping Mama alive, you know?'

'Yes,' said Daniel. 'I know.'

'He had this expression: "We don't believe because we think. We believe because we love." I didn't understand what he meant back then.'

'You do now?'

'Let's just say I've learned I'm not perfect either.' She looked across at him. 'I'm going to find him, you know. I'm going to find them both.'

'I don't doubt it,' he assured her. 'And if you need any help . . .'

'What?' she smiled. 'Apart from driving all the way to Tulear with me to help bring back my boat?'

'Yes,' he said seriously. 'Apart from that.'

'Thanks,' she nodded. 'I might just take you up on that.'

II

It took Boris far longer than he'd anticipated to find a suitable rendezvous spot for his meet with the gun dealer, and he returned to the hotel in a foul mood that quickly grew worse when he saw Davit's empty porch, then heard the unmistakeable creaks coming from inside his cabin. 'Davit!' he yelled, pounding on his door. 'Open up, damn you.'

'One minute,' called out Davit.

'Now!'

There was scuffling. The door opened and Davit appeared, a towel around his midriff. 'Can't this wait?'

'No.' Davit was trying to block his view of the bed, but Boris still caught a glimpse of Claudia lying beneath a rumpled white sheet. He felt an unexpectedly sharp twinge of jealousy; he'd been looking forward to enjoying her himself. 'I told you to watch out for Knox,' he said. 'Can't you do a damned thing right?'

'Relax, boss. I know where he is.' He came out on to the porch, closed his door behind him, picked up the guidebook. 'This place called Eden. Claudia says the track is still closed from the last cyclone, so we can't drive down; but it should be easy to hire a pirogue.'

Boris thought about it as he read the brief write-up. Taking a pirogue would leave him dependent on other people, which he hated. It would mean leaving a trail a mile wide too. On the other hand, his mission would be far easier in a secluded nature reserve rather than here or on a salvage ship. He glanced along the beach at the wooden boat turned turtle on the sand. With the

leave before dawn to reach Eden by nightfall, so he needed to familiarise himself with it now. It had its own inboard, but it was a sailboat first and foremost, designed to be handled from the stern. He opened the main hatch, clambered down into the hold, looked over the engine, propeller shaft, bilge pump and retractable centreboard. There was enough diesel for a couple of hours cruising, though not enough to get them all the way back to Eden. The water tank had a hook glued to its backside, a bunch of keys dangling from it, presumably spares for the lodge. Back on deck, he inspected the anchor and then the bench lockers. Orange life-jackets; flares and a flare gun; a boat-hook; coils of synthetic rope; an inflatable life-raft. There was dive-gear too. A pair of snorkels and masks, a couple of boxes of home-made lead weights, a scuba tank with a red-tag to indicate it was filled with air; a wet-suit, a buoyancy-control device and a regulator. There were also biscuits, canned foods, bottles of water, soft drinks and beer. All valuable stuff, yet not taken.

The bridge was set down in the deck, but offered good views on all sides, though the windows were scratched and tired. It was better equipped than he'd expected, too, with VHF radio, GPS and sonar, a compass in a brass binnacle and a varnished wooden wheel. He turned on the GPS, hoping to find a record of the boat's movements around the time Adam and Emilia had gone missing, but either it hadn't been turned on that day or the information had since been deleted. The bridge was too cramped for a map table, so Adam had instead rigged a corkboard to a system of pulleys that could be raised when needed, then lowered out of sight again. A chart of the Eden reefs was currently pinned to it, protected by a sheet of acetate. It was marked not just with the usual depth lines and tidal information, but also with Adam's own additions, Latin and Greek characters, zodiac signs and dates, some ringed or boxed or in triangles. There was no key to explain these symbols, however, and it was too dark to make them worth the study.

He unfurled the mainsail, checked the mast and rigging, then furled it back up again. A hatch opened on to living quarters. He climbed down a ladder into a cramped cabin with fold-away bunk-beds against one wall, a compact galley on the other, with a fridge and cooker and a small cupboard filled with tinned food and condiments. A framed photograph on the far wall showed Emilia and her son Michel. A sliding door concealed the WC, washbasin and a large chest of medical supplies.

'How much longer?' asked Rebecca, climbing down to join him. 'Only we should probably find ourselves a hotel.'

'All done,' he told her. 'Let's get out of here.'

NINETEEN

I

Boris had to wait to find out about the boat and outboard, because they both belonged to a local tour guide, and he was away for the day. He showed up during dinner, but only shook his head regretfully when Boris asked him to name his price. It wasn't for sale, he assured him. His clients liked to go fishing and hiking and exploring the islands. Boris was welcome to rent it for a very modest sum, but this wasn't just a boat, he must understand, it was his livelihood.

Boris wasn't interested in a rental. He didn't know how long he'd need it, or whether he'd want to come back this way; and there was also a fair chance it would get damaged or destroyed. Besides, it wasn't his money. He fished out his wad, therefore, began slapping fifty-euro notes down on the table. The tour guide trailed off and fell silent, licking his lower lip.

They dragged the boat into the shallows, rocked it this way and that to check for leaks. The outboard was an old Honda four-stroke, simple to fit, start and steer. Not ideal for long journeys, but perfectly adequate for burbling them down the coast, so they shook hands upon it, both happy with the bargain. Now all Boris needed was camping supplies. Oh. And his gun, of course.

II

Zanahary swore blind he knew the best hotel in town; the best at giving backhanders, thought Rebecca, when she saw it. But it was late and she and Daniel were both too tired to go hunting for anything better. What with her father's Jeep waiting for her back at Eden, she didn't need a hire car any more, so she thanked Zanahary and signed off on his paperwork. Then she and Daniel followed the concierge upstairs to neighbouring rooms, huge and grey with wire mosquito mesh over the windows, chunks of plaster gouged from the walls, wardrobes with neither drawers nor rails. 'Fancy something to eat?' asked Daniel.

'I need to freshen up first.' She hoisted her overnight bag on to the double bed. It creaked loudly beneath the modest weight, so she transferred to the single. She could hear Daniel pottering around next door. For some unaccountable reason she remembered how she'd stumbled on the *Yvette*'s deck earlier, and he'd caught her arm. 'Careful now,' he'd said.

Careful now, indeed!

These past few years, she'd grown accustomed to signing the cheques, taking the decisions, being the boss. She couldn't remember the last time she'd spent a whole day with a man whose help she needed, yet over whom she'd had neither authority nor leverage; and she wasn't quite sure that she liked it. She took a shower, was drying herself off when Daniel knocked. 'Ready yet?' he asked.

'Another minute.'

'I'll be downstairs.'

She spread her clothes out on her bed, wishing she'd given a little more thought to her packing this morning. She put on blue jeans and a ruby T-shirt, then did her make-up. The mirror was cracked and dull, and the light above the sink was infuriating, flickering for an age, then springing on abruptly, before breaking into flickers once more. She went out, locked up. Daniel was on a swing-bench chatting to a Malagasy woman with bleached-blonde hair and a turquoise tracksuit. Even as Rebecca watched, she got up on to her knees on the bench and whispered something in Daniel's. He laughed and shook his head. She pulled an expression of mock affront then unzipped her tracksuit top, grabbed his hand and pressed it against her breast.

Sensations both hot and cold warred inside Rebecca. The cold ones won. Her heels slapped the bare concrete as she made her way down. 'Well?' she asked. 'Still want something to eat, or have you found something better to do?'

'This is Mimi,' said Daniel. 'I think she likes me.'

'I'm sure she can be here when we get back, if you ask her nicely.' It came out more tartly than she'd intended. He raised an amused eyebrow, which for some reason infuriated her. She led the way out of the hotel, waved down a taxi, directed the driver to an old haunt. They took a table on the terrace. 'Drink?' asked Daniel.

'Not for me.'

Daniel went to the bar, returned with a large bottle of Stella Gold, ice-cold and sweating, its label peeling free. He poured them each a glass, offered his in a toast. 'Your health,' he said.

'Don't drink too much,' she told him. 'We've got an early start.'

'Come on,' he said. 'That girl was just being friendly.'

'I don't know what you're talking about.'

A young waitress appeared at their table. She had shiny jet-black skin stretched so tightly over her cheekbones it looked as though someone had poked a straw through the back of her skull and sucked all the air out. She took their orders from a distance, as though nervous of touching them by accident. And when she walked between the tables, it was in an apologetic, sideways crouch, one arm in front, one behind, like a figure from an Egyptian tomb painting come to life.

A Malagasy band and dancers began performing. Their music was jangling, primal. Madagascar's humpback topography meant the only station they could pick up on this coast twenty years ago was Radio Mozambique, so Tulear had developed its own distinctive sound, a blend of Malagasy and African. The men strummed furiously while their women wailed and jiggled their buttocks like jackhammers; press down on their shoulders and you could dig up roads. The crude, overt sexuality of their dance soured Rebecca's mood even further. There was still no sign of their food. Their waitress finally appeared with a woven basket of baguette slices and a bowl of nuts. Rebecca's hand hovered above them like a crane-grab in the fairground game, looking for rich studs of salt.

Daniel tore a chunk of white flesh from a baguette, tossed it on to the tiled floor behind her. She turned to look. A ring-tailed lemur was tethered by a long, thin black leash to the limb of a tree. They were delightful creatures, these shrunken kangaroos with their long, hooped black-and-white tails. They had springs in their legs; they bounced all over the place. This one was male; she could tell from the black packet of his crotch. He began bounding up and down with excitement at the sight of the bread, just out of his reach. Daniel got up, walked across, picked up the morsel, held it out. The ring-tail seized it in both forepaws, ate it greedily, then bounced exuberantly for more. Daniel laughed and tore off another piece, crouched low to lure the ring-tail on to his arm, his shoulder and finally on to his head. He looked across at Rebecca and grinned like a schoolboy who'd done something clever.

'Don't do that,' she said.

'Why not?'

'Lemurs aren't domesticated. They're not *pets*.'

He took the ring-tail off his head, set him down. 'He seems happy enough.'

'And how would you know? An expert on *Lemur catta*, are you?'

'That's not exactly—'

'Ring-tails are social animals,' said Rebecca. 'They need their own kind.' Even to her own ears, her voice sounded unnecessarily strained. She was aware of other diners falling quiet around her, but there was something inside her that had to get out. 'They need to groom and be groomed. They need their family. They need to be part of a group, not isolated by themselves and tied on strings for the amusement of moron tourists.'

He looked strangely at her as he came to sit back down. 'I'm sorry,' he said. 'I wasn't thinking.'

'No,' she said stiffly. 'Evidently.'

A forty-year-old tourist with a paunch and thinning brown hair entered the restaurant at that moment, wearing leather trousers and a gaudy shirt, holding hands with a dazzlingly beautiful young Malagasy girl. You found plenty of Europeans like this in Madagascar. They couldn't hack it back home, so they came out here, taking advantage of the poverty to hire themselves a succession of teen dolls and make out like they were studs. He took the neighbouring table, leaned back in his chair, shouted out for a carafe of red wine in a manner designed to let everyone know he was on cordial terms with the *patron*. He glanced across at Rebecca, looked her up and down with approval, then threw Daniel a smirk of congratulation, along with an inquisitive little raise of the eyebrow, as if to suggest they might want to try trading sometime.

Daniel sagged visibly in his chair, as though sensing trouble, but Rebecca felt only an icy calm. She said in a deliberately loud voice: 'Did I ever tell you about the study of sex tourism we did when I was at Oxford?'

The man was clearly startled by her English. He pulled a self-deprecating face to acknowledge and apologise for his gaffe. Rebecca ignored him. 'It was fascinating,' she went on. 'Did you know that men who pay for sex have shorter, thinner penises than normal men? That they masturbate more and earn less. And that they're more likely to live with their mothers into their thirties.'

'Come on, Rebecca,' said Daniel. 'Let it go.'

She frowned in feigned puzzlement. 'It's only a study,' she said. 'I thought you'd find it interesting. I'm sure you'd never use whores yourself. You're not the type, after all. I'm sure that girl at the hotel was just being friendly, like you said. I mean, sex tourists are usually obese, ugly and of subnormal intelligence. And you're not remotely obese.'

'For fuck's sake, Rebecca.'

Their neighbour looked a little sick too. He leaned across, his voice low. 'I think maybe I make offence,' he said. 'I am sorry if this is—'

'Not at all,' Rebecca assured him. 'I'm just telling my friend here about a study I did at university.' She turned back to Daniel. 'Where was I? Yes. Did you know that sex tourists are twice as likely to be bald as normal men, and that they suffer disproportionately from premature ejaculation? It's quite true. And not – as you might think – because they pay by the minute and are too cheap to hold back. No. It's because they're socially inadequate, very low-status, I mean full-blown omegas. They usually only ever have the chance for opportunistic sex, when the—'

'That's enough,' said Daniel.

'—real men are away. Premature ejaculation helps them

deposit their sperm and get away before the alpha males return to kick their—'

'I said that's enough.' He grabbed her wrist and squeezed it so tight she flinched and looked at him in surprise. 'Typical biologist, aren't you?' he said softly. 'Tolerate frailty in every species but your own.'

'We should know better.'

'And you do, I suppose. That must feel good.' He held her a moment longer then let go, sat back in his chair. She could feel her wrist throb where he'd held it, but she didn't look down, she wouldn't give him the satisfaction. Their food arrived at last. They ate, paid and left without exchanging another word.

TWENTY

I

Knox was suffering a little from remorse when he banged on Rebecca's door at five the next morning. That man in the restaurant last night had been a dick; she'd been entitled to her revenge, especially considering the extraordinary strain she was under. His job had been to back her up, not slap her down. But when he tried to make amends by offering to carry her bag down to the taxi, she shook her head and assured him coolly that she could handle it fine by herself, thanks.

The port was already buzzing when they arrived, though the sun wasn't yet up. High on a crane, a welder showered sparks as if celebrating fiesta. Ropes creaked alarmingly as a container vessel unloaded a huge net swollen with wooden crates. Last night's whores boiled up coffee and rice for their men; children huddled beneath blankets on the sea wall, and fished for crabs. Small waves rocked the *Yvette* softly against the tractor-tyre buffers of the port wall. Knox jumped down on to its deck, turned to help Rebecca, but she ignored him, pointedly making her own way down.

He checked over the boat once more. A moderate westerly was pinning them to the jetty. He started the motor and left it idling while he freed the fore and aft mooring ropes from their steel mushrooms, stowed them away. He pushed against the harbour wall, burbled them clear of the harbour and its traffic. Then he turned the engine off again, unfurled their mainsail, took his seat at the stern and adjusted the rigging until suddenly it swelled pregnant with the breeze and they were off, passing through thin banks of predawn mist.

The sky began to lighten over the rocky silhouette of land, revealing thatch shanty towns on the shore, the marooned and rotted carcasses of metal and wooden hulls. Herons, whimbrels and plovers waded the mudflats and shallows with their curious jerky, backward walks. A pair of fishermen pushed their pirogue out into the shallows, then jumped aboard and paddled vigorously out towards them. Knox looked at Rebecca, sitting on the starboard bench, staring out towards land. 'So was it true, then?' he asked.

She turned to him with a raised eyebrow, though he was sure she knew what he was talking about. 'Was what true?'

'That stuff last night. About sex tourists having dicks like betting-pencils, living with their mothers until they're ninety-five.'

Her chin lifted defiantly. 'It was true of him.'

He couldn't help but laugh, and his laughter was so obviously unaffected that it seemed finally to thaw her. Their eyes met briefly but then she hurriedly looked away again, almost in confusion. 'So you're a freelance, eh?' she asked. 'Any particular specialty?'

Knox shrugged. He'd been expecting this, had decided to hew as close to the truth as possible. 'Archaeology and history, mostly.'

'Hence that salvage ship?'

'Yes.'

'The interview I read with that guy. He reckoned the Chinese made it to America before Columbus.'

'Yes,' agreed Knox. 'That's what he reckons.'

Rebecca laughed. 'So weren't the Chinese frightened of sailing off the edge of the world, then, like all the Europeans?'

Knox hesitated. 'That's a bit of a myth, actually,' he said finally. 'No one ever truly believed the earth was flat.' He pointed away to the western horizon. 'Think about it. Any sailor could tell you the world was round. All they had to do was climb their mast and look at the curvature of the sea. You didn't even need a boat, just a high cliff. And if there was no sea to hand, there were plenty of other ways. You could watch the shadow cast by the earth during a lunar eclipse, or measure the different lengths of shadow similar objects left at different latitudes.' He sat forward, his enthusiasm getting to him. 'There was this extraordinary Alexandrian called Eratosthenes. He actually calculated the circumference of the earth that way back in around 300 BC, and he got it right to within a percentage point.'

'Huh. So where did the flat-earth idea come from, then?'

Knox smiled. 'It's the fault of your people, as it happens.'

'*My* people?'

'Sure,' he nodded. 'Darwinists; evolutionists. Though, to be fair, it really started with an American essayist called Washington Irving. He wrote a romanticised account of Columbus's voyages, I guess in around 1830, though don't hold me to that. It praised Columbus for defying the conventional wisdom of his time, risking sailing over the edge of the world for the sake of expanding knowledge. But it was complete nonsense. You've got to remember that Columbus didn't head off searching for a new world; he was just looking for a shortcut to the Spice Islands.

The people who argued against him pointed out that such a voyage was too far to be practicable, because they correctly believed the earth to be about twenty-three or twenty-four thousand miles in circumference; but Columbus refused to accept their estimate, insisting that it was only seventeen thousand miles around, which meant that Japan was just two and a half thousand miles west of Spain.'

'And how far is it really?'

'Ten or eleven thousand miles. Something like that. But the point is, Washington Irving knew all this. Everyone did. He never meant for his version of the story to be seen as historically accurate. But somehow the idea caught on. People began to believe flat-earthers had been for real. And then Darwin came along with all his disturbing ideas about evolution, and a lot of people took fright and tried to rubbish him away. The science got lost; it became a propaganda war. And a couple of Darwin's defenders, Draper and Dickson White, I think their names were—'

'Yes,' said Rebecca. 'That sounds right.'

'They decided attack was the better form of defence. They wanted to make the point that just because an idea is revolutionary doesn't mean it's wrong; and also to poke a little fun at people who insisted on clinging to stupid ways of thinking even in the teeth of irrefutable evidence.'

'So they accused them of being flat-earthers?' laughed Rebecca. 'Nice.'

'Exactly. Pure propaganda. And incredibly effective. *Too* effective. Now anytime someone criticises a new theory, they're just another flat-earther. It's pretty unfair, when you think about it. And unnecessary, too. They could have accused them of being like the people who attacked Copernicus and Galileo for putting the sun at the centre of the solar system. Or they could have even accused them of being bulge-earthers.'

Rebecca squinted at him. 'Bulge-earthers?'

'Oh, man,' laughed Knox. 'This is going to get complex. Maybe that's why they didn't use it, come to think of it. You've got to go back to the Greeks. Everything was made up of four elements: earth, fire, air and water.' The Indians, Japanese and plenty of others had believed in there being just four or five elements, but it had been the Greeks who'd influenced the Europeans, and it had been the Europeans who'd believed in the bulging earth. 'Earth was the heaviest element, of course, because it fell through air and water. It therefore had to lie at the centre of the universe. Second heaviest was water, which surrounded earth; then came air, which surrounded water, and fire, which flamed upwards in air. But Christianity had a problem with this view, because the universe was God's creation, and therefore perfect; and it stood to reason that a perfect universe would be arranged in a series of perfect concentric circles, with earth at its centre, and the sun, the moon, the planets and the stars all revolving around it.'

'Why would that be a problem?'

'Because if you put your perfect circles together with your differently weighted elements, the earth should logically have been an absolutely round ball completely submerged by water.'

'Ah. So we should all have drowned by now? Or be fish?'

'This was a serious conundrum,' said Knox. 'Medieval scholars really fretted about this stuff.'

'And what was their explanation?'

'It'll sound weird, but effectively they decided that God had wanted to create man, and therefore had needed dry land, so He'd arranged the universe's mix of elements and gravitational fields in such a way that the earth bobbed in the great world ocean, rather like an apple in a bucket.'

'So just the top bit is exposed?'

'Exactly. But that creates problems of its own, not least that all of the world's exposed land had to be gathered in one place. There simply *couldn't* be any land on the other side of the world.'

'And people really believed this?'

'Oh, yes. It was pretty much accepted wisdom in Europe in Columbus's time; so the argument against him wasn't just that the voyage he proposed was many thousands of miles longer than he believed; but also that it would be across a wilderness of water, and that therefore they'd have no chance of finding land and restocking on the way. But Columbus *knew* that there was land to the west, because he'd seen Iceland for himself; he'd heard about Greenland, Newfoundland and maybe even the northern US from the men of Bristol, who regularly fished off those coasts. And that was why he dismissed the arguments of the Spanish courtiers, and had the courage to set off.'

'Bulge-earthers,' smiled Rebecca, glowing with the new knowledge. 'I'm going to have to use that in my next series.'

II

The gun dealer wasn't due until that afternoon, so Boris took Davit into town after breakfast to buy supplies. The two-man tents on offer in the camping store weren't designed for people the size of Davit; he could only fit diagonally. They took one each, added it to the growing mound by the counter, then returned to look at sleeping bags. 'Damned things,' muttered Davit, stepping into one and pulling it up to his waist. 'It's discrimination, that's what it is. It's *tall*-ism.'

His good humour needled Boris. He'd been this way all morning. 'So how's the girlfriend?' he asked.

'I really like her,' grinned the big man. 'I'm thinking maybe of staying on a few days after we're done with Knox.'

'I wouldn't make any promises,' advised Boris. He didn't know quite how, but Claudia had got beneath his skin. The evening before, he'd offered her fifty euros for a quick roll. The little bitch had turned him down flat. 'A job like this, we may have to leave in a hurry.'

'I'd just like to do something for her, you know? Show her a good time, buy her some nice clothes. She's had such a hard life, and they treat her like shit at that hotel.'

Claudia turning him down had only aggravated Boris's itch. He'd lain awake last night listening to the two of them going at it like pigmy chimps next door. There was only one thing to do when a woman got beneath your skin this bad, and that was to fuck her until the sight of her made you sick. 'Why don't you ask her to come with us?' he suggested. 'She can cook for us, translate, even scout out Eden for us.' This was a genuine problem that had been weighing on his mind. He and Davit shone like beacons in this place; they'd be spotted in a heartbeat as they approached Eden. But no one would look twice at Claudia if she went to their free clinic complaining of a toothache.

'I don't know, boss,' said Davit. 'I don't want her tangled up in this.'

'We won't ask her to do anything risky. And we'd pay her well. Five hundred euros, say. That's a hell of a lot of money in this place. It could change her life.'

'She'd have to give up her job at the hotel.'

'Make it a thousand, then. I don't care.' It was Sandro's money, and he wouldn't exactly miss it. And if Boris couldn't manage to get Davit out of his way for long enough for him to scratch his itch good and proper, he wasn't the man he knew himself to be.

'Great,' grinned Davit. 'I'll ask her when we get back.'

III

This coast had changed beyond recognition in the eleven years of Rebecca's absence. New villages had appeared, old ones had grown large, and the tangled mangrove of her childhood had all but vanished, leaving it like one long beach. She glanced at Daniel at exactly the same moment he looked at her. It kept happening that way, and it unsettled her. She was here on serious business, not some frivolous jaunt. She folded her arms and looked north. They reached and passed Ifaty, though it didn't feel as though they were racing. Daniel evidently just had the knack. When he stood up to do boat things, he walked in easy harmony with the roll, whereas she spilled all over the place. 'Something to eat?' she suggested.

'That'd be great.'

She unpacked two of the silver-foil packages Daniel

had had their hotel prepare for them the night before. Cold boiled white rice, octopus and vegetables. She tried a mouthful. Bland, even with the tang of sea-salt on her lips. She went below in search of a bottle of her father's home-made chilli sauce, opening cupboards at random, including a chest filled with medical supplies for patients too sick to make it to the clinic, and for anaesthetising and treating animals in the wild. She found a bottle of sauce at last, took it back up and added three drops to her rice, cautious as a scientist with a pipette, before mixing it in thoroughly with her fork. She held the bottle out to Daniel. 'Want some?' she asked.

'Sure,' he said.

'Be careful,' she warned. 'It's very hot.'

He gave her a patronising look and splashed it all over his rice, as if to prove his manhood. She considered saying something, decided against. He took a forkful, nodded approvingly, followed it quickly with a second and then, a little more slowly, with a third. A first sheen of sweat appeared on his brow. He lifted his fourth forkful to his mouth, then hesitated. 'Wow,' he said, putting his fork back down. 'You weren't kidding.'

'I did tell you.'

'Yeth,' he admitted ruefully. 'What'th in thith thtuff?'

She had to fight back laughter. 'It's my father's home-brew,' she told him. 'The shops never make it hot enough for him.'

'Uh huh.' Daniel lifted his fork again, then put it down untouched, stared at it bleakly. 'Ith there any water?'

She looked in the bag. 'Orange juice?' she asked.

'Thankth. That would be gweat.'

'No pwoblem.'

'It'th not funny,' he protested. 'I've weally thcorched my tongue.' He scowled good-naturedly as laughter finally got the better of her, and threw pinches of rice at her.

She passed him her leftovers when she was done, leaned back against the side. The clouds had all vanished; the sun had grown hot. Her legs felt sticky and uncomfortable in her long trousers. She went below to change into shorts. Back on deck, she squirted lotion into her hands, put her foot up on the bench the better to rub it into her leg. She could sense Daniel watching, and his attention felt good. She set her foot back down, put the other one up, taking her time over it, stretching the moment out.

The boat pitched suddenly. She yelped and tumbled into Daniel's lap. He caught her easily, his arm around her waist. She looked into his eyes but there was nothing there to indicate he'd done it on purpose. 'So sorry,' he said, as he helped her back to her feet.

TWENTY-ONE

I

Low sandy islets appeared offshore ahead, and the sea-bed became increasingly visible beneath their hull. Knox showed Rebecca how to hold a course then went to the bridge to check the charts for dangers. They hadn't yet reached Eden's waters, but there were more charts rolled up in a wooden umbrella stand. He pulled one of the tubes out: it actually had two charts back-to-back inside an acetate cover, Tulear on the front, Ifaty on the reverse. He pulled out another pair, of Morombe and Morondava. The third tube also had twin maps, but different in style, and rather startling too – not least because he'd been looking at their twins just three days ago, on the wall of the *Maritsa*'s conference room.

'What is it?' asked Rebecca, who must have noticed his surprise.

'Nothing,' he told her.

'Nothing?'

'Just some old maps.' His answer evidently didn't satisfy her, for she left her position to come look. Instantly, the mainsail started flapping and they began to lose speed. 'The Waldseemüller and the Piri Reis,' he said, showing her the reproductions. She raised an eyebrow that he should be familiar with them, so he added: 'They're pretty well-known in my line of work.'

'Why so?'

'Because they're about the first maps we know of that showed America.'

'Someone had to be first.'

'Yes, but these were both made in the early sixteenth century, and no one's quite sure how they were so detailed and accurate.'

'Why should that be a puzzle? I thought Europeans discovered America in the 1490s.'

'Yes, but they didn't realise they'd discovered it. Not until later. Columbus went looking for the Spice Islands, remember, and he went to his grave thinking that was exactly what he'd found. So did Vespucci and the rest.' It hadn't been until 1513, when Vasco Núñez de Balboa crossed Panama to the Pacific, that they'd finally accepted they'd found a whole new continent. 'So how come these map-makers were drawing South America this accurately so early? Particularly its west coast, which hadn't yet been visited?'

'And . . .? What's the answer?'

'Depends who you ask. That salvage guy I interviewed, for example. He thinks these maps are more proof that the Chinese got to America first.'

'Why would European maps prove that?' frowned Rebecca.

'Because all these old cartographers borrowed from each other. Piri Reis was Turkish, and the Turks ran the spice trade at the time, so he'd certainly have had access to Oriental sources.'

'Sounds plausible enough.'

'Yes,' agreed Knox. 'But there are easier explanations. For example, maybe the Portuguese or the Spanish were much quicker at exploring the new territory than most historians believe. They just kept quiet about it. You have to remember that the pope had just granted the Portuguese all new land discovered southeast of an arbitrary line of longitude west of the Azores, while the Spanish got everything to its south-west. But facts on the ground are what count, so both nations made huge efforts to explore and settle these places before the other, and they only broadcast information that suited their claims. These were the great state secrets of the time.'

'So you reckon there was a mole?'

Knox nodded. 'A lot of people point the finger at Vespucci. He was working for the Spanish at the time. But I guess we'll never know for sure.' He rolled the maps back up. 'Just odd that your father should have these. Is he interested in this kind of thing?'

Rebecca smiled. 'He's interested in everything,' she told him. 'But, yes, geography for sure. He used to say that evolution *is* geography.'

'I guess.' A gust of wind sent their sail flapping. 'Anyway. We'd better get moving again or we'll never make Eden tonight.' He replaced the maps, found the chart he needed, took it back to his seat. Then he adjusted the rigging until the sail swelled again and they began once more to pick up speed.

II

Rebecca trailed a hand in the water as they headed north, and watched the shore. A pirogue drew close, a spear fisherman standing astride its narrow prow, shouting directions to the youngster at the stern. They were important and admired men, these spearmen. The best could spike fifty kilos of fish on a good day. Some held rocks as weights so that they could lie on the sea-bed in ambush for big fish; others brashly chased after the shoals, though you needed to be super-fit to fight the currents. Their bodies, consequently, were exquisitely honed, burned of any trace of fat.

The man looked up as they passed, waved exuberantly. '*Salaam, Becca!*' he cried. He motioned to the youngster and the pirogue tacked and came alongside, holding steady just a couple of metres away. A fat scar glistened on his left hip where a fishing line must once have sliced through his skin, and it was this that gave Rebecca the cue she needed, a sudden memory of the day he'd limped into their clinic with his leg a mess of blood, glimpses of the white bone beneath the flap of skin. '*Salaam, Toussaint!*' she called out. '*Inona no vaovao?*'

'*Tsy misy.*' He was obviously chuffed that she'd remembered him, though he tried not to let it show. 'So sorry about Adam and Emilia.'

'Thank you.'

'Your father is a very good man. Your sister a very good woman. Whatever we can do.'

'You can search.'

'We search already,' he said. But his eyes dropped just a blink. 'Is a big sea.'

'Yes.'

'You come see us sometime, yah?'

'I'd like that.'

201

He pointed at Daniel. '*Vezo blanc, yah*?'

'*Vezo blanc*,' smiled Rebecca.

He made a small gesture to his companion in the stern and they tacked instantly away, waving their farewells.

'*Vezo blanc*?' asked Daniel dryly.

'It's a compliment,' Rebecca assured him. 'It just means a foreigner who knows the sea. It was years before anyone ever called my father a *Vezo blanc*. He didn't stop gloating for days.'

'He looked a bit sheepish,' said Daniel. 'Did you ask him if he's been out searching?'

'Yes.'

'What's the problem with these guys?'

'It's not that simple. They don't like visiting the Eden reefs, not if they can avoid it.'

'Why not?'

She didn't reply at once, for it wasn't easy to explain properly. 'Have you ever heard of the tragedy of the commons?' she asked finally. 'It's a theory about why shared resources don't work. Imagine you live next to a forest full of trees. Under local law, your family owns a section of that forest, as does every other family. You can do what you like with the trees in your section, but if you cut them all down to sell, then that's it, you can't take anyone else's. So you're going to look after your own holding, right? Plant new saplings, protect it from thieves, cut only what you need, because your family's future livelihood depends upon it.'

'Sure.'

'Now imagine a different village next to a different forest, where all the trees are common property.'

'It'll be logged in a heartbeat,' nodded Daniel.

'A short-term feast followed by famine forever,' nodded Rebecca. 'That's the tragedy of the commons. Fishing is a textbook example. No one owns the sea, but they do own whatever they catch, so they'll fish and fish until there's nothing left. It used to be fine here, plenty for everyone. But the villages are growing and the lagoon is silting up and the pressure on stocks has become hopelessly unsustainable. My father tried to get everyone to agree not to fish off Eden, leaving it as a breeding ground to keep the stocks up. It worked for a while, but then some people cheated, and the honest ones grew resentful, and it was a free-for-all again.'

'So what did your father do?'

'There's something called *fady* in Madagascar. It's like a taboo; very powerful. *Fady* aren't just respected and obeyed: they're *feared*. He realised that the best way to stop fishing near Eden was to make it *fady*. The question was how. The people here have always loved stories. Before TV came along, they'd all gather in the evenings, get smashed on rum and marijuana, trade tall tales. My father learned Malagasy so that he could join in. He took the

Odyssey and some other Greek myths and transplanted them here. Boats destroyed by clashing rocks, fishermen snatched and eaten by one-eyed sea-creatures with arms thick as trees, families cursed for generations; giant squids lurking in lairs, their tentacles leaving hideous blisters, causing penises to shrivel up and fall off.'

'Ouch.'

'He even tricked up some photographs and showed them around, and it wasn't long before all the fishermen were claiming to have seen them themselves, except bigger and scarier. No one believes a lie like people who've made themselves part of it. Within a year, they pretty much stopped coming even to our clinic, because they were too scared. My mother had to lay spells on lanes through the water to make it safe.' She smiled. 'A powerful witch, my mother.'

'So what you're saying is, they'll happily look everywhere except off Eden, which is precisely where you need them to search?'

'The *fady*'s grown less powerful over the years, but it's still there. And if I break it altogether, it'll be a disaster for the fish stocks. I couldn't bear that.' She gave a dry laugh. 'Apart from anything else, my father would never forgive me.'

Daniel nodded. 'Then I guess we'd better just search that bit ourselves.'

TWENTY-TWO

I

The meet with the gun dealer was set for four that afternoon, but Boris showed up shortly after three. Buying guns was notoriously risky on missions like these, partly because gun dealers were scum, but also because so much stock came via the military or the police, who'd often make a token arrest just to show that they were taking the problem seriously. That was why he'd taken such pains yesterday over choosing this site. It was deep in the spiny forest, far enough from Morombe that he could test the guns without attracting undue attention. And, while there was just one track big enough for a car to get here, there was also a forest track along which he could make a quick getaway on his bike, if it should come to that. He parked it in cover, then walked around the glade to check for ambush before finding himself a vantage point. He lifted his shirt and taped his hunting knife to his stomach, lest things turn ugly, and settled down to wait.

Four o'clock came and went. Four-thirty. Five. He cursed and wondered if his directions had got garbled. The light was beginning to fade when he finally heard engine noise, and a banged-up blue Mercedes 4x4 trundled into the clearing. There were two men in the front, which immediately put Boris on alert, as he'd only expected one. But the passenger stayed inside while the driver got out. He was short and grossly fat, with a tomato-red T-shirt. Boris relaxed at once. If he couldn't handle this guy, he needed to get out of the business. He put on his sunglasses and went out. The tomato popped his rear door and opened a large steel box inside, revealing three handguns of varying hefts and styles, plus spare magazines, boxes of shells and other gear designed to appeal to Special Forces wannabes: knives, balaclavas, holsters, flexi-cuffs, night-sights.

Boris took the semi-automatic Beretta 92G first, ejected and checked the box magazine, slotted it back in. He'd used one before, and it felt reassuringly familiar, but there was a hairline crack in its frame. He gave the tomato a look and put it back. He passed over the Taurus Raging Bull, which was less a handgun than a midlife cry for help, and took the Heckler & Koch. It was a few years old, but he couldn't see any obvious flaws. It was fitted with a laser sight for competition shooting too, and its elongated barrel was threaded for a noise and flash suppressor. He took up his favoured stance. It felt good in his hands. It felt like authority. 'Silencer?' he asked, miming fitting one to the barrel.

The tomato went to consult. The passenger got out, tall and cadaverous, with hair like melted vinyl. He looked nervous, which made Boris nervous too. He opened the rear door, rummaged inside, then stood back up and shook his head. Never mind. Boris hadn't expected one. He spotted the red dot on a tree across the glade, squeezed the trigger. A chunk of soft flesh exploded from the tree only a little below where he'd aimed. He visualised Knox and fired three more rounds: stomach, heart and head. Perfect. 'How much?' he asked.

'How much have you got?' replied the tomato. And there was enough amusement in his voice for Boris to know, even before he looked around, that the Raging Bull and the Beretta would both be aimed directly at his back.

II

It was late afternoon when the *Yvette* neared the Eden pass. The sea was getting rougher, waves breaking hard against the reef. A squadron of jellyfish passed like ghosts beneath their hull, provoking Rebecca to wonder what horrors might lie beneath. But then she stamped down on the negative thought. Adam and Emilia were alive. If there was anything on the sea-bed, therefore, it could only be of help in finding them: and the sooner she found it, the more useful it would prove. She opened a bench locker, fished out a mask, snorkel and pair of flippers.

'What are you doing?' frowned Daniel.

'I thought you agreed it was up to us to search this area.'

'Yes, but not tonight. It's too rough. And it'll be dark soon.'

'My father and sister had to come out of the lagoon this way. I need to take a look.'

'Tomorrow.'

'No. Now. What if there's something down there? I owe it to them, Daniel.'

'Bollocks,' he said. 'You owe it to them not to take stupid risks that can't possibly do them any good.'

'I'm doing this,' said Rebecca. She stepped up on to the bench before he could stop her, jumped overboard. She took a little water in her mouth, salty and warm. She sank into the trough of a wave, rode it up high. She hadn't realised quite how big the swell was, or how fast the *Yvette* had been travelling. Already she was twenty

A large wave simmered and boiled as it passed her, saltwater splashing down her snorkel into her mouth, making her splutter, while all around her the reef fish mocked her struggles with their serene ballet. The shelf grew steeper; she was near the pass. She warned herself to be careful. The whole lagoon virtually drained and filled with each tide, all that water squeezing through this narrow gap like vast crowds through a single turnstile, creating incredibly fierce currents. A translucent plastic bag floated past. She grabbed for it, lest a turtle mistake it for a jellyfish, as they sometimes did, and choke to death. It eluded her, so she swam after it. She heard Daniel shout a warning and looked around just as another wave struck her obliquely across her face. Water gushed in through her snorkel. She spat it out choking and hacking. A second wave broke over her, taking her tumbling her with it, spinning her out of control. She tried to kick away but her left foot hit something immense and solid, and pain spiked up her leg. A third wave threw her backwards on to the reef. Her left elbow took a bang; the back of her crown smacked dizzyingly hard. The swell subsided, backwash dragging her with it over the coral. She pushed to her feet, clumsy from the blow and from wearing her flippers; but she dared not take them off because of all the sponges, urchins and crown-of-thorns starfish that lived upon these reefs and which would leave you limping for days. She stood sideways to the waves instead, spread her feet wide. Her left shoulder began to throb. She'd dislocated it twice before, was terrified of doing it again; but as far as she could tell it was only wrenched and bruised.

A wave smashed against her thigh and waist, almost throwing her from her feet. Its backwash tried to fold her up like a deckchair. She glanced down. Blood was leaking in thin, watery sheets from grazes in her knee and thigh. Coral was sharp as knives; infectious, too. Her palms were already a lattice of thin red lines that quickly spread and merged. Another wave smashed into her thigh. The sun had already half gone behind the western horizon. Clouds were gathering overhead. Daniel and the *Yvette* were fifty metres away, and it felt like fifty miles.

TWENTY-THREE

I

Boris dropped the Heckler & Koch and raised his hands as he turned around. 'There's no need for this,' he said. 'I'll pay you whatever you want.'

'That's right,' agreed the tall man. 'You will.'

Boris belatedly realised why the man had made him uneasy. His jitteriness wasn't that of someone involved in a risky transaction, but of an addict needing his next fix. 'My friends will be angry with you,' he said. 'They'll send more people.'

'Sure they will,' scoffed the man. 'Now let's have your money.'

'I left it in the trees,' said Boris. 'I'll go get it for you.'

The tall man said something in Malagasy; the tomato nodded and approached Boris carefully, making sure not to block his comrade's line of fire. He patted him down with his left hand, felt the wad of banknotes in Boris's back pocket, pulled it out and held it up in triumph.

There was only one question on Boris's mind: what plans did these two have for him now? If this was just a heist, no problem. He'd get Sandro to wire more money, start over. But that wasn't the impression he was getting. When he'd threatened them with his friends, they'd found it funny. Petr had put this deal together, and Petr was his successor as Sandro's head of security. What if he was worried that Boris might be after his old job? What if he'd put these vermin up to this, and more? Could he take that risk?

It was getting dark, just enough to give him some cover. He stepped abruptly to his side, putting the tomato between himself and the tall man, grabbing his knife from beneath his shirt as he did so, stabbing upwards. The Raging Bull erupted, a blaze of light and noise. The round caught the side of the tomato's head, splattered it, spun him around. Boris grabbed the Beretta from him as he went down, fired blind twice, not to hit anything, merely to buy himself time. The Raging Bull erupted again. Boris threw himself sideways, rolled on to his back, took a moment to steady himself and then aimed at the tall man's torso and pulled the trigger three times. The man

He went to the cabin, started the engine. It gave a dull, unpromising thump, then picked up smoothly. He swung the *Yvette* around parallel with the coral shelf, just the safe side of the breaking waves. When he'd drawn nearly level with Rebecca, he locked the wheel and hurried to the bow, picked up the lead weight and hurled it towards her, but it didn't quite reach. A wave edged the floating life-jacket tantalisingly closer to Rebecca, but then backwash took it away again. He could see her steeling herself to dive for it, but her left arm was injured, and if she failed, she'd be in desperate trouble. He waved at her to let it go.

The sun had set by now, but it still reflected in thin bands of orange and pink off the undersides of the thickening cloud. The sea was growing bigger. Rebecca was having to hurl her hip against the waves to stay upright. He took the *Yvette* around for another pass, but couldn't get as close again. He considered the VHF: but there'd be no one close enough to make a difference. He thought about going through the pass and trying to reach her inside the lagoon, but he wasn't sure he had the time. He drew as close to her as he dared, stilled the engine, dropped anchor. The sea-bed was too sandy here for the anchor to hook on to, which meant that it would drag behind them as the breakers inexorably pushed them towards the reef.

He went below to put on jeans, boots and a sweatshirt. By the time he got back on deck, the *Yvette* had already been swung around by the waves, her bow barely fifteen metres from the coral. He untied the life-jacket and weight-belt, looped and knotted the rope around his own waist instead, stepped up on to the guard-rail and dived into the water, struck out hard, the coil of rope paying out behind him. He turned feet first, let the next wave take him in, bending his knees as he hit, rising up like a water-skier, then wading fast towards Rebecca across the coral. He turned his back. 'Get on,' he said. She did as he told her, clasping her right forearm around his throat, her legs around his waist. 'When we get there,' he told her, 'don't worry about me or the anchor. Just get to the cabin as fast as you can, give the wheel a full turn then throttle forwards. Okay?'

'Yes,' she said, pulling off and discarding her flippers.

The *Yvette* was being dragged closer and closer with every moment. Waves were crashing around her. Knox pulled the rope taut, braced against the next wave, then dived in and hauled them arm over arm through the swell. They reached the *Yvette*, just a few metres from the reef, every wave smashing her closer. Rebecca did as he'd instructed, clambering rudely over his shoulders and head, tipping herself aboard. He hauled himself up after her, ran to the stern, began to haul anchor. The engine stuttered but then failed. A wave pushed them on to the reef so that their hull scraped coral for a moment and their centreboard retracted and they listed violently, but then backwash took them off again and their engine caught and they began to turn. A last wave crashed against their side, water gushing over the deck with enough power to send Knox staggering, but Rebecca opened the throttle to its maximum and they began surging safely out to sea.

TWENTY-FOUR

I

Davit was in bed with Claudia when he asked her to come to Eden with him.

'I can't,' she told him. She was lying on her back, stroking his hand upon her stomach. 'This is my work here. If they hire another girl, they won't take me back.'

'What do they need you for?' he asked. 'There's no one here but us, and we're leaving. Ask them for a holiday.'

That made her laugh. 'No holiday,' she said.

'Please come,' he said. 'We'd pay you well. A thousand euros.'

To his surprise, Claudia looked hurt rather than pleased by this. 'I don't want your money. Not for this.'

'It wouldn't be for this,' said Davit. 'We could really use your help. To cook for us, translate, that kind of thing.'

She turned on to her back. 'You want to pay me one thousand euros to cook and speak Malagasy? How many days?'

'Four. Five. I don't know yet.'

'And what is this job? You look for this Eden man, yes? Why? What do you want with him? Do you mean him harm?'

'The people I work for just want to talk with him, that's all.'

'Talk!' she snorted. 'Then why not just telephone him? Do they not have telephones where you come from?'

'It's not as simple as that.' But then he wondered: *Why not?* He let the thought go, however; it was more enjoyable to stroke her belly. 'Please,' he said. 'We really need you.' He realised suddenly he had a way to prove it. 'In fact, it was Boris's idea to ask you, not mine.'

This didn't please her as much as he'd expected. 'I don't like your friend,' she said. 'He's a bad man.'

'He's okay.'

'Men like him come here all the time. They are not good men.' She turned to face him, pointed a finger at herself. 'Me, I can always tell. That is why I am with you and not him.'

Her words cheered him immeasurably; he felt a rush

219

of tenderness for her. 'Please come,' he begged. 'I don't know how I'll survive without you for five days.'

'Sure!' she laughed. She gave his right hand a little squeeze. 'This is how you'll survive.'

'I'm serious. I'm crazy about you. I really am.'

She looked doubtfully at him. 'You mean that?'

He took her hands and kissed them. 'I mean it,' he told her. 'I want to be with you all the time.'

'Okay,' she said happily. 'Then I come.'

II

Rebecca quickly assessed the damage. Her own blood was smeared over the controls and wheel, and the floor of the bridge was covered in half an inch or so of red-stained water that washed back and forth with each lurch of the boat. She looked outside and saw no sign of Daniel, so for a terrible moment she feared he'd been swept overboard by that last great wave; but then he emerged from the engine hatch, and her heart started beating normally again. He looked her up and down with stony eyes before vanishing below, reappearing in dry clothes carrying bottles of drinking water, a first-aid kit, two towels and some bedclothes. He soaked up water with a towel, then swabbed the floor dry and laid out blankets, sheets and a pillow. He took the wheel from her, put the engine on slow ahead, set and locked a course safely out to sea. 'Lie down,' he said.

She tried nonchalance. 'I don't take orders from—'

'Not one word,' he warned. 'I'm too fucking angry. Now lie down.'

She got down and stretched out on the makeshift bedding. He poured a sachet of antibiotic into a glass, stirred in water, made her drink it all. 'Your hand,' he said, when she'd drained it.

'Therese is—'

'Give me your hand.'

'Therese is a trained nurse. We can be there in—'

'The longer you leave coral cuts, the worse they infect.' He elucidated clearly, as though she were an idiot, a child. 'The worse the infection, the worse the scarring. You want to be scarred for life? No? Then give me your fucking hand.' She let him take it. It was trembling violently with indignation. He held it firm and studied her left palm and wrist, torn and bleeding. He rinsed it with water, cleaned out the grit and sand with cotton buds from the first-aid kit then dried it thoroughly, salved it with antiseptic cream, bandaged it with gauze, cloth and tape. He kept getting up to make sure they were still clear of the reefs. Occasionally, he'd take them a little further out to sea, where it was calmer. Night had fallen fully by now, making the lamplight seem brighter. When both her hands were dressed, he turned his attention to her ankles, shins and calves. It tickled when he examined her soles; she clenched her toes into fists. 'Turn over,' he said.

'What?'

'Turn on to your front.'

'I can do this myself,' she told him.

'Don't be a child. You can't do anything with those hands.'

She turned reluctantly on to her front. He grimaced when he saw the damage, causing her to look around at the back of her right leg and the inside of her thigh, so badly torn by the coral that blood had glued her skin to her shorts. He tried to peel the fabric delicately away, so that he could get at the cuts beneath, but it hurt enough that she sucked in breath. 'Quickly,' she said.

'Are you sure?'

She clenched her legs and buttocks in anticipation. 'Now.'

He ripped the fabric away, scorching her tender skin like a match struck against a wall, but she didn't make a sound. It wasn't as bad beneath as she'd feared, however. She watched him as he cleaned, waiting for him to take some kind of liberty; but he did nothing. It made a woman wonder. Homosexuality was an intriguing topic for an evolutionist. If natural selection insisted on anything, after all, it was the primacy of procreation. She'd had fierce arguments on the subject with colleagues convinced

222

there must be some sophisticated genetic advantage to homosexuality, like co-operative breeding; but dedicated adaptationists were always looking for convoluted explanations where none were needed. They forgot that a drive was distinct from its purpose and effects. The purpose of a car engine wasn't to radiate heat after a long journey; yet it did. Human blood was red because red was the colour of its optimum chemical composition under certain conditions, not because the colour itself was useful. The blunt truth was that natural selection was imperfectly efficient. It left anomalies and glitches everywhere. Nature favoured lustful creatures because they left more offspring; but the mechanisms of lust existed separately from procreation, too. 'So do you have someone special, then?' she asked. 'Back in England?'

'How do you mean?'

'I mean a woman, Daniel. Or a man, maybe.'

He returned to his work, snipping neat strips of gauze, bandage and plaster. 'They call it a private life for a reason,' he said.

'Come on,' she coaxed. 'You can trust me.'

'No,' he said. 'I think you've just proved that I can't.'

Something pulsed inside her. This man wasn't gay. She'd known it from the moment he'd arrived at the lodge, from the way he'd treated her last night, how he'd watched her oiling herself earlier. He was just in control of himself, that was all. He pinned the last bandage in place. 'You'll need to change them tomorrow. Maybe your friend can do it for you.'

'Yes.' She struggled to her feet, refusing to show pain. 'And thank you.' She nodded towards the reef. 'Thank you for everything.'

'It's okay.'

'You need me to guide you through the reefs?'

He nodded at the charts, the GPS, the sonar. 'I can handle it.' He turned his back on her, opened the throttle a little, headed them towards shore.

Rebecca stood there uncertainly, but he didn't look round. She left the bridge and hobbled below, changed into fresh dry clothes. Her cuts reopened as she stretched and turned; the sensation sharp yet not altogether unpleasant. The engine churned into reverse; they came to a stop. Home already. She climbed back up, one step at a time, just as Daniel grabbed the marker buoy with a boat-hook and then secured the *Yvette* to her fixed mooring. When he was done, he stripped down to his boxers and jumped into the sea to test it for deepness. It came up to his chest. He beckoned her over to the stern, gave her a fireman's lift to the beach, set her down. He nodded at the *Yvette*. 'I need to put her to bed,' he said. 'You okay to wait?'

'I'm fine,' she assured him. She hobbled over the dunes, up the dark path to Eden. Black birds screeched and scattered from the lodge's roof. Wild turkeys squawked. She had the strangest sense of being watched as she unlocked and opened the front door. A brown envelope was lying on the floor inside. Her heart gave a double thump. She lit an oil lamp, the better to see what she was doing, grimaced as she picked up the envelope. It had her name written in block capitals upon it. She tore it open, pulled out a colour photograph of her father and sister standing against a whitewashed wall, holding up an English-language newspaper. She turned it numbly over. *Five hundred million ariary*, someone had written. *Independence Square, Tulear, 9 a.m., Monday. Tell the police and they die. Tell anyone and they die.*

TWENTY-FIVE

I

Euphoria. Terror. Joy and relief counterbalanced in Rebecca's heart by the cold fear that if she examined this too closely, she'd find out that it was a hoax. She knew only too well how easily photographs could be manipulated these days. Her own people did it all the time, enhancing the look and sound of footage for her programmes. She limped around and around reception trying not to let her hopes soar too high. Yes. Someone had got hold of an old picture of Adam and Emilia, taken another of some stooge holding the newspaper, overlaid the two and—

She stopped dead, halted by a sudden bout of severe cramps; the birth-pangs of hope. Because she knew, too, how difficult it was to fake photographs convincingly. It took specialist software, experience and expertise. You needed high-quality originals to work with. Light, shadow and perspective had to match exactly, or the result would look phoney; and these didn't. Tulear wasn't Seattle in these matters. There were no graphic design shops, no software houses. Most telling of all, though, was her father's expression as he stared at the camera. He looked trapped. He looked angry.

Oh Jesus Christ, let it be true.

Her mouth opened and a feral sound came out. She felt acid swilling in her stomach, could taste its sharpness in the back of her throat. She rocked backwards and forwards until both had subsided, read the note again. Her eyes were blurred, and when she tried to wipe them, her hand rattled a little against her cheekbones. Five hundred million ariary. She did the maths in her mind: it worked out at fifteen million pounds. The bile rose to her throat and she promptly vomited it out on to the floor. But the evacuation helped her. Her hands steadied and her mind became cold and clear. She'd misplaced the decimal point by a couple of places, that was all. It was actually one hundred and fifty thousand pounds, not fifteen million. The cramps started again, but more gently. There was something almost reassuring about them. One hundred and fifty thousand pounds and she'd have her father back. She'd have Emilia . . .

One hundred and fifty thousand pounds! Oh, Jesus Christ! How in the name of hell was she supposed to—

Perhaps she should take this straight to the police. Kidnappers would always warn against going to them, after all. And Andriama, that police chief she'd met in Tulear, had struck her both as intelligent and sympathetic. But the Malagasy police were famously incompetent and indiscreet, and if word should somehow get back to the kidnappers and they were to . . . Rebecca couldn't even bear to think about it. She had at least to try to raise the cash. She had at least to *try*. If she failed, she could go to Andriama then. But not before.

So. Five hundred million ariary. She read the ransom note again with a growing sense of unreality. The deadline was 9 a.m. on Monday. It was already Saturday night. She had less than forty hours, and tomorrow was Sunday, which meant that all the banks and moneychangers in Tulear would be closed. There was no way she could raise that much cash by 9 a.m. on Monday morning, even if she'd had it in her account. No bank would hand a foreigner that much cash, whatever ID they produced, however good their credit. It was crazy. The kidnappers weren't giving her even a fighting chance. Panic welled again. She had to breathe rapidly to soothe herself.

So, then. She needed help. But whose? Her first thought was Daniel, but there was no chance he'd have that much money on him, or even access to it. And nor would anyone around Eden, except just possibly Pierre. Who else? Delpha, her father's lawyer. You never knew what lawyers had stashed away; and even if he didn't have the money, he'd certainly have contacts and advice. And Mustafa Habib, that Indian businessman from the police station, had made a fuss about wanting to help; it would serve him right if she went to him. She checked for his card. Yes. And he lived on the way to Tulear too. She could stop by on the way to Delpha.

One thing was for sure: she wouldn't find the money here. She fetched the Jeep's keys from behind reception, hobbled outside. The padding of the driver's seat had long since been torn out and replaced by two short planks and an old pillow. Bare earth was visible through a gaping rusted hole in the floor. The windscreen was opaque with smeared mud and flies. Adam had kept it running with a hammer, string and prayer. But it was all she had. She thought briefly of asking Daniel to drive her, but it would mean having to tell him what had happened, and the note had been explicit. She lowered herself gingerly into the driver's seat, twisted the keys. The engine sputtered as though the battery were low, but she revved it hard and thankfully it came to life. She switched on the headlights, carving chiaroscuro rifts in the forest walls, drove over to the generator building and siphoned fuel from the pearly container into her tank until it overflowed.

Then she climbed back in the driver's seat and set off.

II

Knox was lugging his and Rebecca's bags from the *Yvette* back to the beach when he heard the car engine and saw headlights. It could only be Rebecca, though it was hard to believe that she was in any state to drive. He swore and ran up towards the track in an effort to intercept her, but he got snagged on spiny branches as she drove past. He glimpsed her face, however, her expression a strange mix of exaltation and panic, making him think she'd had news of Adam and Emilia.

He picked thorns from his clothes as he walked along the beach to the path to Eden. The lodge's front door was wide open and an oil lamp was flickering inside. He smelled and saw the vomit on the reception floor; more evidence that something extraordinary had happened. He stepped carefully over it, found a mop and bucket to clean it up. Afterwards, however, he felt at something of a loss. The place seemed empty without Rebecca. Hollow. However absurd and reckless her swim had been, he couldn't help but admire the courage and determination that underlay it, her stoicism under pain. She was a fighter; there was no disputing that. He thought suddenly and guiltily of Gaille. The suddenness of the thought was common enough – little things were always reminding him of her – but the guilt was rarer. He'd gone on several dates this past year, cajoled into them by solicitous colleagues, and he hadn't once felt a twinge of guilt, only boredom. Yet something about Rebecca gave him a twinge. He didn't like to think too hard about why that might be.

He wandered out the front door. He felt bad doing nothing, as if he wasn't just letting the Kirkpatricks down but Miles and his MGS colleagues too. He turned on the generator, took a proper tour of the lodge. The computer in Adam's study beckoned, but he couldn't risk Rebecca catching him snooping. He looked along the shelves instead. Most of the books were academic texts, though there were several on carpentry, plumbing and other DIY topics. He glimpsed the spine of a familiar book, a history of the *Winterton* he'd given to Emilia himself, because she'd complained about how difficult it was to get the books they needed out here. It amused him to see it sitting here so openly on the shelves, despite Emilia's insistence on secrecy. A case of hiding it in plain view, no doubt, for the *Winterton* was a celebrated local wreck. He looked around for the other books he'd given her, the copy of the Nautical Archaeology Society's guide, a history of the Chinese treasure fleet. Neither of them were there. There were more shelves in the lounge. They weren't there either. And, now that Knox thought about things that were absent, the Kirkpatricks had shown him photos of pieces-of-eight Emilia had recovered from the reef. Where were *they*? And where was everything else they'd need for the project?

When Emilia had come to England, she and her father had already concocted a plan to keep the salvage secret. A group called the Landseer Trust organised two or three expeditions out here every year, with volunteers paying serious money to spend a month or six weeks surveying the local reef and forests. No one would suspect a thing if MGS Salvage used one of these expeditions as cover, with all the 'volunteers' actually being their own staff and divers, sleeping at Eden and using the *Yvette* as their dive-boat. Not ideal, but certainly workable and cheap. Yet there was a limit to how far one could pare down an underwater excavation. The *Yvette* was too small to do much more than ferry the divers and their gear to and from the site, so they'd need a land-base to store surplus equipment like the caesium magnetometer and side-scan sonar, the water-dredges, grids and mapping frames, their drawing boards and pens, their markers and artefact tags, their trowels, rulers, cameras and laptops. And what about their finds? Where would *they* be stored? Emilia had pestered him with questions about strong rooms and atmospheric controls. She'd assured him that everything would be in place on time, and he'd believed her.

He found nothing in the lodge or cabins, so he took keys from behind reception and checked out the boathouse too. It was an ugly building, newly built from cemented breezeblocks, very different from the local materials used for the lodge. It smelled pungently of brine inside, and looked unremarkable enough. A wooden table stood against the wall near the door, with chairs for divers to write up their notes. There was a small rowboat next to it, presumably for getting to and from the *Yvette*'s fixed mooring at high tide, and a couple of long-handled paddles plus some boxes of lead diving weights. Two disassembled sea-fishing rods leaned against the wall, along with a box of hooks and reels of different strength line. A motley assortment of life-jackets, wetsuits, buoyancy-control devices and other pieces of dive-gear hung from wooden racks, though most of the pegs were empty, presumably for volunteers who brought their own equipment.

A powerful generator was sitting on the bare concrete against the left-hand wall, next to an air-compressor covered by a sheet of brown sacking to keep the damp off, and fitted with beach-buggy wheels so that it could be trundled across the sand. Fifteen or so well-used scuba tanks stood next to it, along with a big red barrel of water to stop them overheating while they were being filled with air. A second barrel was three-quarters full of fuel for the generator and the *Yvette*. And there were more hooks against the far wall, for flippers, masks and snorkels, though most of them were empty. And there were various other bits and pieces: underwater pens and boards, metal grids for laying out the dive-site and the like. But he saw nothing to help answer his questions, so he returned dispirited to the lodge.

III

Pierre's front door opened as Rebecca pulled up in the Jeep, and Therese appeared. 'I think it must be you,' she beamed. 'I tell Pierre that—' But she broke off in shock when she saw all Rebecca's bandages. 'What happen?' she cried.

'I was out on the reef,' she answered. 'But it's fine. I had a friend with me. He fixed me up.'

'*He!*' scoffed Therese, shaking her head at the absurdity of entrusting such work to a man. 'Show me.'

'I'm fine,' insisted Rebecca. 'I just need to speak to Pierre.'

'But I—'

'Please, Therese. Come round tomorrow if you like. Change my bandages then. But right now I need to speak to Pierre.'

She nodded and went inside. Pierre emerged almost at once, as though he'd been standing there listening. He cut a coin-sized slice from a stick of manioc with his penknife, ate it off the stubby blade. 'We look in the forest this afternoon. Nothing, I'm afraid.'

'Thanks anyway.'

'Of course. Whatever we can do.'

'Listen, Pierre . . .' She hesitated, uncertain how to approach this without alerting him to the kidnap. 'Did you hear that I've offered a reward for whoever finds Adam and Emilia?'

'Sure. Everyone has heard.' He flashed her a grin. 'Maybe I'll win it myself, eh?'

'The thing is,' she said, 'I don't have that much cash with me. And it's proving a nightmare to arrange. So I was wondering . . .'

'You want me to provide it?' He blanched and put a hand on his chest. 'I'm sorry, Rebecca. I don't have that kind of money. Truly.'

'It would only be a loan. I'd get it back to you in a couple of days.'

'I'm sorry,' he said. 'If it were possible, yes, of course. But it's not. It's just not.'

She hadn't expected anything else, but it had been worth asking. She thanked him and took her leave, climbed gingerly back in the Jeep, headed south. Mustafa Habib next, then Delpha. The bumpy track tore at her cuts, forcing her to slow down, allowing her to brood on the kidnap. By a strange twist, one of her first ever programmes had included a segment on hostage taking. Surely if anything was an exclusively human behaviour, kidnapping would be. Yet male baboons under attack had been observed taking their assailants' offspring hostage: *Let me go or the kid gets it.* She gave a little shudder at the thought of something similar happening to Emilia. She *had* to raise this money. But how? And how to repay it? Her credit cards and bank accounts were already stretched beyond their limits. Her house was fully mortgaged and had loans of nearly half a million pounds secured against it.

Good Christ! What had she become?

It had started innocuously enough. Years before, an Oxford boyfriend had ridden in point-to-points. She'd hated those afternoons, all those pompous pricks drinking punch, shivering over stale picnics. And she didn't even have the fun of betting. Her allowance was so pitiful she couldn't risk even fifty pence each way. One time, Nicholas had offered her a few quid to take a punt, but she'd been too proud and he hadn't offered again. Or not directly, at least. Instead he'd put £5 on a horse called Madagascar Pride in the fourth race one afternoon. 'Madagascar Pride,' he'd said. 'I had to place a bet for you.' Somehow taking the yellow slip from him hadn't seemed so bad. Madagascar Pride had romped home at 10-1. Fifty-five quid. *Fifty-five quid.* All the money in the world. After that, Nick had manufactured excuses to bet for her on almost every race. Rather than dreading these point-to-points, she'd begun looking forward to them, had lain in bed afterwards reliving the rush of a close race, the way the tendons in her neck stood out in sympathy with those of her horse.

She'd studied evolutionary biology, she'd known all

about game theory, how players could often skew situations in their favour with seemingly perverse behaviour. But until she'd first gone racing, she hadn't understood the first thing about gambling. She'd assumed that it was about money. But it wasn't. It was about getting high. Losses were simply the price you paid for your fix. Her break-up with Nick had put an end to it, however, for she couldn't afford to risk her own money. But then success had arrived, and she'd taken her whole team out for a big night as thanks. Titch had suggested going on to his casino, had signed them all in. She'd known from the first minute that she was in trouble. Her heart had broken into a pleasant canter even walking between the tables, and she'd tasted the delicious metal at the back of her throat. *Get out*, she'd told herself. *Get out while you can*. But it had been too late.

There's something comforting about the word 'addiction'. It's an admission of defeat in itself, a way to make the problem so big that there's no point even trying to fight it. Addictions all work in much the same way, usurping your body's own reward mechanisms, flooding your system with dopamine, oxytocin, adrenaline, whatever your craving might be. Rebecca's problem had been boredom; her fix adrenaline. She'd usually start with blackjack; it gave the illusion of pitting wits. She'd set a limit and vow to leave when she'd reached it, but she never really meant it. Sometimes she'd lose so quickly that she would become convinced the croupier was cheating her, yet she wouldn't even move table; instead she'd become defiant, throwing down her money until it was gone. At other times she'd eke out her defeat, hunching over her chips until the weariness got to her and she'd grow almost eager to lose, before coming to her senses in the cab, nauseous with the knowledge that she had lost – *irretrievably lost* – another ten, twenty, maybe even fifty thousand pounds. And despite that, despite her disbelief at her own stupidity, she'd already be calculating how to put together her next stake. *One hundred and fifty thousand pounds!* Rebecca had lost twice that much in the last year alone. She owed her company over a quarter of a million and as much again to her various banks. She had gambled away her father's and her sister's lives, and now she had nothing left.

TWENTY-SIX

I

Knox fixed himself something to eat then took another wander round the lodge. There were group photographs of all the previous Landseer Trust expeditions on the walls, volunteers glowing with youth and sunshine. He gave a little snort of amusement as he looked them over, for he and his fellow MGS divers were going to look shop-soiled by comparison. The wall behind the photographs caught his eye, its plaster studded with shells, quartz and other stones, decorative touches presumably harvested from the beach. In the gloom, it was hard to be sure, but there was an inch long, scimitar-shaped fragment of what appeared to be pottery, remarkably similar to coarse-ware they'd found on the sea-bed off Morombe. He examined the surrounding walls for several minutes before he found a second shard, then a third; only this one was white with hints of blue. He touched it with his fingertip, wondering how a shard of Ming porcelain could possibly have found its way on to Eden's beach. And then a startling thought occurred to him.

Emilia had told him that she and her father had found silver from the *Winterton*. She'd shown him photographs of dozens of pieces-of-eight recovered from their reef. It was certainly plausible, because of the legend of the *Winterton*'s lost silver. But what if they'd actually found something else? What if that was why the book on the *Winterton* was sitting so openly on the shelf yet there was no sign of the one on the Chinese treasure fleets? Those armadas had been huge, and the Mozambique Channel was notoriously prone to terrible cyclones. If such a storm could have swept one ship on to the reefs, then why not two?

He shook his head at himself. He was being absurd, extrapolating so much from such small shards. Why would Emilia have lied? If she and her father had found a Chinese ship here, surely she'd just have told him. *But would she?* Her overriding concern had always been secrecy, out of fear that treasure hunters would learn about the wreck and dynamite the coral to get at it. Emilia had known

MGS was working with Ricky Cheung; in fact, she and her father had originally heard of them *because* of all the publicity he'd generated around his Morombe salvage. Maybe she'd feared that they'd let this new discovery slip to Ricky, and that he'd announce it to the world, effectively declaring open season on Eden's reefs. So why hire MGS at all? Why not simply go to a rival? But marine salvage was hugely expensive. Adam and Emilia were planning on bankrolling this one themselves, in order to keep control. MGS would consequently have been far cheaper to hire than their rivals, partly because they priced themselves competitively anyway, partly because their divers and equipment would already be in Madagascar, saving a fortune on flights and freight, and also because a salvage like this demanded hundreds of man-hours studying the history of the target ship, its materials and cargo. That was work Knox and his colleagues had already done.

An owl hooted outside. Something rustled. He recalled Emilia sitting across the negotiating table from Miles and Frank, pleading poverty and pointing out how prestigious the salvage of the *Winterton* would be. Frank had shrugged that it wasn't such a big deal, not after a treasure ship. And Knox had seen her smile at that, a private, knowing smile that he'd never quite understood.

Not until now.

II

Rebecca double-checked Mustafa Habib's card to make sure she had the right address. She'd thought him a run-of-the-mill businessman, but he lived in a vast beach-front estate, its perimeter wall topped with broken glass, video-cameras whirring and humming either side of high steel gates. A young man in khaki uniform emerged from a breezeblock guardhouse, lighting one cigarette from its predecessor, then squashing the discarded butt into the dust. 'Yes?' he asked.

'I'm Rebecca Kirkpatrick,' she told him. 'I'm here to see Mustafa Habib.'

'Is he expecting you?'

She showed him Mustafa's card. 'He'll know what it's about.'

He slouched off into the guardhouse. The gates slid silently open a minute later and he waved her through. She drove past outbuildings down a winding crushed-shell drive to a white hacienda lit up by spotlights and topped by satellites, aerials and masts. Two more uniformed men stood to attention either side of the high double front doors, AK47s leaning against the walls behind them. She parked by a marble fountain and got painfully out.

The two guards opened the doors and Mustafa emerged, a phone to his ear, a young woman in gorgeous silks a couple of paces behind. He beamed in pleasure at Rebecca as he bounded down the marble steps, but then winced sympathetically at her injuries, though he was too polite to remark directly upon them. 'You'll have to forgive me,' he said, a hand over his phone's mouthpiece. 'I have to finish this call. Five minutes at the most.'

'No problem.'

'This is my daughter Ahdaf,' he said. 'A zoologist like yourself. Or studying to be one, at least.' He gestured vaguely at the satellite dishes on his roof as he made his way back up the steps. 'She watches *all* your programmes.'

'Is that right?' asked Rebecca.

Ahdaf's eyelashes flickered. 'I watch your programmes, yes.'

Rebecca caught her tone at once. 'You don't like them,' she said.

Ahdaf glanced at her father, waited until he was safely out of earshot. 'You make humans out to be so special,' she said. 'We're just one species among tens of millions.'

'A species that happens to make up my whole audience.'

'Science shouldn't be about ratings,' said Ahdaf. 'If *I* were doing the programme, man would be treated just like any other animal.'

I'll bet they would, thought Rebecca. But she said nothing; she couldn't risk Mustafa's goodwill. She reached into her bag for her mobile. 'You don't mind, do you?' she asked, gesturing at the masts. 'Only I've been out of signal range for two days now.' She didn't wait for an answer, just wandered a little distance off, listened to her messages. She had three from Titch alone, telling her that everyone at work was thinking of her and praying that things were going as well as could be hoped, asking her to call if there was anything he could do. She'd hardly thought of him or the office since leaving London, but his messages did wonders for her spirits, and she found herself dialling his mobile. He picked up almost at once, and his obvious gladness to hear her voice lifted her spirits immensely. She began to talk and then it all came pouring out in an incoherent jumble: her visit to her mother's tomb, her ordeal on the reef and how Daniel had saved her, even the ransom demand. She was still babbling away when a man cleared his throat behind her and she whipped around to see Mustafa standing there with an embarrassed expression. 'Got to go,' she told Titch. 'I'll call soon.'

'Forgive me,' said Mustafa, holding a hand up in apology. 'I didn't mean to overhear.'

'But you did?'

'You cannot know how glad this news makes me. If it's true.'

Rebecca shook her head. 'They sent me a photograph. Photographs are easy enough to fake.'

'Yes,' he agreed. 'But you intend to prepare as if it is for real?'

'I have to.'

'And you're here for my help?'

Rebecca said defensively: 'You said if you could do anything . . . And it's not as if I can't raise the money myself. Just not by nine a.m. on Monday.'

Mustafa frowned. '*This* Monday? But that's crazy!'

'Exactly. They're not giving me a chance.'

'Where?'

'Independence Square, Tulear.'

'How much?'

'Five hundred million ariary.'

He grimaced, but in a way that suggested it could have been worse. 'Who knows about this?'

'Only my business partner. That was him just now. I had to tell someone.'

'Of course. But not the police?'

'No.'

Mustafa nodded seriously. 'You must please keep it that way. Understand, what our police know, everyone knows. You can see for yourself that I already take absurd precautions to keep my family safe. If people think that I pay ransoms—'

'I won't tell anyone, I swear. But is it possible? To raise the money? I'll pay you interest.'

'Interest!' sighed Mustafa. 'How can you talk about interest? Your father is my friend; my interest is getting him and your sister safely home. Listen: I do not keep such sums sitting in my safe. I will have to borrow it myself. The people from whom I borrow will doubtless charge me interest and impose various conditions. What they ask of me, I will ask of you. But no more.'

Rebecca's eyes watered. 'Thank you,' she said.

'It will not be easy,' cautioned Mustafa. 'Even for me, this is a large sum to raise so quickly. But one way or another we will do this. You have my word.' He smiled, gestured flamboyantly. 'Ask anyone: when Mustafa Habib gives his word, he keeps it. But you must promise me one thing in return . . .'

'Yes?'

'You are hurt, you are exhausted. You must be fresh for this battle. So you will go home and rest and get your strength up. And on Monday morning you will be back here at eight o'clock, and I will have your money for you. You have my word on this. And, God willing, together we will bring back Adam and Emilia.'

'It was nothing to do with them. It was something else.'

It was pretty obvious she wasn't levelling with him, but he let it go. 'Are you hungry?' he asked. 'Is there anything I can get you?'

'I could do with some aspirin.'

He helped her to her camp-bed, fetched some painkillers and a glass of water. 'Listen,' he said, 'I don't know what happened earlier. If you don't want to tell me, fine, I trust your judgement. But I can still be useful. Just tell me what needs doing, and I'll do it, okay? No questions asked.'

Her eyes moistened, he thought she was about to crumble. But then she caught herself and her expression hardened, as though he'd been trying to trick her. 'I don't know what you're talking about,' she said.

'Fine,' he sighed. 'Sleep well.' He returned to his bed, lay there listening to her bitten-off cries as she readied herself for bed. It distressed him to hear her pain, to not be allowed to help. He struggled for sleep, turning this way and that on the thin mattress without ever quite finding repose. It grew less dark outside. He tiptoed quietly through the gloom to the washroom, dressed and went out. The sun wasn't yet up, leaving the morning grey and cool. Down on the beach, he kicked off his shoes. The thin, cold crust of sand crunched satisfyingly beneath his tread, like the dried bark of a rotted tree. He bowed his head as he walked, searching the beach for fragments of pottery.

He stopped, crouched, picked up a white shard; but it was only a piece of eggshell. From the size of it, it had to have belonged to an *aepyornis*, a one-time Madagascar endemic, and the largest bird ever to have lived, taking advantage of the island's lack of large predators to become the bully on the block. But then the first settlers had arrived and they'd eventually hunted them to extinction – for their meat, of course, but also for their eggs. The damned things had been the size of rugby balls, so that an *aepyornis* omelette would feed a family for a week. The birds had become well known in the ancient world. Marco Polo had immortalised them as the *rukh* or roc, capable of carrying off elephants in their claws and then dropping them like bombs from a great height; though actually the *aepyornis* had been as flightless as ostriches.

There'd always been a bit of a question mark as to how Marco Polo knew about the birds. He'd never visited the island himself. In fact, he'd actually confused it with Mogadishu, a corruption of which had given Madagascar its name. Most likely he'd heard of them from Arab merchants, who'd certainly been familiar with the place. They'd called it the Island of the Moon, and they'd believed it to be a point of no return for the southern ocean; that he who sailed beyond it was lost. Yet people undoubtedly had sailed beyond it. A Chinese map completed in around 1390 in honour of the first Ming emperor showed the world in traditional fashion, with beyond, still searching the shore as he went. The sand became infested with tiny flies; he set off blizzards of them with every step, cascading ahead of him down the beach. He went down to the sea's edge to avoid them, small waves splashing timidly around his ankles before withdrawing like unctuous servants, his feet leaving shallow imprints that quickly filled with water and then faded into nothing. It was there in the wash that he saw the shard of porcelain. He crouched to pick it up. It was perhaps an inch long, its edges abraded smooth, white with just a trace of blue upon it, the exact same shade he'd seen on the porcelain fragments on the Morombe sea-bed. He tossed it up and caught it, thinking through what it might mean. Then he tucked it away in his pocket and headed back to Eden.

II

Rebecca's cuts had healed enough overnight that every small movement was an agony when she woke. She didn't intend to waste her morning feeling sorry for herself, however, so she gritted her teeth and swung out her legs and used gravity to help herself up, then hobbled through to her father's office, hoping to guilt Daniel into making coffee and breakfast. He was already up and gone, however, but at least that gave her the opportunity for a more methodical search of her father's desk than she'd been able to give it when rummaging around for the *Yvette's* insurance documentation.

His desk had filing-cabinet-style drawers, with multi-coloured hanging folders inside, each tagged with the name of a bank, insurance company, tax authority, stock-broker or friend. One of the tags bore her own name. She pulled a thin sheaf of letters from it, read through them with growing dismay, so obvious was it how absent her heart had been from her words. There were two postcards of London landmarks that she didn't remember sending. She turned them over and with a jolt recognised Emilia's handwriting. She must have gone ahead with her forestry training course after all.

— *You came anyway? You didn't tell me?*

— *You didn't want me there.*

— *No! Don't say that!*

— *You'd moved beyond me.*

— *Never! I made one mistake. How could you—*

'Is something wrong?' She looked up to see Daniel at the door. She feared her voice would sound strained if she spoke, so she shook her head instead. He came inside the room. 'How are you feeling?'

'Better, thanks.'

'You want me to change your bandages?'

'It's okay. Therese is coming by.'

'How about some breakfast, then?'

'That would be wonderful.'

He nodded and went out. She returned her letters and her sister's postcards to the folder, began on Adam's finances instead. They proved astonishing. She'd known he had money in England, for he'd paid her Oxford allowance from an English bank account. But he'd always been so careful, she'd assumed it had been a constant struggle. He'd built the *Yvette* himself, for example, and the Jeep was decades old. Yet these folders told a completely different story.

Daniel reappeared with a tray of coffee and fruit salad, toast and jam, set it upon the desk. 'Is there anything else I can do?'

She shook her head. 'I can't think of anything.'

'What about searching the reefs?'

She smiled and showed him her bandages. 'I can't exactly go diving, not like this. And I'm hopeless at doing boat things.'

'Then maybe I could take the *Yvette* out, see if I can't find something.'

'By yourself? Is that safe?'

'I know what I'm doing.'

'Then thanks. That's really kind.'

'No problem.' He shouldered one of his bags. 'See you later, then.'

Rebecca watched him leave, feeling bad about shutting him out like this when he so clearly just wanted to help.

But it wasn't only the kidnappers who'd insisted on her silence; Mustafa had, too. She resumed totting up her father's assets. Without even taking Eden into account, he had over three-quarters of a million pounds invested in British bank and share accounts, and he still owned a house near Oxford. He had more income than she'd expected too, and not just from rent, dividends and interest. The Landseer Trust ran at least two expeditions a year here, each made up of twelve to twenty volunteers paying through their noses for the privilege of collecting data from the reefs and forest. He'd also written several journal articles, had conducted field trials on a new GPS tracker system, had acted as an agent for local craftspeople, selling their works to dealers in London and Munich. And now that tourists had started visiting this coast in greater numbers, he'd begun taking in paying guests too, offering day-trips on the *Yvette*, even the occasional deep-sea fishing expedition. Everything was scrupulously documented and declared, kept here in these drawers. And it occurred to her then that anyone with access to the lodge could easily have found out about her father's wealth; and that would have made him a very tempting target indeed.

TWENTY-EIGHT

I

Boris sat bolt upright in his bed as he remembered last night's gunfight. It wasn't remorse for the two men that had pricked him, but the belated memory of a mistake he'd made. He'd gutted that tomato with his knife before the Raging Bull had taken his face off, but then he'd wiped off his knife and put it back in its sheath and taken it away with him. *How could he have been so stupid?* The Malagasy police wouldn't be up to much, from what little he'd seen of them, but even they would have to wonder where the knife had disappeared to. And that would surely lead them to conclude there'd been someone else at the scene.

He threw back his sheet, pulled on trousers, went over to Davit's cabin. The big man was still fast asleep, Claudia snuggled against him, holding hands like teenage lovers. He gave their bed an extra-hard kick.

'What time is it?' grunted Davit.

'Time we got shifting.'

They dragged the boat down to the sea's edge, stowed their camping gear, food and other supplies, fixed the outboard. Davit helped Claudia to her seat, then he and Boris pushed it out beyond the breakers and clambered aboard either side to make sure it didn't capsize. With all that weight, however, it sank low in the choppy water.

'Maybe we should leave Claudia behind,' suggested Davit.

'Maybe we should leave you behind,' grunted Boris.

'You'd like that, wouldn't you?'

'It was a joke,' he sighed. 'Look at the size of you two.'

'We'll see how it goes,' said Davit. 'We'll just have to take it slow and stick close to shore in case anything goes wrong.'

'And if it does?'

The big man shrugged. 'Then we'll just have to try something else.'

II

Knox waded out to the *Yvette*, then spent a few minutes studying the chart of the Eden reefs pinned to the corkboard. Nothing he'd learned so far had given much support to his hunch that Adam and Emilia's disappearance was connected to their upcoming salvage; but nothing had disproved it either. And, rather than simply search the sea at random, he might as well look for the wreck-site too, if only to ease his conscience about Miles.

Emilia had been secretive about its precise location, but she'd let slip a few clues all the same. He knew, for example, that it lay a little over thirty metres deep. That cut out all of Eden's lagoon, which was twenty-five metres at its deepest, as well as everything beyond the pelagic boundary. She'd also told him that she and her father had found it during a routine coral check. This involved visiting particular sections of the reef month after month, year after year, to examine them for bleaching and other symptoms of ill health. While their secrecy about the wreck would surely have precluded them from marking its location, this chart appeared several years old, so it seemed probable that the coral they'd gone to check that day would have been marked upon it. But which mark? There were three or four hundred of them on the chart, and he didn't even know which ones represented corals.

He unpinned the chart, looked at its reverse for a key.

Nothing. He turned to the map-stand instead, pulled out and checked the other charts in turn, again without success. He did, however, find another old chart rolled up at the bottom. He hadn't noticed it before because it was shorter than the others, and shorter than the top of the stand. It was a vaguely familiar reproduction of an ancient world map, but of very poor quality, blurred black-and-white printouts cut into a collage and glued to a backing sheet. He took it out into the sunshine for a better look, which was when he realised why he was having trouble recognising it. He was holding it upside down.

It was a commonplace, these days, to blame Western arrogance for the orientation of maps with north on top and Europe at the heart. But Knox had little truck with that view. Apart from anything else, it would be perverse to expect a map-maker to place their home anywhere but at the centre. As for putting north on top, that was less to do with arrogance than with rivers. The ancient Egyptians, for example, had based their lives around the Nile. The Nile had flowed from south to north; water flows downhill; it had followed that the south had been Upper Egypt, and the north Lower. Claudius Ptolemy, on whose great work *Geography* modern maps are indirectly based, had lived in Alexandria, and so he might easily have adopted the Egyptian style. But he was also Greek, and the Greeks put north on top. For many centuries after the schism that split Rome from Constantinople, however, Ptolemy fell into obscurity in Europe. And when medieval Christians started making maps of their own, they put *east* at the top, not north, for they had seen the world as a cosmic metaphor for Christ, in which the rising sun represented his haloed head. The Arabs, meanwhile, put *south* at the top of their maps; and, because they were the great seafarers of the age, the many cartographers who borrowed from them did likewise. One of these was a Venetian monk called Fra Mauro, and it was a copy of his 1459 map that Knox was holding now.

The map wasn't just notable for being upside down, however. Fra Mauro had written notes to accompany his creation, even crediting his sources, though often leaving them unnamed. According to one of these, a huge ship had arrived at the Cape of Good Hope from the east in around 1420, then had sailed off westwards for two thousand miles or so before giving up and coming back. It was hard to be sure from the terse description, but it certainly could have been a treasure ship, especially as the dates tallied so perfectly with Zheng He's sixth voyage. If so, it was the only recorded sighting of a treasure ship that far south, that far east. And it had been on its own.

Knox's working assumption had been that, if Adam and Emilia had really found a Chinese ship on these reefs, then it had been a second ship from the same fleet as the one Cheung had found further north. But the presence of the Fra Mauro map suggested that the Kirkpatricks, at least, had considered a simpler explanation: that there was only one ship, the very same one that had been seen twice at the Cape of Good Hope.

Ricky Cheung had been dismissive of Fra Mauro and his source. A single treasure ship hadn't fitted his preferred narrative of a vast Chinese fleet making it to the New World, mapping it and establishing settlements before sailing back home. Besides, Fra Mauro's source had been emphatic that the ship's crew had found nothing at all on their two thousand mile voyage west. Nothing but sea. Yet Knox had always wondered about that.

After all, they would have said that, wouldn't they?

III

Rebecca finished looking through her father's desk, turned on the generator and started up his computer instead. His document manager was testament to his extraordinary range of interests, with folders on zoology, geology, geography, astronomy, medicine, anthropology, anatomy and linguistics. Each contained many dozens of academic articles downloaded from his favourite journals once a month or so at an Internet café in Tulear, where he'd also catch up on email and post new photos, podcasts and text to Eden's website.

She ran a search for files he'd been working on recently, came across a draft of his most recent letter to her mother.

Yvette, my darling, another year gone, I can't believe it.

I start with the big news, of course. We have our first grandchild, Michel, named for your father. He is beautiful; he looks like you. Both he and Emilia are flourishing. Emilia will fill you in on the details and say Hello for herself when I am finished, and update you on all our projects, which progress well. A word about her, though: motherhood suits her, as we always knew it would. She is fulfilled, she is confident, she is prepared to fight her corner. She reminds me how becoming a parent for the first time fixes your place in the world and gives you a full explanation for your life. And she is so strong. She was walking within twelve hours of delivery. And already she insists on taking Michel sailing with us, can you believe! I tell her he's just an infant; the sea can wait. Your namesake is a fine boat, my love, but I'm not sure about trusting our first grandson to her! Emilia wins her argument, of course, as she always does, though I cannot help but sermonise a little when she trips on the top rung as she is carrying him aboard and both of them go tumbling on the deck; and, ow, poor Michel is bawling still!

261

You used to watch me hammering and sawing at the cabins with a look of profound disapproval, as though manual labour were beneath the dignity of an Oxford Professor of Biology. Michel gives me this same look; he gives everyone this look, it's how he views the world. Every time he looks at me this way, my heart lurches, I think of you, I can't help it. I miss you so much, more than before even, more than I can ever say. It's not healthy. I know this. People come and go like tides. Scientists, zoologists, do-gooders, tourists. Some of the women are very forward. They offer themselves openly. They feel sorry for me, perhaps, or maybe they're just lonely; maybe that's why they travel. Yet I have no appetite for them at all. At least, it's like visiting a library in a country whose script you cannot read.

The books remind you of the joy of reading, but in themselves are nothing.

Our beloved Rebecca continues her triumph. She has grown beautiful. She has your sumptuous dark hair that she mostly ties up in a bun when she is on her treks, but sometimes she lets it loose and then she runs her fingers like combs through it, the way you used to do, and it takes me back to the moment I first saw you and I knew instantly what I wanted from my life. Everyone should have such a moment; our stay here is meaningless without it. Sometimes she sends me recordings of her programmes. It frightens me to watch her. She approaches crocodiles and snakes and tigers as if they were pets, then turns her back on them to talk to the camera. She is quite fearless. No, that is not quite right. Fear adds a glow to her, like the candle inside the pumpkin. She stands among those savage creatures and burns the screen with intensity. She writes her own scripts, I understand. They make me so proud: clear, insightful, witty and delivered with perfect timing. My only worry is how bleak her view of human nature has become. Behaviourism is a most dangerous discipline. It puts a window between you and the world. You observe, you diagnose, you put other people into your little boxes and then think yourself superior to them. It's a miserable way to live. I know this because it was me before I met you. Sometimes when I'm in Tulear, I browse the Internet for stories about her. She seems to be out on the town with some new man every few weeks, but none of them last. I can't help but fear she's been too badly scorched by my terrible anger ever to put down her guard completely. It grieves me more than I can say that this might be so, but still I hope that maybe one day she'll lose her heart before she even realises it's in danger.

She was kind enough to track down and send some

copies of my own old programmes. At least, she
didn't exactly send them herself. She had one of her
people send them. They put in a compliments slip and
signed it in her absence, or pp'ed it, as they say – a
most telling acronym. I cringed when I watched them.
I'd forgotten how wooden I was, how patronising. I
used to believe that knowledge was enough, that
wonderful ideas were in themselves contagious.

Rebecca raised her head and stared at the far wall. Adam
was right about his programmes. They'd been academic,
patrician, stilted, hideously dated. And yet, when she'd
watched them, she'd been aware of an elusive quality
missing from her own work, and which she'd envied deeply;
something like integrity, or even love. Watching him,
listening to him, she'd been reminded that the study of
animals in their environment was a demanding discipline
in which new knowledge was gained only by years of
patient fieldwork that rarely produced headline results.
Her father had put in those years of graft and grind. The
BBC had commissioned his radio broadcasts and then his
television series not for his looks or screen presence but
because he'd been one of Britain's leading biologists.
Thankfully for her own career, TV had since realised it
didn't need substance. But Rebecca herself had been quite
capable of telling the difference.

Of course Emilia and I dare not say anything to her. She is so close to snipping even the slender threads of communication we have that we cannot risk giving her an excuse. One day she will be ready, and she will let us know. At least, that's what I tell myself. But there are times I fear she will never forgive me. Why should she? My anger with her was unforgivable, and I will never forgive myself. True remorse doesn't seek forgiveness anyway. It seeks expiation. You made me vow to you, when you told me your secret, that I would never reveal it to Rebecca. But you believed then that I was a good man, capable of self-control. I cannot imagine that you would have wanted it to tear our family apart like this. I cannot imagine that. I want to tell her, Yvette. I want to explain myself to her, to have her at least understand. I need her forgiveness. Please, my darling; you must find some way to let me off my vow, or she'll be paying for it all her life.

The sins of the father, indeed.

It was too much for Rebecca. She stood and hobbled to the front door. Outside, a warbler was singing its heart out. It took her back vividly to a childhood afternoon, pestering her father with that hackneyed yet fundamental question: nature or nurture? She'd asked such questions less from curiosity than because it had given Adam such intense pleasure to answer them, and making him happy had still been her greatest joy.

Typically, Adam had answered her question with an experiment. Never tell when you can show. Together with Emilia, they'd purpose-built a huge aviary in the forest, then they'd pillaged eggs from some nearby Thamnormis warbler's nests, had hand-reared three male chicks. The local adult warblers sang *tew-tew-tew-tee-tew-tee-tew-tew-tee-tee*. Rebecca had known their song well; you couldn't escape it during the mating season. If their captive warblers sang this, it would show that song was innate. If they remained silent or sang something different, then the song was learned. It had taken many months for her question to be answered, when their captive warblers had finally broken into song, a truncated *tew-tew-tew-tee-tew-tee*.

Behaviour was nature and nurture fused.

Outside her window the warbler continued to sing, as though it simply had too much life to contain within its breast. It seemed cruel in retrospect to cage such vibrant and exultant birds for an answer Adam could have told her in a minute. It hadn't seemed so at the time. The world had grown absurdly sentimental. You couldn't tread on a cockroach these days without some hippy yelling in your face. And you'd never be permitted to experiment with humans, of course. Yet life sometimes threw up serendipitous examples: identical twins separated at birth; fostered and adopted children, the offspring of illicit affairs. You could learn a great deal about nature and nurture through cuckold children, who were far more common than many people thought. Genetic sampling showed that perhaps as many as one in ten children born within seemingly stable relationships were in fact the products of infidelity. *One in ten!* Sometimes, when meeting large family groups, she'd wonder which of them might just get a shock from a DNA test. It was not a subject to broach lightly, however. Parentage was so fundamental a component of identity that when it was brought even tentatively into question, people often reacted with anger and extraordinary denial, refusing so much as to consider the possibility that they were the product of an affair, however compelling the evidence.

It never failed to amuse Rebecca, the obtuseness of some people.

Her musings were interrupted by the bawl of an aggrieved infant. She looked towards the path just as Therese arrived carrying Xandra and Michel, honouring her promise to change Rebecca's bandages.

TWENTY-NINE

I

'Watch what the hell you're doing,' yelled Boris, as water splashed yet again over their bow and on to his hip and lap.

'Sorry,' said Davit.

'What use is sorry? Stop doing it.'

'I can't help it,' shrugged the big man. 'Not if you want us to make any decent progress.'

Boris glared at him; but Davit refused to back down. It was having the girl dozing in the crook of his arm, no doubt; wanting to impress her. Boris's irritation with her was increasing all the time; but, unfortunately, so was his desire. She was wearing a knee-length white dress with nothing but knickers underneath, and every time water splashed over her, the fabric would go a little translucent. He remembered the way she'd spurned his offer, generous though it had been, and his irritation increased another notch. She needed taking in hand, that was the truth of it. She needed to be taught who was boss.

He flapped out his map, checked their position against the low islets that lay like upturned oyster-shells upon the water. Their progress was hopelessly slow. At this rate, they'd never get to Eden by nightfall, or anywhere close. And if they weren't going to make it there tonight, then they'd have to stop even earlier so that they could make camp before it got too dark. He put away his map again, let his eyes drift back to Claudia. The hemline of her dress had ridden up a little, showing off her thighs. He licked his lower lip.

Their bow plunged into another wave, splashing more water into his lap. He glared furiously at Davit. The big man was looking innocent as an angel, holding up a hand in apology, but Boris knew better.

He was going to enjoy taking Claudia from him. By Christ, he was.

II

Knox sailed out to a cluster of symbols marked at between thirty and forty metres on Adam's chart, then dropped anchor, checked his equipment and suited up. Diving solo on a re-breather was a bad habit to get into, but he'd be fine as long as he stuck to his disciplines, kept checking his equipment and took breaks. He tipped himself backward over the edge, exploded into the sea. The water was cold but visibility was excellent, though it grew darker as he descended. The sea-floor here was rich with brain and stag-horn corals, but there was no way to tell which in particular Adam had been interested in, or why he'd marked his map as he had. He swam in a widening spiral around the *Yvette* before deciding he'd seen enough and beginning his ascent.

The sun was high and warm. He unzipped his wetsuit, the better to enjoy it, opened a bottle of drinking water and sat on deck watching the waves breaking gently yet relentlessly upon the reefs, just as they'd done day after day for centuries now; for millennia.

The *Winterton* had spent three days upon these reefs before it had broken up. *Three days*. What a bizarre time that must have been for crew and passengers alike, praying for a berth on one of the few lifeboats that had plied back and forth to the shore, or with the native fishermen who'd come out to help, as their ship slowly fell apart beneath them. They'd tried to save it, of course; their immediate response to collision, indeed, had been to throw everything overboard to lighten it and so float it off the reef.

He sat forward a little. It was a sailor's first instinct, when they'd run their ship aground, to try to refloat it. Was that what had happened to the Chinese? He closed his eyes, the better to picture that leviathan on a shortcut from the Cape crunching its keel upon this reef. He could only imagine the chaos and terror. Giving orders on a ship that big was hard at the best of times, but infinitely harder in the aftermath of a reef-strike, particularly if it had happened – as they mostly had – at night or during a storm. But deckhands knew the drill even in the absence of command: toss overboard anything and everything you can to lighten the ship and make it easier to refloat. The most obvious things to jettison would have been its anchors and cannons, the very things they'd found at Cheung's site. And if a cargo hold had been torn open, it would explain the pottery and other artefacts too.

Chinese ships had been fitted with watertight bulkheads to survive moderate hull damage. But even once they'd refloated themselves, they'd still have been stuck outside the reef, badly damaged and shipping water fast, shrouded in darkness or buffeted by a storm, facing a desperate race to find a pass before they sank.

A pass just like the one right here.

III

Rebecca went across to greet Therese. Michel smiled up at her as she took him in her arms, and his smile did strange things to her heart. They walked together through to the clinic, laid the infants down in matching wooden cots. 'I don't suppose you have medical records for Adam and Emilia?' she asked.

'Of course,' said Therese. 'What for?'

'The police found some blood on the boat. They want to see if it belongs to Adam or Emilia.'

Therese gave her a dismayed look, but she flipped through a drawer of handwritten cards without a word, jotted down the information for Rebecca. 'Okay,' she said, gesturing at the examination table. 'Now show me what your boyfriend do.'

Rebecca entrusted herself to Therese's care without a qualm. Many Malagasy struggled with Western medicine, for it was widely believed that much sickness was caused by *gris-gris*; malevolent, voodoo-like spells and curses that could only be cured by countervailing magic. But Therese had grasped the principles from the first, and had only grown more knowledgeable, intuitive and energetic with the years. 'You do this on coral?' she murmured, as she saw the extent of Rebecca's injuries. 'You away too long if you forget coral is dangerous.'

'Yes.'

'Why you away so long? Why you cruel to your papa and sister like this? You like to hurt your fambly and frens maybe?'

'I never had time to come back.'

Therese snorted. 'You hab time now, all right. Too late now. You break your papa's heart, you know. First Mama, then you. Eb'ryone he lub go away.' She removed the dressings on Rebecca's palms, examined the multicoloured mess beneath. But she nodded in approval. 'Your boyfriend's a good nurse,' she said. 'Where he learn to nurse like this?'

'He has some quite bad burns,' replied Rebecca. 'Maybe he learned from doing his own dressings.'

'Burns?' frowned Therese, taken aback. 'Where?'

'On his shoulders and back. Why?'

'No reason. No reason.'

Rebecca wasn't convinced, but she let it go, watched Therese clean her wounds, apply more antiseptic cream and iodine, dress her with fresh bandages. 'I come back tomorrow, yes?' she said, when she was done.

'Not tomorrow,' said Rebecca. 'I'll be away. The day after.'

Therese pulled a scolding face, but evidently knew Rebecca too well to argue. They picked up the infants again, and Rebecca walked her out, entrusting Michel once more to her care before returning to her father's desk and his letter to Yvette.

*Enough melancholy. Time for my round-up of gossip.
Pierre is our most regular guest, of course, still as
bemused by life and by his own nature as ever. He
sits there with one eyebrow cocked as things happen
around him. He ordered colour leaflets from a print
shop in Tulear and now refuses to pay, if you please,
because two of the pictures are slightly fuzzy! I know
I should disapprove of him more, but he's a child
and entertaining company and it's difficult to hold
him responsible for the messes he creates.*

*Therese asks me to remember her to you. She has
had her child now, too, of course, christened
Xandra Yvette after you. I pray every night that this
one lives. She is wonderful, Therese, completely
selfless. She looks after Michel whenever Emilia and
I take out the boat. And she still won't take
payment for it, or her work at the clinic, though
Pierre comes around afterwards and asks for it on
her behalf.*

*I head into Tulear more than pleases me. I would
stay at Eden always if I could. I am like that
tree-frog who cannot stand the croaking of its own
species. Our friend Mustafa Habib inevitably finds
me within minutes. His intelligence system is second
to none. He even dragged me and Emilia to lunch
at his wretched palazzo, then spent all day pestering
me to let him invest in Eden, so that Ahdaf might*

work for such a worthy venture! I keep telling him that he is talking to the wrong person, but I don't think he believes me.

The letter ran on for three more pages, chronicling the activities of people she didn't know or barely remembered. When Rebecca had finished, she read others in the folder, one for each anniversary of Yvette's death. Fifteen years on, Adam's adoration of his late wife was extraordinary and moving. As a specialist in behaviour, it was almost an accepted truth for Rebecca that love was merely an adaptation designed to bind together a male and female long enough for them to procreate and rear. As her father's daughter, however, it was difficult to sustain such belief. There's a species of anglerfish in which males physically embed themselves in the females, becoming entirely dependent upon them for nutrition, survival and procreation. Adam had sometimes seemed like that to her, so completely had he subsumed himself and his former career into his marriage.

As young girls, Rebecca and Emilia had pestered their parents endlessly for the story of how they met and fell in love. Adam had been a typical bachelor professor, scoffing at the idea of marriage; but then he'd come filming in Madagascar, and had found himself in need of a translator for his south-western leg. Yvette had been recommended; she'd taught languages in Tulear's international school. The moment Adam had set eyes on her, he'd known. He'd found talking to her so difficult, she'd thought him mentally afflicted (she'd taken his producer aside to ask why an organisation as respected and wealthy as the BBC would employ an idiot as their presenter). He hadn't been able to sleep or eat. He'd driven his crew crazy with his mistakes. Within four days he'd asked her to marry him. She'd had a fit of the giggles, had pointed out justly that he was a funny-looking man (they'd all laughed uproariously every time he'd come to this bit; it had become their catchphrase whenever some unfortunate had turned up at the camp) and anyway she'd never leave Madagascar. Adam had returned lovesick to England, where he'd waited to get over her, as all his knowledge of the world had assured him that he would. But time had passed and his condition had only worsened. Everything had drained of meaning. Success and fame had become irrelevant. He'd fallen seriously ill. In the end, he'd given in. He'd resigned his chair, chucked in his TV career, and flown back out.

They'd married one month later.

the shelf. He swam north along it for a few minutes, until, away in the deep waters to his left, he glimpsed something the fluorescent orange of a life-jacket. His heart gave a little lurch; he feared the worst. But when he swam closer, it proved to be only a cluster of four buoys held down by a cable that vanished into the depths. A fish aggregating device, most likely. He'd read about these things, though he'd never seen one before. They were an occasional tool of marine biologists, who'd tie one end of a long cable to a job-lot of broken truck axles; the other to some kind of flotation device, then sail the whole rig out over deep water and dump it. The idea was that the axles would sink to the sea-bed while the buoys would stay near the surface, and the cable would stretch out between them. Algae would grow upon this cable, drawing shoals of algae-eaters that in turn drew bigger fish, and so gave marine biologists a fixed point to study changing pelagic fish populations, and local fishermen somewhere to ply their trade that wouldn't damage the reef. This one was certainly doing its job. The cable beneath him was surrounded by a pointillist haze of small fish, and the larger shadows of their predators. A juvenile white-tip shark saw him and lazily headed his way, curiosity rather than menace. He retreated to the relative safety of shallower waters. Back through the canyons again, he reached a place like an underwater rubbish tip, where tides and currents had brought together a great mass of detritus over the centuries. He floated inches above it, careful not to stir up sediment, scoured it for artefacts. It didn't take long for him to pick out several fragments of porcelain and coarse-ware, though he'd never have spotted them unless he'd been looking, for they lay in an almost perfect camouflage of old shells, dead coral, cartilage and bone. He didn't find a wreck, however, or any sign of Adam or Emilia. And the day was getting on, and he'd still barely put a dent in the vast expanse of the Eden reefs.

The search area was too big for him alone, that much was clear. He needed help. There were fifteen other divers on board the *Maritsa*, searching urgently for the wreck, but surely in the wrong places. He needed to bring them down here. But before he could even broach that with Miles, he needed to speak to Rebecca.

He couldn't lie to her any longer. It was time to tell her who he was.

II

Adam kept hundreds of personal photographs on his computer, with many more burned on to a set of CDs on his shelves. Rebecca started looking through them to see if any could have been used as the source shot for the ransom photo. There was nothing remotely like that, but she found herself getting hooked by all the family history she'd missed out on these past eleven years: sorrows and joys, friendships and partings.

When she'd finished the CDs, she turned to his old photograph albums. Her hand trembled a little when she pulled out the album for the year she'd left for England, and she soon came across the first photograph of herself, standing on the veranda with Emilia, arms around each others' shoulders. There were abundant photographs of her after that: on her own, with Emilia, with her father; in the woods and on the beach. She couldn't believe how happy she looked. Photograph albums suffered from publication bias, of course, in that you only kept the ones you liked. Even so, it was hard to reconcile these glowing portraits with her darker memories.

The afternoon drew on. She turned her mind to the following morning. She topped up the Jeep with oil and fuel, then wondered what else she might need. A bag for the money, though presumably Mustafa would have his own. The thought of simply handing it over made her feel sick. It wasn't just the money in itself; she hated being cheated. If only there was some way to . . .

She frowned at a recollection, went back to her father's desk. Yes, his income statement showed that he had been running field trials for a wildlife GPS system. She went through the lodge room by room, finally found two boxes in a cupboard in the clinic, one full, one empty.

The transmitter was a thin white cylinder about two inches long, like a cigarette with its filter torn off. The tracker was bulkier and had an inset screen. Also in the box were a collar, a harness and some glue for attaching the transmitter to animals, and instructions written in such terrible English that she gave up on them, and instead turned everything on and figured it out by trial and error. The transmitter used lithium batteries to cut weight and space, sending off small bursts of data at adjustable intervals. She set it to one hour, regular enough to make tracking practical, yet without straining the batteries. Then she switched it all off again, and wondered how best to use it.

Kidnappers weren't stupid. They'd surely search the money before handing over Adam and Emilia. If they found the transmitter, it would be the end of them. If she kept the transmitter on her, however, she could plant it when opportunity presented, yet also use it as a safeguard should she be taken too. But that meant leaving the tracker with someone she trusted, with instructions to take it to the police should she vanish. She could leave a note for Therese in the clinic, for she was due here to change her bandages the day after tomorrow. Or she could leave it for Daniel instead. Alternatively, she could just tell him everything right now, explain why she'd been acting so distantly. And she realised that was what she wanted. She wanted him by her side.

She went outside, but there was no sign of him. She climbed the steps on to the lodge's roof. It afforded a wonderful view over a low fringe of forest down to the lagoon. Her father had set up a spotting scope here, partly for watching the night sky, but mostly to monitor Eden's reefs and make sure no one was fishing in the protected waters. She removed the dust cover and lens cap, looked out along the shore. The resolution was extraordinarily good. She could see young boys gleaning shellfish from the rocks on the beach far away to the south, while their mothers gossiped and washed clothes in the shallows. Three shore fishermen dragged in their nets then brained their catch against the rocks. She turned the scope out to sea, searched the waters until finally she found the *Yvette* way out beyond the reef, her sail furled, seemingly at anchor.

She adjusted the focus as Daniel climbed up the stern ladder. He was wearing a wetsuit, but with a black-and-yellow pack upon his back rather than a scuba tank. She recognised it immediately – a closed-circuit re-breather, much like the one her underwater cameraman Anton used, because it let him stay underwater forever, and because there were no annoying exhalations of air bubbles to spoil his shot. But it stunned her that Daniel would have one. Re-breathers weren't just hideously expensive to buy and operate, they also took hundreds of hours of training to master, which was why only elite professional and military divers used them. And they were a pig to fly abroad, because they used such volatile chemicals that airport security often refused point-blank to allow them on their planes. No way would some itinerant journalist just happen to have one in his bag. No way.

She stood up tall and replaced the lens cap, certain of one thing: Daniel had been lying to her. The knowledge was a gash in her heart. She hobbled down from the roof and back into the lodge, heaved his bag on to the camp-bed, unzipped and opened it. She caught a whiff of yesterday's shirt as she took it out, pungent yet not unpleasant. At Oxford, years ago, investigating the nature of male sexiness, she and her colleagues had asked twenty men to wear identical white cotton shirts continuously for two days, then they'd passed the soiled shirts to a panel of women to judge for attractiveness, based only on their smell. Later, those women had also judged photographs of the same men for looks. The correlation between the scores had been remarkable. Handsome men smelled better. But why? Some of her colleagues had contended that there was a positive correlation between the perceived sexiness of smell and androsterone, a pheromone that indicated high immunocompetence. But when Rebecca had smelled the shirts herself, she'd been startled to discover that ugliness had an acrid sourness to it, disconcertingly like failure. Ugliness stank; or, at least, anxiety and low self-esteem did. They'd discussed this question with a celebrated theorist and philosopher, one of the ugliest men Rebecca had ever seen. She'd suggested mischievously that maybe self-assessment was an adaptation designed to let sexual failures appreciate and so address their shortcomings. Wasn't it Socrates who'd remarked that the unexamined life was not worth living? Now *he'd* been famously ugly, a goblin of a man. Perhaps extreme ugliness was exactly what it took to be a successful philosopher, the ability to see one's own blemishes and yet not flinch. She'd felt terribly pleased with herself for this until he'd met and held her eyes with such perfect equanimity that she'd had to look away in shame. It had been a humiliating, levelling experience, the first time she'd properly understood the ordinariness of her own intellect. And all of this came flooding back to her as she sat on Daniel's bed holding his shirt.

She removed his other clothes, stacking them carefully so that she'd be able to replace them as she'd found them. Right at the bottom she found a heavy, mottled grey box-folder. She pulled it out, undid the catch. It was packed so tight that the lid jumped slightly, like a broken jack-in-the-box. She flipped through the papers inside: passenger lists, manifests and newspaper reports about the *Winterton*. She set the box back down. She knew the *Winterton* well; everyone around here did. The local fishermen still found the occasional piece-of-eight that they'd sell to her father for the going rate. She knew the wreck-site too; she'd sailed there often as a girl. The wood and other organic material had long since rotted away, but there were still several huge cannons, anchors, cannonballs and iron ingots lying just a few metres deep, along with some copper and iron sheets that had been too heavy to move, but which everyone had wondered about, imagining great stashes of silver beneath. A French salvage ship had arrived one day, had blasted through the sheets with dynamite. To everyone's delight, they'd found nothing. But the rumours had persisted, and every year or so some foreigner would come to find and plunder it, thinking they alone knew the secret. Daniel, it seemed, was just the latest of them.

It galled Rebecca to remember how *grateful* she'd been when he'd offered to sail the *Yvette* up from Tulear. She'd thought he'd been trying to help her, but the blunt truth of it was that he'd just wanted a dive-boat for his search.

THIRTY-ONE

I

Boris decided to call it quits for the day while they were still some four miles north of Eden. They heaved the boat up above the tide-line, then found a clearing in the spiny forest in which to make camp. He had Davit bring up their baggage while Claudia went scouting for firewood, then he set up the laptop and IP terminal a little distance away, and called in to Georgia.

'I have some distressing news,' said Sandro, when he appeared. 'About my father.'

'He's not . . .?'

'No,' said Sandro. 'We have that to be thankful for. But he suffered renal failure last night. His medical team have put him into a controlled coma while they work on solutions.'

'I'm sorry to hear that,' said Boris.

'Thank you,' said Sandro, who seemed to be dealing with the bad news commendably well. 'But of course it has implications for our current project. You saw for yourself how eager he is to be part of it. I therefore think it best to put everything on hold until he is better.'

Boris had to fight not to show his dismay: people with terminal cancer didn't just recover from renal failure. He said: 'I imagine your father would want us to continue our preparations. After all, we don't know how long his next remission will last. We should be ready to act swiftly.'

Sandro's eyelids flickered. 'That's true,' he acknowledged. 'Yet I can't see how to arrange things unless we know my father will—'

'Leave that to me,' said Boris. 'That's what you sent me here for.'

'I'm not sure that that's really the best—'

Boris looked around, as though he'd heard a noise. 'Someone's coming,' he whispered. 'I have to go.' He cut the connection before Sandro could say anything more, then sat there brooding. He'd come to think of those half-million euros as already his. No way was he going to let Sandro weasel out of it now. No fucking way. He packed up the laptop and IP terminal, headed back to camp. Davit was setting up the tents while Claudia was preparing dinner. In need of a lift, Boris cracked open a bottle of cheap rum, splashed it liberally into a glass, sweetened it with a dash of coke. He knocked it back, poured himself another, then watched Claudia stirring some crushed garlic into a small bowl of oily sauce that she smeared on the silvery skins of three filleted fish and set upon a metal grill that she placed above the open flame to cook.

'So you and Davit, eh?' he said. She glanced up, but didn't answer, except to sprinkle the fish with herbs. 'I said you and Davit, eh?' said Boris more loudly. 'You like each other.'

'Yes,' said Claudia. 'We like each other.'

'You're a better person than me,' he told her. 'If I had to spend the night with someone who snored like that . . .'

'I don't mind,' she said.

'Well,' he said. 'If it gets too bad for you, you know where I am.' She threw him a glare, but said nothing. He glanced around to make sure Davit was out of earshot, still putting up the second tent. 'A hundred euros,' he offered. 'I can't say fairer than that.' She wouldn't even look at him. 'Fine, you bitch. Two hundred.'

'Leave us alone,' she said.

Davit finished the tents, came over to join them, wiping his hands on his trousers. 'All done,' he said cheerfully.

'About time.'

Claudia turned over the fish. The hot grill had blistered

black lines on their silver skins, spitting out oily fireballs of yellow and pale-blue. Davit pinched off some flesh, tossed it from palm to palm before popping it in his mouth. 'God, that's good,' he said, giving Claudia a proud kiss upon her cheek. He turned to Boris. 'Try some, boss. Heaven on a tongue.'

'I'll take your word for it.'

Davit put his hand upon the small of Claudia's back. She turned and smiled up at him with a warmth that made Boris's heart twist. 'Did you ever get to Gori before the Russians came?' he asked Davit, in Georgian.

Davit frowned. 'Once or twice. Why?'

'They've got some cracking whores down there. My God! There was this dancer in this nightclub I went to – I couldn't take my eyes off her. Or my hands.'

Davit's face went stony. 'Claudia's not a whore,' he said.

'I never said she was. I'm just telling you about this place down in Gori.'

'Claudia's not a whore,' said Davit, walking around the fire.

'Of course she's a fucking whore,' spat Boris. 'What do you think? That she's suddenly just fallen in love with you? Are you really that stupid?'

'You take that back,' warned Davit.

'She's a whore,' said Boris. 'Face it. She just offered to blow me for a hundred euros while you were doing the tents.'

'That's it,' said Davit. 'That's fucking it.' He bunched his fist and came swinging. Boris ducked beneath it, threw a right to his ribs, but it was useless, the man was a ogre, like punching a fucking wall. Davit swung again. Boris jumped backwards to evade him, stumbled over a root. Davit came after him. On hands and knees, Boris scrambled to his bags, pulled out his Heckler & Koch, took off the safety and swung it round at Davit. 'That's enough,' he yelled. 'Now back off.'

'What the hell's that?' asked Davit, blanching and putting up his hands.

'What the fuck does it look like?' retorted Boris.

'Sandro said no guns.'

'Well, Sandro lied, didn't he? What do you think this is? Girl scouts?'

'I don't do guns. Not after last time.'

'You do whatever the fuck I tell you to do,' said Boris. 'I'm in charge of this operation, and I'm going to do what I've been tasked to do, and you're going to help me.' He raised the gun at Davit's face. 'Is that clear?'

'Yes, boss,' said Davit. 'It's clear.'

'Good. Good.' He felt a little foolish as he tucked the Heckler & Koch away in his belt. 'I'm sorry if I upset you. But we go back a long way, you and me; I'd hate to see you get hurt.'

'I'm a grown-up,' said Davit. 'I can look after myself.'

'Fine. Then we'll say no more about it, okay?' He put

on as bright a smile as he could muster, rubbed his hands together in an effort to lighten the atmosphere, walked over to Claudia. 'How about serving us up some of this delicious food of yours, eh? I'm starving.'

II

Knox was in a good mood as he moored the *Yvette* and headed up the track to Eden. It would be a weight off his back to tell Rebecca what he was doing here and why he'd kept it secret until now. But he sensed trouble when Rebecca, sitting at her father's desk, didn't even look up at him. Then he noticed his overnight bag up on his camp-bed, papers spilling out of his box-file on the *Winterton*.

He turned to Rebecca, spread his hands, put on his most contrite face. But it was pretty obvious that she was in no mood for his contrition, partly from her stony expression but mostly because she chose that moment to pick her father's shotgun up from behind the desk and aim it vaguely his way. 'A freelance journalist, eh?' she asked.

There was no point lying. 'No,' he confessed. 'I'm a marine archaeologist.'

'A marine archaeologist!' she snorted. 'A treasure hunter, you mean. Just another fucking treasure hunter come looking to plunder the *Winterton*.'

'It's not how you think,' he said. 'I was going to tell you everything.'

'Sure!'

'I swear. Let me tell you now. Just put that gun down.'

'So I can listen to more of your bullshit?' Her eyes glittered. 'I *trusted* you. My father and my sister went missing and I needed help and I told you *everything*. I thought you were on my side. How could you betray me like that?'

'I had no choice. I gave my word to—'

'I don't want to hear it. I don't want to hear another word.' She stood and motioned him towards the door. 'Just get out. Go on. Get out. I can't bear to look at you any longer.'

'Rebecca, please.'

'Get out.'

He backed on to the veranda; she slammed the door in his face. He could hear her shooting bolts and then the diminishing sound of footsteps. Christ, what a mess. He considered shouting out his story so that she'd hear him through the walls, but she was still too angry. Better to give her a night to calm down, come back first thing tomorrow with apologies and the truth. But where to sleep? Rebecca was too sore for him to risk taking one of the cabins. He could trudge down to Pierre's place . . . but there was a bed on the *Yvette*, and Rebecca was unlikely to come looking for him out there.

He waded out, climbed aboard, sat on deck as it grew dark around him, watching the shore, lulled by soothing sounds, the creak of wood, the soft splash of distant breakers. Away to the south, someone lit a beach bonfire, perhaps Pierre's women cooking dinner. Confrontation and guilt had robbed him of his own appetite; he dined on biscuits and beer. His thoughts kept drifting to Rebecca, though he tried to stop them. Her anger had upset him more than he'd have imagined possible, not least because it was justified. Gaille would never have erupted like that, however; she'd have given him at least a chance to explain himself. But Gaille had been a conciliator by nature, always wanting to think the best of people. Rebecca, on the other hand . . . he gave a rueful laugh. Yet there were similarities between the two women too. Their vitality, their intelligence, the way they both came alive when talking about their passions. One of his most treasured memories of Gaille was an evening in Alexandria when she'd shown him photographs of an ancient mural she'd coaxed back to life. The way her skin had glowed had been one of the things that had first enchanted him about her. Rebecca lit up in the exact same way whenever she talked about animal behaviour. And they were both resourceful too, as well as scientifically minded, loyal and courageous, prepared to risk everything for the people they loved. And they both looked so damned good, too.

by then, she'd got pregnant by him too, and had since become the mother of his . . .

Knox frowned. Emilia had assured him that she was on the pill, that he needn't worry about consequences. Yet she'd come back to Madagascar and had got pregnant within a couple of months at the most, depending on Michel's precise date of birth. His breath came a little faster; he felt slightly dazed. There was a photo of Emilia with Michel on the wall of the cabin. He set down his beer, got to his feet, climbed down the companionway ladder, switched on the light. It ran off the ship's batteries, and was therefore so dim that he had to remove the photograph from the wall and hold it up close to the bulb to see much of anything at all. Squint though he might, he couldn't reach any firm conclusion one way or the other. But that meant that the possibility had to remain.

Maybe Michel wasn't Pierre's son after all.

Maybe he was his.

III

Davit lay on his back, his arm around Claudia, and looked up at the walls of the tent above him, the way they flapped in the occasional gusts of breeze, the way the moonlight glowed through the blue fabric. Things scuttled outside; things screeched and crept. He turned to look at Claudia, kissed her on her brow.

'I don't want to be here any more,' she whispered. 'I don't want to be part of this.'

'It'll be okay,' he assured her.

'No, it won't,' she said. 'Why has your friend brought a gun? What has he done, this man you're looking for?'

'It's complicated.'

'You mean you don't want to tell me,' she said. 'You mean you're ashamed of what you're doing here, but you're still going to do it anyway.'

'You don't understand. My life back home . . .' He shook his head. 'I have to change it. I *have* to.'

Her body began to heave and hump against him; he could tell that she was sobbing. It distressed him to hear her so unhappy. He tried to comfort her by stroking her hair, but she only shook her head. 'Why don't you want to change your life *here*?' she asked. 'Why don't you want to change it with *me*?'

Davit didn't reply at once. He'd thought about staying on a few days, enjoying Claudia, the sea, some sunshine. But he'd never thought about staying on for good. He was a Georgian through and through; he couldn't give up his homeland and family and friends. But then he realised with a jolt that he'd *already* given them up; or, rather, they'd given him up. He just hadn't accepted it yet, like the ghost who refused to leave his corpse. 'What would we do?' he asked. 'How would we survive?'

A moment's silence as they both contemplated this. 'Work, work, work?' she suggested.

Davit laughed. 'Work, work, work,' he agreed.

THIRTY-TWO

I

It was pitch black when Rebecca's alarm sounded the next morning. She threw off her bedclothes and fumbled for the matches to light the candle she'd left out for herself, then washed briskly, dressed and went out to the Jeep. Despite the cool, it started first time. A good omen, perhaps. She drove as fast as conditions allowed, the world growing light around her, villages coming to life. She kept checking her watch, measuring her progress, a little panicky until she saw the first signs promoting hotels in Ifaty, and knew she was nearly there.

She pulled up outside Mustafa's gates. The guard was expecting her; he hurried to her window to let her know that Mr Habib's daughter Ahdaf was coming out. Rebecca felt a twinge of alarm, but the guard knew nothing else and only shook his head at her questions. Ahdaf then appeared, looking flustered. 'What's going on?' Rebecca asked her. 'Where's your father?'

'He went to Ilakaka last night,' Ahdaf told her. 'He just called to ask me to tell you that he had to go there on your behalf, and that he's been successful. He said you'd understand what that meant.'

'Yes,' nodded Rebecca. Ilakaka was the shantytown hub of Madagascar's recent sapphire boom. If you needed cash in a hurry, Ilakaka was an obvious place to try.

'He said to tell you he's finalising everything now, but he'll be setting off very shortly. He says he'll meet you in Tulear. Do you know La Terrasse? It's on Independence Square?'

Rebecca nodded. Independence Square was where the kidnappers had told her to wait with the ransom. 'When will he get there?'

'He couldn't be sure. As soon as he can.'

Rebecca thanked her and sped off south. Anxiety came in hot spasms as she drove. She passed a petrol station. It was as well to fill up while she could. A doddering antique of a man held a hose-pipe in her tank while his great-grandfather turned a rusted hand-crank. They changed places every five litres, the effort too much to sustain. When they'd finally filled her up, one of them produced a pocket calculator on which he tried to multiply volume pumped by price per litre, while the other watched over his shoulder and chided him for doing it wrong. It took them five attempts and still they couldn't agree. She checked her watch. Eight fifty-six. She was supposed to be in Independence Square in less than five minutes. She wailed in exasperation and thrust twice what it should have cost at the two men, then sped off in a cloud of dust.

II

Boris woke to a pounding headache as the sides of his tent grew light with dawn. They needed an early start, but he decided to give himself another five minutes. With luck, Davit or Claudia would get up and start brewing coffee. But there was no sound from the other tent.

Not even snoring.

He pushed off his sleeping bag, grabbed the Heckler & Koch, hurried out. Their tent was still there, but that meant nothing. He strode over, pulled back the flap. Davit's sleeping bag was still inside, but the man himself had gone, Claudia with him. There was a note lying on the bag: an apologia from Davit, claiming that he'd never have signed on to this mission if he'd known there'd be guns; that he'd decided to take Claudia on a tour of the island, see how things worked out between them. Sorry.

The sleeping bag was still contoured from the weight of Davit's body. Boris touched the synthetic fabric; it still felt slightly warm, as though they'd slept here last night, and had only left at first light. But it was still first light right now. Maybe the sound of their departure was what had woken him in the first place.

He took a moment to listen, heard a faint noise. Yes, the outboard. He swore and took the safety catch off the Heckler & Koch as he ran down to the beach, holding it out to the side lest he trip and shoot himself. But even as he reached the sand, he saw them already well out to sea, heading north back towards Morombe.

He splashed out several paces into the sea. 'Come back,' he yelled. 'Come back.' Davit heard him or, more likely, saw him. He pushed Claudia down in the boat, then ducked down himself. 'Come back,' yelled Boris for the third time. But they couldn't have heard him over the motor, and wouldn't have obeyed even if they had. He aimed the Heckler & Koch, but they were already out of his effective range; all he'd achieve by shooting was wasting ammunition and drawing attention to himself. He yelled out in frustration as he walked back ashore; but in truth it wasn't that severe a blow. He hadn't wanted Davit along in the first place; he'd just been slowing him down. He still had his gun, his bags, the laptop and IP terminal. And he was close enough to Eden that he could walk from here.

He trudged back to the camp, then began to pack what he needed.

III

Knox made his way early to Eden, hoping that Rebecca had calmed down overnight, but instead he found the Jeep gone and the lodge locked. He needed to get inside; his bag was in there, as well as the information about Michel's date of birth. He circled it looking for an open window, but without result. That was when he remembered the keys dangling from the hook on the backside of the *Yvette's* water tank.

He waded back out. They were wrapped in sticky tape to stop them jangling. He peeled the tape off as he made his way back to shore. All bar one were standard issue house, car or motorbike keys; but that one intrigued him. It was a double-bit key, modern and highly sophisticated, similar to the one MGS had for its safe-room, where they kept their most precious discoveries and confidential documents. Emilia had asked him several questions about it during his office tour. He ran his finger along its edge. Surely it had to open something both important and recently built.

The boathouse was ugly and blockish, but it was also new and large and close enough to the *Yvette* to make it an appropriate mission control for the salvage. He hadn't seen anything unusual on his previous visit, but then he hadn't looked very hard. One of the standard keys fitted its front door. It was so gloomy inside that he couldn't see much. He took the tour nevertheless, looking for anything he might have overlooked. He was about to give up when he noticed the air compressor's rubber wheels. Mobile compressors typically came with their own generators; there wasn't much point to them otherwise. He pulled off the brown sacking and yes, there it was. So what was the second generator for? It was quite modern and powerful enough to run a number of appliances simultaneously. He checked behind and beneath it, saw a single fat grey cable that vanished into the concrete.

On his hands and knees, he went over every inch of floor, found nothing. He paced out the boathouse's length, inside and out. It was a full pace longer on the outside. He went to the rear internal wall, took the dive-gear from the pegs, knocked on the plasterboard panels. The right one was solid; but the left sounded hollow. He put his shoulder to it and pushed. It gave an inch or two, then slid to one side, like a closet door opening, revealing empty space behind.

A solid steel door gleamed dully to his right. The three-bit key fit perfectly in its lock. He turned it, heard the elaborate internal mechanism smoothly cede, then pushed

Her café-au-lait arrived, a jug of steaming black coffee, a small steel bowl of condensed milk. She scooped up a bulb of the sweet white treacle with her teaspoon, dangled a thin strand to make patterns in her coffee. She wiped it off with her finger, then licked it clean: sickly yet delicious, just what her body craved. She stirred in a whole spoonful, gulped the coffee down greedily before it lost its pleasurable heat.

Rebecca had suffered several bouts of negative thinking over the years, but the worst had been during her first few months in England. She'd never before spent time in a town larger or more sophisticated than Tulear. Oxford had bewildered her. All those brilliant, beautiful, shiny and learned young people. Adam's old friends had tried to make her welcome, but it wasn't the faculty who determined your acceptance, it was your peers. And she simply hadn't known how to behave around them. The humiliations had piled up. Many now seemed trivial. In retrospect, they *were* trivial. But, at the time, they'd been mortifying. A buffet dinner had been thrown in her honour. She'd been invited to serve herself first. Everyone had gawped when she'd piled her plate high with rice from the bowl, as you did in Madagascar. A fellow guest had remarked upon it in that peculiarly hurtful put-down manner of the pompous Englishman. It hadn't sounded like an insult, except that everybody had sniggered. And when another guest had later earned laughter by telling everyone that his grandfather had left him nothing but invoices in his will, Rebecca had tried to redeem herself by joking that her grandfather had left her only bills. The embarrassed silence had been broken by a law student with wretched skin who'd explained with great gentleness that invoices *were* bills. Rebecca had smiled blandly as though she'd known this all along, had spent the rest of the evening in tears in an upstairs bathroom. It had been like that for weeks. In her imagination, her fellow students had spent their lives trading jokes about her behind her back.

Rebecca didn't crack easily; she'd have ridden her blues out in time. But while at her lowest ebb, something else had happened, rooted in an incident from the torrid years after her mother had died, during which Rebecca had sought solace in the beds of the local Malagasy boys. Shortly before her sixteenth birthday, she'd realised she was pregnant. Jean-Luc was the most likely father, but he'd denied it furiously, denied even having slept with her. He'd been sufficiently fearful of her father finding out, however, that he'd taken her to an elderly Sakalava witch east of Tulear. She'd spilled hot wax upon Rebecca's thigh while examining her with a candle. A *candle* for Christ's sake! She'd stirred a white powder in a dirty glass of water. It had tasted so bitter that Rebecca had had to hold her nose as she'd chucked it down, but she'd aborted in agony that same night.

At the end of her first term in Oxford, Rebecca had

picked up an abandoned magazine from a bus seat, just for something to read. She'd chanced upon an article about women who'd had botched abortions and then subsequently been unable to conceive. She'd tried to set it aside, but she hadn't been able to, she'd had to know the worst. Some of the women in the article seemed blasé, as though it didn't impinge on their life-plans, but Rebecca had always yearned for children. She'd gagged suddenly on the remembered wormwood of that poison, had doubled up with cramps so violent that she'd collapsed to the floor of the bus. A passenger two rows back had pulled the emergency cord. In hospital, with trepidation bordering on despair, she'd revealed enough about her situation to a nurse with huge, empathetic eyes for a gynaecologist to be summoned. When she'd learned the news of her own likely barrenness, it had pushed her into something of a tailspin. It being the Christmas holidays by now, she'd taken to her bed, had barely got up for a fortnight. She'd felt *gutted*. Such an expressive word. It had left her hollow, and she'd needed something, anything, to fill her up again, to give her the sensation of substance. Her landlady, a kindly Caribbean widow, had provided her with a portable black-and-white TV that she'd kept by her bed. She'd watched it all the time, forever adjusting the wire aerial to improve the reception. It had given her an excuse not to think. And gradually, watching day after day, she'd come to realise

THIRTY-THREE

I

Knox arrived at the foot of the steps to find himself in a large room of much the same size and shape as the boat-house above, tall enough that he could only just touch its ceiling with his fingertips. To his immense relief, there were no horrors waiting for him. In fact, the place looked rather dull. A dehumidifier and an air-conditioning unit stood at the far end. There was metal-rack shelving against the near wall, wooden bookshelves against the far, and a spine of processing tables running down the middle, fitted with power-points for computers and other equipment, buttressed by a three-drawer filing cabinet. The top two drawers were empty, but hanging folders in the bottom contained salvage licences, correspondence and contracts with MGS, and a report Emilia had written about her visit to England in which she noted the promises of secrecy she'd exacted from all MGS project members. Knox couldn't have asked for a better way to explain himself to Rebecca than by bringing her here and giving her this to read.

He put it back, glanced at the shelves either side of him. He could see the books he'd given Emilia on the treasure fleets and on underwater archaeology, along with rows of other textbooks and printed out articles. But it was the metal shelving that drew him. Most of the racks were empty, awaiting the start of salvage. But there were a dozen or so white plastic tubs, a few boxes too. The first tub contained several handfuls of silver pieces-of-eight; but that was the only sign of the *Winterton* he found. Everything else was distinctively Chinese or impossible to attribute. Tubs of shattered ceramics sat next to others of rusted nails, ironwork and Ming coins. Elsewhere, several pieces had somehow survived largely intact. Most were rough-and-ready coarse-ware, but two were of a different order altogether. With great care, Knox picked up a blue-and-white bowl, turned it around in his hands. It was as fine a piece of eggshell porcelain as he'd ever seen, let alone handled. And it was flawless, as far as he could tell, without chip or crack, only the very slightest discolouration in the exquisitely painted pomegranates, grapes and lychees that decorated its exterior. One quite similar had sold for over two million dollars at auction a year or so before. Cheung had kept gloating about it, how rich they were all going to be. And here this was, just sitting on a shelf.

He set it down, picked up an enamelled flask instead, gorgeously decorated with dragons front and back. He walked a little further on. At the end of the shelf, he found an ornately carved wooden box filled with tissue paper. He pulled it aside to expose a fragment of black ceramic. His heart began to race a little as he reached in and carefully picked it up. It was evidently of a kneeling man, though he was missing his head and his feet and much of the left side of his body. A broken stem protruded a millimetre or so from his back. It wasn't the piece itself that so shook him, however. It was the *style* of it. Because it didn't look Chinese at all.

It looked Chimu.

II

Rebecca glared at Andriama, hoping that hostility might send him on his way; but he didn't even seem to notice as he pulled out a chair for himself and sat down, raised his hand for a waiter, called out for a hot chocolate and a pastry. 'You're here early today,' he said. 'You stay last night in Tulear, perhaps?'

Rebecca had passed a police checkpoint on her way in. They were so common in Madagascar, she hadn't given it a second thought. Yet something in Andriama's manner made her suspect that this meeting was no accident. 'I've just come from Eden,' she told him.

'From Eden?' He pretended surprise. 'You must have set off early.'

'Yes.'

'You bring me perhaps the blood information for your father and sister? Perhaps that is why you come so early?' Rebecca had forgotten about that. She rummaged through her bag for the slip of paper Therese had given her, passed it across. Andriama studied it briefly, then frowned in genuine perplexity.

'What is it?' asked Rebecca.

Andriama glanced up at her. 'We find two blood-types on the boat,' he said. 'One blood they tell me is woman blood. Two blood they tell me is man blood. I do not understand how they know this blood is man blood and that blood is woman blood, but they assure me—'

'It's to do with chromosomes,' said Rebecca.

'Yes,' smiled Andriama. 'That is what they assure me.' He set down the paper she'd given him, tapped it significantly. 'This woman blood matches your sister.'

'But the male blood doesn't match my father's?'

'Exact!' Andriama beamed like a proud teacher. 'This is strange. I think for sure this will be your father's blood.

It is AB negative blood. According to my doctors, you do not find this AB negative blood at all among Malagasy men. You do not find much in foreigners, either, but never in Malagasy.'

'It's rare?'

'Yes! Exact! It is rare. It is rare foreigner's blood.' He smiled wolfishly, and she saw his shrewdness suddenly, why he'd become a policeman, how he'd made his way up through the ranks. 'You tell me maybe who it come from, this rare foreigner's blood?'

Rebecca shrugged. 'Pierre?'

Andriama shook his head. 'No. We know already the blood of Monsieur Desmoulins. This is not it.'

'You know Pierre's blood?'

'Oh yes. For sure we know Monsieur Desmoulins and his blood.' He gave her a mischievous smile. 'He is sometimes our guest after his nights out in Tulear, you know.' His order arrived. He clapped his hands with delight, plopped four rough sugar-lumps into his hot chocolate, then took a huge bite from his pastry, leaving his lips glossy with icing.

'How about the South Africans who found the boat?' asked Rebecca. 'Maybe the blood came from one of them.'

'No. We ask already. Is not them.'

'Eden often has foreign guests,' said Rebecca. 'So does Pierre.'

'You will give me perhaps a list of visitors?'

'Of course. Next time I'm in Tulear. Now if you'll excuse me—'

'Anyone else?'

'No. Not that I can think of.'

'But you are seen in Tulear yourself with a foreigner two nights ago. A tall man. English, I'm told.'

'Daniel?' For some reason, even the suggestion made Rebecca freeze a little. 'No.'

'How can you be sure?'

'I just am,' she told him stiffly. 'That has nothing to do with him. But why all these questions? I thought you believed it was just an accident.'

Andriama gestured vaguely. 'I am a mountain man. These nights in Tulear are too hot for me. I cannot sleep. My brain makes circles; it makes patterns. I tell you, I think, that people are sometimes taken for money near here.'

'Kidnapped?'

'Exact! Yes! Kidnapped.'

'But you also said that hadn't happened with my father and sister. You gave some very good reasons. I forget exactly—'

'Yes. Three reason.' He held up his thumb. 'People know your father not have big money.' Up came his index finger. 'Why take your father *and* sister? Kidnappers need someone back home to raise money for them.' The middle finger. 'No one receive a ransom demand.'

'That sounds convincing to me.'

'But!' Andriama spread all his fingers now. 'What if these kidnappers never mean for your father to pay?'

Rebecca swallowed. 'I don't understand.'

'What if they mean for *you* to pay? You are success. You are rich. Your father is proud man, he tells everyone how big success and rich you are. Perhaps these bad peoples hear of this. Perhaps they think, if they take him, you will come home and they will make you pay.'

'Wouldn't I have heard from them by now?'

'Yes!' beamed Andriama. 'You would.'

There was silence. Rebecca could hear her heart pounding. 'What are you suggesting?' she asked, trying to be imperious, but her mouth was so dry that it came out as a treacherous croak.

'I think it is clear exact what I suggest.' He leaned forward. 'We find no bodies yet. In a drowning like this, we expect to find bodies by now.'

Her outrage was genuine. 'How dare you say that?'

'I sorry.' He didn't look it. He dipped another sugar-lump into his hot chocolate until it had soaked brown, then he popped it in his mouth and crunched it with evident pleasure between his stubby molars. 'You visit my good friend Mustafa Habib two nights ago. You stay with him two hour.'

'You've been watching me?' He shook his head to deny her charge. Rebecca frowned. 'You're watching Mustafa.'

Andriama shook his head again, but his grin betrayed him. She asked: 'Why are you watching your good friend Mustafa?'

'Is privilege of being police that *we* are the ones who ask the questions,' answered Andriama. 'What you talk about with Mustafa?'

'That's private.'

'Mustafa very busy man this weekend. He visit people. He ask for money, big money. My people hear whispers that this money is ransom money.'

'I know nothing about any money Mustafa might be raising,' said Rebecca. 'I suggest you ask him, not me.'

Andriama nodded. 'We will.'

'Anything else?' asked Rebecca. 'If not, I'll—'

'Sit! Sit!' he said. 'Listen: We not like kidnapping in this country. We make it stop, everyone safer. But very difficult to make stop when people pay. It encourage others. So! We pass new laws. You know these laws?'

'This has nothing to do with me.'

'These laws say is criminal not just to ask money for kidnap, but also to *pay* money for kidnap. We put people who pay in jail.'

'You're lying,' said Rebecca weakly.

'Oh yes, is true.' He held up his hand, spread his fingers. 'Five years.' He dipped more sugar into his chocolate, watched greedily as it turned brown. 'You know our jails? We have one in Tulear.' He turned and pointed down one of the nearby streets. 'I show you, if you wish. They not like English jails, nice, lots of room, bathroom and shower, one television each, doctor, lawyer, family, friends visit every day. Our jails nasty jails. Men, women all together, wash and make shit together.' He shook his head sadly. 'A pretty girl like you, I worry for her.'

'Are you threatening me?'

'Me? No. I give information, travel information. And is not just jail you must think about. If *we* know Mustafa collects money, bad peoples know also. Greedy peoples. They think maybe this their chance to make themselves rich. When Mustafa gives you money, they—'

'I've had enough of this.'

'—they come for you,' insisted Andriama. 'Guns, knives. They cut your throat, here to here, for money like this.'

Rebecca rose to her feet. 'How dare you talk to me this way!'

'Because I want to help you,' said Andriama. 'Tell me what happen and I do everything I can. What chance have you, alone?' He leaned forward, tapped the tabletop. 'Listen – these kidnappers watch what you do. Already they see you talk with me today. They think now for sure we work together.' He spread his hands to show her the obviousness of what he was saying. 'You have nothing to lose.'

'Jesus!' exclaimed Rebecca. She walked unsteadily

away, hands on her head. What a mess this was becoming! She consulted her watch. Nine fifty, still no sign of Mustafa or the kidnappers. Andriama was finishing his pastry, watching her closely. She hurried for her Jeep, her nerves jangling. A stone had got into her right shoe and now pressed against her heel. She tried to pick it out but lost balance, had to put her hand against the wall.

A phone began to ring nearby. Rebecca looked around. Some Madagascans eked out a tenuous living renting out their mobiles. One such man was sitting at a school-desk on the pavement, fanning himself with an old newspaper. He had no chin at all, as though a team of crack surgeons had cut out his jawbone and stitched his Adams apple directly back to his lower lip. Rebecca watched with a sense of premonition as he answered his phone, listened for a few moments, then held it out to her. '*C'est pour vous,*' he said.

THIRTY-FOUR

I

Knox had too much to do to spend the morning in the boathouse basement, but he was still in something of a daze as he went back up the steps, locked the steel door then hid it again behind its plasterboard façade.

First things first: he was anything but an authority on Chimu ceramics. He certainly couldn't make a determination of so small and damaged a fragment with any confidence. And even if it was Chimu, it didn't mean it had come from the same wreck as the Chinese ceramics. It could theoretically have come from some other wreck, or even just have been brought here by a collector, and then been lost.

But the chances of that . . .

Knox had occasionally come across the Chimu while working as an Egyptologist. The Early Chimu – better known as the Moche – had been pyramid builders too, and so once or twice he'd been asked about the possibility of cultural crossover. On such occasions, he'd usually smiled politely and pointed out that the Early Chimu had built their pyramids well over a thousand years after the Egyptians. More to the point, they'd lived in Peru.

It was one thing to imagine a Chinese ship sailing west from the Cape to within sight of South America, then turning back. It was another altogether to have them heading south down the east coast and then reaching the Pacific through the Straits of Magellan *a hundred years before Magellan did*. Yet that was what this fragment implied.

The Chimu of the black ceramics were a much later people than their pyramid-building forebears. They'd first come to notice in the early tenth century, but it had only been in the fourteenth that they'd become a major regional power. They'd worshipped the moon and the sea, had sacrificed their own children. When Francisco Pizarro and the Spaniards had sailed south from Panama on their voyage of discovery to Peru, it had been off the port city of Tumbez that they'd first anchored; and though the Chimu had themselves recently been absorbed into the Inca Empire, Tumbez had still been in essence a Chimu city.

A colleague of Pizarro's called Pedro de Cieza de León had written a vivid account of that first contact. It had always struck Knox as curious. Dozens of men had paddled balsa-wood rafts out to Pizarro's ship, bringing fresh fruit, fish and llama meat to trade. Once on board, they'd exclaimed excitedly over the crowing of a rooster, the beards of the Spanish men, the blackness of the slaves. That is to say, it hadn't been this great foreign ship in itself that had so amazed them, but the *detail* of it. Pizarro was the first European to venture so far south; and though Magellan and his fleet had already passed Tierra del Fuego on their circumnavigation, they'd left the coast behind far further south. Maybe word had already reached the Chimu about these strange people from across the seas, but, if so, they'd been impressively relaxed about it, for the Spanish had taken death and disease and the brutal pursuit of gold with them wherever they'd gone. So maybe, just maybe, other strange visitors had arrived in great ships before. Visitors without beards or black skins.

Knox was an archaeologist. He enjoyed a good speculation as much as the next man, but he liked evidence he could see and touch before taking it seriously. Aside from the Norse settlement at L'Anse aux Meadows, there were just a few bare scraps of evidence of pre-Columbian contact with the New World. A Roman-style terracotta head had been discovered in the foundations of a pre-Columbian Mexican house. Carved Olmec heads appeared to reflect African features; a Malinese fleet was known to have sailed westwards across the Atlantic; and Columbus himself had been told by the natives of Hispaniola of previous visitors with black skins. There was evidence from the plant kingdom too. The sweet potato, an American endemic, had spread across Polynesia long before Columbus. The resin in Peruvian mummifications came from New Guinea trees. African gourds had been found in Central America, and there were claims of cocaine and tobacco in ancient Egyptian contexts. American peppers had been described by Aristotle's pupil Theophrastus, and there was a pineapple in a Pompeii mosaic. Chicken bones carbon-dated to the fourteenth or fifteenth century had been found on the Chilean coast, far to the south of Tumbez, even though chickens were supposedly introduced by Europeans. But, when all was said and done, it was a fairly meagre catalogue of evidence, especially as every scrap of it could be explained away by natural causes, fraud or coincidence. Extraordinary theories needed extraordinary proof, after all.

And maybe he'd just found it.

II

Rebecca took a moment to calm herself before she took the phone. 'This is Rebecca Kirkpatrick,' she said.

'You have the money?' A man's voice, but the signal was too weak and the crackle too loud for her to tell much more than that.

'Yes,' she lied. 'Yes I do.'

'You have one hour. There is—'

'I want to speak to my father.'

'You have one hour. There is a sheet—'

'I speak to my father or you get nothing,' she yelled. She ended the call and stood there clutching the phone in trembling hands, waiting for it to ring again, praying for it to ring. The phone's owner reached tentatively to take it from her. She held up a palm to fend him off. They'd call back. For five hundred million ariary, they'd call back. If they didn't call, it meant they didn't have Adam and Emilia, it had all been a sham. She'd go straight to Andriama and tell—

The phone jumped suddenly in her hand. She almost spilled it. 'Do that again,' said the man, when she answered, 'and we kill them both. You understand?'

'I want to speak with—'

Another man's voice came on. 'Rebecca,' he said. 'Rebecca, my darling.'

The sound of his voice transfixed her. She'd have recognised it anywhere. 'Dad!' she wailed. 'Dad.'

'Please, Rebecca. Do as they ask. We're both well but—'

There was the sound of scuffling and then the kidnapper came back on. 'You have one hour,' he told her curtly. 'There's a map beneath your windscreen wiper. Follow its directions to the place marked. Travel alone. We will be watching. You understand?'

'Yes.'

'You will find a yellow bag there. Put the money in the bag then return to Tulear. Tell no one. If the money is all there, we will release your father and sister. If not—' The phone went dead. Rebecca stared at it dumbly. The trader took it back from her, asked apologetically for money. She reached into her bag and thrust some banknotes at him. She couldn't concentrate, she couldn't think of anything but the echo of her father's voice. *Rebecca, my darling!* He'd never called her that before! Yvette had always been his one and only darling. She felt euphoric, drunk and terrified all at once. *Rebecca, my darling!* He was alive. Emilia was alive. She was going to get them back. She walked unsteadily to the Jeep. A map. The man had said something about a map. But where? She couldn't remember. She searched anxiously until she found it tucked beneath her wiper.

'Hey!'

Rebecca turned to see Andriama hurrying towards her. She threw the map on to her passenger seat, climbed in and roared away. Andriama chased her for a few paces before giving up and waving down a taxi. She swung left at the first opportunity, left again, hiding herself in the maze of streets. She looked in her rear-view, couldn't see anyone following. She unfolded the crude map on her steering wheel as she drove, but it was difficult to read, what with her eyes blurred and the roads bumpy and her hands shaking wildly. She pulled to the side. It directed her to take Route Nationale 7 through Andranohinaly, past an orange road-side stall and then down a track to her right. Andranohinaly was on the way to Ilakaka, the same road Mustafa would currently be driving along in the other direction. A stroke of luck at last! She took out his card and dialled his mobile. It rang and rang but nobody answered. She called his home instead and made Ahdaf describe her father's car: a blue Mercedes 4x4 with tinted windows. She was putting her phone back in her bag when she noticed the GPS transmitter. She'd forgotten all about it, but now she switched it on and put it in her pocket, set off again for the Ilakaka road.

Traffic was mercifully thin, but she'd only driven about eight miles when the Jeep began to limp and then she heard the distinctive flapping of a flat tyre. She gave a cry and pulled to the side. The Jeep's tyres had been popping forever; she'd changed them often in the distant

'There's no time.'

'You must count,' he insisted.

She shrugged her shoulders helplessly, tipped the money out, stacked up the bundles. She kept glancing down the road, expecting the police at any second. There were fifty bundles in all, five piles of ten. She tested two at random. Each comprised ten wads of twenty brand-new 50,000 ariary notes stapled together. It took her a few moments to do the arithmetic, then she nodded at Mustafa. 'Good,' he said. 'Now you remember what I told you about interest?'

A knot of stress tightened in Rebecca's nape. 'Can't we sort this out later?'

'I had to sign a contract to get this money,' he told her. He took two sets of papers from his jacket pocket, rested them on the side window. 'That is what took me so long, because my lawyer had to make sure—'

'For heaven's sake!'

He said apologetically: 'Please. You must understand my situation. This is a great deal of money. I had to give certain undertakings before I could borrow it. I need to secure myself against any loss, but I wouldn't want you to think I'd take advantage of you. If you read then sign each of the pages, as I've already done, then we can—'

'I don't have the time.'

Mustafa spread his hands. 'I'm sorry, but I must have some form of receipt. Surely you can see that.'

Rebecca put a hand to her forehead. 'What does it say? Tell me what it says.'

'Certainly.' He took one of the contracts and began to read it aloud.

'No!' she cried. 'How much interest?'

'Ah. Let me see.' He leafed through the pages. 'Yes. Here it is. Five per cent, with two weeks to repay. But if it goes over two weeks, there are certain penalties.'

'What penalties?'

'Give me a moment,' he said, shuffling through the pages. Rebecca shook her head in dismay. She had no time for this. 'Your pen,' she said.

'But you should read this before you—'

'Give me your fucking pen!' She peeled the bandage from her right palm, signed the pages of both contracts, stuffed one copy in her holdall. The fresh air felt sharp and good upon her lacerated but healing palm, so she tore the bandages from her left hand too, then packed the money back in the holdall. It was so heavy she had to heft it across to the Jeep. She threw it on the passenger seat, ran round to the driver's door. Mustafa came across. 'Thank you,' she told him.

He waved it away. 'Is there anything else I can do?'

Rebecca shook her head. 'They told me to go there alone. They said they'd be watching.'

'Good luck, then.'

She nodded and sped away, horribly aware that she was already late, praying that the kidnappers would cut her a little slack.

THIRTY-FIVE

I

There was still no sign of Rebecca at the lodge. Knox unlocked its front door then went in search of Michel's medical records. When he entered the clinic, however, he noticed the handheld GPS tracker on the examination table, pinning down a folded handwritten note that Rebecca must have left for Therese. He knew he shouldn't read it, but he did so anyway. He went a little numb at her dry account of receiving the ransom note, of everything she'd done since. He read through her plans for the day, her request that Therese get the GPS handset to Chief of Police Andriama in Tulear if she didn't reappear.

If she didn't reappear . . .

His heart clenched; he felt sick. *What was she thinking, taking this on all by herself?* He needed to help her. Michel would just have to wait. He turned on the GPS handset, checked for recent transmissions. Nothing since last night, presumably when Rebecca had tested the equipment. He checked his watch. Damn. It was past ten already. He'd used up half the morning in the boathouse. He went out, locked up behind him, pushed Adam's track-bike over to the generator building, filled it with fuel, straddled it and kicked it into life. Then he swung it around in a tight circle, opened up its throttle and roared away along the track towards Tulear.

II

Many of the villages Rebecca passed were too small and straggling to have name signs. She had to stop every few miles to ask for Andranohinaly, only to be pointed further down the road. Eventually she reached it, however, and set about looking for the orange wayside stall. She passed a broken-down, one-room shack. In the hazy midday sun it looked nut-brown, but she could imagine it might look orange at sunset. She pulled in. Several planks bore peeling flecks of orange paint. If this was it, there should be a turning to the right immediately afterwards. Sure enough, a thin track led off the road fifty metres further along, but it was rutted and narrow, more footpath than proper road.

She pulled into its mouth, sat there clutching her steering wheel for the best part of a minute before deciding it couldn't be right. She pulled back out on to the main road, drove on for another four kilometres before cursing out loud, swinging around and driving back to the track. She lurched along it to the base of a wooded hill, then snaked upwards in increasingly steep hairpins. Her doubts grew stronger and stronger, but she was too late to second-guess herself again. The surface kept deteriorating; the vegetation grew thicker, branches reaching out at her, thorns screeching on the Jeep's flanks like fingernails on a blackboard. This couldn't be it. It just *couldn't*. She wanted to turn around but the track was too narrow; and the hillside was too steep and the corners too sharp to make reversing practicable. She pressed on in increasing dismay until she reached a heap of broken rock and loose debris left across the track by a small landslide. She crossed it at crawling speed, leaning almost sideways in her seat. Her relief at making it safely to the other side lasted only to the next hairpin when the track turned back on itself and she reached the place from which the landslide had fallen. The surface was completely gone. There was no possible way forwards. She was trapped.

She gave a yell of frustration. Her cry echoed forlornly. A wild dog barked. Her father and sister were depending upon her, and she was already grotesquely late. She needed to get back to the main road right now. With no way to turn, she had no choice but to try reversing. Negotiating the hairpin backwards was a nightmare. She kept hauling on the hand-brake and leaning out the window to check her wheels weren't over the edge. Even after she'd successfully made it, she still had the buttress of rock to cross. It had been difficult enough going forwards. In reverse it was unbearable. Pebbles cascaded from beneath her wheels, clattering down the steep hillside until they were netted by the undergrowth. Each time she heard another miniature avalanche, her heart leapt. The Jeep was tilted so far over by now that she was pressed against the driver door, could see nothing in her mirrors.

And then, perhaps inevitably, the steady trickle of earth turned to a cascade, and the ground simply sheared away beneath her, and the Jeep began sliding down the hill like a ship launched sideways into the sea.

THIRTY-SIX

I

Knox sped south as fast as the track would allow him, the bike's balding tyres slithering on the dust, forcing him every so often to throw out a foot to save himself. But he reached Tulear in good time, stopped to check the GPS handset. Rebecca had turned on the transmitter at last; and though the tracker's map of Madagascar was rudimentary, it was evident she'd taken the Ilakaka road. He followed signs for it, passed out of the suburbs. The road grew better; he opened the throttle wide. It didn't take him long to reach the place from where the most recent signal had been sent, but there was no sign of her. According to her note, she'd set the transmissions for once every hour. He'd just have to wait. With nothing else to do, he turned on his mobile. It found a signal, notified him of messages. Most were from Miles, sounding increasingly strained, wondering what had happened to him, begging him to get in touch as soon as he could.

'About bloody time!' he erupted, when Knox complied. 'Are you on your way back?'

'Not yet,' said Knox.

'Things are turning ugly here,' said Miles. 'We've found jack shit, our new tests have come back negative and the Chinese have sniffed something. They're sending a delegation.'

'Christ! When?'

'The day after tomorrow. And I need you here. No excuses. We're going to have to blind them with science and archaeology. I can do the science, but I need you for the archaeology.'

'I'll be there,' Knox promised him. 'But listen: I think I'm on to something.'

'What kind of something?'

'I need your word first. You're not to tell Cheung or anyone else. Not yet.'

'Whatever you say. Now spill.'

He gave Miles a digest of what he'd been up to since he'd left the *Maritsa*. The shards in Eden's wall; Adam's interest in medieval charts; the boathouse basement and the Chinese artefacts. He outlined his theory about the treasure ship floating itself off the reef and sailing down to Eden's waters; and why the Kirkpatricks might have lied about it.

Miles was silent for a second or two after he'd finished, as though struggling to take it all in. 'Any chance you can get us proof?' he asked. 'Something to show the Chinese?'

Knox thought of the blue-and-white porcelain bowl, the enamelled flask. 'I'll need to clear it with one of the Kirkpatricks first.'

'And when will you be able to do that?'

He checked the GPS tracker again. A new signal had just come in, about ten miles to his east. 'With any luck,' he said, 'maybe pretty soon.'

II

Once the ground started to give way beneath Rebecca, everything became reflexive, something she couldn't stop, only manage. She sat up straight and buckled her seat-belt. Her rear-end cannoned a tree and the impact turned the Jeep face-on to the slope. She stamped hard on the brake and clutch, thrust her gear-stick into reverse, but something snapped and then the Jeep was bounding down the steep gradient, wheels barely in contact with the earth, punching a way through the thin vegetation, branches and tendrils slapping the windscreen. A baobab loomed. She wrenched the steering wheel around but it had no effect. She braced her feet against the floor and threw up her forearms to protect her head. The front left hit hard. She heard the crunch of metal and the tinkle of a headlight. The Jeep flew up on to two wheels and then fell back. The brush opened up in front of her; the hillside simply dropped away. The Jeep plunged down an embankment and smashed nose-first into the compacted earth of the track which had wended back on itself. The bonnet buckled like a concertina against her knees. The windscreen and side windows shattered. Pebbles of glass spat everywhere. She slammed against her seat-belt, her head flew forward and she felt her left shoulder dislocate. The Jeep tumbled over itself before settling on its passenger door. It rocked for a few moments and then was still.

Rebecca's head slowly cleared. She checked her arms, legs, head and torso, was relieved to find scratches and bruises but no serious damage except for her shoulder. She looked out. Smoke and water vapour rose in clouds from her crumpled bonnet. The slope was so steep that the Jeep was only held in place by a tangled net of spiny brush, creaking and groaning beneath the strain. She could smell diesel and oil. She needed to get out quick. She tried to unfasten her seat-belt, but the buckle had jammed. She shimmied out sideways instead, keeping her shoulder as still as possible, retrieved the holdall and her bag, dropped them through the empty windscreen and followed them out. She had to jump down to the ground. The jolt was so exquisite on her left shoulder that she cried out, both from the pain itself and from knowledge of what lay ahead. Her shoulder had dislocated twice before, once after an awkward parachute landing, once deep in the Australian outback, trying to grab the reins of a snake-spooked horse that had bucked her. Catching that damned mare and riding her six miles back to camp had taken Rebecca three hours. For the last two of those, her shoulder muscles had been in spasm. It had been the most gruelling ordeal of her life, the kind that ages you, that makes you understand why patients in chronic pain seek to die. They'd had to cut open her shoulder to fix it. God only knew what would happen in Madagascar.

She took her mobile from her bag, but it had no signal. She breathed deeply to quell her rising panic. On safari in Kenya last year, a knuckle-head South African had tried to impress her with all his scars, so she'd retorted with her shoulder. He'd laughed at that. Dislocations didn't count. Christ only knew how many times he'd dislocated his shoulder; he just slammed it against the nearest tree. If some loudmouth guide could do it, thought Rebecca grimly, then she could, too. She held her left arm with its ball as near its socket as she could figure, then threw herself hard against the front bumper of the Jeep. She screamed in agony and failure. She stood, wiped away her tears, gritted her teeth and hurled herself even harder. The pain was so fierce and prolonged that she screamed and carried on screaming, her screams turning into cries of frustration. It wasn't going to work. Your body would tell you these things if you listened. She squatted down. As a zoologist, she understood the rudiments of primate anatomy. The shoulder wasn't a typical ball-and-socket joint, because it needed to facilitate such a wide range of movement. The ball therefore sat upon the socket rather like an egg upon its cup, held in place by muscles, tendons and ligaments. That made it all the more prone to dislocation, but it also made it easier to fix. Reduction was a matter of angles, torque and traction. That South African had been a braggart, but not a liar.

The carry-straps of Mustafa's canvas holdall had detachable metal buckles at either end. She took them off with her teeth and her good right hand, clipped them together into a single, long rope. The muscles in her left shoulder were beginning to twitch and fibrillate. In ten minutes, it would be too late. She tried not to let panic hurry her into mistakes. She tied slipknots in either end, tightened one loop around her left wrist, the second around her left foot. Then she stood up tall, lifting her leg so that the strap was taut, but no more. Satisfied, she now pressed down and outwards with her foot, pulling her wrist, arm and shoulder forwards. She could feel the ball getting closer and closer to its socket, but it still

didn't stop at once, lest it was being watched. Then he saw wisps of smoke rising from the hillside and had a sudden dread that he was already too late, so he turned around and drove back, hid his bike in the trees and continued on foot, keeping to the verges so that he could take cover should anyone—

Rebecca came charging out of the trees to his left, yelling and swinging a rock. He put up his arms to protect himself, but she'd already recognised him. 'You!' she said. 'What the hell are *you* doing here?' But then she saw the GPS handset and her question answered itself. 'I left that for Therese!' she protested.

'For God's sake,' he said. 'You can't take on this kind of thing alone. Why didn't you tell me?'

'They told me not to.' Her eyes filled with dismay. 'They've got Adam and Emilia. They said they'd kill them if I told anyone at all.'

'They're alive? You're sure?'

'I spoke to my father. He said "we're both well". He said "*we*".'

'That's fantastic!' said Knox.

'But I'm late,' she said. 'I'm so late.'

'Then let's get moving, eh?' He took the holdall from her, led her down to the motorbike, pulled it out of the trees. 'Where to?' he asked.

'They said to turn right after an orange roadside stall. There was a stall. It looked sort of orange.' She started breathing fast, fighting down panic. 'I must have got it wrong.'

He could see how close to the edge she was. He put his hand to her cheek. 'Listen to me, Rebecca,' he said. 'Kidnappers have strong nerves. They have to, by definition; they wouldn't be in the business otherwise. They're greedy too. Five hundred million ariary is a ton of money. So this isn't over. Not by a long shot. You understand?'

She nodded, covered his hand with her own. 'I'm sorry about last night,' she said. 'Things got on top of me.'

'It was my fault,' he told her. 'I should have told you the truth about myself that first night. I had good reasons not to, I swear, but even so I should have—'

'It's okay,' she said. She gave his hand a squeeze. 'Explanations can wait. Right now we need to get going.'

He nodded, straddled the bike, balanced the holdall on his lap. Rebecca climbed on behind, anchored herself to him with her right arm. He drove to the main road, turned towards Ilakaka. It was about ten minutes before they reached a vividly orange roadside stall with a thinly grassed avenue on the right just after it. He didn't look around, lest she take it as reproach, just swung right down the track, followed it to a bright glade with an ancient tamarind at its centre. He circled it once, idled to a stop, waited for Rebecca to get off, then rocked the bike up on to its stands.

'There should be a bag,' she said. 'A yellow bag.'

'They must have been back already. Write a note. Explain what happened. Assure them you have the money and want to give it to them. Give them a way to contact you.'

She nodded and took a pen from her bag, uncapped it with her teeth, was scribbling her note when she hesitated and looked around. 'There's no mobile signal in Eden,' she said.

'So we'll stay in Tulear tonight.'

'What was the name of that hotel?'

He told her. She wrote it down, pinned the note with a stone at the base of the tamarind. He couldn't help but notice that she was doing everything with her right hand. 'What's up with your left arm?' he frowned, as she walked back to the bike.

'My shoulder,' she told him. 'I dislocated it when I crashed the Jeep.'

'For fuck's sake! Why didn't you say?'

'It's okay. I put it back.'

'You *what*?'

'It's no big deal,' she assured him, as she climbed back astride the bike. 'You just slam it against the nearest tree.'

THIRTY-SEVEN

I

Boris reached Eden mid-afternoon. He saw the boat first, then the boathouse and the sign. He set down his bags and walked along the edge of the trees, the Heckler & Koch in his pocket ready for a quick draw in case anyone should appear; but no one did.

He made his way up the track to the compound. There was no one there either. The main building was locked and all the cabins were empty. There was no sign of Knox at all. He went back down to the beach, stripped off his trousers, waded out to the boat. There was a bag on deck, tagged as belonging to Matthew Richardson, Knox's alias. Boris opened it up and rummaged around.

There was dive-gear inside, expensive-looking stuff, not the sort you'd just forget about, or leave lying around for the benefit any light-fingered passer-by.

No doubt about it, Knox would be coming back aboard this boat some time very soon.

And Boris intended to be waiting.

II

Knox took it slow on the drive back to Tulear, now that he knew Rebecca had a sore shoulder. Even so hampered, however, she was a good pillion passenger, taking her cues from him, leaning as he leaned. Her chin was on his shoulder, her mouth against her neck, her breath upon his throat. Every time he braked to avoid a pothole or rock in the road, deceleration pressed her against his back.

The afternoon had sped by. The sun began setting as they approached Tulear. Knox turned on the headlight only to discover that it was broken. Gloaming turned into night. There was a cacophony ahead, a wedding party blocking the road, tooting horns and yelling exultantly out their windows. He could have pushed and wended his way through, but instead he waited until the long train had finally passed. It made him realise that he didn't want this ride to end. Maybe Rebecca felt the same; he could feel her arm tightening around his chest.

They reached their hotel. She climbed gingerly off the back. 'Why don't you sort out our rooms?' he suggested. 'I'll go get some bandages and things for your hands.' He found a chemist open a couple of blocks away, bought all the first-aid supplies that could possibly be of use, added a bag of ice from a general store. He could hear water running when he arrived outside her room, knocked. The water stopped and she opened her door a few moments later, a towel wrapped around her waist, her blouse unbuttoned but clasped closed with her right hand.

He held up his bags of shopping. 'You want me to do your dressings?' he asked.

'Please,' she said. She walked to her bed, stretched out on her back, still holding her blouse. He closed her door, went to kneel beside her, rested the ice-pack upon her left shoulder. He inspected her hands first. They were still dirty from the day, despite her efforts at washing them, but at least the coral cuts seemed to be healing well. He cleaned her left palm with gel, then painted it with iodine and put on new dressings. He motioned for her right hand. Her blouse fell open a little way as she held it out. She made no effort to close it. He looked down at her, then up into her eyes, already there waiting for him. She reached out and touched his cheek, stroked it with her thumb.

He said softly: 'You asked me the other day if I had someone special.'

'You're married,' she said. 'You have a wife.'

He thought of Emilia, of the strong possibility that he was Michel's father, of the complications that would surely ensue if he let temptation get the better of him. 'I have a family,' he told her.

Her face fell; she looked stricken. 'Stay with me,' she said. 'Just for tonight.'

'I can't.'

'You mean you don't want to.'

'No,' he said. 'I mean I can't.'

Her mobile rang at that moment, its buzzer making it shiver and rotate upon the bedside table. They looked at it and then at each other with the same thought: the kidnappers had found the note. Rebecca breathed in deep as she picked it up and answered it. 'Yes?' she said. Colour seemed to drain from her complexion as she listened. Her expression hardened. She gave directions to the hotel, ended the call and set her phone back down on the bedside table.

'Well?' frowned Knox. 'Who was it?'

'My business partner, Titch,' she told him. 'He's just flown in from England.'

III

Rebecca clutched the ice-pack to her shoulder when she went down to meet Titch, dribbles of water running coldly down her flanks. His taxi pulled up. He took his time paying the fare and then retrieving his luggage, as though apprehensive of his welcome. Rebecca went over to greet him, kissed him on either cheek. 'What are you doing here, Titch?' she frowned.

'Your phone-call,' he said, shouldering his overnight bag. 'It sounded like you could use some help.'

'You flew all this way because of a phone call?'

He glanced over at Daniel, standing a few paces away in the hotel entrance, lowered his voice so that he couldn't be overheard. 'You said you'd had a ransom demand. What with our recent conversation about the company finances, you know, I thought you might need a hand putting it together.'

She laid her hand on his elbow, touched beyond words. 'I don't know what to say,' she said. 'But it's okay, I've been able to borrow it. You should have called.'

'I tried. You never answered. Besides, I figured you could use a friend anyway.' He glanced over at Daniel again, gave her an interrogative look, as if to ask whether he could speak freely in front of him. She assured him he could, led him across and performed the introductions.

'Daniel,' said Titch, as they shook hands. 'So you're the one who rescued Rebecca from the reef?'

'He had to rescue me again today,' she said with a wry smile. 'It's becoming rather an irritating habit of his.'

'Is that right?' asked Titch.

Something in his voice reminded Rebecca of the uncomfortable night he'd taken her hand and made his
declaration. Maybe there was more to his flying out here
than he was letting on; but she put the disloyal thought
aside. 'You must be starving,' she said. 'I know I am.'

'You want to go out?'

She shook her head. She dared not leave the ransom
money unguarded in her room, but nor did she much
fancy lugging it around town.

'I'll pick us up some pizzas,' said Daniel. 'Give you
two a chance to catch up.'

'Thanks.' She led Titch up to her room, out on to her
balcony, talked him through everything that had
happened since they'd last spoken. She was just finishing
up when Daniel arrived back with beers and some boxes
of pizza: thin, scorched crusts smeared with tomato sauce
and sprinkled sparingly with toppings. Titch tore off a
strip that he rolled up like calzone and stuffed into his
mouth. Then he turned to Rebecca, flapping his hands
from the heat of it, evidently wanting to say something,
but struggling to swallow. 'So what now?' he managed
finally.

'I guess we wait for the kidnappers to contact us,' said
Rebecca.

'Can't we *do* something? I mean, what about that mobile
phone guy?'

'What mobile phone guy?'

'The one the kidnappers called to give you your instructions.'

'Someone just knew his number, that's all.'

'Yes, but how did they know to call just when you were passing? I mean, either he gave them the nod or they had someone watching.' Rebecca frowned, a little worried she'd not thought of this herself. 'Maybe we could talk to him in the morning, see if he knows anything.'

'It's a good idea,' acknowledged Rebecca.

'And there's something else,' said Titch. 'The kidnappers originally contacted you up at the Eden Reserve, right?'

'So?'

'So what if they didn't get your message in the clearing? I mean, what if they still think the best way to contact you is by slipping a note beneath Eden's front door?' Rebecca glanced at Daniel, who nodded. 'The thing is,' continued Titch. 'Perhaps one of us should be there, just in case. I mean, it can't be you, Rebecca. You've clearly got to be here in case they try to contact you or call your mobile, right? But *I* could go.' He glanced back and forth between her and Daniel. 'It's been a while since I've ridden a motorbike, and you'd have to give me directions, but—'

'I'll go,' said Daniel.

'No!' protested Rebecca.

'He's right,' said Daniel, getting to his feet. 'One of us should be there. It makes sense for it to be me.'

'You're not leaving now, are you?' asked Rebecca, dismayed. 'You can't. Your headlight doesn't even work.'

'Yes, but I can leave at dawn, and that means filling her up while the petrol station's still open. Besides, I'm bushed. It's been one hell of a day.' He put his hand on her shoulder as he made his way past her to the balcony door, and she felt the jolt of contact run right through her. But if Daniel felt it too, he gave no sign. He merely nodded at Titch. 'It was good to meet you,' he said.

'Likewise,' said Titch.

THIRTY-EIGHT

I

Daniel's departure, and a stomach full of pizza, made Rebecca realise how tired she was. Titch began making noises about getting himself a room, but Rebecca's had a spare bed and she felt the need for company, not least because of all that ransom money in the holdall. They washed and went to their separate beds, turned out the lights. She lay there on her back, watching the headlights of passing cars painting yellow lines upon her ceiling, making desultory conversation with Titch about the office and their various projects. She couldn't help thinking, while they were talking, how *remote* London seemed, how indifferent she was to news and gossip of it. They

352

fell silent for a little while, then she said: 'I'm going to stay here.' She hadn't consciously considered remaining in Madagascar until then, but the moment she said it, she realised it had been inevitable.

In the neighbouring bed, Titch drew in breath then pushed himself up on to his elbow. 'How do you mean? For how long?'

She heard anxiety in his voice, decided to allay it. 'Just until I can sort things out properly.'

'What about America?'

'Fuck America,' she said, more vehemently then she'd intended. 'This is family.' She waited for him to respond, but he remained quiet so long that she realised there was a question he dared not ask. 'Yes,' she said. 'I'll stay whatever happens with my father and sister.'

'And what about us? What about our company?'

'You'll be fine.'

'It won't work without you.'

'Yes, it will.'

'It won't. You know it won't.'

'Let's talk about it in the morning.'

He seemed to accept that. They wished each other goodnight and within fifteen minutes or so, his breathing pattern indicated he'd fallen asleep. Rebecca found it harder to drop off. Her soft tissues ached from the day's ordeals. Apprehension about tomorrow was exacerbated by not having Daniel at her side. She strove for soothing thoughts, for happy places, but it wasn't easy. She kept picking up her mobile to check the time, make sure the battery still had some juice in it; but each time she checked it, its dial would light up, draining it a little bit more. Her recharger was in Eden. Daniel was about to head that way. She wondered if she could justify going with him to collect it, but then she heard a motorbike outside. She slipped from the bed and went out on to her balcony, only to find his bike already gone.

She returned to bed, dozed off, woke a little later to find that it had grown light outside, and that the town was coming slowly to life. She still felt tired but she got up anyway, took out her copy of Mustafa's loan agreement. She hadn't had a chance to go through it properly before, and the more she read, the more it alarmed her. She kept setting it aside, telling herself not to worry about it now. But then she'd pick it up again. Mustafa hadn't stinted himself, that was for sure. He'd told her about the five per cent interest, but not about his agent's fee, nor that he'd demarcated the loan amount in its euro equivalent, according to the previous day's tourist exchange rate; and that he wanted the principal paid back according to the exchange rate at the time of the repayment. The way she figured it, that would mean she'd have to pay the spread between the buy and sell rates *twice*; and the spreads here were notoriously punitive. She did a rough-and-ready calculation on the back of one of the pages; she'd borrowed five hundred million ariary from him: yet under the various terms, she already owed him getting on for seven hundred and fifty million. He was, in effect, charging her a £70,000 management fee for arranging a ten-day loan. She felt a little sick, not just at the money, but also because it felt like she was being scammed. Her immediate instinct was to stiff Mustafa in return. Once she was back in England, after all, he'd never be able to sue her. But that was too easy an out; he'd surely have anticipated it. It took her a minute or so to find the sting in the contract's tail: a clause stipulating her stake in Eden as security for his loan. That puzzled her, for she had no stake in Eden, not while her father was alive, at least. Suddenly she had a very bad feeling about this.

She shook Titch awake. 'I need your help,' she told him.

'Of course,' he said, stifling a yawn. 'What?'

'A hire car. Preferably a 4x4. And see if you can get them to rent you one without a driver.'

He nodded and threw back his sheet. 'I'll get on to it at once.'

'We'll meet back here in an hour or so, okay?' she said, zipping the contract up in the holdall. 'Only there's a lawyer I need to go see.'

II

Next door, Knox had also slept poorly. He'd expected Titch to take a room for himself, but he'd been able to hear him and Rebecca preparing for bed then talking through the wall, though their conversation had been too muffled for him to make out what they were saying. It gave him a twinge anyway to think of the two of them together, for it had been obvious from the first that Titch was infatuated with Rebecca, and that she was fond of him too, though it had been less clear how fond. They finally fell silent, except for the creak of bed-joints as they tossed and turned, sounds that he found equally disturbing.

It came as a relief, therefore, when it finally grew light enough outside for him to be able to drive. He rose, paid for his room, then pushed his bike out on to the road so as not to wake the other guests when he started it up. A yellow dog dozed against a yellow wall, as if using it as camouflage. A family of four wobbled by on a ramshackle bicycle, the father standing up on the pedals, the mother sitting side-saddle nursing an infant, a boy balanced precariously upon the handlebars, giggling joyously. For a few miles, the road was busy with smallholders carting produce to Tulear's markets, but soon he was beyond them and making quick progress, slaloming the track's pitfalls. He passed a paradise beach, the golden sand bevelled by footprints and scarred by the broken husks of old pirogues. The sun rose above the trees, grew warm. By the side of the road, two men sawed up an old truck tyre to make sandals. Everything had residual value here; everything was squeezed dry. A young boy dragging a snow-white goat by its hind leg grinned and waved. He waved back. Then he saw Pierre's cabins ahead, a concrete reminder of the revelation that had been haunting him these past twenty-four hours, that he was quite possibly a father. It was an extraordinary thing, like discovering a new dimension in the world. He told himself to drive on, that this was no time for distractions, that his job was to check Eden for ransom updates. Yet he found himself turning off the track up towards Pierre's house all the same.

The noise of his arrival brought Pierre to the door. 'Yes?' he asked. 'What do you want?'

'I have a message for Therese,' he said. 'From Rebecca.'

'Tell me. I'll pass it on.'

'It's personal,' said Knox. 'She asked me to give it to Therese myself.'

He scowled but went inside. A minute passed. Therese came to the door carrying an infant in her arms, its face to her chest so that Knox couldn't see. His heart gave a double thump all the same; he beckoned Therese to follow him out of sight and earshot.

'Yes?' she asked.

Now that the moment was upon him, Knox didn't know quite how to proceed. 'Is that Emilia's son?' he asked.

'Yes,' she said warily.

'So that would make him Pierre's?'

Therese didn't say anything at first. She looked instead at his face, as if assessing his state of knowledge, his intent. 'Who are you?' she asked. 'Why you ask me this?'

'I knew Emilia,' he told her. 'We became close when she came to England. *Very* close. Maybe she mentioned me?'

Therese's eyes watered a little, but happily. She wiped a finger beneath them. 'I think it must be you,' she said. 'When Rebecca tell me this Englishman is here, with scars upon his back . . .'

'It's me.' He nodded at Michel. 'So he's mine?' he asked.

She seemed to hesitate, as though still bound by some vow of confidentiality; but the situation had gone beyond that, and she must have realised it. 'Yes,' she said. 'He's yours.' She held him out. Knox took him in both hands and raised him up a little awkwardly, as though he'd just been presented with some undeserved trophy. Therese was talking rapidly; he didn't take in a word of it, too numbed by those big brown eyes. Michel's face clenched as though he was about to start bawling; but then he thought better of it, he looked up and away, as though mildly puzzled by some anomaly in the world. Knox saw his sister in him, then, and his father too. And in that moment, accepting Michel as his responsibility, all the dead tissue around his heart was simply excised and thrown away, allowing what remained to breathe freely again. He remembered a simple truth he'd somehow forgotten in the loss of Gaille: that life was only worth living when it was lived for someone else. His vendetta against the Nergadzes was instantly over; they just weren't worth it. And he realised, too, that his first duty now was to find Emilia, one way or another. Everything else could wait.

He passed Michel back to Therese. 'I have things to do,' he told her. 'Will you look after him a little longer?'

'Of course,' she said.

'Thank you,' he said. 'Thank you for everything.'

She nodded and headed back to the house, carrying Michel against her shoulder. He walked with them and watched them safely back inside. Then he straddled his bike and turned it towards Eden, profoundly aware that his old life was over, and a new one had begun.

THIRTY-NINE

I

Delpha didn't pick up Mustafa's agreement. He simply turned it to face him on his desk. His half-moon reading glasses proved inadequate for the small print, so he produced a magnifying glass from his desk drawer and used that instead, sliding it with such agonising clumsiness across the paper that Rebecca longed to do it for him. When he was finally finished, he looked up at her with the most melancholic eyes. 'You signed this?'

'Yes.'

'Why?'

'I had no time. It was for a ransom. I was late and I—'

'A ransom.' He looked stunned. 'Your father? Your sister?'

'I spoke to him,' she said. 'He's alive. They're both alive.'

Delpha's eyes glistened. He convulsed once, like a sob, put a hand to his brow. 'Heaven be praised,' he murmured.

'Mustafa's been after a stake in Eden,' said Rebecca. 'My father mentioned it in a letter. He also remarked that Mustafa was pestering the wrong person. What did he mean by that?'

Delpha gave himself a few moments to compose himself, then said: 'You must remember something about Malagasy law,' he said. 'Since Independence, only citizens have been able to own land here. Your father has never become a citizen.'

Rebecca frowned. She'd always taken it for granted that her father owned Eden, yet Delpha was right: her parents had bought Eden after Independence, and her father had never become a Malagasy citizen. Then she realised how it must have worked. 'My *mother* owned Eden? But what about when she died?'

'We set up a trust together, to hold the reserve in trust for you and Emilia when you attained majority. You have dual citizenship, after all, so you're legally able to own property here.'

'But why didn't anyone tell me?' Again Delpha was silent, allowing her to work it out by herself. 'My father didn't trust me, did he?' she said bleakly. 'He was worried I'd sell my share just to get back at him.' She put a hand to her forehead. 'But what if either Emilia or I should . . . I mean, what if one of us . . .?'

'Then their interest in Eden passes to the other.'

'Will Mustafa know this?'

'Mr Habib usually knows everything it is in his interest to know.'

'What are you saying?' frowned Rebecca. 'Is he a crook?'

'A crook is a person who has been convicted of something. Mr Habib has never been so convicted.'

She gave a dry laugh. *Now* she found out! 'So that's why Andriama's having him watched. But why does he want Eden this badly? It can't be worth *that* much.'

'There have been rumours,' said Delpha. 'I do not know that they are true. But they say a German hotel group wants to build an ecotourism resort upon this coast. Eden has beautiful beaches and bays. It has virgin forest, reefs and plentiful fresh water. Can you imagine a better site?'

'How much?'

'Two million euros at minimum. Perhaps as much as four.'

Rebecca stood and went to the window, looked out into the street. After Yvette had died, Eden had become her father's life. He'd *never* sell it for development, or forgive anyone who did. She had to find some way to undo this. She was about to ask Delpha his advice when her phone beeped, sending her heart into overdrive, thinking it was the kidnappers; but it was only to warn her that her battery was almost dead. *Damn it*. Her phone was the most likely way for the kidnappers to get in touch; she needed to sort this out now. She made her excuses to Delpha then grabbed the holdall and hurried off in search of a solution.

II

Knox arrived back in Eden hoping to find some message from the kidnappers inside the door; but there was nothing. He went through the lodge and all the cabins just in case, then headed down to the boathouse, but again without success. While he was there, however, he decided to take another look at that ceramic, make sure his imagination wasn't running away with him. And there was something else he wanted to check out too.

The Kirkpatricks were self-evidently an intellectually curious lot. If a subject was of interest to them, they'd acquire books and articles about it. That was no doubt why Adam had the charts on board the *Yvette*, so that he could study them while out on the water. And it was why they kept those books on the treasure fleet and underwater archaeology in the basement. Knox had been following in the Kirkpatricks' footsteps so far. Everything he'd discovered about the Chinese wreck, they'd got to first. So maybe they'd figured out other things that he still hadn't. If so, it was a good bet that they'd have bought reading material on those subjects, and that they'd have stored it in the basement. The shelves, in brief, might be his shortcut to their state of knowledge.

He turned on the generator, slid open the panel, unlocked the door and went down, walked along the shelves. There were textbooks and articles on Zheng He and his treasure fleets, on the Ming Dynasty and Chinese shipbuilding techniques. There were archaeological works on the Chimu, the Incas, the Aztecs and other New World civilisations. There were books on the Renaissance, on the history of mapmaking. Several volumes were ageing badly, missing their spines. He pulled one down, opened it up. It was a biography of Ferdinand Magellan, the man widely credited as being the first to circumnavigate the world. A slight fiction, of course, because he hadn't completed the circumnavigation himself. He'd died in the Philippines, leading an attack on islanders who'd had the temerity to refuse conversion to Christianity. But eighteen of his men *had* made it all the way. Eighteen out of two hundred and thirty-seven, sailing the one ship that had survived from the original fleet of five.

Since finding the Fra Mauro map, Knox had had a scheme in his mind, of a treasure ship sailing west to South America from the Cape and then returning. Even his discovery of the Chimu ceramic hadn't changed that scheme; he'd just thought they'd found the Magellan Straits first. But what if they *hadn't* turned back east? What if they'd kept going west? Why else sail so far north up South America's western coast if they'd been planning to turn around again and head back across the Atlantic? The Chinese had known the world was round. They'd known circumnavigation was possible. And they'd been on a voyage of discovery. What greater discovery than circumnavigation, than achieving Chinese mastery of the globe?

Sailors, when faced with crossing large bodies of water, often sailed to the latitude of their destination port, then aimed directly east or west towards it. Running the latitude like this not only made navigation easier, it also minimised time spent on the open seas, and therefore offered the crew their best chance of reaching their destination before their supplies ran out. The Straits of Magellan were a good thousand miles south of the Cape of Good Hope, and far, far further south of Beijing. It would have made perfect sense, therefore, for them to head north along the Chilean coast to Peru, trading with any natives they found and thus restocking their holds with provisions for the long

own email. On an impulse, she went to his hotmail provider, plugged in his email ID, tried 'Yvette' as his password. No luck. She tried 'Emilia' and 'Michel' without success. Then she tried 'Rebecca' and it welcomed her to his home page. She put a hand to her mouth, closed her eyes to prevent tears. She went to his in-box, noticed immediately that he'd checked his messages the day before he'd gone missing; and also, that one of the very last messages he'd read was from Pierre. She opened it herself.

Meeting went well, though they want new photos of white sifaka. Please send by Thursday if at all possible.
All best,
P

She frowned. Pierre hadn't said anything to her about any such meeting, or about sending emails to her father before he vanished. She made a mental note to ask him about it, then checked the other messages. There were half a dozen or so unread, one of them from someone called Braddock at the Landseer Trust saying he'd just heard that Adam and Emilia had gone missing. He was of course hoping devoutly that it was just a misunderstanding, but please could Adam let him know as soon as possible, or they'd have to alert Matthew Richardson and his colleagues at MGS Salvage.

She stared in disbelief at the screen. *Daniel knew her father? What the hell was going on?* She typed MGS Salvage into the search engine. The company had its own website. She went to it. Her screen refilled with a background shot of an underwater wreck, overlaid with corporate pap about expertise and reputation, dedication to ecosystems and archaeological context, plus a link to updates about their Madagascan treasure ship project. She went to the 'our team' page, two rows of thumbnail photos, with Daniel's second from right on the lower row, captioned as Matthew Richardson. The photo was of poor quality, but there was no question it was him. It made no sense to her. She couldn't get a grip on it at all. Who was he? How did he know her father? Why hadn't he been straight with her? Could she trust him? She touched a fingertip to the screen, fuzzy with static, ran her finger down his face, along the line of his jaw—

A reflection in the monitor's screen. She whirled around to see Titch standing behind her. She couldn't tell how long he'd been there, but his face was pale and he looked a little dazed. He spun on his heel, hurried out. Rebecca grabbed the holdall from between her feet and chased after him, catching him outside, grabbing his arm. 'What's wrong?' she asked.

He turned and shook his head bitterly. 'It's him, isn't it?'

'What's him?'

'The reason you're staying here. The reason you're blowing off America, even though you know how important it is to us.'

'Don't be ridiculous, Titch. I'm staying here because of my father and sister.'

Anger clouded his face. 'Don't bullshit me,' he cried. 'I saw the way you were with each other last night. I saw how you flinched when he put his hand on—'

'The way I flinched!' she scoffed.

'Yes,' yelled Titch. 'The way you fucking flinched.' All around them on the streets, people stopped to stare, but Titch, normally the most reserved of men, didn't even seem to notice. He stabbed a finger at his chest. 'The things I've done for you,' he said. 'I've put my whole fucking life into your fucking company, and this is how you repay me? For Christ's sake, Rebecca! You know how I feel about you: don't you care for me *at all*?'

'You've got this all wrong,' she assured him. 'I was just checking up on him, that's all. I need to make sure I can trust him.'

'Sure!' scoffed Titch.

'It's the truth, I swear it.'

'So this is about trust, is it?'

'Yes.'

'And you trust me, don't you? We've been together three years, after all.'

'Of course I trust you.'

'Then tell me you're glad it's me here with you, not him.'

'For goodness' sake, Titch!'

'Tell me!'

She had too much to do to be wasting time like this. She said glacially: 'I'm glad it's you here with me, not Daniel.' But her eyes flickered as she spoke his name; her voice rang hollow. She steeled herself to say it again, with conviction this time. 'I'm glad it's you . . .' She trailed off. Her frown deepened. She looked at Titch in genuine bemusement.

A vein throbbed in his forehead. He clenched a fist and for a moment she thought he was going to hit her; but he controlled himself, shook his head, fished the hire-car keys from his pocket, tossed them to her. 'It's the white Toyota,' he said, gesturing vaguely to his left. Then he turned his back on her and walked away.

IV

Knox didn't have a chance for either flight or fight. All that was open to him was bluff. 'Who the hell are you?'

he asked, raising his hands above his head. 'What do you want with me?'

'You know who I am,' said Boris.

'If it's money you're after, it's inside the main building,' he said. 'I'll get it for you.'

'Sure,' said Boris. 'I flew all the way from Georgia just to lift your wallet. Let's not waste each other's time, eh? I know who you are. You know who I am, and who sent me. If I was here to kill you, you'd be lying on your back right now with a hole in your forehead. So isn't it logical to assume I don't want you dead?'

'I don't know what you're talking about.'

Boris came a little way inside the basement. 'Ilya Nergadze is dying,' he said. 'Sandro's boss now. He knows what kind of person Mikhail was, what he did to your fiancée. He doesn't blame you for what you did. He just wants to move on, restore his family's reputation and strength. But your Black Sea survey has got him spooked. I'm sure you can understand that. He sent me to talk to you, get your word you'll drop it. Do that, you'll never hear from any of us again.'

Knox hesitated. Boris's story sounded plausible enough. Rumours had been swirling that Ilya was sick; and while Sandro was no saint, he was known as a pragmatist. And, as Boris said, if they wanted him dead, he'd be dead already. 'Okay,' he said. 'You can tell Sandro he has my word.'

Boris smiled. 'I think he'd rather hear it from you yourself.'

'How do you mean?' frowned Knox. 'Is he here?'

'In a manner of speaking,' said Boris, nodding at the steps. 'We're going to go talk to him right now.'

FORTY

I

Rebecca went back into the Internet café for her recharged mobile, took it over to the computer, which still had MGS's website up. On a whim as much as anything, she punched in its telephone number. A young woman answered, her voice bright and keen to please. 'Good morning, MGS Salvage,' she said. 'How may I help you?'

'Daniel Richardson, please,' said Rebecca.

'I'm sorry. Daniel's out of the country at the moment.'

'Where?'

A first small hesitation. 'Let me put you through to Frank. Frank deals with Daniel's work while Daniel's away.' Silence for twenty seconds or so, then a man picked up. 'This is Frank. Who's calling?'

'My name's Cecilia,' said Rebecca, putting on a breezy airhead voice. 'I'm a friend of Danny's.'

'Danny's?' He sounded like he was picking up dogshit with his teeth.

'He promised to call last week but I haven't heard a word.'

'He's away.'

'When's he back?'

'Why d'you want to know?'

'It's personal.'

'Why don't you try him on his mobile?'

'I lost the number.'

Frank laughed. 'Sure you did, love.'

She dropped the phoney voice. 'So what's the deal with the Eden Reserve?' she asked. 'Are you doing a job there?'

Silence from Frank. When he spoke again, his tone was markedly different. Hard, shrewd and a little bit disquieted. 'Who is this? I want your name. I want your full name now.'

'It's the *Winterton*, isn't it?' she said. 'You've found the silver.'

'Who the fuck is this? Are you a journalist?'

'You have, haven't you? You've found the silver.'

'I'm warning you, if one word of this leaks—'

She killed the call. A muscle began going crazy along

the line of her jaw. So Daniel hadn't come here *looking* for the silver. He'd already found it. No. Scratch that. Adam and Emilia had found it. That was surely the only way to explain the involvement of the Landseer Trust. They'd found the silver and had taken advantage of MGS doing a job just up the coast to ask them to come here afterwards. And then Landseer had emailed Daniel to let him know her father and sister had gone missing, and he'd headed straight on down. But with what purpose? Had he come to help find them, or to take advantage of their absence to plunder the silver? She recalled, a little hollowly, how quickly he'd accepted Titch's suggestion last night that he go back to Eden. She settled her bill and went out, trying to put Daniel out of her mind, focus back on the important stuff, on her father and Emilia, the kidnap and the ransom. But another part of her brain was whirring independently away. The *Winterton*'s lost silver, her father's investments, the hotel group's interest in Eden – all these millions swirling around, yet the only people playing for small stakes here were the kidnappers.

She stopped walking abruptly, sensing the outline of a larger picture, wanting to give it the chance to reveal itself. Mustafa coveted Eden; the kidnap had given him the opportunity to win it. But had that been just pure chance, or was there more to it than that? Was it possible, in short, that Mustafa had been behind the kidnap himself, that he'd planned the whole enterprise simply to get her to sign

'Peace of mind,' Boris told him. He placed the laptop on the work-table, opened it up, established a broadband connection, called Georgia, carried out the security protocols. This wasn't his usual time-slot; it took over a minute for Sandro to appear. 'I've got someone for you,' Boris told him, pulling Knox into shot.

Sandro leaned forward, squinted at his screen. 'Daniel Knox?' he asked.

'It's me,' said Knox.

'See?' said Boris.

Sandro ignored him, addressed Knox instead. 'You're planning a salvage project off our coast, I believe,' he said.

'Not any more,' Knox told him. 'I've called it off.'

'And why should I believe that? You've effectively just admitted you were coming after us.'

'Yes,' admitted Knox. 'I *was* coming after you. I was coming after you because you sent your fucking son to Greece where he murdered my fiancée in cold blood; and then put a price on my head and turned me into a fugitive. I couldn't even visit Gaille's grave; I couldn't even *mourn*.' He seemed to catch the anger rising in himself; he took a long breath. 'But it's over. It was over before this. I've got more important things in my life now than your family.'

'Such as?'

'Such as none of your business.'

'So you'll give me your word, then? If we leave you alone, you'll leave us alone?'

'Yes. I give you my word.'

'What is this?' demanded Boris in Georgian.

'We're going to let him go.'

'But your father told me to—'

'My father is dead, Boris. He died early this morning.'

Boris went numb. 'We had a deal.'

'That deal was with my father. My—'

'It was with you both. It was with the both of you.'

'My father is dead. I am now head of the Nergadze family. The deal is off. My decision on this is final.'

'You can't do this.'

'I promised you one hundred thousand euros for finding Mr Knox. You have found Mr Knox. I will pay you your fee in full. On your return, so long as Mr Knox remains unharmed, I will also authorise a bonus for—'

'No way,' said Boris. 'No fucking way. I'll never get home if I let him live. He'll go straight to the fucking cops.'

'He's given us his word.'

'His word!' spat Boris. 'What good is that?'

'I trust him.'

'Of course you fucking trust him. I'd trust him too if I was safe at home in Georgia.'

'I'm warning you, Boris.'

'Fifteen months I spent in that fucking Greek prison!

378

Fifteen months! Do you have any idea what that was like? Do you know what they *did* to me there?'

'I'm sorry that—'

'Sorry!' he scoffed, anger roiling up his heart. 'What good is sorry? Your father hired me to do a job, and I'm going to do it, and you're going to pay me the full fee, just like you promised.' He held up his camera-phone which he'd been holding down low. 'Did you honestly think I wouldn't record our little conversations? Is that what you thought? I've got video of us discussing this job. I've got video of you arranging my gun. I'll give it to the police if you try to stiff me, I swear I will.' He slammed down the laptop lid, breaking the connection, then stood there breathing heavily, a tumult of emotions inside him: anger, fear, frustration, the longing for revenge. He glared at Knox, pressed the Heckler & Koch against his temple, pushed him towards the basement steps.

'What is this?' asked Knox. 'I thought we had a deal.'

'Sure!' scoffed Boris. 'So you can hand me to the police again.'

'I give you my word.'

'And you think that carries weight with me, do you?' He pushed Knox ahead of him down the steps. When they reached the bottom, he kicked Knox behind his knees so that he went down upon them.

'This is crazy,' said Knox. 'You don't need to do this.'

Boris aimed down at him, his finger on the trigger.

Enough of his anger had subsided for him to become aware again of consequences. Sandro would never forgive him for what he'd just done; there was pragmatic and then there was soft. Georgia was dead to him now; he'd therefore have to start all over. But with what? Something on the shelves caught his eye at that moment, like the answer to a prayer. A blue-and-white porcelain bowl, just like one in the press-cuttings Sandro had given him – and that had sold for millions at auction. He edged across, keeping his gun on Knox, picked it up. It was perfect, flawless. And next to it was an enamelled flask that looked to his uneducated eye even more valuable. With the right fence, he could get maybe twenty cents on the dollar. If these pieces were worth what he thought, then he'd—

He whirled around as Knox took advantage of his distraction to leap to his feet and sprint for the steps. Boris brought up his gun but he was too late. He cursed and set down the bowl and ran after him, grabbing the end of the shelving to swing himself around. He reached the stairs just as Knox tripped on the top step and went crashing into the wall, twisting on to his back as he fell. Boris arrived at the top, his anger fully restored, along with his hunger for revenge. He aimed down at Knox's face, put his finger on the trigger and began to squeeze.

convinced herself she was being ridiculously paranoid, that Mustafa was her ally. But then her suspicions would reassert themselves. And there was too much at stake to take them lightly. Thus far, Mustafa only had legal claim to Rebecca's share in Eden. For him to own it all, Emilia would first have to die. And if Mustafa thought it worth his while to kill Emilia, then he'd surely kill Adam too. Her actions now might determine their fate; she couldn't afford a single misstep.

She tried to put herself in Mustafa's mind, work out whether he was the kind to cut his losses at the first setback, or hold his nerve. She still had his five hundred million ariary. If he was greedy, he'd keep Emilia and Adam alive while he arranged a second handover, just in case she insisted on speaking to them again. Yesterday's fuck-ups might actually have saved their lives. But maybe not for long. She needed to find them fast. The trouble was, she didn't have the first idea where to look. She couldn't believe Mustafa would risk holding them at his home, not with his wife and daughter there. Besides, he was an importer–exporter, he'd have warehouses and other such properties all across the town and region. Andriama would surely know of some of them, but the moment they started nosing around, Mustafa would realise they were on to him and take steps to cover his tracks. She couldn't risk that. She felt helpless. But then she realised she didn't actually need to find Adam and Emilia at all.

If she could somehow get compelling evidence or even proof that Mustafa was behind the kidnapping, it would give her such a hold over him that she'd surely be able to barter for Adam and Emilia's release.

A minor incident from her original visit to Mustafa's house came to her mind. After he'd agreed to help her put together the ransom, she'd asked to freshen up before setting off back to Eden. When he'd led her inside, one of his staff had called him to an important incoming phone call. He'd begged her to excuse him, then opened and closed his office door in such a way that she wouldn't be able to see inside.

She hadn't thought anything of this at the time, other than that he valued his privacy; but now she wondered whether there might not have been something in his office that he hadn't wanted her to see. It wasn't much to go on, but it was better than sitting here doing nothing. She thrust the Toyota back in gear and accelerated away.

II

It was the metallic shrieking that stopped Boris from shooting Knox. He knew what it was and what it signified and the world seemed to stop for a moment as he waited for and then heard the crash of shelving that he himself had precipitated by swinging himself around on it. A cacophony of ceramics shattered on the concrete floor. He closed his eyes briefly, then opened them again with renewed hatred of Knox. 'If those two pieces are broken . . .' he warned.

'There are more of them,' said Knox, his hands above his head. 'Lots more.'

'Where?'

He nodded towards the sea. 'Out there.'

'Bullshit.'

'I swear. I found them yesterday. I'll take you out there.'

'Like you were going to take us to the golden fleece?' he scoffed.

'The golden fleece existed,' said Knox. 'So does this. You saw those pieces downstairs. Do you think they appeared out of nothing? They came from a Chinese ship that sank outside the reef.'

'That's further north.'

'No. We thought it was, but we were wrong. It made it down here before it sank. That's where the bowl came from. That's where the flask came from. And there are dozens more pieces like them. Hundreds. And not just porcelain. Gold and jewellery too.'

'And you just left it all on the sea-bed?' sneered Boris.

'I'm an archaeologist, not a thief.'

Boris coloured, raised the gun at Knox. 'Where exactly is this place?' he asked. 'Describe it to me.'

384

'It's forty metres underwater,' protested Knox. 'How am I supposed to describe that?'

'Then what use are you?'

'I can show you. I can take you out there.'

He's a liar, said a voice in Boris's head. *A proven liar. Don't fall for him again.* But the Chinese pieces downstairs had looked real enough. And what if he was telling the truth this time? What if others came down here and found all this wealth that could have been his? He'd be cursing himself for the rest of his life. He motioned Knox to his feet, marched him back downstairs. If either the bowl or the flask had survived the carnage, then he'd have no more need of Knox. But neither had. 'Okay,' he told Knox. 'You're going to take me out there. But if you try anything, anything at all, by God you're going to pay.'

III

Rebecca drove briskly north, anxious to make good time yet without drawing attention to herself. A bank of smoke from some charcoal makers drifted like fog across the road, making her eyes smart and her throat tickle enough to send her into a coughing fit. She came out the far side to find a bus unloading passengers, forcing her to brake sharply and swerve. A pair of panicked goats scrambled over each other to squirm through sliver-thin gaps in the fence, while a girl in a cut-down wedding dress snatched up a scrawny black chicken from almost beneath her wheel.

The guard on duty outside Mustafa's house flicked away his cigarette as he sauntered across, blowing smoke out his nostrils in twin plumes, like a cold-weather bull. Mustafa was in Tulear, he told her. She asked for Ahdaf instead. He slouched back to his hut, then beckoned Rebecca over so that she could speak to Ahdaf herself on the intercom. 'I'm afraid my father had some business in Tulear this morning,' said Ahdaf. 'But he should be here in an hour or two, if you'd like to come back.'

'That's okay,' said Rebecca, who'd anticipated this possibility. 'It's actually you I wanted to talk to.'

'*Me?* What about?'

'You made some very perceptive comments about my programmes the other night,' she said. 'I've been thinking about them a great deal. I'd like to talk to you about them, if that's okay.'

'Oh!' Ahdaf sounded thrown. 'Then yes, come on in.'

The gates slid open as Rebecca returned to her Toyota. She drove up to the house, looking all around her for anything out of place. The front doors opened as she parked, and Ahdaf emerged, swathed in silks. She led Rebecca around to a shaded veranda with a long glass table. Two maids appeared from nowhere to lay a tablecloth,

napkins, cutlery and bone china. 'I don't have long,' said
Ahdaf. 'My studies, you understand.'

'Then let me get straight down to it,' nodded Rebecca.
'I feel the same way about science as you obviously do.
Truth *should* be enough. But it isn't. Natural selection
operates on TV just like in any competitive environment.
The weakest programmes are ruthlessly killed off. You
need special qualities to survive, let alone prosper. My
programmes succeeded because they were fresh and startling and they looked damned good. But audiences grow
bored. They crave the new. What you said the other
night—'

Ahdaf had the grace to blush. 'I didn't mean to—'

'It's okay. You were right. My last few programmes
have been flat. I hate to admit it, but it's true. And I've
been thinking about moving to the other side of the
camera anyway. Maybe now's the time.' She looked Ahdaf
straight in the eye. 'But do you know what I'll need most,
if I'm to become a successful director or producer?'

Ahdaf's mouth turned sour, as though suddenly she
understood what was going on. 'Money, I suppose?'

'No,' laughed Rebecca. 'Money's easy. Money's
everywhere. *Talent* is what I need. Specifically, I need
a qualified zoologist with zest, youth and beauty. A young
woman of forceful ideas, and with the confidence to
express them. Someone who can dazzle a screen; someone
exotic. And preferably someone fluent in French as well

as English, because my programmes do very good business in France.'

Ahdaf placed a hand on her chest. 'You can't mean—'

'Ahdaf,' said Rebecca earnestly, 'have you ever considered a career in television?'

Ahdaf looked up and away, her eyes glinting. Rebecca remembered the moment she'd got her own series; the intoxication of it, the absurd conviction of how perfect life would now be. 'It's not . . .' stammered Ahdaf. 'No, that is, I have sometimes thought I might be . . . but my father wouldn't—'

'This isn't an offer, you understand,' said Rebecca. 'I'm only asking hypothetically.'

'Hypothetically.' Ahdaf seized gratefully on the word. 'Yes. I think I can say that hypothetically I'd be interested.'

'Good. Then may I ask you some questions?'

'Of course. Of course.'

'Thank you. When do you finish at university?'

'This summer.'

'Are you planning postgraduate studies?'

'Yes. In Antananarivo.' Then she added hurriedly: 'But that's not definite.'

'If I could arrange for a scholarship to Oxford, would you consider that?'

'Oxford?' Ahdaf swallowed. 'Yes. I think I could—'

'Do you drink?'

'No.'

'Drugs?'

'No.'

'You have a boyfriend?'

'No.'

'A girlfriend?'

Ahdaf blushed furiously. 'What are you suggesting?'

'If I'm to put my reputation and my business behind you, I need to know what I'm getting. Do you have a girlfriend?'

'I . . . No.' She shook her head. 'I'm not like that.'

'Good. Is there any reason you wouldn't live in England?'

Ahdaf made fists of her hands. 'I don't know . . . Wouldn't there be immigration and work permits and—'

'I have people to take care of all that,' said Rebecca airily. 'I mean personal reasons. Would you get home-sick? Are you promised in marriage to some nice Indian boy? Would your family stand in your way?'

Ahdaf said defiantly. 'They could try.'

Rebecca stood up, walked around the table, tugged back Ahdaf's silk head-scarf, combed her fingers through the wiry, shoulder-length black hair. She tilted back Ahdaf's chin, examined her throat, her profile, her pierced but empty ears. She asked: 'What about your hair? Would you want to keep it covered on TV?'

'I . . . Yes. It is . . . That is, yes, it's part of—'

'That may be a problem,' said Rebecca. She took a pinch of Ahdaf's sleeve, rubbed the silk between her fingers. 'And these clothes wouldn't do at all.'

'But your programmes aren't on fashion,' protested Ahdaf. 'They're on science.'

'No,' said Rebecca. 'They're on television.' She shook her head. 'Oh well. Best to know early. Too bad, though. I really thought you—'

'I'm sure something can be arranged,' said Ahdaf quickly.

'How do you mean?'

'I'm sure we can find a compromise.'

Rebecca snorted. 'Oh yes. I know compromise. You pretend you'll do what I tell you until the last moment, and then I'll be screwed.'

'I wouldn't be like that.'

'How can I be sure? You're implying you'll agree some time in the future. If so, why not now? Don't you realise what I'm offering you? Do you imagine I'd risk my reputation on someone who thinks her hair too precious to—'

'Okay,' said Ahdaf.

'You'll go bareheaded if I tell you to?'

Ahdaf twisted her hands in her lap. 'Yes,' she murmured.

'Sorry? I didn't hear.'

'Yes,' said Ahdaf, more loudly.

'Yes, what?'

'Yes, I'd go bareheaded if you told me to.'

'Good.' Rebecca reached to take Ahdaf's hands from her lap. She separated them, examined the stubby fingers artificially lengthened by false nails of burnished brown; the smudges of ink on her index finger and thumb. 'You'll wear what I tell you to wear?'

'Yes,' said Ahdaf.

'Clothes that showed off your figure?'

'I . . .' Ahdaf bowed her head. 'Yes.'

'That flattered your breasts and waist and hips?'

Ahdaf's head drooped lower and lower. 'Yes.'

'That showed your cleavage?'

'Yes.'

Rebecca pushed back Ahdaf's sleeve and jangling silver bracelets, revealed dark forearms soft with downy black hair. She reached up inside the material all the way along Ahdaf's arm to her shoulder. 'Clothes that showed your legs and arms?'

'Yes.'

'You'll put yourself completely in my hands?'

'Yes.'

Rebecca leaned backwards. 'Why do I get the impression you'll be too proud to take orders?'

Ahdaf said softly: 'I can take orders.'

'From me?'

'Yes.'

'You'll obey me?'

'Yes.'

'Look at me, Ahdaf.' Ahdaf raised her eyes slowly, reluctantly. Their gazes met and locked. Ahdaf seemed to quiver, almost to shrink. 'Sometimes, to succeed,' said Rebecca, 'we must do things we wouldn't want to do, things that clash with our image of ourselves. I need to know you'll do such things, if I tell you they need to be done.'

'What kind of things?'

'I can't predict that,' answered Rebecca. 'Each person balks at different obstacles. I only know that if you want to succeed, you must be willing to sacrifice everything else, including your pride. Are you willing?'

'Yes,' said Ahdaf quietly.

'Your family? Your friends?'

'Yes.'

'Without protest? Without bitterness?'

'Yes.'

'Good,' said Rebecca. 'Then take me to your room. I need to see you in some other clothes.'

FORTY-TWO

I

Boris had been diving several times in his life, on holidays in Bali, the Red Sea and the like, but it had been a while and he'd forgotten much of what he'd learned, particularly on equipment set-up and safety. He and Knox were much the same size and build, however, so he removed the man's flexi-cuffs, had him turn on the compressor to fill a pair of scuba tanks with air, then made him assemble two complete sets of dive-gear. 'I don't need any,' said Knox. 'Mine's already on the boat.'

'What I dive with, you dive with,' Boris told him. 'And I'm not saying who's getting which set until we suit up. So no tricks, eh?'

Knox shrugged. 'Whatever you say.'

The compressor took forever. Boris made Knox carry the dive-gear out to the boat while they waited, keeping the gun on him all the time, half expecting him to try something; but he didn't. When they returned to the boathouse, the reels of fishing line gave him an idea. He cut off several metres, coiled it up and put it away in his pocket. The second tank was still filling; Boris took Knox to collect his belongings from the lodge, so that he wouldn't have to return here once this was done. The compressor finally finished. They turned it and the generator off, locked up the boathouse, carried everything out to the boat then motored through the pass and north-west, navigating with GPS and a local chart until Madagascar was just a dark line on the horizon behind them, and Knox finally cut the engine.

'This is it?' asked Boris.

'This is it,' nodded Knox, deploying the anchor. 'See what I mean about trying to describe the place?'

It was true enough. The water was too deep here to see the bottom, and they were too far from shore for landmarks. 'You fuck with me down there, you're going to regret it.'

'Then let me go collect some pieces for you.'

'Sure!' Climbing into a wetsuit was an awkward and ungainly process, during which Boris knew he'd be at his most vulnerable. He had Knox suit up first, therefore, then tied his wrists behind his back again with another set of flexi-cuffs. He took out the fishing line he'd cut earlier, looped it around Knox's neck and then knotted it tight enough to cut into his throat a little, whiten his skin.

'What's that for?' asked Knox.

'You think I'm going to let you swim around loose? What kind of idiot do you take me for?' He suited himself up, chose a BCD and tank, weight-belt, mask and fins, then he knotted the other end of the fishing line around his left wrist, so that Knox was like a pet dog on a long leash. If he tried to get away now, all Boris would have to do was give the fishing line a good sharp tug and it would choke Knox, bring him within the business range of his knife. He picked up the Heckler & Koch again before releasing Knox from his cuffs so that he could finish suiting up. There was no way of cuffing his wrists behind his back again, not with his scuba tank on, so he cuffed them in front instead.

'Okay,' he told Knox. 'In the water.' He waited until Knox was down, gave a little tug on the fishing line to remind him who was boss. No point taking the Heckler & Koch down with him. It was useless underwater, and cumbersome too. On the other hand, he didn't want just to leave it on board, lest Knox somehow make it back here first and use it against him. He ejected the magazine, therefore, and zipped it away in his wetsuit's waterproof pouch.

He hid the gun itself in a side-pocket of Knox's dive-bag, on the basis that it was the last place he'd look, then he took his knife in his right hand, climbed down the stern ladder and joined Knox in the water.

II

Rebecca was thinking furiously as she followed Ahdaf through a vast atrium and up a marble staircase. Ahdaf might be vain enough to buy her cover story, but no way would her father fall for it, and he was due back here within an hour or so. She needed to find her proof and get away fast.

Ahdaf's bedroom was pastel pink with spectacular views of the beach and lagoon. She led Rebecca into a walk-in closet, a narrow aisle several paces long between rails of dresses and blouses on her left, shelves of folded silks on her right. It wasn't perfect, but it was too good an opportunity to pass up. Rebecca stepped back out, closed the closet door with Ahdaf still inside, then pinned its handle with a leaned chair.

'Rebecca?' asked Ahdaf tentatively, as though suspecting some curious joke. 'What are you doing?'

'Just give me a moment,' said Rebecca. She picked up a remote control at random, pressed buttons. The flat-screen TV came on. She flipped through until she found a music channel, turned the volume up just enough to muffle Ahdaf's increasingly panicky pleas of claustrophobia, then hurried back down through the atrium to Mustafa's office. The door was locked. She tried to force it but it wouldn't give. She heard footsteps approaching, so she hurried the other way into a plush drawing room. The footsteps drew closer. She went to stand before a vast acrylic family portrait to make it look as though she belonged there. There were more Habibs than she'd realised. Mustafa, of course, was the focal point. Dominant, serious and kindly, sitting on a high-backed red armchair. His wife stood in a floral dress beside him, somehow managing to look down on the artist, despite her own low starting position. Ahdaf stood on Mustafa's other side, her face half shadowed by her scarf. And there was a young man on either flank too, presumably Mustafa's sons. The first looked athletic and handsome, with arrogant hooded eyes. The second was thin with high cheekbones and wavy hair, his hips thrust out like a model at the end of the catwalk.

'What are you doing here?'

Rebecca turned. One of Mustafa's guards was at the door. 'Ahdaf asked me to wait,' she told him. 'She's fetching something from her room.' He stayed a few more seconds, then walked off. She hoped he'd go back outside, but she heard his footsteps on the stairs. *Damn it*. She went to the French windows, slipped outside, went around to

Mustafa's office. There was no external door and his windows were locked. She cupped her hands to look inside, but saw nothing that might help. The guard would find Ahdaf any moment now. The alarm was about to go up. She needed to get away while she could. She walked briskly but quietly towards her Toyota, not wanting to draw attention. The front gates would be locked but maybe she could drive down to the beach, cut back on to the coastal track further north. But then she stopped. Leave now and Mustafa would know she was on to him. If he decided to cover his tracks, she'd never see her father or sister again. She couldn't leave here empty-handed. She just couldn't.

She turned and ran back into the house.

III

The water felt colder to Knox today, though maybe that was just the old wetsuit he was wearing, or even apprehension about what lay ahead. There was no dispute that visibility was worse, however, the sea a thin particulate soup roiled up by waves and currents. He checked constantly behind him to make sure Boris was keeping up, because the noose was already biting into his throat. That said, he wanted to set a decent pace. The only thing in his favour was that he was the better diver; he needed to make the most of that.

The deeper you dived, the greater the pressure upon your body. One effect of that pressure was to enable your bloodstream to absorb more air. In such increased volumes, nitrogen had a heady effect, much like alcohol; and the faster, deeper and longer your descent, the worse it became. Nitrogen narcosis wasn't in itself particularly dangerous, but it made divers overconfident, impaired their judgement and motor-function, rendered them as prone to stupid mistakes as a drunk behind the wheel. And that was what Knox needed: he needed Boris making stupid mistakes.

They reached the sea-floor. Knox checked his gauge. Thirty-one metres deep already, yet he needed to go deeper still. He led Boris past the underwater tip, pointing out shards of porcelain as he went, giving credibility to his account. They followed a canyon to the pelagic shelf. With the reduced visibility, he only barely saw the orange marker buoys of the fish aggregating device. He swam towards them, continuing the descent to forty metres, then fifty, feeling a mild buzz as the narcosis kicked in. You never grew immune to it, however much you dived. You simply learned to manage it.

Dark shadows ahead. He swam towards them. Boris gave a tug on the fishing line, constricting Knox's windpipe, making it hard for him to breathe. He stopped and turned so that the line slackened. Boris was treading water some five metres away, holding up his gauges, his expression making it plain he wanted to know what the hell was going on, where the porcelain was. Knox pointed ahead. Boris shook his head. Knox checked his gauges. Fifty-five metres deep, just fifteen minutes of air left. No wonder Boris was getting nervous. If they didn't start their ascent soon, they'd be at severe risk of decompression sickness. It was now or never. But how the hell to get close enough to Boris to—

The bull shark surged up from the turbid depths, its maw already open, murderous rows of white stalagmites and stalactites within, rolling up its mean black eyes to show its whites. Knox lifted his feet, thumped its snout with his flippers. It turned and swam away. He glanced around at Boris, watching it in rapt horror, giving Knox his chance. He propelled himself across, grabbed for the knife with his cuffed hands, but Boris was too quick for him, he turned and slashed at Knox's face. Knox ducked beneath the blade, reached for Boris's buoyancy-control device, inflated it to its maximum, then stripped him of his weight-belt.

At once Boris began rising like a runaway hot-air balloon. The fishing line quickly played out and pulled the noose tight around Knox's throat, cutting into his windpipe, dragging him upwards with him so fast that it put them both at risk from the bends. The moment Boris reached the surface, Knox slammed on the brakes, coming to a halt at just four metres, deep enough for him to decompress safely, not that that would be much use if he couldn't breathe.

Above him, Boris began thrashing wildly. Symptoms of the bends typically took an hour or so to present, sometimes even a day or more. Only in the very worst cases was onset immediate. His struggles pulled the makeshift garrotte ever tighter around Knox's throat, so that he couldn't breathe at all, his lungs screaming for air. He needed to get rid of the fishing line now, but he couldn't even get a fingernail beneath it. He looked upwards, almost in prayer, at the very moment that a spasm of pain wracked Boris so severely that he let go of his diving knife. And Knox watched spellbound as it began fluttering down through the water towards him like a silvery leaf in an autumn breeze.

IV

Rebecca hurried back through the drawing room to the atrium. Upstairs, she could hear Ahdaf wailing like a two-year-old while the guard shouted into his walkie-talkie. Mustafa's office was locked, but maybe there'd be something in his bedroom. She took the steps two at a time, slipped through a half-open door into a large bedroom with a basketball hoop screwed high on its wall, a pool table with a unblemished cloth. One of the son's rooms. Not what she was after. The passage was empty; she slipped back out and tried another door. The second boy's bedroom, a geek rather than a jock, his desk stacked with sophisticated-looking computer equipment. She was about to go out again when she heard guards arriving on the landing outside, opening doors, beginning a search.

Rebecca cast around for somewhere to hide. The only other door opened on to another walk-in closet, suits to her left, shirts to her right. She pulled it softly closed behind her, though leaving it a fraction ajar to give herself some light. Two guards ran into the bedroom a moment later, shouting at each other where to search. She slipped between two suits, grabbed the rail and lifted up her legs. The rail bowed beneath her weight, but held. The door banged open a moment later and a guard rushed in. She could hear him panting for breath as he flipped through the suits then got down on to hands and knees, yet somehow didn't see her. He ran back out, leaving the closet door open. She let her legs back down, her left shoulder aching from the strain. The voices grew fainter as the guards ran off to search other rooms. She got out her mobile and tried Andriama again, was again transferred to voicemail. As loudly as she dared, she told him where she was and why, recasting her suspicion as certainty. The signal cut off before she could finish her message, however. Someone had turned off the mast.

She knew she wouldn't have long before the guards

came back for a more diligent search, so she looked around for salvation. There were caps and scarves hanging from hooks behind the closet door, but she'd scarcely be able to disguise her way out of here. She risked a peek out. The bedroom was still empty. She went to the window just as Mustafa pulled up in his blue Mercedes immediately behind her Toyota, pinning it in. The driver door flew open; he stepped out and strode purposefully into the house. A moment later she heard him shouting abuse at some hapless guard.

She edged back towards the closet. Something about the baseball caps and scarves was calling out to her. Those two intruders her first night at Eden had been wearing caps and scarves. Could they have been Mustafa's sons? But that made no sense. Why bother to break in if they already had Emilia and Adam? She felt a little nauseous as she recalled Mustafa bursting in on her meeting with Andriama, how she'd patted her heart and insisted that Adam and Emilia were still alive. Now that she thought back on it, she recalled raising the possibility of a kidnap herself, and had even told them that she'd be staying at Pierre's that night, so that Mustafa would have expected Eden to be deserted. And he'd likely have had keys for the lodge, too; he'd have been the most likely supplier of the new steel door.

It was with a tremendous feeling of relief, then, that she remembered her father on the phone. 'Rebecca,' he'd said. 'Rebecca, my darling.' Her skin began to tingle, but not in a good way. Her mother had been Adam's one and only ever darling, then, now and forever. Even if it had been her father's voice, so what? It was stored on dozens of CDs and cassettes in his office. And that was all the intruders had been after: the raw material with which to fake a convincing kidnap, and so take cruel advantage of Rebecca's own conviction that she'd get Adam and Emilia back alive.

Outside, she heard the wail of approaching sirens. Andriama must have got her messages. She walked out on to the landing, looked down into the atrium, Mustafa and his guards staring anxiously out the front doors as three police cars swept up the drive. None of them even noticed Rebecca as she strode down the stairs. She was almost upon Mustafa before one of his guards shouted out a warning. He whirled around, saw the knowledge in her eyes, and the way he blanched was full confirmation of her fears. Even as Andriama and his men ran up the front steps and inside, the fury and grief welled up within her. 'You gave me hope,' she yelled at Mustafa. 'You gave me hope.' She made claws of her fingers and went for his eyes.

FORTY-THREE

I

Knox kept his eyes fixed on the knife as it tumbled in slow motion through the water towards him, all too aware it was his one hope of escaping death. He reached up for it but it caught on an eddy and bumped the heel of his palm then bounced down his forearm and shoulder before vanishing behind his back. He spun around but it was already level with his waist by the time he saw it again. He grabbed for it but it was elusive as soap in a bath and then he reached the end of his fishing-line tether and was jerked back. He watched in horror as the knife fell past his knee and calf, but he reached out a foot beneath it, trying to keep his movements slow so as to avoid creating eddies.

The knife hit his flipper point first, then fell on to its side, half the hilt hanging precariously over the edge. He reached for it but again his tether held him back. He was out of air now, running on fumes, so he lifted up his foot. The knife tumbled over the side but he grabbed it and caught it and instantly brought it up to his throat, laying the blade sideways so that he could get its tip beneath the fishing line, then twisting it and pressing out and suddenly it snapped and he was free, able to breathe once more, sucking great draughts of air back into his starving lungs.

It was a good minute before he was sufficiently re-covered even to think of next steps. He carefully turned the knife around in his hands then used it to free his wrists of the flexi-cuffs. He looked up again. Boris was still thrashing around above him. Despite everything, he felt wretched for the man. The bends were as painful as anything on earth, like having spikes hammered through all your joints. Yet there was nothing he could do for him right now; he had to give his own body time to adjust to the lesser pressure or he'd suffer a similar fate himself.

When finally he surfaced, Boris was whimpering and weeping in the water, the pain too great to manage. Mild cases of the bends could be treated with pure oxygen, which was why Knox kept a small tank of it in his dive-bag, but Boris was beyond that. His one hope was the decompression chamber on board the *Maritsa*. Knox grabbed his collar and tried to drag him to the *Yvette*, but he was thrashing so wildly that Knox finally let go of him and swam over to the boat himself then motored it back across, trying unsuccessfully to raise the *Maritsa* as he came, hoping to get them to meet him halfway.

Boris's cries had diminished by the time Knox pulled alongside, exhaustion rather than slackening of the pain. Knox snagged him with a boat-hook, dragged him around to the stern, hauled him aboard. He curled up on the deck like a foetus, his teeth stained red with blood, more blood and mucus leaking from his nostrils. Knox took his oxygen from his bag, attached its breathing mask and clamped it over Boris's mouth. 'I need to get you to my dive-ship,' he told him. 'You're going to have to hold the mask, okay?'

Boris reached up and took Knox's wrist, dragged it down so that he could speak. 'You lied to me,' he said.

'Yes,' said Knox.

'I knew it,' he said, tears of pain and regret streaming from his eyes. 'I knew it and I still couldn't let it go.'

'Keep breathing,' Knox told him.

'What for?' asked Boris. Pain wracked him; he arched and clenched Knox's hand, then he fell limp with exhaustion. Blood began dribbling from beneath an eyelid, and from his left ear too, some terrible trauma taking place inside. His head lolled back and he looked up with what seemed like puzzlement at the afternoon sky. 'I used to be a soldier,' he said. Then he let go of Knox and his hand fell lifelessly against the deck.

II

With Rebecca's guidance, it didn't take Andriama and his men long to find evidence of what the Habibs had done. In the second son's room, beneath the desk, were a number of CDs of voice recordings made by her father: field-notes, podcasts and his most recent message to his late wife. A selection of these had been copied into a new folder on the son's computer, and several snippets had been rearranged into a familiar yet heartrending message, the splices disguised by static.

'Rebecca. Rebecca, my darling. Please, Rebecca. Do as they ask. We're both well but—'

Each syllable a dagger in Rebecca's heart.

They found the original for the ransom photograph too. It had been taken during a lunch party months before, at which Mustafa had corralled his guests against the stables then photographed them in groups, pairs and individually. Emilia had looked bored throughout; but Adam had looked increasingly angry at the imposition; and it showed most in the photograph of him with

Emilia. They also found a separate image of one of Mustafa's sons holding up a recent newspaper; and the blended image, too, cropped and doctored for the ransom demand.

Rebecca handed Andriama the ransom money and her copy of the loan agreement, and was giving him her statement too when a call came in on his mobile. His expression grew increasingly sombre as he listened. He kept glancing at her. He scratched his chin uncertainly and then switched to a patois she couldn't follow.

'What is it?' she asked, when he'd finished.

He pulled a face to warn her of bad news. 'They've found a body.'

Her heart clenched. 'Where?'

'Tsiandamba.'

She nodded. Tsiandamba was just a little way south of Eden. 'Who?'

'They didn't say.'

'Male or female?'

He touched her gently on her arm. 'Let's go find out,' he suggested.

III

Knox sat by Boris a little while. It was partly out of respect for the dead, partly from exhaustion, but mostly to buy himself time to think through what to do next. He could see two paths open to him. The first was to take Boris's body back to shore, turn himself in, throw himself on the mercy of the Malagasy criminal justice system. But he'd heard terrible things about the courts and jails here, and he didn't much fancy betting his future on them. Besides, while he'd done certain things in his life that warranted judgement and penance, this wasn't one of them. He'd acted in self-defence.

Option two, then.

He stood up, looked around. There was a trawler on the western horizon and a pirogue far to his south. But that was all. The *Yvette* was low on fuel, but there was a decent southerly. He took off his wetsuit, unfurled the mainsail, sailed out to deeper water. He retrieved the boathouse keys from Boris, bled the air from his buoyancy-control device and scuba tank, packed a weight-belt with as much lead as it would take and strapped it around his waist. Then he grabbed him around his chest, hoisted him up and dumped him over the side, consigning him to the deeps.

He watched the bubble trail until it had died away, and then a little while longer. If this was revenge, it certainly tasted sour. He wanted no more of it. He sailed on a little way, then weighted down Boris's bag and dumped it too. When he picked up the laptop case, it made him wonder what the Nergadzes would do about this. Nothing, he suspected. But that was Sandro's decision to make, not Knox's. He held the case out over the water and let it drop. Then he took his seat at the stern, brought the *Yvette* around, and headed back to shore.

FORTY-FOUR

I

Rebecca was in no state to drive, so Andriama took the wheel of her Toyota, with one of his men following in a police car. Everything seemed out of sync to her, numb and surreal. She pressed her hands between her knees and remembered Pierre calling just a week ago, her certainty that she'd get both Adam and Emilia back alive, that force of will would be enough.

But the world didn't work that way.

It was late afternoon when they reached Tsiandamba. Villagers lined the route, staring at Rebecca with mournful expressions that couldn't quite disguise their underlying curiosity and excitement. They reached a whitewashed chapel, the largest and coolest building in the village. Rebecca's legs were so unsteady that Andriama had to help her out of the Toyota, and she kept her hand on his shoulder as they walked together into the tall, cool, dark interior. After the bright sunshine, she had to blink to adjust her eyes. To her right, a vast wooden crucifix was hanging on twin steel chains from the roof-beams above the altar. Two oblique arches of afternoon sunshine fell through narrow frosted-glass side-windows on to the red-tiled floor. To her left, along the rear wall, benches had been pushed together to form a low table, and lying upon it was the unmistakable form of a human body covered by a white altar cloth. A bowl of aromatic petals had been set beneath it, and at each corner, an incense stick burned in a glass jar.

Andriama walked across to lift the altar cloth and peer beneath. He turned to her and nodded sadly.

She took a deep breath. 'Who?' she asked.

'Your father.' He laid the cloth back down.

She walked forward, stumbling a little over the edge of some matting. Andriama caught her, tried half-heartedly to hold her back, but she pushed past him. Now that she knew the worst, her hands were strangely steady. She pulled the altar cloth down to his shoulders, and there he was, instantly recognisable despite the eleven years, despite his bloated appearance, the way his body arched slightly, as if he'd been electrocuted, but in reality merely bowed by his constricting wetsuit. His face and throat had been torn open in places, but elsewhere his complexion was pale, with tints of blue, green and yellow that suggested he'd been dead for days.

A cloying smell rose to her nostrils, sea-water and the onset of decay, distinctive more than unpleasant or over-powering, mitigated by the perfume of the incense and flowers. A drop of water splashed down, creating a grey circle on the white altar cloth that quickly grew almost translucent. It was only then that she realised she was crying. Andriama laid his hand gently upon her back. She stepped away from his false comfort, around to her father's other side, pulled the cloth down to his waist. His arms were down by his side, a GPS unit on his right wrist, a diver's watch on his left, along with what looked like the strap for a camera, only there was no camera attached. But what took her breath away was the blood-encrusted puncture wounds in the fabric of his wetsuit. They were all over his torso, and there were two on his right forearm as well, as though he'd been trying to defend himself from a furious assault. And they weren't shark bites, or coral tears, or any other such natural phenom-enon. They were too clean and straight to have been made by anything other than a sharp knife.

Her left leg gave way beneath her. Andriama caught her and helped her to an empty pew. A stooped and grey-haired priest, Latin American from the look of him, pulled the altar cloth back over her father then came and sat on her other side. He took her hand and pressed it. His fingers were dark, gnarled and hairy, she noticed, his nails torn and dirty with soil. A man, like her father, who'd practised his religion in hard work. 'Who found him?' she asked.

'He was on the reef. Everyone saw him together.'

'I promised a reward.'

He hushed her. 'This is no time for that.'

'We must take his body to Tulear,' murmured Andriama from her other side. 'Cause of death, you understand.'

'We know the cause of death,' said Rebecca. 'Didn't you see? Someone butchered him with a knife.'

'With respect, Rebecca, the sea can often make an accident look like—'

'He was stabbed to death,' stated Rebecca. 'You know it. I know it.' Andriama's eyes dropped; he looked away. She sensed immediately that he was holding something back. 'What is it?' she asked. 'What aren't you telling me?'

Andriama gave a heartfelt sigh. 'There has been an incident,' he acknowledged reluctantly. 'In Morombe.'

A tiny shiver ran through Rebecca. Morombe was where Daniel had come down from. 'What kind of incident?'

'A serious one. We found two bodies.'

'Bodies? You mean they were killed?'

Andriama nodded. 'We thought at first that it was just

an argument that had got out of control. They were gun dealers; they'd shot each other. It made a certain sense. But one of them had been stabbed too; and there was no trace of a knife at the scene. And we've since learned that they were supposed to be meeting a foreigner.'

Rebecca nodded. 'And you think their deaths are connected to my father's?'

'Murder is very rare in Madagascar,' said Andriama. 'Stabbing is very rare. To have two such incidents so close in time and place, both involving foreigners . . . But it is still only a possibility. Coincidences happen. We don't even know for sure yet that your father was murdered.'

She gave an expressive snort, glared up at him; but this time he met her gaze, and it was Rebecca who looked down. 'I suppose you're right,' she said.

He touched her arm. 'If your father was murdered, we will get his killer. I swear this to you.'

'Thank you.' She glanced at where he lay. 'May I have a minute alone?'

'Of course.'

Both men left together. She listened to their fading footsteps. When they were gone, when the door had swung softly closed behind them, she stood and walked back over to her father. She pulled down the altar cloth once more, removed and then pocketed the GPS unit from around her father's wrist. Then she kissed his forehead and made her pledges to him, and laid the cloth reverently back down.

II

It was dusk by the time Knox moored the *Yvette* and waded ashore. He heard the engine then saw a white 4×4 approaching along the track, Rebecca at the wheel. He hurried up to Eden to greet her, but the moment he saw how pale she was, how raw her eyes, he knew she'd had bad news. 'Oh, no,' he said, taking her in his arms. She wept into his shoulder, as though she'd been holding her grief back during her drive, but now could let it out. 'Both of them?' he asked.

'My father.'

'What happened? Was it the kidnappers?'

'No. That was just a scam. Nothing but a scam organised by that fuck Mustafa and his sons. They never even had him or Emilia. He's been dead several days at least.'

'I'm so sorry, Rebecca.'

'He wasn't just dead,' she told him. 'He was *murdered*. And I'm going to find out who did it.' She pushed herself free of him, her expression stern and resolved. 'So I want the truth. Who are you? What are you doing here? No more equivocation; no more half-truths. I want to know everything.'

He nodded, buying a moment to think this through. He'd have loved to show her the basement, give her Emilia's report to read; but then he'd have to explain how the shelves had been pulled over, and that would inevitably lead to Boris, and this wasn't the time for that. He therefore gave her the bowdlerised version instead, about how he worked for a company called MGS who'd been hired by Ricky Cheung for a salvage a little further north, and how Emilia had invited them on afterwards for another salvage, ostensibly the *Winterton* but in truth a Chinese treasure ship. He told her of the email from the Landseer Trust telling him that Adam and Emilia had disappeared, and how he'd been so worried for them that he'd come straight down here to check it out.

'Why didn't you just tell me all this that first night?'

'Because your sister made us all swear not to. She was beyond adamant that if we told anyone at all, we'd be out.'

'I'm not anyone.'

'I'm sorry, Rebecca. But she made a special point of warning us not to tell you.'

'*Me?*' Her cheeks coloured. 'Why me?'

'I don't know, not for sure. But you're a celebrity, and people act like idiots when celebrities are involved. I think she was scared that one of us might approach you maybe, or shoot our mouths off; and that you'd hold it against her. She was terrified of doing anything to spook you, I know that much. She told me she'd got in touch with you when she was thinking of coming over, hoping to see you; but you put her off.'

Rebecca buried her face in her hands. 'What have I done?' she wept.

He took half a step towards her. 'I was going to tell you all this two nights ago, I swear I was; but you threw me out before I could, and then you headed off to Tulear. And I was trying to broach it last night when your partner showed up.'

Rebecca wiped her eyes dry with her thumb and forefinger, then assumed a stern expression as though there'd be time for mourning ahead, but right now she had work to do. 'My father was in a wetsuit,' she told him, fishing a GPS unit from her pocket. 'He was also wearing this. It logged his movements the day he and Emilia disappeared. As far as I can tell, he headed out to sea around seven-thirty that morning. At eight-forty the connection was dropped. The GPS wasn't turned off, mind; it just lost coverage.'

'He went underwater,' said Knox.

'Yes,' she agreed. 'And this tells us exactly where.'

Knox nodded. 'We'll go out first thing tomorrow.'

'No,' said Rebecca. 'I want to go now.'

'It's too dark, Rebecca. The sea's getting up. Seriously, if we wait until—'

She held up the GPS. 'This is where my father was

murdered. This is where my sister went missing. Maybe this is where I'll find information to help me get her back alive. Do you really think I'm going to sleep on it?'

He sighed, weary from his day; but he knew she was right. 'Okay,' he said. 'I need to get some more fuel.'

'And I need dive-gear.'

He looked at her in alarm. He hadn't realised she meant to go that far. 'Have you been night-diving before?' he asked.

'Sure. Several times.'

'By yourself? On a reef? In a rough sea? With unfamiliar equipment?'

'I'm doing this. Don't try to stop me.'

He shook his head. 'It's too dangerous,' he told her. 'If anyone's going diving, it's me. It's what I do for a living, remember. And all my gear's already on board.'

'I can't ask you to do that.'

'You're not asking me. I'm volunteering. And that's the end of it. Okay?'

Her eyes watered again. She reached out and touched his arm. 'I don't know how I'll ever thank you,' she said. 'Not just for this. For everything.'

He was about to tell her there was no need for thanks when he heard noise along the track, looked up to see headlights approaching, a pickup weaving erratically towards them, pulling to a stop. Pierre threw open his door and almost tripped over his seat-belt in his haste to get out. 'Becca!' he sobbed. 'I hear terrible news. Is it true? Have they found your father?'

'It's true.'

He gave a low wail, enfolded her in a hug. 'I can't believe it. The best of men. The very best of men. And your poor sister!'

'Emilia isn't dead yet,' said Rebecca tightly. 'We're going to look for her now.'

'How do you mean? In the forest?'

She shook her head, showed him the GPS. He gave it the baffled look of someone who refused even to engage with modern technology, so Rebecca talked him through how it had logged her father's movements on his final day.

'I come with you,' he said. 'I help you look.'

'Forget it,' said Rebecca. 'You've been drinking.'

'One glass, that's all. Thirty-four years I know your father. Thirty-four years! You expect me to stay here and do nothing? Besides, I know your father's boat. I know our reefs. Even at night, I know them.'

She glanced at Knox. He shrugged to let her know it was her call either way. 'Fine,' she sighed. They fetched the fuel, waded out. Knox released them from their mooring and took the wheel to steer them through the pass, Rebecca beside him plotting the GPS co-ordinates on the Eden chart.

'So this is where we're headed, yes?' asked Pierre.

'Yes.'

He frowned and opened his mouth as if to say something; but he checked himself and gave his earlobe a little tug, went outside.

Knox glanced at Rebecca. 'What was *that* about?' he asked.

'I don't know.' She was silent a few moments, then asked: 'You said my father arranged the salvage licences, right? Do you know who with?'

'The Culture Ministry, I think. Though don't hold me to that.'

'But someone in central government, right? Not some local guy.'

'Yes. Why?'

'My father and sister both hated Antananarivo. They never went there if they could avoid it.'

'They couldn't have avoided it. Not for this.'

'They could have if they'd sent Pierre instead.'

'Is that likely?'

'He was always doing stuff up there on my father's behalf. Giving lectures, attending meetings, making sure the right people got their "commissions".' She rubbed her fingers and thumb together in the universal symbol of corruption. 'My father *loathed* that side of Madagascar. Emilia, too.'

'Would your father have trusted Pierre?'

'Not enough to have told him where the wreck was.

But that he'd found something, and needed licences . . .
Yes, I can certainly believe that. And I know he's been
struggling to pay his bills recently. Imagine if you'd never
done a day's work in your life, and then you found yourself running out of money.'

'And your best friend found a fortune on the sea-bed,
but wouldn't tell you where. Worse, he was intending to
turn it all over to the government.'

'Pierre was at a conference in Antananarivo all last
week,' said Rebecca. 'If there were any details to finalise
about the salvage, that would have been the perfect
opportunity. He sent my father an email asking for new
photographs of the white sifaka. But you don't find sifakas
here. You only get them south and east of Tulear.'

'You think it was a code?' frowned Knox. 'You think
he sent your father out to photograph the wreck?'

'It's possible, isn't it? And my father certainly saw the
email. It was one of the last he read.'

'Why would Pierre ask for more photos?'

'To trick my father into giving away the wreck's location, of course. So that he could plant a GPS on board,
plunder it himself before the salvage started.'

Knox shook his head. 'You saw how baffled he was
when you showed him your father's GPS. That wasn't
faked. Besides, you said yourself that your father was
murdered. He couldn't have done that from Antananarivo.'

'Then maybe he came back. Listen, his lecture would

have taken him one morning or afternoon, but he stayed there the whole week, then met me at the airport. But what if all that was just to establish his alibi?'

'You think he came back here midweek? It's a hell of a drive.'

'Yes, but he could have flown. I mean, let's go back a few days. He's desperate to find out where the wreck is, but Adam won't tell him. He's got this conference in Antananarivo, and he makes up some story about going to see the Culture Ministry about the licences. Or maybe he really does have a meeting. Whatever, he tells my father to check his email on a certain day, in case he needs anything, then he sets off in his pickup. But instead of driving up to Antananarivo, he goes to a local airport instead. Not Tulear: he's too well known there. But Manjo or Morombe, somewhere like that. He flies up to Antananarivo, checks into his hotel, gives his talk, shows his face around. He emails my father for new photos of the wreck, then he flies back down, gets his pickup and . . .' She broke off, shook her head in frustration. 'No. He'd still need a way to get out to the *Yvette*.'

'He could have stowed away in the hold.'

'That wouldn't explain how he got back to shore afterwards. The *Yvette* was found way out at sea, remember?'

'What about his zodiac?' suggested Knox. 'He could have taken it with him in the back of his pickup.'

'Yes,' said Rebecca. 'Of course. He flies back down,

drives as close to here as he dares, then gets in his zodiac and motors down here and waits outside the reef for the *Yvette*. Maybe he approaches them; maybe they spot him. There's a confrontation; it gets out of hand. He kills them, dumps them overboard. He lets the *Yvette* drift off, then gets back in his zodiac, races back to his pickup, drives up to Antananarivo before anyone even realises he's been away.'

'It's a hell of an ask,' said Knox.

'But it works, right?' asked Rebecca. 'I mean, in theory.'

'Yes. It works in theory.'

Their eyes turned to Pierre, sitting at the stern. Maybe he sensed something, because he glanced up at that moment. He gave one of his ghastly smiles, pushed himself to his feet, came to the bridge, his nervousness only made the more obvious by his efforts to conceal it. 'What?' he asked. 'What is it?'

'It was you,' blurted out Rebecca, unable to stop herself. 'You murdered my father and my sister.'

FORTY-FIVE

I

Pierre looked aghast at Rebecca's accusation, but Knox couldn't tell whether it was guilt or shock. '*Me?*' he protested. 'How could you say such a thing?'

'You set them up,' insisted Rebecca. 'You sent them out here.'

'No! This is crazy!'

'Then you murdered them.'

'No!' Pierre pointed a trembling finger at Knox. 'It's him. He's been poisoning your mind.'

'White sifaka,' said Rebecca.

A look of unmistakeable guilt appeared on Pierre's face. He must have realised it too. His eyes watered, he tried to say something, but it stuck in his throat. The boat plunged into the trough of a wave at that moment, his left leg gave a little. He lurched out of the doorway, stumbled away along the deck. They ran out after him. Pierre picked up the boat-hook, turned and waved it at them. 'Stay back,' he warned. 'Stay away.'

'Or what?' asked Knox.

'I did nothing,' insisted Pierre. 'I swear. I'd never lie to you, Becca. Not to *you*. You're a daughter to me.'

'Like Emilia was?' asked Rebecca. 'Get her pregnant and then murder her so that your son could inherit Eden?'

Pierre's face crumpled. 'How could you even think that of me?'

Knox motioned to Rebecca to edge to her left, to make it harder for Pierre to watch them both. She nodded and did so. 'Then tell me what happened,' she said to Pierre.

'Nothing happened,' insisted Pierre.

'You sent my father an email. You wanted him to lead you to the wreck.'

'No!'

'Then you came out here and murdered him and Emilia and dumped their bodies overboard.'

'Stay back! Stay back!'

'But my father's body drifted back to shore.'

'I was in Antananarivo all week, I swear it.' And he gestured towards the land behind him. It wasn't much of an opening, but Knox went for it anyway, launching himself at Pierre, trying to get the boat-hook from him before he could do any damage with it. But Pierre swung it backhanded and caught Knox a glancing blow on his crown. His momentum still took him into Pierre, sent them tumbling together into the starboard lockers, the wood splintering. Knox tried to press his advantage, but the blow had left him groggy. Pierre threw him off, raised the boat-hook above his head, swung it down. Knox rolled aside; the boat-hook thunked into the deck. Behind his back, Rebecca pulled a scuba tank from the broken locker, crashed it down on Pierre's skull. He collapsed instantly, fell sideways on to the deck, saliva leaking from his mouth. Rebecca knelt beside him, searched his throat for a pulse, nodded in relief at Knox when she found one.

Knox was still a little dazed as he got to his feet, but he found a coil of rope in the locker, hog-tied Pierre wrist and ankle. He was just finishing up when Pierre groaned and opened his eyes. He strained impotently at his knots, then glared furiously up at Knox, spat at his face. Knox took a hand-towel from the locker, wiped himself off with it, then twisted it into a rope and, with Rebecca's help, used it to gag him. 'Try spitting now,' he said. He opened the main hatch above the engine hold, dragged Pierre over to it, dropped him feet first down into it, shot the bolts. 'That'll hold him until we get back,' he told Rebecca.

'Are you certain?'

'I know my knots,' he assured her. He put his hand on her arm. 'But enough, eh? Let's take him in, come back out first thing.'

Rebecca shook her head. 'She's my sister, Daniel. I have to look. I *owe* it to her.'

'I know, but—'

'You don't have to do the dive. There's plenty of gear aboard. Just stay on the boat while I go down.'

Knox sighed, exasperation matched only by admiration. 'Fine,' he said. 'I'll make one dive. But only one. And then that's it for the night. Agreed?'

'Agreed,' she nodded. 'And thanks.'

FORTY-SIX

I

They reached the GPS co-ordinates, dropped anchor. The sea was getting frisky, but it wasn't quite rough enough for Knox to call it off. He unpacked and prepared his equipment, checked it thoroughly before putting it on. The deck was rolling enough that he had to sit down to pull on his wetsuit and booties. He consulted his watch, made a note of the time, calculated a rough dive plan. He strapped his diving lamp and knife to his wrist, then sat on the rail, pulled on his flippers, held his breath and toppled backwards into the dark water in an eruption of bubbles. He'd weighted himself enough that it was an effort to stay afloat as he breast-stroked around to the stern. Then he let gravity go to work, the anchor chain running through his hand as he descended.

For all his experience, diving alone at night on such a macabre quest proved unnerving. There were shadows everywhere. At sea, as on land, predators were at their most dangerous in the darkness. A sudden memory of that bull shark looming up at him earlier: they were blessed with excellent eyesight, sharks, but they weren't dependent upon it. They could track their prey instead through minute vibrations in the water, through their extraordinary sense of smell, through fluctuations in the electromagnetic field. His re-breather and other dive-gear would light up like fireworks in the electromagnetic field.

He sensed something behind him, spun round and lit up the darkness, but there was nothing there. The bottom came into view, ridged with canyons much like his earlier dive, though that had been a good distance away. His feet touched down, kicking up glowing emeralds of biolu-minescence. The currents were strong, but the weights held him. He swam above gulches and canyons, looking for anything out of the ordinary. A shoal of shadows ahead scattered as he headed towards it, barracuda glinting like thin strips of silver foil. He swam down a canyon, overhangs of rock either side of him forming shallow grottoes. The floor was buried beneath white sand and dead coral, but also by vast quantities of pottery and porcelain shards. Ground Zero at last. He propelled himself along, probing crevices with light. A boulder lay half buried in sand ahead, covered not just in algae and barnacles, but also by a lattice of fine white veins. He drew closer and saw they were the filaments of a gillnet. Knox hated these wretched things with a passion, partly for the perverse cunning of their design, in which the mesh was almost – but not quite – big enough for their target species of fish to wriggle through. By the time the fish had realised for themselves the mesh was too narrow for them, it was too late for them to back out, their gills trapping them there like the barbs on a hook. But he also hated them because trawlers so often cut them loose when they got snagged on anything, leaving them to drift on the currents, or to lie on the sea-bed in deadly ambush for anyone unlucky enough to get tangled up in them.

He shone his lamp around, could see nothing save for a thin cascade of fine white sand falling in a steady stream to his right. It shouldn't be falling like that, not unless something had recently happened here. He swam upwards to find a black gash in the rock, a tunnel into darkness. He looked back down at the boulder. Though it was hard to be sure, it certainly looked an almost perfect fit. If it had once plugged this mouth, and if it had recently fallen away, it would explain how come all this sand was leaking out, slowly burying it.

The tunnel was just wide enough to take him. He pulled himself along it. It opened up abruptly and he found himself in a vast underwater cavern. The water was exponentially stiller and clearer here, so his diving lamp just about illuminated the far wall and ceiling. It had, remarkably, the approximate shape and size of a great ship. And maybe that was more than coincidence: he could picture in his mind's eye the great treasure ship sinking into one of these limestone canyons, or perhaps being nudged there by the tides and current. Sand and sediment and rock would soon have covered it, and coral would have grown atop it. And, as each generation of coral died, their husks would slowly have formed a great carapace above it, hermetically sealing everything inside, protecting the ship and its cargo from the surrounding currents. But the sea and its creatures would still have gone to work, decay inside a tooth, eating away all the wood and anything else organic, until there was nothing but minerals and metals left.

He swam into the cavern. Strange pillars protruded from the sand, reaching upwards like the buildings in a miniaturised city skyline. He drew closer and realised he was looking at stack after stack of dishes. With immense care, he picked up a bowl, tipped away the sand within. It was white with blue dragons around its rim, one of the most exquisite pieces of porcelain he'd ever seen; yet here it was, sitting on a tower of such pieces, surrounded by thousands of others, with who could guess how many more still buried in the sand. Presumably they'd once been packed in wadding in wooden chests in the cargo hold; but the wadding and the wood had rotted away around them, leaving them in a cocoon of sand instead. But that too was now trickling away, released by the fallen boulder, exposing these treasures for the first time in six hundred years.

The stacks of porcelain swayed as he swam between them, moved by the small eddies he was himself creating, leafless trees in a winter wind. He came across the golden statue of a giraffe, only its head and neck protruding from the sand. The Chinese had believed giraffes to be unicorns of myth, bringers of great good fortune. Not this one. He swam on, reached down for a gold bracelet set with rubies. Part of the ship's great cargo, perhaps, or the treasure of some favoured courtesan. A great golden sphere glinted ahead. He swam over to it. It took his breath away: a globe of the world as the Chinese had seen it, lands enamelled upon it: China itself, of course; the scattered archipelago of the Spice Islands and then Australia; the fat daggers of India and Africa. Europe and the Mediterranean. He rolled it a little way to expose the Atlantic and then further underneath, his excitement intense. And there was America. The new and old worlds all captured together for the very first time, and on a globe too.

Movement caught his eye; he whirled around. But it was only the swaying of the stacks of porcelain. Their whiteness and their motion put him irresistibly in mind of ghosts, and that made him realise that this wasn't just a shipwreck, it was a tomb too, the final resting place of perhaps hundreds of passengers and crew, for only a few would have made it into lifeboats and to shore. He felt a mix of privilege and guilt for intruding upon their rest. But it was also a salutary reminder of why he'd come down here; and it wasn't for the wreck. That would have to wait for another time.

He turned, swam back to the tunnel mouth and out. The boulder had been the cork in this ship's bottle. It was covered in netting and had recently fallen loose. It was certainly possible that it had no connection to Emilia's disappearance, but the odds surely pointed the other way. Much of the sand that had been trickling from the cavern had been swept away by the currents, but enough had fallen on to the boulder to half bury it and anything lying around it. The sand was wet and packed; he had to sweep it away with his arm. He was starting to hope that he might be wrong when he felt something soft and yielding. He snatched his hand away, then steeled himself and dug back into the sand. His fingers met other fingers, bloated and cold. He brushed away sand until he'd uncovered a hand, wrist and then forearm. A woman's. It had to be Emilia. He kept at it until he finally revealed her face and confirmed his fears. Her skin was discoloured and torn, her mouth gaping, sand trickling from it. But it was her. An angel fish darted in and gave her eyeball a little kiss. Knox tasted bile at the back of his throat and hurriedly turned away. Vomiting was lethal this deep underwater. He breathed in and out until he'd regained his calm, then he resumed the patient work of freeing her. He reached his arms around her chest and gently pulled, but there was no give at all. He felt around, touched some netting with his fingertips, unsheathed his diving knife and tried to cut through it, but it tangled in the mesh and he couldn't get it free.

Emilia wasn't wearing a wetsuit, only blue denim shorts and a disintegrating T-shirt, but she did have a buoyancy-control device on, along with a scuba tank, regulator and gauges. He undid the buckles of her BCD, freed each of her arms in turn, then tried again. This time he felt a little give. He kept at it and at it until finally he pulled her out. Her body wanted to rise, though she was still held down by a packed weight-belt. He took firm hold of her, then began a measured ascent to four metres, where he decompressed before surfacing.

The night had clouded over and the sea had grown rougher while he'd been below. Another storm was coming. He rose on a swell, saw the lights of the *Yvette* a hundred metres or so away. Holding Emilia with one arm, he paddled across and around to the stern ladder. He let go of her then threw his flippers aboard and called out to Rebecca that he was back.

FORTY-SEVEN

I

Time had been a torment for Rebecca. After half an hour, she'd begun to fear that something dreadful had happened to Daniel. After an hour, she was sure of it. She paced back and forth on deck, checking on Pierre and doing purposeless things in the bridge and cabin, just so that she wouldn't have to think. But she thought nonetheless, berating herself for putting Daniel at risk on such a futile errand. She'd never forgive herself if he came to harm while—

She heard his voice, gave a sob of relief and ran to greet him. She was going to throw her arms around him, but the way he pulled a face and spread his hands, she knew at once. For a moment, she felt unsteady on her feet, but then she forced herself to be strong. 'Where?' she asked.

'I want you to listen carefully,' said Daniel. 'Your sister was trapped by a rock-fall. She's been underwater several days now. It shows. I don't think you should see her like this. I don't think she'd want that.'

'She's my sister,' said Rebecca. 'I don't care how she looks. Where is she?'

'Nearby. Are you sure?'

'Yes.'

She watched him climb back into the sea, take hold of a shapeless form. When he returned to the ladder, she couldn't help herself, she gave a cry and looked away. He brought Emilia aboard by himself, then took her to the cabin. Her left arm spilled from his hold as he did so, a digital camera around her wrist dragging along the deck. He had to turn around to carry her down the companionway steps, but they were so steep that he missed his footing anyway and both he and Emilia tumbled to the floor. Rebecca gave a low sob. 'I'm sorry,' said Daniel, the strain in his voice betraying how hard he was finding this. Rebecca waited on deck until he climbed back up and out. 'I'll get us back to Eden, okay?' he said, touching her elbow in sympathy.

'Yes. And thank you. I know how hard that must have been.'

'It's okay. I'm just so sorry.'

She went below. Daniel had laid Emilia out on one of the beds and covered her with a thin white sheet that was already translucent with moisture, the button of her denim shorts showing through, along with fragments of some bold slogan on her T-shirt. For the second time that day, Rebecca pulled down a makeshift shroud to reveal a member of her family. She glanced at her sister's ravaged pale face, then looked away again, only able to bear the horror of it in blinks.

— *I'm so sorry, Emilia.*
— *There was nothing you could have done.*
— *I should have been here.*
— *There was nothing anyone could have done.*

She pulled the sheet down to expose Emilia's ragged T-shirt and bare arms. She noticed something odd then. The camera strap was still biting into Emilia's left wrist, but the camera itself had gone. She searched the cabin, on and under the bed, but she couldn't find it. Had Daniel taken it? He must have. But why? Was he trying to protect her somehow? Was there something on the camera he didn't want her to see? But why then wait until Emilia was back aboard? Or had he simply not noticed it until he'd brought her down here and arranged her body on the bed?

The engine started up. It was louder down here than she'd expected. The light grew stronger and the boat

439

shuddered and then began to move. She remembered, suddenly, all the troubling unresolved questions she'd asked herself these past few days about Daniel: how smoothly he'd fabricated and then kept up his cover-story; how he'd tried to dissuade her from coming out here tonight, then had insisted on being the one to dive, perhaps to make sure there was nothing down there that could incriminate him. She remembered how he'd assaulted Pierre before he could have a chance to explain himself, then had trussed him and gagged him to keep him quiet. She remembered what Andriama had told her about those two men killed at a meet with a foreigner, one of whom had been stabbed just like her father. Daniel had a knife; she'd watched him strap it to his forearm before making his descent. And the blunt truth was that he'd been only a few miles north of here when Adam and Emilia had disappeared; and he'd known that there was a shipwreck here, and that it was valuable too.

She shook her head at herself. She was letting the horrors of the night get to her. Maybe Daniel hadn't told her the full truth about himself, but he'd explained everything to her satisfaction. Besides, telling a few half-truths were a long cry from being a killer. He'd have to be made of stone to have behaved as he'd behaved towards her these past few days if he'd murdered Adam and Emilia. But that gave her pause. She'd read the

440

literature on psychopaths and so knew that they had certain traits in common, for example how *plausible* they were, how charming and completely without guilt or remorse, how famously hard they were to distinguish from the surrounding population, until they'd been caught and had their basements searched.

There was one other trait that psychopaths typically had in common: the capacity for rage. It was a valuable attribute, rage, an anger so intense that it overrode the instinct for self-preservation. Animals had a keen sense for it in others. They placated it, flattered it, steered clear of it. Because if they triggered it . . . For her father hadn't simply been murdered, Rebecca realised. He'd been *butchered*. Savagery like that wasn't a crime of greed. It was a crime of *rage*; a psychopath's crime.

She covered Emilia once more, climbed the companion-way steps. Daniel was in the bridge, steering them towards home, but his dive-bag was against the port locker. She kept low, beneath his line of sight. Maybe Daniel would have simply tossed Emilia's camera over-board. But maybe he wouldn't have risked that, lest it be found by some future diver. So maybe he'd have packed it away in his bag for later disposal instead. She crouched to unzip each of the side-pockets in turn. In just the second, she found a handgun. She felt hollow as she pulled it out, turned it around disbelievingly in her hands. Those two dead men in Morombe had been gun dealers.

Was that where Daniel had got this? She could see no other explanation. At least it gave her a way to defend herself; but then she saw that it had no magazine and so was functionally useless. She searched his bag for it but without success. She did find the empty sheath of his diving-knife, however, which made her wonder whether he'd ditched it lest it be matched against her father's wounds.

If she couldn't use the gun herself, she could at least deny it to Daniel. She hid it in one of the lockers, then searched his bag again, just in case. Her fingertips brushed something cold at the bottom of a side-pocket. She fished out a medallion on a silver chain and remembered that first night back at Eden, watching Daniel as he'd showered in the storm, the way the links had glinted in a burst of lightning. She looked down at the inscription.

MATTHEW DANIEL RICHARDSON
ATTENTION: RARE BLOOD TYPE

She closed her eyes before she could read any more. She clutched the medallion so tight she could almost feel it imprinting on her palm. The blood Andriama had found on the *Yvette* had been AB negative. It had belonged to a foreign male, but not Pierre. It was too rare for co-incidence. If Daniel had AB negative blood, then he'd been on the *Yvette* before, whatever he claimed, whatever her heart told her. She lifted each finger in turn.

Not AB negative, she prayed silently. *Please God, not AB negative*. She took away her last finger.

It was AB negative.

FORTY-EIGHT

I

Rebecca put back the medallion and was zipping up Daniel's bag when she heard him coming out of the bridge. She stood up and turned, but not quickly enough to escape his notice.

'Looking for something?' he asked.

'No,' she told him.

He shrugged, let it go. 'I'm taking us south-east,' he said. 'We'll be back at the pass soon.'

'Good,' she said. 'And thanks.'

He gave her a slightly puzzled look. 'You don't have to keep thanking me, Rebecca,' he said.

She nodded, aware she was behaving strangely and

was bound to arouse his suspicion; but it was hard to stop herself. 'Maybe I should check on Pierre,' she said.

'He'll be fine.'

'He took a blow to the head,' she said.

Daniel shrugged. 'As you like,' he said, returning inside the bridge.

The roll of the deck threw her a little. The breeze had grown strong, rousing the sea with it. She unbolted and opened the main hatch. It was dark inside, but the deck-lights were strong enough to see Pierre lying on his side, still securely trussed. She lowered herself into the hold. 'Are you awake?' she murmured. He gave a grunt of acknowledgement. She put a finger to her lips to ask for quiet. He nodded. She untied his gag.

'Please, Rebecca,' he begged. 'You have to believe me. I didn't do anything to Adam or Emilia. I swear I didn't. They were my friends, my closest friends. I loved them both.' He was weeping and snuffling piteously. She found his protestations unnervingly convincing. 'Please, Rebecca,' he said. 'You can't trust that man. He's the one! He's the one!'

He was hog-tied, his ankles and wrists separately bound, then knotted together behind his back. She examined the knots more closely. By undoing one knot, she could leave his wrists and ankles securely bound, just not to each other. It would make him more comfortable and enable her to release him quicker in an emergency. In the half-light, with the wet rope, unpicking the knot was hard. She was so concentrated on it that she didn't even hear Daniel approaching across the deck above until he appeared at the hatch. 'What are you doing?' he frowned.

'I was just making sure his knots were secure,' she told him.

'And?'

'I don't know. I'm not very good at this kind of thing.'

'Let me have a look.'

'It's okay. I can—'

'Come on, Rebecca. If there's something wrong with his knots, I need to see for myself.'

The hold was too small for them all. Daniel helped Rebecca out first, then lowered himself down. He knelt beside Pierre, looked up and around at her in surprise. 'Did you untie this?' he asked.

'I told you it was getting loose.'

He shook his head. 'I know knots, Rebecca. No way he did this himself.'

'What are you suggesting?'

'Rebecca?' asked Daniel. 'What the hell's going on?'

She moved as quickly as she could, slammed closed the hatch before he could reach it, shot the bolts. 'Rebecca!' he yelled, pounding the underside of the hatch. 'Let me out!'

'You've been on this boat before,' she said.

The pounding stopped. 'Of course I have. I sailed it up from Tulear with you.'

could. She remembered the anaesthetics in the cabin's medicine chest. She hurried down the steep steps, opened it up. Yes. A full bottle of ketamine, now a party drug of choice, but originally for anaesthetising mammals in the wild. It was perfect for dart-guns because it was so fast-acting, even if not injected directly into a vein. She tore a new syringe from its plastic wrapping as she hurried back up the steps. She'd used ketamine plenty of times herself over the years. Dosage was proportional to body-mass. She made an estimate of Daniel's weight, sucked up the requisite amount. The wood splintered. Daniel reached out an arm and fumbled blindly for the bolts. The *Yvette* pitched over a wave. Rebecca stumbled and went sprawling. Daniel found the first bolt, slid it back. She scrambled on all fours along the deck as Daniel found the second bolt. She stabbed the needle as high up his arm as she could reach, plunging the ketamine into his system with her thumb. He yelled as the hatch flew open, slammed back on its hinges. She fled to the cabin, down the steps, pulled the hatch closed above her, shot the bolt just as Daniel arrived, stamping down hard on the wood. 'What have you done to me?' he cried, fear in his voice. 'What the fuck was that stuff?' He stamped down again, harder. The wood splintered, his foot came rushing through, catching her on the forehead, throwing her sprawling backwards, tripping over the medicine chest, falling against the cot, knocking a pole out of its slot, bringing Emilia tumbling down on top of her, cold and clammy, and the sound of her own voice screaming, screaming, screaming at this waking nightmare, pushing her sister off her, brushing at her tainted skin.

It was a while before she stopped screaming, and noticed the silence.

FORTY-NINE

I

Rebecca looked up. Daniel's leg was still plunged through the hatch, but he wasn't moving. The ketamine had worked. She got to her feet, pushed his foot up and out through the gaping hole, unbolted the hatch. Daniel had fallen across it, so she had to heave to clear him away. Her heart played all sorts of tricks on her as she looked down at him. Sorrow and fear; love and hate. But she had no time to second-guess herself. Ketamine was a temporary solution. It would buy her maybe twenty minutes. She needed to make the most of that time.

There was plenty of rope left in the lockers. She tied his wrists together behind his back, then his ankles, emulating as best she could what Daniel had done to Pierre. But Daniel knew knots; she didn't. She gagged him and tied him to the rail, so that she could keep an eye on him from the bridge. Then she went to check on Pierre too. He begged her to release him, but she shook her head. One of these two men was a murderer, but she still wasn't sure which. Get back into the lagoon, raise reinforcements, then Pierre and Daniel could plead their cases all they liked.

The sea was growing rougher. There was no obvious direction or pattern to the waves. Each time the *Yvette* rose on the swell, she'd glimpse the pass and steer back towards it; but then they'd pitch into a trough and it would corkscrew her all over the place, so that whenever she next rose, they were off course again.

Daniel raised his head a little, looked around. He caught her eye and froze for a moment, as if his memory had returned. He started rubbing his hands and ankles back and forth to gain some play. 'Stop that!' she shouted. But he didn't stop. 'Please!' she cried. 'Just let me get us home. Then I'll let you free.' But he looked at the turbulent sea and shook his head. The bottle of ketamine rolled across the deck. She picked it up; there was still a little left. She went down into the cabin for a fresh syringe, came back up to find Daniel working furiously at his wrists, getting some decent play in them now. She sucked up the last of the ketamine, plunged it into his arm. Blood bubbled on his skin. They both looked at each other for a moment, before Daniel resumed his frantic efforts to escape. Rebecca took a step back. One hand free, two hands, pulling off his gag, scrabbling at his ankles. But then his hands stopped obeying him, his movements slowed, he groaned and was out again.

She approached him warily. His wrists were free, his ankles almost so. She checked his pulse. Faint and slow, but regular enough. She retied his knots as well as she could, aware they wouldn't hold him long. The hatches were broken. She was out of anaesthetics. She needed some other plan. Daniel's bag was close by. She fetched it, opened it up. It had his dive equipment inside, the re-breather, wetsuit and a small tank of oxygen. She pulled out the wetsuit to make space, then added the handgun and all the lead weights she could find in the bench lockers. By the time she was finished, it was so heavy she could barely pick it up, but it still had too much air in it for her purpose, so she scooped up sea-water in a bucket and splashed it into the bag until it spilled glassily on to the deck. Then she zipped it up and lashed it to Daniel's ankles with a coil of rope.

It was growing a fraction less dark. Night would be over soon. Back inside the bridge, rising and falling on the swell, she lined up the *Yvette* for the pass once more, glancing around regularly to check Daniel for signs of life. It wasn't long before he raised his head groggily. She went out, knelt beside him, waited until he focused and looked her in the eye. 'Listen to me,' she told him. 'See this rope around your ankles? It's tied to your bag, which I've filled with weights. If you cause me any more trouble, I'll throw it overboard, and it'll take you with it. I really, really don't want to do that. I swear I don't. All I want to do is get us safely back to Eden. But I'll do it if you make me. Do you understand?'

He nodded. She hurried back to the bridge. The sea was getting higher all the time; the boat kept skewing on the swell. A great wave crashed over their side; she looked around to see Daniel working again at his knots. 'Stop it!' she shouted, but he kept at it. She ran back out, lifted up the bag. He stopped struggling at once, nodded compliance. But then the *Yvette* began sliding from the crest of a swell, and kept on going. His eyes went past her; he blanched and redoubled his efforts to get free. Rebecca glanced around. The foamy crest of a freak wave towered above them, bearing down fast. The *Yvette* was already deep in its trough. She stared at it in horror for a moment, then back down at Daniel, struggling furiously now, helpless at her feet, bound and weighted and doomed, utterly dependent upon her. And she realised, in that one fraction of a second, that all the incriminating evidence in the world didn't matter a damn. She threw herself down upon him, straddled her arms and legs around him, grabbed hold of a davit to pin them both to the deck, took a deep breath and held it as the wave swept them along, tipping the *Yvette* almost on to her side and hurtling them along with it for several seconds, so that Rebecca was certain they'd capsize. But Adam had built her for stability and safety rather than speed. The wave crashed over them and the *Yvette* bobbed aright, drenched and creaking but afloat, Daniel still in her arms. She buried her head into his shoulder, hugged him and began sobbing in relief.

It was a moment later that she heard the hiss. She looked around. The weighted bag had washed overboard and the rope tying it to Daniel's ankles was paying out. It reached full length and dragged Daniel and her both against the sopping deck to the rail. She held on to him grimly, a tug-of-war in which she struggled to gain ground, but wasn't losing either, buying him time to free his hands. Her arms began to tire. Her shoulder throbbed. The knots around his wrists and ankles had soaked and pulled tight. The *Yvette* tilted again. Rebecca looked up, appalled. Freak waves sometimes came in pairs. This one, if anything, was even bigger. Daniel began breathing fast and deep, packing his lungs with air. Then it crashed over them, picking them both up and sweeping them overboard. Rebecca still had hold of Daniel, but the weighted bag pulled him down and took her with him. They sank quickly; he began slipping through her fingers. She grabbed his elbow but her fingers slid down his forearm to his wrist. She tried to hold him, but he was too heavy for her and he fell away. He must have freed his hands, however, for at the last moment he grabbed her ankle, pulling her down with him, her lungs bursting for air, both of them doomed unless she got away. But before she could kick free, he simply let her go.

She swam for the surface, gasping in air the second she breached it, then looking around for Daniel, praying he'd pop up beside her; but there was no sign of him. She waited for him to resurface, riding the swell of waves, searching all around her, but in vain. She dived down, again and again, flapping her arms in hope, but it was futile in the enormous darkness. Her heart turned to lead inside her as seconds accumulated into minutes. She could still feel his grip around her ankle. She could still feel the way he'd let go.

The *Yvette* had righted herself. She was maybe fifty or sixty metres away, being swept towards the reef. Rebecca needed to get back to her now. The highest waves had passed, but the swell was still steep, and took real effort to negotiate, so that her injured shoulder ached wretchedly by the time she made it. She worked her way around to the stern ladder, hauled herself aboard. Pierre was banging and yelling in terror in the hold. She'd forgotten all about him. She glanced down through the broken starboard hatch. He was sitting up in a foot or so of water, having spat out his neckerchief, his wrists and ankles still tied.

'Let me out!' he begged, when he saw her. 'Let me out! Please. I meant no harm. I swear it.'

The waves were taking them ever closer to the reefs. She didn't have much time. 'Tell me what happened,' she said.

He looked cowed, beaten. 'It was a gift from God, Becca,' he said. 'Your father was just going to give it away.'

'You sent him that email, then came back to watch.'

'No.'

She turned and walked away. He yelled out desperately behind her: 'I swear it, Rebecca. It was only a sudden idea to send that email. I meant to ask Lalao and Marie-Claire to watch where your father sails. From different places, you know.'

Rebecca went back. 'Triangulation,' she said flatly.

'Yes. But I never even got hold of them, I swear. Nothing happened.'

'Nothing except my father and sister dying,' she said bitterly. 'They were your *friends*. They did everything for you. How could you betray them like that?'

He had the grace to look ashamed. 'All my women, my children. You think my life comes free? Please, Becca.' He got on to his knees to show her his wrists bound behind him. 'Untie me. *Please*.'

She shook her head, too angry even to look at him. She had no time anyway. The waves were still pushing them inexorably towards the reef. The floor of the bridge was swilling with water. The engine had stalled. Her heart was in her mouth when she tried and failed to restart it, but thankfully it came alive at the third attempt. She swung the *Yvette* around and away. It was growing lighter all the time, and her anger made her decisive, which in turn made steering easier. She reached the pass, steered them back into the relative calm of the lagoon.

The eastern sky was pale with dawn. She felt a terrible weariness. Daniel must have been guilty after all. He *must* have been. She couldn't bear to contemplate anything else. He'd been greedy for the treasure, he'd made his way down here and murdered her father and sister. He'd deserved everything he'd got. But each time she drew close to convincing herself, she remembered the feel of his hand around her ankle, the way he'd let her go, sacrificing himself so that she could live. Was that the action of a murderer? Of a psychopath? In a daze, she steered the *Yvette* back to Eden, until the hull scraped sand and she cut the engine. Her hands began trembling wildly, as though her body were demanding back-payment for everything she'd put it through.

Pierre was still bawling to be let free, but she couldn't face him, not yet. She went down into the cabin instead, where Emilia had tumbled face-down in a couple of inches of water on the floor. She righted the bed, hauled her back up on to it, trying not to look at the trickles of sand that leaked from her nostrils and mouth. The *Yvette* lurched suddenly on its keel, sending a low wave of water washing across the cabin, carrying all kinds of flotsam with it, including Emilia's camera, the very camera whose disappearance had set her worrying about Daniel. She felt hollowed as she picked it up, turned it over. A hook at the back had broken, allowing the strap to escape. She remembered how Daniel had stumbled when bringing Emilia down the companionway steps into the cabin. The camera must have snagged on something, snapping the hook. She turned it on. It was a digital camera, its display allowing you to view your most recent photographs. She went through them one by one. Adam outside the lodge, a scuba tank on his shoulder. Emilia with Michel, playing on the sand. Then one of Therese holding Michel and waving them off. Out on the boat now, sunlight on turquoise waters and the white sail of a distant pirogue. Adam grinning at the camera as he zipped up his wetsuit, then another with him in the full gear, about to make a dive. And not a sign of Daniel anywhere, or of Pierre, or of anyone but Adam and Emilia themselves.

She looked over at Emilia. Now that the sheet was off her, she noticed her pulped left leg and the fine-meshed gillnet around her ankle. It was dreadful stuff, all too easy to get tangled up in. She tried to think back to her father, whether there'd been any on him. She couldn't remember seeing any, but his lower body had been covered by that altar cloth, and she couldn't be sure.

She shivered, suddenly, as she remembered Andriama warning her not to take the seeming stab wounds at face value. A sudden mental image of how that day might have gone assailed her. Adam and Emilia had never deployed their anchor near the reefs if they could possibly avoid it, because they did the coral such unnecessary damage. Typically, therefore, one of them would stay aboard while the other dived solo. The photographs showed that Adam had been that day's diver, Emilia staying on board the *Yvette*. But what if Adam had somehow got tangled in this wretched netting and hadn't resurfaced on schedule? What if Emilia had got nervous? What if she'd seen a sudden eruption of bubbles in the water, say? What if she'd panicked and suited up in such a hurry that she hadn't even taken the time to pull on a wet-suit? What if she'd gone down herself and found her father tangled up in this fucking netting, almost out of air? Without any time for subtlety, Emilia would have hacked and hacked at that damned netting until she'd cut him free, slashing his wet-suit in the process, leaving the marks Rebecca had misread as rage. But she'd got tangled up in it herself, or maybe her efforts had brought down the rock Daniel had told her about, pinning her against the sea-floor.

Bile rose in Rebecca's throat; she swallowed it back

down. It *couldn't* have happened like that. It just couldn't. What about Daniel's blood being on board the *Yvette*? Yes! She seized gratefully upon it. He was the killer after all. He had to be. She looked up at that very moment, and a first shaft of dawn sunlight slanted through the open cabin door and fell upon the photograph of Michel that had somehow remained hanging upon the facing wall, despite everything the night had thrown at it. And she remembered, then, her father's last letter to her mother, how Emilia had brought Michel aboard the boat, how she'd fallen and both their heads had banged the deck, and *ow*, how Michel had only just stopped bawling.

That was where the blood had come from, the male and female both.

Above her, footsteps, mutters, Pierre's face appearing through the hatch. Evidently Daniel hadn't been quite so good at knots as he'd believed himself. 'There you are!' he scowled, rubbing the back of his head. 'What happened? Where's your English friend? What did you—' But then he saw Emilia lying on the bed; his face crumpled in grief and tears sprang from his eyes.

Rebecca turned to him. 'Why did you lie to me?' she asked.

His face assumed that self-pitying look again. 'I told you. Your father was going to give everything away.'

'Not about that,' she said. 'I'm talking about why you told everyone that Michel was your son.'

'Oh,' he said. For a moment, she thought he was going to deny it. But then he saw her expression and thought better of it. He nodded at Emilia. 'She made me.'

'Go on.'

'It was after she went to England to meet her salvage people, you know. She liked one of them very much. She thinks, ah, yes, this man will make a good father for her child. You know how she is about men. Always she wants to be a mother, but never to share her child. Well, this one lives in England, he has good genes, he won't be part of the salvage. *Parfait!* So she takes him to her bed and assures him not to worry, that she has taken every precaution. But of course she has taken no precaution at all. At first she refuses to tell anyone who the father is, but then our country goes to shit, and the salvage is delayed, and now the father is to be part of it and Emilia is scared he will find out about his son and insist on being part of his life. She does not want him to be a part of Michel's life, so she begs me to pretend to be the father myself. "Why me?" I ask. "Because the father is a European," she says, "and you're the only European here." I don't like this, I tell her. A man is entitled to know his son.' He gave an expressive shrug. 'But you know Emilia. When she makes up her mind on something . . .'

Rebecca bowed her head. She began to weep.

EPILOGUE

Three months later

Rebecca held Michel against her hip as she waved farewell to Titch. Her former partner did not look at all happy. He'd come to have one last go at persuading her to return to London, but he was going home alone. He couldn't understand it; he'd kept telling her how their company was on a roll. Their US run had been a triumph. Canada and Australia had both picked up options, and she'd won some kind of award in France. The money was flowing in again. Chat-show hosts were clamouring. She was *hot*.

She'd tried her best to explain to him. She really had. But after a while she'd realised that he'd never get it, it went so against everything he thought about the world. He couldn't see that his kind of success meant nothing

to her any more, or that she'd gained a new and suffi-
cient vision of herself: as a strong, stern, selfless and
formidable matriarch; handsome, erect and proud; feared
and loved by her Malagasy friends; admired yet considered mildly eccentric for having had everything the West
could offer, then choosing to give it up. She'd appointed
an agent to sell her Notting Hill house, lawyers to settle
all her debts. She sweetened the pill for Titch by telling
him that she intended to divide her equity among their
employees; and that he'd be getting the largest chunk
himself. He'd have control of the company at last. Wasn't
that what he'd always wanted?

'There won't be a company without you,' he'd sulked.

'Of course there will be. You just have to find the right
talent, that's all.'

'You'll be bored to tears in six months. You'll be
begging to come back.'

She'd laughed so loudly at that, he'd looked affronted;
but she knew he was wrong. She had plenty here to
occupy her. She'd started teaching French, biology, math-
ematics and history in the school. She helped Therese in
the clinic. She watered the orchids around her family's
expanded tomb, and had planted more. She talked
constantly on these visits, telling her sister and her parents
everything that was happening in Eden. And often she'd
talk out loud to Emilia, too, just walking around the
village or along the beach, so that people thought she

was slightly mad. Her hard certainties about death had softened. She hadn't found God so much as rediscovered the childhood awe of nature that she'd mislaid for a time, too busy mining it for nuggets. Adam had been right: We don't believe because we think. We believe because we love.

She'd made him a second pledge that day in the church in Tsiandamba when she'd kissed him on his brow. Eden would remain the sanctuary he'd created, whatever it took. She'd lie awake at night, watching the moon-shadows in the eaves, her hands folded behind her head, making plans to bring him honour. She still didn't know why he'd turned on her during her teenage years, but she'd put that behind her. All that mattered was that he'd felt the shame of it, and had wanted her forgiveness. She'd given it with her whole heart.

With her renewed respect for nature had come a re-kindling of her eagerness to learn. Knowledge for its own sake. Her chance to contribute something solid and lasting to the world. She planned to pick upon some obscure local endemic (a toad, perhaps, or maybe a millipede; something small and a little bit ugly) then study it intensively for the next ten years, writing papers on it that only twenty-seven people would ever read, and only fifteen would understand.

She was happy.

When Titch was gone, when even his dust trail had

resettled, she took Michel down towards the beach. She was crossing the track when she saw Pierre hurrying towards her, waving for her attention, great dark pools of sweat on the underarms of his blue shirt. 'You said *voavy* for the roof, yes?'

'That's right.' She'd hired him to supervise the building of the new Emilia Kirkpatrick schoolroom, not least to feed him enough money that he'd leave the reef and the wreck alone.

'Jean-Luc says *cassave* is better,' he said. 'Cheaper, too.'

'Fine. *Cassave* it is.'

'Good.' He stood there for a moment or two, mopping his brow, gathering his breath. He crouched a little to chuck Michel under his chin, then glanced up at Rebecca. 'More like Emilia every day.'

'Yes,' agreed Rebecca.

'Therese ask me to give you a message,' said Pierre. He stood to his full height again, gazed at her in a slightly unsettling way he'd developed these past few weeks. It was nothing she could rebuke him for, avuncular and fond rather than lustful, akin to the way he gazed upon his children when they'd done something to make him proud. 'She says yes, this afternoon is no problem.'

'Great,' nodded Rebecca. 'Thank her for me.'

He turned and walked away, raising his right arm in acknowledgement. Michel stirred, stretched his arms, yawned. His eyes opened briefly, then closed again, a soft smile on his lips. Her heart twisted as she looked down at him. She still hadn't decided what to tell him about his parentage. A small part of her yearned to keep him entirely for herself, though the far larger part was ashamed that she could even contemplate such a profound betrayal of her sister.

She was far from the first to face such a dilemma, of course. An extraordinary number of people, after all, went their entire lives without ever for one moment suspecting they weren't the biological child of the man and woman they'd always taken it for granted were their parents.

Titch had known about her gambling. That had been a surprise. Apparently everyone had known. He'd thought that maybe it was why she was so reluctant to come back, and so he'd assured her that it wouldn't be a problem; she could join some group, get the best counselling money could buy. She'd laughed again and assured him that gambling wasn't a problem, that she hadn't even thought of it in weeks. And it was true.

Something cramped in her stomach. She placed her palm flat upon it. The days since her last period kept ticking by, and still nothing. And she'd felt distinctly nauseous this morning. Not sick, exactly, but certainly queasy. There was an unopened test kit in Emilia's cabin, but it was still way too soon, she couldn't risk losing her hope just yet.

Sometimes the possibility so overwhelmed her, she had to do something to distract herself until it went away.

There was one final thing that Titch had failed to grasp, however many times she'd tried to explain it. It was this: even if she did go back, she wouldn't be any use to him. She'd succeeded on television because the fire of evangelism had blazed within her. She'd been so certain that she knew the truth about how life worked that she'd needed to convince the world of the rightness of her vision. But the fire inside her had since gone out. It had gone out during her search for Adam and Emilia, when she'd come to realise how magnificently more complex the world was than her perception of it. And, worse, she was *glad* of this.

It had happened barely two hours after she'd consigned Daniel to the deeps. She and Pierre together had carried Emilia from the boat back to the lodge. Pierre had tried his best to console her, to tell her that she'd done nothing wrong, that she had to be strong for when the police came to talk to her, as they surely would, and ask what had happened to the missing Englishman. For all their sakes, she mustn't implicate herself. What good would confession do now?

She'd known he was right, but it had been unbearable all the same, to pretend that Daniel hadn't existed, that his life had meant nothing, that she'd have no penalty to pay. It had been too much for her; she'd run out of the lodge, out of Eden, down the track to the beach, using the heaviness of the sand to exhaust herself, make herself too weary to grieve. But then she'd glimpsed something far out in the lagoon, and yes, it had been a man swimming with long, measured strokes towards the shore, a black-and-yellow pack upon his back; and something had crumpled inside her as she'd realised that Daniel hadn't let go of her ankle so that she might live. No. He'd let go of her to get at the re-breather and the small tank of oxygen in the dive-bag she'd tied to his ankle.

She made her way between the last of the spiny trees on to the soft white sand. The *Yvette* was already through the pass; she'd be back at her mooring within a couple more minutes. Daniel had been out to check the wreck-site was still secure, in preparation for the return of Miles and his other former MGS colleagues. Now that they'd secured new funds from the Chinese government and other investors, and had bought off Ricky and his triad friends, they were hoping to get in several weeks of salvage before the weather turned. He glanced shore-wards, saw her, stood and waved. She waved back. He reached the mooring buoy, leapt down into the water to secure the *Yvette* to it. She couldn't wait any longer, she splashed out to meet him, soaking her trousers. Michel sensed his father, he grew fractious. Rebecca passed him across and instantly he soothed.

'Your friend left yet?' asked Daniel.

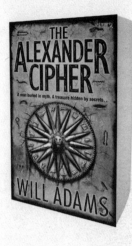

Will Adams
THE ALEXANDER CIPHER

Outcast archaeologist Daniel Knox believes he has found a clue which leads to the whereabouts of the burial place of Alexander the Great, history's most enigmatic warrior king. His fabled tomb was a wonder of the ancient world, in a catacomb of chambers each packed with diamonds, rubies and gold.

But when a construction crew unknowingly rip open the mouth of the tomb, it triggers a deadly race for one of the greatest treasures of all time. Knox's lifelong fascination with the legend could be the cause of his own demise – because the discovery has alerted two of the most dangerous men in the world, and Daniel is suddenly a marked man...

ISBN: 978-0-00-725087-5

Will Adams
THE EXODUS QUEST

When a chase ends in the tragic death of Alexandria's senior archaeologist, Daniel Knox becomes the main suspect. Knox is on the trail of a Dead Sea Scroll when he stumbles across an ancient temple being secretly excavated by evangelical Christians. Meanwhile, his partner Gaille Bonnard is abducted by rogue soldiers and appears in a hostage tape on TV where they threaten to execute her.

Knox is certain she's hidden a message for him in the broadcast but he is locked in a police cell half a country away, under arrest on suspicion of murder. With time running out, Knox must race across Egypt to the mysterious tomb of a heretic pharaoh that may just provide the answer to the greatest riddle of the Exodus itself.

ISBN: 978-0-00-725088-2

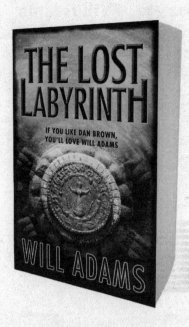

Will Adams
THE LOST LABYRINTH

Twenty years after vanishing without a trace, French archaeologist Roland Petitier makes a dramatic reappearance at a major Athens conference, promising an astonishing find. But on the eve of his sensational announcement, he is found dying in an Athens hotel room. Petitier's former protégé Augustin Pascal is the chief suspect, but a policeman beats him into a coma. Only Augustin's two closest friends, Daniel Knox and Gaille Bonnard, can clear his name and uncover the truth.

However, rumours of Petitier's findings have spread, and ruthless Georgian oligarch Ilya Nergadze is determined to take them for himself. He sends his psychopathic grandson Mikhail to Athens with orders to bring back whatever has been found. Knox and Bonnard venture deeper and deeper into a dark labyrinth of mystery and political high-stakes, while Mikhail closes in on them, ready to kill. The only way to escape certain death is by cracking one of the greatest unsolved mysteries of all time...

ISBN: 978-0-00-728631-7